Praise for *The Mise-en-Scène*

"One of the best as well as the most influential of the French New Novelists. . . . Skillfully translated by Dominic Di Bernardi. . . . The novel is a demonstration of the complexity of reality, and the impossibility of knowing for certain the true meaning of a chain of events. . . . A rich voyage of discovery of the human psyche . . . by one of the most original authors in modern France."

Washington Times

"The minute description of every sight and sound is a send-up of 19th century French realism; in this case appearances reveal nothing but their own appearance. . . . Claude Ollier remains one of the most significant writers among the New Novelists in recent French literature."

Choice

"A beautiful and mysterious story . . . which enriches the reader with a whole new experience of adventure and anguish."

Le Journal de Geneve

"*The Mise-en-Scène* is close to being the masterpiece expressing that most subjective of human passions: anguish."

Les Lettres Francaises

Works by Claude Ollier that have been translated into English

Disconnection

Law and Order

Mise-en-Scène

The Mise-en-Scène

Claude Ollier

Translated with an Afterword by Dominic Di Bernardi

Dalkey Archive Press

Originally published © 1958 by Éditions de Minuit; copyright renewed © 1982 by Flammarion.

Copyright renewed © 1988 by Claude Ollier
English translation and afterword © 1988 by Dominic Di Bernardi

First hardcover edition, 1988
First paperback edition, 2000

LC: 87-73069
ISBN: 0-916583-26-0 cloth
            1-56478-232-8 paperback

Partially funded by grants from the National Endowment for the Arts, a federal agency, the Illinois Arts Council, a state agency, and the French Ministry of Culture.

Dalkey Archive Press
Illinois State University
Campus Box 4241
Normal, IL 61790-4241

www.dalkeyarchive.com

Printed on permanent/durable acid-free paper and bound in the United States of America.

The Mise-en-Scène

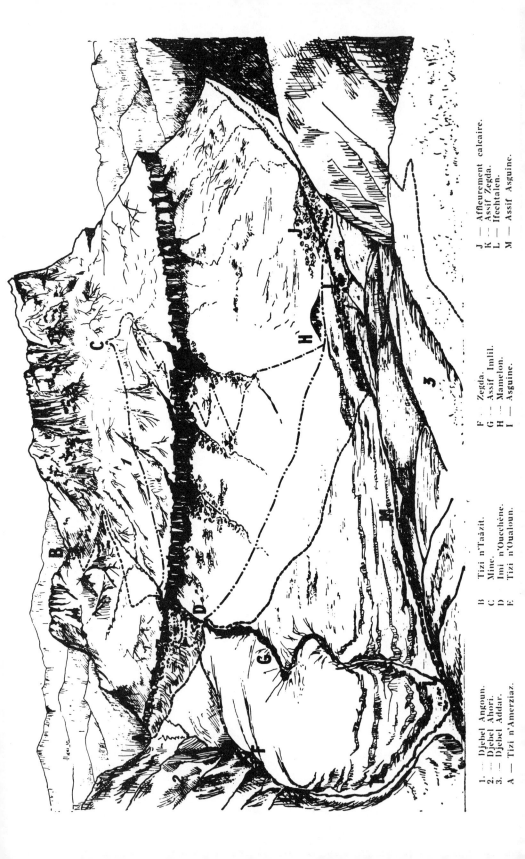

1. — Djebel Angoun.
2. — Djebel Ahori.
3. — Djebel Addar.
A — Tizi n'Amerziaz.

B — Tizi n'Taäzit.
C — Mine.
D — Imi n'Ouechêne.
E — Tizi n'Oualoun.

F — Zegda.
G — Assif Imlil.
H — Mamelon.
I — Asguine.

J — Affleurement calcaire.
K — Assif Zegda.
L — Ifechtalen.
M — Assif Asguine.

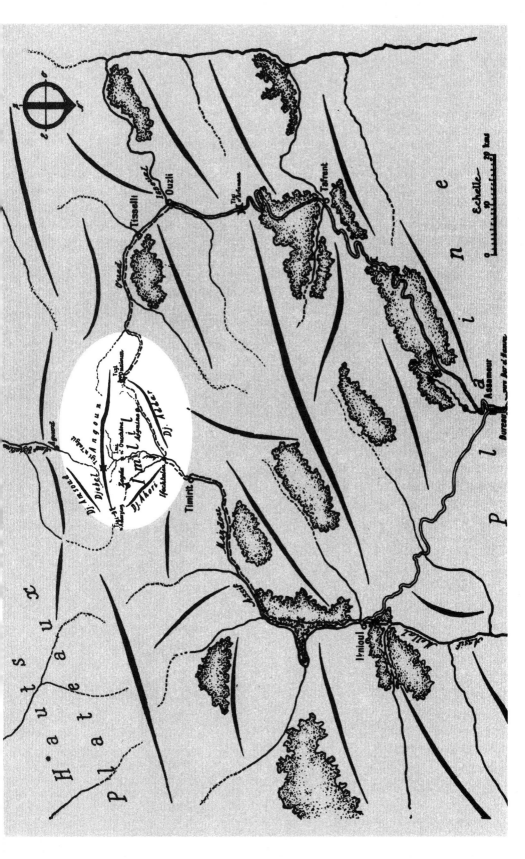

I

I

FOR A LONG WHILE, for a few moments perhaps, reclining on the bed in the white corner, the window at his feet, the wall to his left, to his right the night table and the vestibule door, motionless, alert, he has been observing the room: it is somewhat as if he were observing it from without, crouched against the balustrade bordering the garden: on this side of the walls, the room is this transparent cube coated with a dull, grainy, very clean whitewash. Of course, it is not strictly cubical, even if the corner fireplace on the other side of the window is disregarded. But the fireplace is in the shadows, the bed as well, and the illusion persists.

As a result of his listlessness, point of view splits in two, multiplies. Between eye and object, sleep interposes itself; attention gradually focuses, analyzing perspectives, improvising variations on the simplified outlines which ordinarily meet his gaze. Contours dissolve, planes dilate; upon the threshold of darkness, partitions disintegrate: upon these novel elements the white space restructures itself.

In this drowsy state, it is somewhat as if he were observing himself from without, in close range of his reflection in the right-hand corner of the walls.

From the window, a beam of pale light crosses the room and casts itself on the opposite wall, where two dark surfaces are hanging: on the right, the door leading to the bathroom; on the left, the twin flaps of the closet whose dark brown glinting paint is marred by streaks of roughly scraped-off plaster. A map is pinned to the wall, equally distant from the door and the closet; from the bed, some grayish patches are discernible, furrowed with curving lines: it is probably a map of the mountain where only the salient features of the relief emerge, but from a short distance it might be taken for a large insect or a creeper with branching offshoots.

[3]

Even though the remaining portion of the room is engulfed in darkness, he relocates the position of the objects without effort: the painted wooden night table against the bedstead; the wicker chair, between the window and the fireplace; a little farther, on the shelf above the hearth, the two terra-cotta candle holders.

On the floor, the black-and-white tile squares alternate in a checkerboard pattern: several are cracked or badly joined; the white ones are rather yellowed.

The ceiling is as white as the walls, and as empty. There is no electrical outlet in the room. But a sort of glazed Roman lamp, in which a piece of candle is stuck askew, has been placed on the night table. This is all he has at his disposal to light his way: he has forgotten the flashlight in his bag, which has been left in the bathroom with all the equipment.

Lying on his right side, the sheet pulled up under his chin for fear of mosquitoes, his eyes follow the dividing line between light and shadow, which runs to the foot of the wall, over there, along the small yellowed tiles of the plinth, then scales the entire height of the closet, stops in the vicinity of the ceiling, heads back toward the bathroom door, proceeds down along it, but disappears before touching the ground, concealed by the night table.

By raising his head, he perceives, behind the night table, the door to the vestibule, which is merely a narrow hallway: a portico leads to the front steps and, beyond, to the pebbly lane crossing the garden, to the left of the dust-covered palm tree. Is night beginning? Will it soon draw to a close? Determining the time is no simple matter: the wristwatch is on the night table, within reach, but the light is not strong enough to allow the hands to be discerned, yet is too intense for the phosphorescent clockface to stand out. The solution consists in getting close to the window, watch in hand—thus in pulling back the sheet and crawling to the foot of the bed, a complicated and daunting procedure. The heat is so heavy that the slightest movement sets off a fresh flow of sweat, and the sheets are already soaked through.

When he got up to close the window—because of the lizards scurrying over the lattice work of the mosquito net, making the mesh rustle under their claws—the whole room was plunged into darkness. Meanwhile, the moon rose behind the mountain, lighting up the hill. It is most probably this brightness which has made him reopen his eyes.

The light and noise, no matter how faint, disturb his sleep. With the window closed, the howls of the dogs and jackals still penetrate the room, coming from the hollow of the olive grove or the foothills of the mountain, answering each other endlessly; at times the answer is long in coming, but come it does without fail—haunting, uniform.

Right cheek pressed against the pillow, and the iron bed so low, he has the impression of lying at floor-level. Every time he opens his eyes, he spots the wall map which is reduced, at this hour, to the schematic outline of a plant, of an animal or a dwarf tree: a lush ball on the left, another sparer one on the right, linked to the former by an almost horizontal network of fibers.

But this makes short shrift of a night's rest. How to fall back to sleep under such conditions? It is better to turn over on your left side, nose against the wall. It is the only way he has of escaping the light, since he cannot prevent it from coming in: the blinds do not close. They informed him of this as soon as he arrived: the first one has broken blades, and the second is clinging to the wall by only a single hinge—he verified this himself during his tour of the house.

With each shift in position he experiences the same short-lived relief, a soothing sensation which fades very quickly. The window is shut, the air inert, the heat damp and unremitting. He would gladly throw the sheets off, but for the few mosquitoes which a while ago successfully edged their way in and are now hovering about in the vicinity of the bed. All the same, by enclosing himself, he made up for the defects in the mosquito net: the movable frame, badly fit together, is off kilter by nearly an inch; several links of the mesh have been snipped or torn open. But this satisfaction is fleeting. Caution would dictate methodically checking every path of entry: the chinks between the badly fitted tiles, the gaps under the doors, the condition of the roughcast, the inner covering of the closet, not to mention the great weak point of the system —the fireplace. The first precaution to take would be to have it blocked off for the duration of the torrid season. For all that, this room is exposed to every kind of surprise and, when all is said, in its present state does not offer the slightest protection.

He had nevertheless been notified, on several occasions, of the minor hazards, spiders being among them. They described various species to him: those with black bodies and long hairy legs, others with a yellowish hue, very dangerous. The majority were supposedly harmless. But the very idea of touching their legs with his lips or his eyelids was enough to terrify him—as was the thought that they could remain motionless for hours at a time, clinging to the ceiling, before dropping themselves down onto the sheets. With the reptiles, the problem was more complex, more controversial. How many stories had he been told, and among them, how many secondhand accounts, with several sources, some of which were beyond question, others suspect . . .

It always happens at siesta time, during a long listless afternoon. You are not really asleep, not quite awake either, but in a state of receptivity where you shift alternately between waking and sleep at a moment's notice, without lingering. Perhaps you really do fall asleep, although generally you claim the opposite. It begins with an ill-defined, rough rubbing, similar to the rustling of cloth, perceived as a purely aural phenomenon propagating in an abstract space. The sound is there, very close, but your attention has slackened, or is trained on several disconnected planes. The rubbing, however, grows more precise, intensifies, becomes so threatening that it triggers an abrupt about-face: the creature has slipped down onto the bed, its head as high as the bolster. Its thin spindly body undulates to the foot of the bed; its coat—green and black diamonds—has the texture of canvas. The details do not appear all at once: the image is global, instantaneous. Later, the diamonds come into view, set out against the black-and-white tiles: or the rings, wrapping the iron bed frame; the head as well, which cranes up, on the watch for danger. Later still, on the veranda, the narrow strip of cement comes into sight, very clean, hemmed with a double grayish border: the dust which the rings have swept along in their escape toward the wall of dry stones.

So runs the most frequent story. The essential elements are there: the first warning signs, the permanence of the danger. Then follows the standard advice: the inspection of hidden corners, glancing under the bed, stuffing the cracks under the doors, examining shoes, sheets, the mattress . . . failing this, the threat establishes its hold, surreptitiously and persists until a tiny creature is discovered under the pillow, motionless the whole time of sleep, a tarantula perhaps, or something else— some other name . . .

Naturally, in his rush, he neglected to take the most elementary precaution: looking under the bed. It is the shock of surprise which so often comes into play; therefore he ought to first guard against this by turning his back to the wall, for instance.

He finds himself precisely in this position, without remembering just when he assumed it. The zone of light has swung leftward: the wall opposite the window is once again in darkness, the outlines of the map are no longer distinguishable without difficulty. The blurred outer edges of the drawing have blended into the grisaille; only the bold central feature still stands out, chopped into short juxtaposed stumps. By contrast, the whole wall space between the closet and chimney is now lit up: spindly shadows undulate on the large white rectangle, intertwine, untangle themselves . . .

The periodic recurrence of the phenomenon intrigues him: a long branching vine shoots at regular intervals along the base of the panel, unfurls itself halfway up, then vanishes. Others, shorter, and more delicate, sway parallel, and merge into the first. At certain very brief moments, the whole panel is completely empty, that is to say, inanimate. But soon the shadows reappear and recompose their dance, retracing the familiar figures as if they could form only a limited number of patterns.

It is most likely the shadow of the palm tree: its leaves intercept the slanting light which strikes the villa. Or else it is a palm branch which, blown along by a gust, has lodged in the lattice work of the mosquito net, in which case the remedy is within reach.

He throws back the sheet, kneels, and inches across the bed toward the window. Reaching the end, still on his knees, he leans forward: then he sees the mountain in the distance, the enormous olive grove at the foot of the hill, flooded with a whitish light, the garden fence, and to the right of the lane, the palm tree, much smaller than he imagined it, squat, stunted. The moon comes into view between the leaves from time to time, just above the ridgeline. He remains there for a while, his forehead against the window, his hands leaning on the whitewashed ledge. Suddenly an inch or so from his face, on the other side of the pane, he spies a huge black spider, belly pressed against the lattice. Its legs are working at the mesh links—he hears them scratching the iron wire. Its body is very elongated, antennae-like objects jut above its head. The double screen prevents the details from being clearly distinguished.

Perhaps it is not a spider ... But he has no inclination to open the window. He is only thinking about falling back to sleep ... He draws himself up, retraces backward the path he has traveled across the bed and once again slips under the sheet, which he pulls up to his chin.

Yet again he crouches in the corner, flush against the wall, and buries his head under the sheet. His body is soaked with sweat. He shifts the position of his legs several times, to little avail. The rectangular frame of the window emerges from the blackness of the closed eyelids, with its cross-shaped uprights marking out the location of the four panes, and behind the upper left pane—the present sketch eliminating the mosquito net—the schematic silhouette of the spider: the body two or three centimeters long, the legs hook-shaped and, higher up, what might have been taken a moment ago for antennae, now resembling a pair of pincers. He reopens his eyes, closes them: each time the image recomposes itself. He believes that once again he is aware of the rustling of legs on the links of the lattice work, despite the thickness of the sheet and despite the windowpane. Or else it is the memory of the sound which strikes his ear, so like that of the image behind his closed eyelids. Perhaps other creatures are cutting a path through the darkness, along the black-and-white tiles, grazing the legs of the chair or the night table as they pass.

After a certain amount of time has passed, the window frame has disappeared. Other images have taken its place, gray lines crisscrossing upon a white screen. They converge toward the center, then, the motion quickening, trace at full speed a series of circumferences with short radii. When total confusion reigns, when the gray lines have merged into an opaque ball that seems to turn on itself with a calculated slowness—is this the visual consequence of the tangle of accelerated rotations?—an iridescent glow runs along the rim, at first indistinct, then of a garish red streaked with violet bands. The hue spreads as upon a washed-out watercolor, and the more surface it covers, the fainter it becomes. When it begins to contaminate the central disc, it has turned to a pale pink, the violet stripes to blue. The disc, shriveling, is soon no more than a thin black circle moving about against a colored backdrop with a flexible structure: the bluish effusions gather together in a myriad of small square blocks arranged in staggered rows: upon this pink-and-blue checkerboard, the black circle sets itself in motion. It penetrates the first blue cubicle; its passage is accompanied by a slight crackling. The pawn pursues its course. At the second blue cubicle, the crackling takes place more dryly, more insistently.

At the third crackling, he jumps up with a start: something has moved, very close to the bed. He leans with his elbows upon the bolster. Perhaps it was merely the squeaking of the bed springs . . . For peace of mind, he bounces his body sharply: the bed springs do indeed squeak, but was that really the sound? The room is in pitch darkness: a very feeble glow on the window side, when the eyes are trained in the opposite direction. On the night table the clockface stands out legibly, the hands indicating two-thirty . . . He must have slept an hour, perhaps more. And the sound fills the air once again, like a scraping along a smooth, resonant surface. It is surely not the lattice work of the mosquito net. It is within the room. He leans over the floor tiles: the sound is there, under the bed.

Sitting up in bed, he gropes for the matches. His unsteady fingers push the box away twice, inadvertently. He catches it at last, strikes a match and brings it toward the candle.

He passes the lamp above the floor tiles, along the bed, from the window to the night table, then along the narrow space between the bed and table, until he reaches the wall. The creature is there. He recognizes it instantly: the scorpion is scraping the metal upright with its pincers. The legs are working furiously, drawing close to the cylinder each time that the pincers, in a fruitless effort to hold their position, loosen their grip and fall back down. They are gaping open, far longer than the legs, and flattened out toward the middle. But it's the elongation of the body, yet again, which surprises him, this caudal apparatus out of proportion with the rest, these angular rings you would think were slipped end to end along a curving steel shaft, and at the tip, almost above the head, raised up in the opposite direction, the stinger, lying flat, needle-sharp, seeking its prey skyward. The wavering candle glow makes the shadow of the pincers dance on the plinth.

He jumps from the bed, lamp in hand, grabs hold of one of the sandals set against the door, squats down: the scorpion is no longer there. Quickly he drops to his knees, sets the lamp on the floor, looks about. But he must shield the flame, which blinds him, and is barely able to make out the stinger at the very instant it is disappearing behind the foot of the chair. In the time it takes to get up and spring to the corner fire-place, it is already too late: the scorpion has escaped.

He moves the chair, searches again under the bed, in case the creature might have made an about-turn, but all his efforts are in vain. It cannot be found . . . It has surely fled through the fireplace, whose timeworn facing bears several poorly set bricks. For a long while he inspects the hearth in the candle glow, sandal in hand.

Yet perhaps other scorpions are there lurking in the room; he has not the least inclination to get stung. Conscientiously he makes the round of the walls, inspecting as he passes the closet, which is empty, the bath-room door, the vestibule door. He finds nothing, comes back toward the window and leans with his elbows on the whitewashed ledge: outside, it is pitch dark. The mountain is no longer visible, nor the olive grove, nor the garden, not even the palm tree branches . . . The creature would certainly not have succeeded in clinging to the iron upright: its legs could not get a grip on the metal. But it could climb along the wall and from there scurry across the pillow. The scorpion could surely climb along the wall . . . At any rate, the best thing is to move the bed away.

He sets the candle on the fireplace mantel and pulls the bed to the middle of the room, wheeling it around, so that he will be lying with his back to the window. To set his mind at rest, he turns the sheets around, the pillow, the bolster, lifts the mattress. Finally, he replaces the lamp on the table, lies back down and blows out the candle.

He still has at least four or five hours left to sleep . . . He shuts his eyes.

Behind his closed eyelids a black-and-white grid soon takes form, over which a pawn carved with an unusual design is running diagonally, with a halting and uncertain motion, similar to that of a tiny mechanism, barely wound up.

II

The greater part of the tile floor is concealed by a garishly blue, deep-pile woolen carpet, so filthy that at every step small particles of dust are raised by the shoe tips. The sun, already high, penetrates within the room through a large bay window: the rays, striking diagonally, light up two rows of black-and-white tiles which extend slightly beyond the carpet fringe.

The captain's desk is facing away from the mountain. It looks out upon a terreplein bordered with shrubs and, beyond, upon the northern slope of the hill, planted with almond trees, carob trees and Aleppo pines. A double row of eucalyptus highlights the winding line of the road which descends toward the olive grove on the plain, at the very bottom, then slips between the stands of trees and recedes out of sight into a sheet of purple mist from which emerges, at the horizon, a string of pyramidal outcroppings and, closer, a column of red sand propelled upward at full speed, vertical upon its whirling pedestal.

Three armchairs with adjustable backs are set up side by side on the rug, opposite the fireplace, where glazed ocher candle holders have been placed alongside a pitcher and a red earthenware utensil which, from the other side of the room, could be taken for a club or an incense burner.

Three frames are hung on the wall above the fireplace: two global views from above of a Moorish city with its ramparts and minarets, and the portrait of a general in three-quarter profile, probably executed during a ceremony: the mask-like expression is full of energy, the eyes bright, the moustache bushy, the right hand raised horizontally to the cap-visor.

Behind the desk, along the whole breadth of the panel, an enormous map is on display, including the mountainous massif in its entirety, a triangular portion of the plain in the northwest and in the southeast, the onset of the high desert plateaus.

The desk, which is very long, has been furnished with two series of side drawers. A lamp to the right and a telephone to the left frame a leather blotter diagonally crossed by a gilded metal ruler, solid and sharp-edged, with which Captain Weiss, leaning over the desk, has been playing mechanically since the start of the interview. Seated in the swivel chair, elbows firmly propped at the table edge, he begins by pressing two fingers at each end of the ruler, then flips it from one side to the other, then runs it forward and backward and then sideways across the blotter, in such a way as to sweep the entire leather surface, and finally lifts it an inch or so, swinging it from right to left and then releasing it: the ruler drops with a muffled thud. Then his forehead is raised and two gray eyes scrutinize his interlocutor for a brief moment. But this means nothing: almost instantly his glance darts away, and the officer, his nose lowered, eyelids half-closed, resumes his monologue:

— You'll see that the people of Imlil are very friendly. Very independent-minded, naturally, as are all the high mountain tribes. Perhaps wary is the word, fiercely guarded the moment they suspect you of meddling in their affairs. But on the other hand amiable, hospitable when you have gained their confidence . . . And they quickly make up their minds about you: your appearance, the look in your eyes . . . your gait . . . It often comes down to trifles.

Seated across from the fireplace in the middle armchair, whose orientation he cannot adjust, Lassalle forces himself with varying degrees of success to display the conventional signs of polite attention: head tilted a quarter-turn toward the desk, left elbow planted on the armrest, his hand propping his chin, legs crossed, his right-hand fingers tapping the nailheads exposed at the end of the other chair-arm . . . He quickly finds he cannot maintain this posture. But to transfer his center of balance to the right would result in twisting around his neck at a wider angle, sharpening the cramp and ultimately increasing his discomfort. The only thing to do is to bide his time until a pretext to change his seat arises.

— You have never been here before, am I right? . . . And you don't know Arabic? . . . That's a shame, obviously, even though your work does not require constant contact with the population . . . Besides, Arabic would not be of much help to you: the tribe speaks mostly dialect. Those who understand Arabic in the high mountains are few and far between. I have even visited douars where no one spoke it . . . Despite everything, naturally, Arabic would have made things easier for you . . . Well, you'll grasp in no time a few essential words . . . words of dialect probably . . .

Once again his fingers have clutched the ruler, which they run along the leather, parallel to the rectangle's sides, then they raise it just a fraction, release it, grasp it again, run it along the leather, raise, release . . .

Lassalle, fixed in a pose which is more and more self-conscious, seems to be following the maneuvers of the fingers better than the thread of what is being said. If the time had been given him for his part in the dialogue, he would make do with monosyllables:

— Yes (it's the first time he has come to this country).

— No (he doesn't know Arabic, where would he have learned it?).

— Yes (his work will allow for this gap).

— Yes, Captain, thank you. It's been of great use.

— Think nothing of it, it's quite natural . . . I came back very late last night. I was wondering if they had thought to bring it up to you.

The ruler drops once again, and the gray, tired eyes settle a moment on the newcomer.

Without relinquishing the attentive tilt of his head, Lassalle stretches his legs out in front of him, slides his left elbow along the armrest and crosses his hands over his belt.

— Speaking of which—it's the room which made me think of it—a foreign geographer came to the Office the other day . . . Or a geologist, I'm not quite sure. Like you, he was heading toward the Angoun, on his way to Imlil, or perhaps farther along the southern slope . . . I was out on an inspection tour. My assistant was the one who spoke with him . . . This was about two weeks ago . . . A certain Hessing, or Gessing, or something very close to that . . . Perhaps he is here on the same business as yourself?

— No, certainly not, Captain . . . I've never heard of him.

— He came through Iknioul, I think . . . But it's not much shorter than the road through Ouzli. You make time on the paved roadway, you lose it on the mule path: two or three hours of road and two days on mule . . . The high mountains are a godforsaken region. That's the reason the road to Imlil interests us in many respects. Everyone will benefit from it . . . But you must take into account the months it is snowed under, the loose soil, the shortage of manpower, the autumn storms . . .

Footsteps crunch on the gravel of the terreplein, flush against the rosemary bush, then along the wall: a shadow slowly advances from right to left, from the armory to the office. Although the windows have been closed, the shutters have not been drawn and so the heat is intensifying in the room almost as quickly as if they had been left wide open. The only difference is that the air is not circulating at all: sweat is beading on nape and forehead, especially on the nape, turned toward the terreplein.

— Do you have a vehicle at your disposal?

— No, unfortunately, I don't anymore. The truck from the Company had to continue on again immediately after bringing me from Dar el Hamra last night. It had a long road to travel through the south today . . . I was hoping to rent some mules and make the climb in three or four days, in small stages.

— Yes, of course, but it's very long . . . If only you could locate an opportunity . . . someone who would be going up today on one or another of the trails . . . Hold on a moment, I'm going to ask right away, in case there's any chance you might save some time . . .

Captain Weiss picks up the receiver and calls the operator. Lassalle takes advantage of this to get up and take a few steps around the room. Then he comes and sits back down on the seat closest to the desk.

The captain has tilted himself back in his armchair. He has kept the ruler in his right hand and at one moment taps it repeatedly on the edge of the table, at another wipes the sweat from his forehead with his shirt-sleeve. At first, the conversation revolves around something which is apparently rather far off the point: the affluence of vehicles in the Assameur souk—or the influence of a certain person on the Assameur souk. But only a part of the dialogue is audible, and the sentences are broken up with unknown proper names, references to local happenings, new words, most likely Arabic, which perhaps designate familiar objects. Then the captain falls silent for a long while, nose in the air, his gaze lost in the ceiling . . . The fireplace, directly opposite, is covered with small white tiles, exactly like those of the room. The iron grill in the hearth is overflowing with crumpled papers rolled up in balls. The globe-shaped, red earthenware object has been placed flat on the mantelpiece, between the jug and the candle holders. It is furnished with a short handle with stippled ribbing. It is most certainly not a weapon: the globe, pierced with myriad round holes, appears hollow . . . The captain has begun to speak again. It has to do with a small minivan which must be returned to a tribe this afternoon; but its destination remains obscure, unless this was established at the very beginning of the communication, within the series of incomprehensible names.

— Fine then, it's perfect! All right! See you soon!

The captain hangs up the receiver, sits up straight, and once again leans on the table:

— You see, everything's working out for the best: the forest rangers have to make a stop-off in Tafrent early this afternoon. The sergeant will take you in his minivan. At least it will bring you closer. Tafrent is halfway to Ouzli . . .

He gets up, looks for something in front of him, hesitates, finally grabs the ruler and turns toward the survey map. The ruler follows the blue line of a stream, skirts around a range of mountains, crosses a mountain pass . . . Standing in front of the map, but on the other side of the desk, Lassalle traces in imagination the same itinerary, just as he has been doing every evening for quite some time already, on the same map and on the documents that the Company has transmitted to him: maps and charts drawn up during previous missions, surveys of the future trail, descriptions of the chief obstacles with supporting photographs, and above all, topographical studies of the Imlil basin—of particular value, since Imlil and its high surrounding ranges in the deep south of Assameur are invisible on the survey map, lost somewhere in the center of a vast uncharted zone.

The ruler, upon leaving Assameur, traces a vast half circle westward and reaches Imlil by way of Ouzli. Continuing eastward in a roughly symmetrical half circle, it rejoins Assameur by way of Iknioul.

— The new map will be out this year, supposedly. Naturally, it will be complete. Until then, we must make do with approximate sketches . . .

Captain Weiss seems to have finished his business with the map. He contemplates it silently a few more moments, then turns halfway around and passes his hand across his forehead absently.

— Let's see . . . It's now eight-thirty. Do you want to come back at ten? I have to go down to the souk. I'll take you along . . . The sergeant will be there: you'll settle the departure time with him.

Leaving the Office, Lassalle finds himself directly on the small rectangular yard around which the administrative buildings are grouped: barracks on the left—a long wall coated with red roughcast, bracketed by towers on each end, with an entrance in the center where a sentinel in a khaki gandoura keeps watch; a cube-shaped edifice with a covered courtyard under which white figures are dozing at the foot of the arcades; a villa with a green tile roof, an acacia bush, a tamarind tree and a clump of aloe. The leaves are covered with a film of gray dust. All the walls are of the same purplish red, crumbling, filthy, with long black streaks under the waterspouts.

Lassalle crosses the square diagonally and retraces in the opposite direction the path that led him to the Office an hour before.

A hundred meters away, the small villa rises opposite the mountain, on the southern slope of the hill. A wooden fence leads into a dirt courtyard. Not a single blade of grass is growing from the hard, cracked soil.

The door opens directly onto the bathroom where, during the interval he was gone, all his belongings have been gathered together and repacked: against the bathtub the three large leather bags have been set side by side, crammed with supplies and equipment: the tent, the accessories and the camp bed are in the first; in the second are the mattress, the sleeping bag and the food; jacket, some clothes and a change of sheets are in the third, as well as the measuring instruments, the maps, papers, the leather briefcase and the blotter. Only the first is heavy; the two others, despite their size, are relatively light: it ought to be possible to hitch all three onto the same animal.

Lassalle goes over to the sink, turns on the faucet, and lets a little water run across his forehead: the water is hot. Mechanically, he takes the clothes brush from the glass shelf and begins to clean his pants, but it is a pointless process: in no time at all the souk dust will have soiled them again.

Standing in front of the mirror, he checks his attire: linen khaki pants, long-sleeved linen shirt, leather sandals, light and flexible, the large boots reserved for scaling rocky terrain. The problem of headgear greatly preoccupied him. All yesterday morning in Dar el Hamra, he weighed the pros and cons, reluctant to buy a hat, doubtful that he had any real need. Since he didn't usually wear one, he was afraid of not knowing what to do with it, of leaving it behind, of forgetting it at their stops, finally of losing it. He could not come to a decision. After all, in an emergency, he could use his imagination to come up with an expedient alternative.

The inventory of his pockets is quickly accomplished: wallet, pipe, tobacco pouch, matchbox, key ring, pipe cleaner, pen, pocket diary. This small tablet, bound in green leather, comes with a miniature pencil. It is in here that he plans to summarize his daily activities in a few words, without going into details, with one sole purpose: to avoid mixing up dates, or recording information in overlapping blocks, or mistakenly ascribing one day's happenings to another, or facing the abrupt void of memory. Later, when reading these short sentences, remembrance will weave a tighter web of facts. The most difficult part, once the principle is accepted, is to acquire the habit of making an entry every evening . . . In fact, flipping through the tablet, he notices that he wrote nothing the night before. Therefore he jots down, under the heading "Thursday, August fifth": "Morning in Dar el Hamra. Left at 3 P.M. Arrived in Assameur at 7 P.M. Night spent in the guest room at Headquarters." At the bottom of the same page, an analogous block is assigned to Friday, August sixth. He is about to write: "Visited the Assameur souk. Left . . ." After a moment's hesitation, he replaces the pencil in its holder and closes the small tablet.

In the room, the tiles have been swept, the bed made and pushed back into the corner of the wall between the window and the vestibule door. Even though seen against the glare, the fireplace reveals a dilapidated inner coating: the plaster is cracked everywhere, the bricks are badly fitted and crumbling. Obviously, all sorts of tiny creatures could edge their way in.

The four walls are bare except for the panel opposite the window, embellished with a grayish image which distance and darkness caused him to mistake last night for a map of the mountain. But it is not a map. It is an engraving that represents a low coastline covered with broom and, below, a handle-shaped beach, bounded to the east and west by unapproachable jutting cliffs. The rocks advance seaward in two symmetrical arcs. In the background, at the horizon, a larger mass emerges, at the summit of which rises a skeletal tree with a marked eastward slant. This piece of land seems inaccessible either from one or the other of the rocky points. The outline of the shore remains indistinct, disappearing in the waves whose ridged edges merge into each other. Overall, the drawing is murky, softened, blurred. It was most likely the dark mass of rocks which created the night's illusion. The picture bears neither title nor place name, and its presence in this room has no clear explanation.

Lassalle moves away from the wall, stretches out on the bed, but the fear of dozing off—he did not get such a good sleep last night—soon forces him to his feet and to the window ledge, where he sits down.

The narrow window is shut, so as to keep the room as cool as possible.

Even though the temperature is almost the same as it was at night, it seems more bearable at this moment, perhaps because it is so much hotter outside. The mosquito netting, despite its flaws, filters the light somewhat. The sky is not unsullied, but furrowed with long white streaks which diffuse the sun's rays in a dull glare that is very hard on the eyes.

To the left, the dwarf palm looms over a plain hemmed around with holly bushes, even more wretched than in the moonlight. Farther on, a large eucalyptus takes up the southwestern corner of the garden, surrounded by a stone wall with a green balustrade along the top. Immediately beyond the wall, the hill drops down into the olive grove, whose trees seem to have been planted haphazardly, with no sense of alignment. Most of them are very old; many are dead.

Three quarters of a mile or so from here, at the other end of the olive grove, bluish smoke is rising above a vast pink quadrangle—the ramparts of Assameur—and immediately behind them begins the mountain: three lines of crests, with well-defined edges, stretch in tiers from north to south, and are crushed at the horizon by a gigantic steep-sided bastion.

Lassalle does not need to consult his map: this distant rocky prow that stands out against the white sky, looming four-thousand meters over the entire range, is the Angoun itself, at ten leagues distance, always snow-covered in photographs, drawings, and postcards. Today Angoun is gray, leaden, and the lighting accentuates the deeply incised gullies of its northern face.

Imlil is located at the foot of the long terminal ridge, along with its three valleys, its terraced fields, its high-walled casbahs slit with loopholes and its few scrawny trees, vestiges of forests, landmarks in the rocky terrain.

The Angoun appears quite near but it is several days away by foot, several days away from these slopes above Assameur, where slabs of schist gleam in the slanting sunlight.

III

At the other end of the souk, in the slaughter yard, pools of blood are spreading out at the foot of the beams, under the iron hooks which were used for hanging up the animals. A pack of ten or so dogs is pouncing upon shreds of meat covered with flies, their tongues lolling, their fur sticky, as if they had first rolled around in the pools, then dried off in the dust, upon which fresh drops are trickling.

A short man draws near: he has a shiny scalp, a black beard, and a djellaba spattered with brownish stains over the whole front of his body, as well as over his sleeves, his shoulders; even the bag slung over his shoulder has not been spared. With both hands clutching a bludgeon behind his back, he moves within range of the first dog, brandishes the weapon, rears up and with all his might strikes the animal on the skull. A cry rises, which promises to become piercing. But the sound is choked off: the dog whines, flattened on its side in the puddle where it had been splashing about. Its paws are flailing, its belly swells up in convulsive bursts. The man raises his arm again: the bludgeon sweeps down and strikes for a second time. The paws grow still. The man next takes out his knife, leans over the dog and cuts off its ears, which he stuffs into his bag. Then he takes a step forward. Several dogs have fled, but not all of them: a few have remained behind, still rummaging around in the scraps.

Sergeant Pozzi lifts his cap and wipes the back of his neck with a large green handkerchief which has long since been soaked through.

— It's because of the rabid dogs, he explains to Lassalle, standing beside him. Then he turns on his heels, passes in front of the butcher's stall and goes back toward the main thoroughfare. After a few steps, he stops once again, lifts his cap, wipes. He adds, as if in answer to a protest:

— Somebody has to do it.

In the broad avenue, two streams of strollers confront each other in a disorganized mob through which the sergeant slips with a surprising ease. Following him, but already at several breast-lengths distance, Lassalle works his elbows to edge his way through. His only landmark —not counting the sergeant who, being of very small stature, might well escape from him—is a red bed rampart running parallel to the avenue, capped with wobbly crenels. A stork has built its nest upon one of the cubes of dismantled cob. Behind the rampart a sort of gallows rises at the tip of a minaret. This is all he discerns beyond a rolling wave of blue, white, and gray fabrics, from which only a few of the privileged rise into view on the backs of donkeys or mules, along with wicker baskets, and two-handled pitchers set on women's heads. The wooded side of the mountain that appeared from time to time on the left has become invisible.

A little later, the sergeant, in turn, disappeared, his cap swallowed up in a swirl of turbans and djellaba hoods. But the central traffic circle must not be very far off. The crucial thing is to manage holding your course approximately along the axis of the avenue, despite the crush of the crowd.

Luckily the nearness of the rampart greatly helps matters. Progress is slow of course, but sure and steady. About thirty yards to go and the avenue meets the traffic circle.

The sergeant is not there. He has continued on his way, either in a straight line or else along one of the branch roads running at right angles. Considering the situation, obviously the wisest thing would be to stay and wait for him here: he will not fail to about-turn as soon as he notices he is no longer being followed.

The intersection is laid out in a traffic circle, with large road markers rounded like sugarloaves on the top set around the circumference. The crowd pouring in from four different directions is jostling and merging with the greatest possible confusion. Donkeys caught in the center of the commotion are circling around themselves in spite of threats and switch-blows. A bicycle is vainly attempting to extricate itself.

This is where the captain, having arranged to meet the sergeant, showed up an hour earlier to make quick introductions: he parked his car at the souk entrance, beside the path, crossed through the portal, strode up the avenue leading to the traffic circle, went up to meet the sergeant, held out his hand . . . He passed through the courtyard after leaving his office, crossed the porch looking out on the administrative square, strode forward, stretched out his hand, stationed himself behind the steering wheel of his car, pointed to the empty place next to him in the front seat, started the motor and, after a quick glance at his wrist-watch, was on his way.

The car joined the main road at the other end of the square, went down the hillside by following a ramp to the right after two short turns, and at the very bottom of the slope passed through the first curtain of trees. The road began winding back and forth between tiny plots, from one clump of olive trees to another, an irrigation ditch running along the left, and on the right a dusty verge where people on foot, on bikes and on horseback rushed to make way at the first sound.

Then the crowd must have taken a shortcut because the way suddenly emptied, and the road plunged into a gully. On a single-lane bridge, far below, they were moving once again, the donkeys, bicycles, horses, and a camel loaded down with enormous baskets, behind which they were forced to crawl along until the roadway opened up to its normal width. At the bottom of the dry wadi, tufts of oleander bristled between the rocks.

The road climbed again immediately after the bridge and rejoined the olive grove at the middle level of the basin. Two hundred meters farther on, a herd blocked the way, having drawn even with a flat single-level structure, apparently new, which the captain referred to as an "infirmary." Groups lingered out in front, some composed, while others wrangled, their sleeves sweeping eloquently through the air. Mules were hitched to the wall in the corner of the building.

The car slowed down and stopped under an olive tree. "Let's go see what's going on," the captain said as he opened the door.

The people cleared a path when he reached the stairs. He climbed the three steps and penetrated into a long narrow room, furnished with benches on the side, at the end of which a cracked open door revealed a second smaller room, and, within this room, a man in a white coat, leaning over a bed.

At the sound of footsteps, the man turned his head and opened the door wide. At the captain's question, he motioned them in, stepped aside and pointed toward the bed:

— They brought her in not even a quarter of an hour ago . . . She was lying on a mule.

A very young girl is reclining on the bed, naked to her belt—unconscious, or asleep. Her head is straight and firmly propped on the pillow. Her arms are dangling along the metal uprights.

— She was stabbed twice . . . They say it happened the day before yesterday, but the wound's surely older than that.

Once again the attendant leans over and finishes tying a strip of cloth around her waist, which is then fit over a large bandage above the right breast.

The only furniture in the small room is a table on wheels and a cabinet where vials are set in rows on glass plates. On the floor, black-and-white square tiles in staggered rows form a vast rectangular checkerboard, shiny and spotless. There is no one else in the room except for the three men standing around the bed.

The nape of the neck is slightly raised by the headrest. The hair is very black and parted down the middle, with braids which, from behind the ears, fall to the shoulders on either side of a necklace made of silver coins strung upon a silk thread. She has a broad, very prominent fore-head with a tapering lower face, and hollow cheeks. The full protruding lips twitch subtly. The eyes, set unusually far apart, seem to be located at the borders of the temples, past the jut of the cheekbones. The eyelids are closed, the lashes perfectly still.

— Where did you say they come from?

— From the Aït Andiss, sir . . . Normally it takes more than two days to come down from there. And with a wounded girl on muleback, over such pathways . . .

The attendant pushes the table against the wall and puts a bottle back in the cabinet.

— Did you take her name?

— Her name's Jamila, I think, Jamila . . . I'll check the exact details with them shortly: they're in front of the door out there . . . I barely had time to clean the wound.

— Have you informed the doctor?

— I've had him sent for. He had left for the médina.

The captain takes a few steps in the room, wipes the sweat from his forehead, looks at his wristwatch.

— Fine . . . Let them stay there while waiting. I'm going as far as the souk, then I'm coming back.

He casts one last glance upon the bed, then heads for the door, followed by the attendant. As the captain goes out, the other motions to pull both sides of the door shut.

Through the cracked open door the only thing which remains visible is the head of the bed, between a panel of the wall and two rows of black-and-white tiles and, upon the pillow, the delicate triangular face, extremely pale, still motionless. The braids fall on each side of the necklace and reach the base of the throat. The lips are still twitching imperceptibly, but the eyelashes have been raised and the eyes, wide open, are now looking toward the door, effortlessly, the sudden light not appearing to bother them, each set at the outer edge of the face, one of them alert, close, piercing, the other faraway, calm, impersonal.

Behind, the sound of footsteps is growing faint; an emptiness is establishing itself, along the whole length of the waiting room, between the two men who are withdrawing and the wall at the far end, the door cracked open in the threshold of the small room, and there, very near, discovered by chance, emerging suddenly from unconsciousness or sleep, the sidelong pale green gaze, clouded over with fever and exhaustion.

Bursts of speech filter in from outside: the captain has paused at the top of the stairs and is talking with an old man bent upon a cane. He seems on the point of leaving . . .

Upon the pillow, slightly raised by the headrest, the head is still very straight, but the eyes have closed again, the long curling lashes are once more lowered, motionless. Upon the breasts, the tips of the braids are almost joined below the necklace.

On the stairs, the captain is in the midst of shaking the old man's hand . . . In the time it takes to stride across the waiting room, he's already at the bottom of the steps. He immediately heads toward his car. On the road, the curious crowd begins to drift away.

The captain opens the car door, stations himself behind the steering wheel, starts the motor:

— I'm going to drive you to the souk, I'll drop you off there with the sergeant. Please accept my apologies but, as you can see, I have to come back.

The car begins to move. In front of the facade wall only a small group of three men is left gathered around the old man: two among them have their backs turned to the road; the third, a cigarette in his mouth, is leaning against a mule in a corner of the building: his eyes follow the car as it rejoins the roadway, passes in front of the infirmary and, gathering speed, disappears around the first bend.

Several hundred meters further on, the city walls of Assameur become visible at the end of a long straight line. But the car, leaving the main thoroughfare, turns onto a dusty dirt road full of potholes.

At the souk entrance, the captain maneuvers his car so that he is in position to leave, then steps out, crosses through the portal, walks up the avenue toward the intersection where the sergeant is waiting for him.

The sergeant waves as he spots him, raises his cap, wipes his nape, takes a few steps forward . . . The sergeant suddenly emerges from the crowd, waves, reaches the center of the traffic circle, wipes his nape:

— I really thought I'd never find you again! As soon as somebody disappears from sight, in this crush . . .

He takes Lassalle along the side avenue, the left branch which leads to a square building lined with arcades.

— We have to climb on the roof of the mahakma. It's the only place where you have a good view of the souk.

The avenue is only fifty meters long, but it is jammed with merchants selling tea, sugar and spices: the smell of mint, cumin, pepper, and cinnamon is intermingled with that of olive oil, sweat, urine and dung.

Beneath the arcades, in the shadow of the inner courtyard, Sergeant Pozzi negotiates with a guard wearing a pointed red cap. He quickly obtains satisfaction: the guard takes a large key out of his bag and opens a double-sided, rib-shaped door.

The interior is empty. A table and two chairs are placed on a platform, benches arranged along the walls; a huge mass of paper scraps strew the ground.

— There was a hearing yesterday, the sergeant explains, heading toward a ladder attached to a corner of the wall.

The guard climbs the ladder, pushes open a trapdoor in the ceiling and hoists himself onto the roof. Lassalle clambers up after him, then the sergeant, who breathes heavily while getting a foothold.

— Stay close to the edge, above all. You have to be careful about these sorts of terrace roofs. They're never very solid.

The view from the terrace was indeed very beautiful, upon the souk as well as the médina, the olive grove and, naturally, the first range of mountains.

In the other half of the souk, hidden until now, a vast enclosure is used as an animal market, a smaller one as a grain market. Packed earth huts are lined up on each side of a circular avenue set aside for craftsmen: coppersmiths, cobblers, blacksmiths, potters ... These latter display numerous objects upon the ground: candlestick holders, lamps, yellow and brown glazed jugs, and other utensils, among which Lassalle thinks he recognizes that club-like thing decorating the mantel in the captain's office—but it may only be a large wooden ladle.

Trucks are parked along the rampart wall, in the crenels of which several storks have established their nests. Every hundred meters or so rises a tower, more or less in disrepair. The red walls curve to the north and south, encircling the médina, then disappear behind the terrace roofs that ascend from the perimeter to the raised city center, dominated by a large casbah with windowless walls.

This overall imposing panorama would be worth photographing. Lassalle, motionless at the roof edge, is sorry for the first time that he forgot his camera.

Imagining how to frame it is an easy matter: without moving from the spot, you would simply bring the viewfinder to eye level. A classic subject, with picturesque background, "local color" in the foreground, everything contributing to the success of the shot, except for the lighting, far too uniform in the middle of the afternoon. It would have been necessary to come this morning, around six o'clock, when the first rays, slanting down upon the city, create dramatic contrasts ... But the problem, at any rate, does not present itself.

Sergeant Pozzi walks back toward the trapdoor:

— It's about time to go back down ... it's well past noon. I don't want to get too late a start.

He already has set a foot on the first rung of the ladder, but he raises his head:

— Will you accept an invitation to share my lunch? I would never forgive myself if I let you eat at the canteen: it's full of flies, the food is rank and there's no room to turn around.

Lassalle accepts, thanks the sergeant and takes one last glimpse of the souk. But the spectacle has already lost its attraction. And all this commotion dazes him; the heat knocks him out; the odors go right to his head; the intense glare burns his eyes.

More specifically, recalling the countless zigzags through the olive grove makes him queasy.

He feels a slow migraine stationing itself behind his forehead.

IV

Since the temperature has reached 45 degrees centigrade, the main thoroughfare of Assameur is completely deserted, but in the side streets white shapes are reclining along the foot of walls in the dust.

The minivan slowly passes under the ramparts on its way out of the city, then pulls onto the asphalt road. It picks up speed. In the front seat to the right of the sergeant, Lassalle, dazed by exhaustion and the sunlight, jiggles his head at every jolt and twist of the steering wheel. Waves of sleep rise to his forehead, his eyes close, his head bows. When crossing over certain especially sharp bumps, images of trees still impress themselves on his attention from time to time: gnarled trunks, dead branches, silvery-gray leaves.

A sudden swerve sends him flying against the door: the minivan has just made contact with the gradient at the foot of the hill and is forging up and ahead. But the slope is steep, the motor is wheezing, and they slow to a crawl as they ascend.

At the very top, the administrative square is sunk in listlessness. There is not a living soul within the vicinity of the Office. Only the sentinel is walking back and forth under the barracks' portal.

The minivan makes a circuit of the square, slows down and parks in front of the gate to the small pavilion.

Lassalle steps out at the same time as the native corporal jumps out of the back, then opens the gate, crosses the courtyard in the bright sunlight, enters the house, indicates to the corporal two of the bags lined up against the bathtub, glances around in a circle to check that he has left nothing behind, hoists the third bag onto his shoulder, goes out, closes the door, crosses back through the garden.

The Arab packs the three bags in the back, on top of the picks and shovels, and squats down on the biggest bag. Lassalle resumes his place in the front seat. The minivan starts up, goes back to the road, and then down toward the olive grove.

At the end of the ascent, after the bridge on the wadi, a flat structure rises to the right in a clearing. Lassalle recognizes the infirmary, whose long, dazzling white facade wall should have already caught his eye a short while ago when he was riding in the opposite direction: but perhaps he was turning his head at that instant, or he was dozing.

The outskirts of the edifice, so crowded this morning, are now clear. The minivan draws near, passes in front of the wall, reaches the front steps, level with the bay window: the waiting room comes into view for a fraction of a second along its entire length, including the small door opening into the other room. There is no one inside. Everything seems calm and silent.

And already the road is turning: the building is veering away into the distance. In the middle of a bend, it slips behind a curtain of trees.

A few minutes later, the minivan once again rolls through the chicane door at the entrance to the city, progresses a few hundred meters into the main avenue, then brakes, stopping in front of a gas pump.

The sergeant gets out and walks over to knock at the door of a gourbi labeled "Garage." At the third try, a boy comes out, wearing a yellow shirt and red trousers, and he heads toward the pump with a yawn.

The corporal has let himself slip down from the bag onto the roadway: with his back against the wagon's tarpaulin, he talks with the boy while the smell of gas begins to spread around the vehicle. The sergeant nods his head and says a few words of Arabic in turn. Then each returns to his starting point: the corporal climbs onto the bags again, the boy reenters his gourbi, the sergeant restations himself behind the steering wheel.

The main road goes around the casbah at the city center and one more time cuts through the fortified walls, especially tumbledown at this point.

Beyond is a dirt trail crossing the southern part of the basin, hemmed in between Assameur and the first mountain range. Upon leaving the olive grove, the trail forks: the branch to the right scales the red bed spur on which the forest warden's house has been built in the midst of pine trees. To its left the minivan leaves behind the shady road it went down an hour earlier to reach the Office—actually running far behind the planned timetable: the sergeant had decided to cancel the nap and leave right after lunch, but he had already settled into a lounge chair "to have his coffee," had fallen asleep almost immediately and had snored on until three o'clock, at which time he had stretched out, glanced at his wristwatch and shouted to the corporal to start up the van.

— Still, a person feels better all the same after a little nap . . .

Sergeant Pozzi stretches out with obvious satisfaction. He has his work cut out for him along this narrow trail strewn with potholes, deeply grooved almost everywhere by the furrows of runoff streams. He proceeds nevertheless, wiping his neck and forehead from time to time. To make things easier he leaves the handkerchief on the seat: his right hand runs from the steering wheel to the handkerchief, then to the gearshift, once again to the steering wheel, the handkerchief, his forehead, the gearshift, the handkerchief, to his neck, the steering wheel, also to the horn, whenever a donkey suddenly looms up in front of the car after it comes around one of those many blind turns.

The trail climbs along the mountainside and soon dominates the entire médina, the souk—a quadrangular expanse to the west of the city —the olive grove and its offshoots in the adjacent valleys, the line of hills edging the plain, and, upon one hill, the administrative buildings with their purplish-red walls.

Then all at once it disappears: the minivan plunges into a ravine, along a wadi which, devoid of any water, is nothing but a heap of pebbles and rocks.

Behind, the Arab has laid back upon the bags and is sleeping, impervious to the jolts as well as to the racket made by the tools jumping around on the metal floor.

The trail zigzags at the bottom of the gorge, now on the right bank, now on the left bank, moving from one to the other across cement overpasses. At certain points the platform, reinforced with a triple row of gabions, directly overlooks the torrent bed.

They are moving at a moderate speed, due both to the steepness of the inclines and the slower speed imposed on them by the sudden presence of a series of ruts: the springs squeak, the gears grind, the motor weakens, then thrums as the vehicle breaks clear and continues on in first gear.

The heat is stifling, the sun blinding, and the objects touched by its rays are so scalding that one's fingers cannot rest upon them. As for the steering wheel, it is protected by a slip sheet.

The dust stirred up by the wheels settles inside and coats the leather of the front seat, as well as clothes, hair, face. The stones struck on an angle by the tires fly loose with a dry crack and ricochet off the shoulders.

Gradually the trail pulls out of the ravine. Following a very hard gradient interspersed with hairpin turns, it reaches a shelf on the right bank, where clumps of grass and bushes cling to the rocks upon the talus slope.

The gorge, down below, is no more than a corridor between two vertical walls, curving rapidly westward and vanishing behind a fold in the terrain.

The incline becomes more gradual, the bushes more dense, the turns wider: the road opens onto a plateau.

— Here's the forest, the sergeant shouts, loud enough to drown out the roaring of the motor, and his hand describes a vast semicircle encompassing a landscape with an uneven, compartmentalized relief, where stunted copses grow with difficulty in the fissures of a rocky crust.

Lassalle stares at him in disbelief. But the sergeant is perfectly serious. He even elaborates, with a certain pride:

— The leafy ones are holm oak. The others, juniper or thuja. There are also a few cypresses here and there, clusters of maritime pines above Ouzli and thurifiers, almost all dead, burnt down by the shepherds . . .

Here, the trees are hardly over six feet high. As for the leaves, they are coated with an ocher film which makes them difficult to discriminate.

The minivan has gathered speed and stirs up even more dust than a little while ago at the bottom of the gorge. The plateau gently undulates; the view extends rather far. Toward the south the high ranges should be soaring up, but they have become invisible.

The Arab has awoken in the wagon. He is once again sitting up and watches the road shooting backward under his feet. Sergeant Pozzi, ensconced in the front seat, seems to be very much at ease.

Lassalle is the only one who hasn't slept since this morning. He fought his sleep for an hour after lunch, smoking cigarette after cigarette, sitting up straight in his armchair, not daring to awaken his host slumped upon the lounge chair; and if, since they set out, the double foray into the médina, the stops, and the array of sights have kept him awake, at present the monotony of the journey leaves him defenseless: his head drops toward his chest, lifts, leans to the left, the right, and finally falls against the upright of the door where, inert, it remains jiggling, like a bag of sand.

Behind his closed eyelids the road continues to fly toward the vehicle, the shrubs to block the way, and then to veer to one side or the other at the last second, the driver's hand to manipulate the black ball of the gearshift, the handkerchief, the cap, the padded circle of the steering wheel. Later, imperceptibly, new images infiltrate and substitute themselves for the first ones: a blade of straw caught in the stem of the windshield wiper, the smooth trunk of a fig tree, a casbah on a terreplein, a tower pierced with loopholes, a frightened chicken which flees flapping its wings, a dog flying after the intruders, constantly barking; then barefooted children, with shreds of cloth or canvas bags on their backs, running along cob walls; and again, flashes of white sky, as hard, as blinding as at high noon, shriveled leaves, dead branches, pebbly roads crunching under the wheels—and in the intervals, like the punctuation of silent pauses, vast stationary screens which are opaque, uniform.

Suddenly the roaring stops—unless it has already been stopped for a few moments: the minivan has pulled over to the right of the roadway, at the very edge of a bare slope which the route scales methodically: fragments of "loops" appear at different levels, more or less in every direction, but the overall layout of the course does not reveal itself definitively at first glance.

The sergeant has gotten out of the car, raised the hood and remains planted in front of the motor, his fists on his hips, his cap pushed back over his neck. He waves with his hand:

— The motor's overheating . . . We have to let it cool off a bit.

He leans over, stretches out a finger which he quickly and promptly pulls back and sucks, observes the motor once again and walks back toward the door.

— At any rate, we're not very far from the pass. It's fifteen, twenty minutes away . . .

The pass is still not in sight, but the road has gained enough altitude to give a view of the whole wooded plateau just upstream from the gorges, the first range cut by the ravine, and much further northward—for the last time most likely—the pale blue blur of the olive grove. Assameur is hidden by the mountain. Nevertheless, upon one of the rises bordering the plain, Lassalle believes he can make out dark red points. But the hills are suffused with a pinkish mist and the distance is too great for the naked eye to identify anything whatsoever. Only the binoculars could remove all doubt. But the binoculars are at the bottom of the clothing bag, in the minivan, and this is hardly the time to disrupt everything.

The motor is running again, more slowly, while the corporal pours the contents of a water can into the radiator.

Then the sergeant sits in the front seat, slams the door, and the van is off once more.

A quarter of an hour later, while coming off a turn, the mountain seems to split into two equal parts and the road, suddenly level, shoots off into the empty air.

— We're at the pass! the sergeant shouts, pointing toward the open space before him.

Behind, already, everything has disappeared, from the wooded plateau to the pink streak at the horizon. Toward the south rise very high mountain ranges, but the angle is such that they are unrecognizable.

— Tafrent is all the way at the bottom, downstream from the irrigated zone . . .

Below, in the valley, columns of smoke rise above the douars. Two rows of vivid green plots of land are layered in terraces on each side of the wadi.

— We'll be there in a half-hour; the road is good, the way down is easy . . .

The sergeant looks at his wristwatch: it is a quarter to seven.

— You see, it'll be just forty-five minutes . . . That's what it takes in normal weather.

The descent is steep, but the ground is in much better condition than on the way up. The entire slope is in the shade and the sudden briskness is surprising.

The route does not extend to the valley floor, but cuts along the mountainside above the cultivated fields, at a good distance from the douars which, on the other bank, are enjoying the last moments of sunlight.

At a quarter after seven, the minivan stops in front of the forest warden's house in the midst of pines, similar to the one in Assameur, with its walls of exposed stone, a red tile roof and green shutters.

The sergeant shows Lassalle into a rectangular room serving simultaneously as a dining room, living room, and bedroom.

Shortly afterwards Piantoni arrives, the warden at Tafrent, tall, skinny, with a bony face, and on his head a battered cap sinking sideways across the line of his eyebrows. The sergeant makes the introductions, adding that "Mr. Lassalle, who is here for the Angoun mining trail, is heading up toward Imlil."

The guard reaches out his hand without saying anything.

— If you could put him up for the night, you'd be doing him a great favor: it would spare him setting up his tent.

The guard nods his head affirmatively, offers a seat with a wave of his hand and leads the sergeant into a miniscule office almost entirely taken up by a desk, armoire and safe.

Maps are pinned to the walls of the large room: a map of the railway lines, the section of the administrative map labeled "Assameur" upon which thick red pencil strokes encircle a green crosshatched polygon named "Tafrent Shunting-Station." There is also a geological map and a picture painted on a piece of oval wood depicting sunset over the bay of Naples.

The seat offered to him is a large cane armchair. Sitting in the corner between the two windows, Lassalle has a view to the right on the front of the house where the corporal, helped by another Arab, is beginning to unload the minivan: he hitches the bags over his shoulders and sets them down along the wall.

The office door has remained open a crack: the two men are talking official business. The sergeant takes bundles of paper money out of his shoulder bag, which the guard stores away in the safe. Then they set about checking off names on a list: it is always the same ones that come up—Mohammed, Salah, Ahmed, Salah, Brahin, Ahmed, Mohammed —and Lassalle wonders how the two manage to tell things apart.

In front of the house the two guards have turned to the picks and shovels, which they pile up behind the vehicle, then transfer to a shed thirty meters away.

In the office the talk is now about tree-felling areas, tree marking, about official reports, grazing violations, the installation of fences, charcoal burners, boundary lines in effect for ten years . . .

In the chair Lassalle has allowed himself to slip down slightly, his arms propped on the armrests, in such a way that his forehead has come level with his hand. He still feels dazed. The motor's roaring, the jolts, the heat, the smell of the gas revived a migraine that lunch had succeeded in relegating to the background, and naturally his mid-journey nap was ill-timed and merely worsened the pain. The only remedy is to retire as soon as possible.

Outside, it is almost dark. The two Arabs have finished their work and have gone off. The air is dry, warmer than at the pass, but clearly less so than at Assameur, and the temperature is very mild. Everything is calm in the valley, allowance made for the constant chirring of the crickets around the house, and of the locusts, further in the distance and rarer, but more piercing.

Shortly after eight o'clock, the two men come out of the office vying with each other in politeness: the sergeant declares that he should not wait any longer to leave if he wants to get back to Assameur before midnight; but the guard insists that he has more than enough time to "have a bite."

Lassalle makes his apologies: exhaustion . . . headache . . . lack of appetite . . . All the same he agrees to have a little soup.

Meanwhile, a young Arab woman has made her entrance into the room, lit the oil lamp hanging from the ceiling, spread out a cloth over the table and set places for three. Then she brings in the soup tureen and the three men take their seats around the table.

Between spoonfuls, Sergeant Pozzi gives news of Assameur. Piantoni swallows his soup silently, his nose in his bowl, at times raising absolutely inexpressive heavy eyes toward his superior. It's doubtful that he's listening. Presently he turns toward Lassalle and says in a very calm voice, with a youthful lilting tone:

— I do believe I met one of your colleagues two years ago . . .

Lassalle gives a start:

— Someone from the Company?

— Yes, a tall blond man, in his thirties.

— It was Moritz, probably.

— Perhaps so . . . I haven't retained his name . . . He had come through here on his way down from Imlil. To hear him tell it, everything was ready, the studies had been completed, the picks were to start swinging next spring . . .

— It was Moritz, most likely.

— Perhaps so . . . The following year, at any rate, we didn't see anything come . . .

The sergeant interrupts:

— The same thing happened with the mine at the Sidi Meskour jebel . . .

He tells the story of the Sidi Meskour mine, then the one about the trail from the Aït . . . that never got off the ground, the one about the vein at Ouled . . . that was not able to be exploited. The conversation is nurtured by several analogous stories and revolves around the difficulties associated with this sort of enterprise, hazards of every kind, the overly optimistic assessments, the bad weather, the disappointments, the renouncements.

— There is talk about something for years and suddenly the initial project is abandoned, another idea is brought up, or new studies are made, new maps are drawn up, there are discussions, then doubts, and finally things aren't any further along than they were before . . .

— Or else the matter passes into other hands . . .

— And then one fine day you realize that it's not worth the trouble.

And, after a long pause, the expected conclusion:

— Be that as it may, if your company were to decide to open the trail from Angoun, it would be to everyone's benefit.

— Certainly, it would be to everyone's advantage . . .

After the soup, Lassalle was not able to refuse a slice of meat with some salad, nor a bunch of grapes for dessert. The subject "Mines and Mining Trails" being exhausted, the sergeant began to give more news of Assameur, about the Kaid who left for vacation, about the troubles his Caliph had with unruly neighbors, about the heat, about the storm which is not breaking, about the congestion in the souk . . .

— There was some trouble this morning: a woman died in the infirmary. They had brought her down from the mountains a few hours earlier . . . I can't even remember who told me . . . Oh yes: the boy at the gas pump.

— I saw them yesterday: three or four fellows with an old man. They came from the Aït Andiss. They stopped at the house to ask for water.

— She died at noon . . .

— But she was quite young: she looked like a child.

— They say she was seriously wounded.

— Yes, they told me she had been stabbed twice . . .

. . . She died at noon, in the small room all the way at the end of the waiting room, reclining on the white bed, arms dangling along the metal uprights, lips quivering, large eyes calm, exhausted, turned toward the door, cracked open . . .

— That sort of thing happens rather often, incidents like that. Especially in the summertime, with this heat. It begins in a harmless quarrel and then things turn vicious . . .

— Not counting those they settle among themselves and which you never hear about.

The sergeant gets up from the table:

— A quarter to nine, I must be going. Piantoni, would you mind helping Mr. Lassalle to find some mules tomorrow morning? You know the people of the douar. By himself he would run into problems.

Lassalle shakes the sergeant's hand:

— You put me a day ahead of schedule. I probably wouldn't have been able to leave Assameur until today.

— But no, think nothing of it, it's a pleasure . . .

The sergeant heads for the door. Outside, the corporal is ready to leave, seated on the running board of the minivan.

The sergeant stations himself behind the steering wheel, starts up the motor, puts on the headlights, goes forward a few meters, shifts into reverse, comes back . . . Passing in front of the door he waves. The minivan moves down the lane through the pines, whose rectilinear trunks loom forward for an instant in the headlights' glare, then pulls onto the road, turns to the right and rapidly recedes into the valley.

Once back inside, the guard shows Lassalle into a bedroom under the roof, where he has had his luggage brought and a cot set up.

Wake-up is set for six.

The guard withdraws: his steps echo on the stairs, then in the dining room below, and finally in the kitchen. The guard's voice makes itself heard for a few seconds, then a woman's voice, somewhat louder, once again the guard's voice, and finally the sound of a door banging.

The bedroom looks out on the valley. The window is wide open. There is no mosquito netting, but perhaps it is because there are no mosquitoes.

The pine tree branches advance nearly within reach. The night is very dark and the moon is not supposed to rise for several hours yet.

Joining the crickets and locusts are several toads at the very bottom of the wadi bank. Then a roaring is heard in the distance, very faintly but clearly through the darkness, easy to recognize: the minivan has just gone past the last douar and is beginning its climb up the pass. Soon the trail will veer westward and the sound will die quickly.

As for the migraine, naturally the dinner had no effect on that. But this is not important now: it will fade away in the first hours of sleep.

V

Hugging the mountain wall, the road rises, narrow, difficult, and furrowed. But the mule adapts to it wonderfully. In fact, most of the time, it is able to choose between five trails: the two parallel ruts hollowed out by wheels, the space in between where the mud has accumulated, finally the two strips along the borders, limited on one side by the ravine and on the other by the ditch or the embankment.

But every time that circumstances dictate making use of the whole available width—coming onto a curve for example—the inside rut folds up in the middle of the roadway, whereas the other rut, drawing as close as possible to the outer edge, for several meters brushes up against the rock or the precipice, depending on the direction. The side strip is then virtually eliminated, and the mule following along it moves on its own accord to the adjoining span, something it never does normally without first yielding to a tug of the reins.

More rarely, when the shelf has been carved directly into the rock, the ruts and humpbacks give way to an uneven platform, bristling with outcrops that the sledgehammers did not manage to flatten out, flanked with schist-ridden slabs where the animals' shoes slip, even without the slightest hint of moisture present.

But on loose ground the ruts are always there, dating from the last storm or the last spring rain. When the furrows are deeply gouged, the central rib, cambered and chaotic, is unusable. This uncertainty, added to the intermittent but frequent disappearance of the extra space along the margins of the road, makes the rut the most dependable path: this is the way holding the fewest surprises. It is eventually in the rut, then, where the mule almost always walks.

The trail goes up along the side of the mountain, slowly, methodically. At times a bypath breaks the sinuous line: the guide pulls off unexpectedly to the side, jumps over a ditch, leading his animal along into an almost invisible footpath. The second mule follows the example and squeezes itself between the bushes. In front, the large bag on the pack-saddle sways with every movement of the spine, while the two other bags, passing through in the straw baskets on the animal's sides, force down the holm oak branches which spring up again behind them. At the top of the narrow rise, the mule again gets a foothold on the trail and heads out on a new straight segment, or one so slightly inclined that a shortcut no longer imposes itself.

The elevation is sufficient to permit the morning's itinerary to be recomposed with a single glance: the high valley still close by, where the two wooded slopes meet; farther to the north, the defile where the trail ran along the torrent; finally the "useful" valley, irrigated by two large ditches—two "séguias" coming out of the wadi at the end of the defile. The shimmering green of the plots where corn is raised gives a moment's rest to eyes wearied by the extreme aridity of the slopes. Trees are set in rows at the borders of the terraces, which the guard named this morning on the pathway to the douar: fig trees, pomegranate trees, peach trees, willows, black poplars, white poplars, a few walnut trees, even grapevines, intermingled with the carob trees and ashes. The forest warden's house is hidden in the midst of pines, but the hamlet from where the guard, after patient bargaining, brought back the mules spreads out in the bright sunshine, as well as the two douars upriver, at the edge of the trail, the first one gray upon gray earth, and the second, a little farther on, red upon red earth, from which half-naked children have dashed toward them to act as a brief escort.

Since then, the road has been deserted. Not one car has passed by in either direction—nor a pedestrian either, nor anyone on horseback.

From time to time, the guide turns around and shouts something at

Lassalle, who motions his approval. But the man is insistent and punctuates his pointless repetitions with profuse gesticulations. Lassalle attempts, in turn, several symmetrical movements, but without much conviction: the man bursts out laughing and begins tugging on the reins again, shaking his head and talking to his mule, and order is reestablished.

Ever since the trail left the valley floor, the forest has become more and more sparse, to the point of being reduced to a few scattered tufts on the ledge: every trace of greenery has fled the slopes ravaged by runoffs.

A rocky crest stands out to the north, far above Tafrent—the one the minivan crossed over yesterday evening at the last stage of the journey. Gradually as new ranges rise into sight on the horizon, the valley farther down sinks imperceptibly lower, as if buried under the first rises of the sides. The last portion to be seen is located downstream from the defile: the route runs parallel to the torrent, and in the very middle of the roadway a man on horseback in a blue djellaba stands out, very tiny but as distinct as a toy lead model, riding southward.

A little higher, the whole valley has disappeared. The guide has gotten ahead and stopped at the beginning of a curve. He brandishes his bludgeon, shows something ahead of him and shouts triumphantly: "Tizi! Tizi!"

"Tizi," the pass, figures just about everywhere on the maps. It is the name that occurs most often. Even when implied, it always winds up by imposing itself, from one valley to the next, at a given point: it is the true "password," valid throughout the mountains.

Lassalle gives his mount a kick and catches up with the guide as they are coming out of the turn: strewn with stones and scree, the pass opens up very wide between two barren peaks. The route crosses it in a straight line and dips down the opposite slope.

The guide points out a tree one-hundred-and-fifty meters to the left of the trail and heads for it straightaway.

The gnarled and leafless tree resembles a large mushroom. It is most likely one of those old thurifers that Sergeant Pozzi mentioned: the trunk, split, hollow, half reduced to cinders, is supporting a dusty dark-green round ball.

Lassalle jumps to the ground without mishap, fastens his mule's reins to the lower branches of the tree and goes over to help the guide undo the bags. Then he rummages through his provisions, grabs a can of pâté and a box of cookies, sweeps off a flat surface at the foot of the tree and settles down without further delay.

The shadow of the juniper allows exactly two men to stretch out, and it is positively the only shadow cast over the entire length of the pass: huge boulders have tumbled up to the trail edge, but the sun at zenith leaves no hope of finding shelter in their perimeter.

The heat is more bearable than yesterday, without it being possible to say, for want of experience, whether this progress is due to the altitude, to the overall improvement in atmospheric conditions, or to simply having grown accustomed to it.

Squatting over the pebbles, the guide unknots a fold of cloth containing pieces of meat and a slice of black bread. Near him, Lassalle laboriously chomps at his solidly packed indigestible fare. He begins to imagine the landscape as it once was, wooded, and the route—the mule path—crossing through the pass between two rows of respectable trees, and along the border of the slopes, hidden in the grass, a spring flowing between flat rocks... For he has brought nothing to drink from Tafrent, persuaded, rather thoughtlessly, that a stop could only be made in the vicinity of a water source; likewise, later, he neglected to fill his flask in the wadi; and since that time, naturally, he has not spotted the slightest trickle of water. The guide does not seem to have made any allowances either: questioned with a gesture—clenched fist, thumb between the lips—he makes do with stretching out his hand in the direction of the other valley . . . It would have been better, in such conditions, to continue on to Ouzli without stopping. But Ouzli is still two hours away; the animals must need rest—the guide as well what's more, since he has maintained his brisk pace the whole morning.

As for Lassalle, despite letting himself be carried along on muleback, he nevertheless is feeling a great weariness. But it is another sort of fatigue: the general body-ache resulting from a prolonged absence of exercise. His lower back is especially throbbing, as well as his thighs which for the past four hours had been continually rubbing up against the thick blanket, folded across the front, simultaneously serving to protect the packsaddle and to provide a foothold—yet far too high for the position to be comfortable. Step by step, the stiffness spreads to his calves, ankles, shoulders, neck . . . He stands up cautiously, takes a few steps to limber up his legs, swallows the last mouthful, tosses the empty can rather far off and watches it bounce on the stones. Then he opens his clothing bag, takes the map out of the leather briefcase, returns to sit down, leans his back up against the tree trunk and spreads open the map across his lap.

To facilitate the reading, he has outlined the streams in blue, underlined the forest stations in green, framed the location of the passes with a brown cross-hatching, filled in with red pencil the space between the double black lines representing the trails. South of Tafrent, the red line follows the valley for a kilometer or so, but soon deviates from it and loops back and forth up to the pass. The elevation is marked: 2,100 meters, and the name: tizi n'Arfamane.

— Tizi n'Arfamane?

The guide raises his head and confirms, his face beaming. Then once again he points with his index finger in the direction of the other valley —"Ouzli! Ouzli!"—waits for the sign of assent, bursts out laughing and begins chewing again.

Along the extension of the index, Lassalle merely makes out for the moment a sheaf of slanting lines converging toward an invisible center: Ouzli, eight hundred meters below, on the Issoual wadi. But farther to the south, looming up in one burst, just a little while ago, through the gap of the pass, high mountain ranges rise in tiers as far as the eye can see, the closest ones rugged and tortured, the others more harmonious, with long rectilinear ridges and plateaus where the snow must accumulate during the few weeks of intense cold. The highest one, on the left, can only be the Angoun, but its present position, perpendicular to Assameur's, shows the mountain in the unexpected guise of an imperfect, paltry, truncated pyramid. Imlil must be located more toward the left, on the northern declivity of the pyramid, beyond which other crests emerge toward the northwest in the direction of Iknioul, crests which in all likelihood will strew the road back in two weeks time, once the work is completed.

Meanwhile, it is necessary to go down to Ouzli and up the Issoual over a stretch of nearly fifteen kilometers, rejoin the Imlil basin by way of the tizi n'Oualoun, set up camp in the vicinity of the douar and wander around the rocky terrain for whole days at a time, along the whole northern slope of the Angoun, in quest of a satisfactory route. By chance, Imlil is at 2,500 meters: the heat will perhaps not be too depressing . . .

The guide went off to the other side of the tree to kneel in the dust, facing the Angoun: he draws his thoughts inward, forehead lowered, arms hanging down against his body, then prostrates himself several times, with hands stretched toward the eastern horizon. After a new period of meditation, he rises, returns with measured steps toward the tree and begins to replace the bags in the baskets.

Lassalle goes over to his mule, unties the bridle and finds himself as helpless as this morning in front of the guard's house, when, in an attempt to straddle his mount, the animal broke into a sudden and uncoordinated gallop. The guide finishes his work and comes to his rescue: he takes the bridle in hand and holds the rider's left foot high enough to allow his right leg to swing over the rump. On this occasion, furthermore, the mule displays much less impatience.

Shortly afterward, abandoning the shelter of the thurifer, in the broad sunshine the two men travel the short diagonal distance separating them from the road.

At the moment they reach the trail, a sound of more steadily trampling hooves makes them turn their heads: a tall fellow in a blue djellaba emerges from the entrance to the pass, riding a mule whose trot he maintains with precise, energetic strokes of his switch.

In a few seconds the newcomer has caught up with Lassalle. He arrives alongside, draws very close to him, holds out his hand: "Hello!" Lassalle, taken off guard, returns his greeting and holds out his hand, but the contact is brief, for the stranger, who is moving at a brisker pace, has already moved ahead of him, and all he saw of the face so quickly turned away was a thin close-trimmed blond beard rimming the jaw.

The man has joined the guide and is chatting with him. Since he leans to the right so as to be better heard, his features stand out in silhouette with perfect clarity: his nose is straight, rather short, his forehead high; his beard, blond with streaks of red, almost entirely covers his cheek and the rim of the chin. The white turban of the mountain dwellers has been replaced by a khaki chèche, such as the one worn by the sentinel in front of the barracks, at the Office. The djellaba hood is thrown back over his shoulders; lower, the folds of cloth partly hide the saddle rug, whose design intermingles circles and diamonds on a background checkered in black, green, red, yellow, gray . . .

His feet deliver clipped kicks to the belly of the mule, which, much sturdier than the two others, has already drawn the guide along at its own pace: the poor fellow jogtrots between the two animals, but his shortness of breath does not prevent him from speaking.

Soon the third mule also breaks into a trot. Disconcerted, Lassalle instantly has the hardest time maintaining his balance: unable to squeeze his knees together tightly enough to control the bouncing of his mount, he flies up at the slightest jolt and thumps back down into the saddle, sometimes to the left, sometimes to the right, often too far up on the rib of leather bruising his inner thighs.

All at once the stranger, who has let the guide go on ahead, finds himself alongside Lassalle; he speaks in an even voice, as if he was happy to provide a commentary for the events:

— You are going to Imlil . . . It's to work at the mine . . .

Lassalle assents, caught unawares. It is not so much the informal "you" which throws him off—he has already encountered that at Dar el Hamra—as it is the speaker's flawless pronunciation, his accurate and uniform accentuation and, still within the same order of ideas, his pale complexion, his regular features and, now that he is looking at him full face, his gray-blue eyes.

— You know, I've already seen all those who came to the mine, those other years . . . I live in Imlil . . . If you want, I will travel along with you: you don't speak Arabic, so I can help you out. And in Imlil, if you need anything, you come find me: everybody knows Sergeant Ba Iken, in Imlil.

Lassalle accepts, perhaps without understanding, on the spot, all that such a proposal has to offer, but he has just discovered by accident a new position and is entirely absorbed in making adjustments: sitting squarely back in the saddle, on the rump, he leans his torso forward, so that his elbows touch his knees; his hands hold the bridle up very close and come together at the edge of the blanket: the mule, better steered, forgoes its shying, the jolts are softened, and his buttocks only budge a few centimeters. It was about time: the bouncing was beginning to become unbearable.

— You know, you mustn't stop at Ouzli, you must keep going to Tisselli. That way it makes it better for tomorrow: you get to Imlil more quickly in the evening.

— Is Tisselli far from Ouzli?

— No, it takes two hours walking fast . . . You see, it's one-thirty . . . We are in Ouzli at three-thirty, we have a little rest, and we get to Tisselli at six-thirty . . . It's a big douar. The sheikh is my friend. If you want to, you come with me to the sheikh's . . . He has a big house. He is happy if you are coming to his home.

— Thanks, but I have my tent for spending the night . . .

Ba Iken smiles, showing two perfectly symmetrical gold teeth at each corner of his mouth:

— A house is better than a guitonne . . . And what's more, when the sheikh invites you to his home, he is not happy if you sleep under a guitonne!

Lassalle approves and raises an arm to indicate that he is giving in to Ba Iken's arguments. But his gesture, a bit too insistent, makes him lose his balance and he catches hold of the blanket with great difficulty.

— If we walk fast, we are at the sheikh's at six, I just told you.

— But I only have the mules to Ouzli. They didn't want them to go any farther . . . It was just arranged only as far as Ouzli.

— We can always make arrangements . . . Listen — Ba Iken points toward the guide ahead of them — I know him well. If you pay a little more, it works out.

— But he didn't want to hear a word about it this morning!

— No, no, you're going to see. How much did you promise?

— One hundred reals by mule, as far as Ouzli.

— If you give one-hundred-fifty, I'm sure he goes as far as Tisselli.

— Agreed. The hundred-fifty's fine.

Ba Iken breaks into a gallop, catches up with the guide, leans toward him. The guide raises his arms to the sky, speaks very loudly in turn, shakes his head, counts on his fingers, slaps his mule, raises his arms to the sky once more . . . Finally Ba Iken leaves him and waits for Lassalle.

— It's all right for the hundred-fifty. He accepts . . . It's fine this way: tonight we are in Tisselli . . .

He takes out a pack of cigarettes.

— . . . In cha'Allah! he adds, mechanically.

VI

The sheikh's casbah is built upon a red bed peak cutting through the valley at a slant. It is therefore visible for several kilometers around, from the rocky constriction dominating the Ouzli basin, upstream, as far as the bend downstream, where the torrent slips between two cliffs placed one behind the other as in the scenery of a diorama.

Three of the four windows of the reception room look out on the casbah entrance, the fourth on the terraces on the bank of the wadi: the foliage of the walnut trees stands out in the half-darkness against the brighter streaks of the round pebbles and sand dunes. A large lantern lights up the terreplein in front of the porch, where the steep incline opens out.

The room is long and narrow. A carbide lamp hanging from a hook casts an uneven white light which illuminates, depending on the intensity of the sputtering, the whole or part of the walls and ceiling. A young boy is squatting, at the other end of the room, in front of a low table where, on a copper tray, a teapot and several small porcelain cups are set alongside mint leaves and a half-crushed sugarloaf. Upon another tray, placed on the rug, a brazier supports an ornately embellished kettle. From time to time the young man rises, crosses the room and comes over to present Lassalle, upon a matching saucer, a cup filled with a scalding tea. As he leaves, he takes away the empty cup.

Lassalle is on his fifth cup. He swallowed the first without the slightest reserve, at the risk of burning his throat. He was dying of thirst: his last hope had vanished into thin air shortly before Ouzli, when the footpath to Tisselli, veering off to the left from the trail, passed very far above the irrigated zone, only to later go around the gorges of the Issoual, at the bottom of which white water was swirling between the rocks.

Reclining in the corner between the two windows, he savors the tea in sips, with the back of his hand smoothing his cheeks which his beard is beginning to itch: but the decision made this morning not to shave until he got back is irreversible. It is one less thing to worry about, and from tomorrow on most likely the discomfort will have disappeared.

Every five minutes he shifts into a new position, upsetting the arrangement of the cushions, with no success in soothing his aching back and calves, so folded up and stretched out by the eight-hour trek, three or four hours of which was at a slow trot, that after dismounting, a short while ago, in the courtyard of the casbah, he could hardly stand up: with his legs trembling, and thighs throbbing, he wobbled through the porch, where a white hand stencil-painted in the very middle of the door flap seemed to forbid him entrance, then bumped his forehead against a thick beam, took a thousand precautions climbing the stone steps of a low and narrow staircase, and finally crossed, on the second floor, a kind of vestibule strewn with trays and babouches, opening onto a rectangular room which the carpets, windows and cushions spread around the perimeter identified as the reception room at first glance.

Ba Iken crosses the vestibule, takes off his shoes, pushes them with his feet against the wall and penetrates the room. Two men follow him, carrying the bags, which they set down on the carpet.

Ba Iken sits in the corner between the windowless wall and the window facing the terraces.

— The sheikh will be here very soon. He's overseeing dinner.

Lassalle offers him a cigarette. Ba Iken accepts with a reserved smile, as if in apology:

— I got into the habit in the army, you see . . . He lights his cigarette.

— The sheikh really likes having guests. Not many foreigners pass this way.

— Is he the only sheikh at Tisselli?

— No, he's sheikh of the whole valley. He has all the douars along the Issoual . . . Agouram's his name. El Haj Agouram . . . He made the pilgrimage three times.

Footsteps echo in the stairway, then a sound of babouches sliding along the uneven floor. The distended shadow of a turban is cast upon the ceiling, then upon the wall opposite the door. The sheikh steps out of his slippers, crosses through the doorway and strides forward with a joyful expression. He bows before his guest, shakes his hand—Lassalle has not even had the time to get up—and goes over to sit down beside Ba Iken, with whom he immediately engages in an animated discussion, as if he had not seen him for a very long time. But Ba Iken soon turns toward Lassalle:

— The sheikh says that he is very happy to see you. He has already seen your colleague, two years ago . . . It pleases him very much.

Lassalle thanks him, asks Ba Iken to assure the sheikh that he is extremely grateful for the welcome provided him, that he is very honored, that he greatly appreciates . . .

Leaning forward, his elbows on his knees, his hands joined, the sheikh lends such an attentive ear that he gives the impression he understands, but it is most likely a particularly well-executed facial expression, a temporary congruity of his gaze—those large round brilliant eyes—and the seeming fixity of his features—fleshy lips, plump cheeks, a full face with glistening black skin.

When he is conversing with Ba Iken, he leans to the right upon the cushions, and his left hand plays with the chiseled handle and sheath of the dagger slung over his shoulder.

At times the lamplight abruptly dims, almost goes out, and for a brief moment gestures and objects dissolve in the darkness, while within the window frames the glow of the lamp on the terreplein below brightens. But the carbide sputters again, the flame flutters madly and the bright whiteness repossesses the premises.

A servant comes up to them with a kettle and a copper twin-bottomed basin with an openwork design, which he places on the rug before the guest of honor. The water is boiling. Out of tact, Lassalle only washes his fingertips. The basin slides in front of Ba Iken, who lathers himself generously as far as his wrists, then in front of the sheikh, who does likewise after having folded back his sleeves above his elbows.

A second servant sets up a low table between the three guests and brings in succession flat rounds of rye bread, a terra-cotta plate, and saucers filled with salt, pepper and cumin. Then he takes the cone-shaped cover off the serving plate, revealing a kind of stew, where a half-dozen hard-boiled eggs and as many slices of tomato are swimming in oil upon a bed of boiled meat.

The sheikh breaks up the bread and arranges the pieces along the perimeter of the table. Then he pulls out a piece of the soft insides between the thumb and index finger of his right hand and thrusts it into the oil:

— Bismillah!

Lassalle, a novice in such matters, carefully labors to imitate him gesture by gesture: he grabs hold of a tomato round and pulls it up out of the sauce.

Ba Iken leans over to him:

— The sheikh apologizes: he didn't know you were coming. He didn't have the time to have a mechoui cooked . . . If you come this way on your trip back, you must stay longer. That way he has the time to prepare a real diffa.

The sheikh points his index toward the plate, and to encourage his guest to serve himself more heartily, he pulls off a big piece of meat which he without fuss plops in front of Lassalle upon his piece of bread. After which, he begins chatting again with Ba Iken. Sometimes, while still listening, he briefly stares at the foreigner's eyes, and if the latter happens to meet his gaze, he smiles, shows him the plate with his finger and turns back to his neighbor.

The sound of voices and muffled laughter now and then reach them from the vestibule or the adjoining rooms; and from below, the sound of the pawing mules hitched in the casbah courtyard; also from below, but closer, a few notes of an indistinct song, and sometimes someone calling out in the distance, a shout, from the other side of the valley. Darkness has now fallen and the two banks of the torrent are invisible.

Lassalle conscientiously eats the big piece of meat, then dips small squares of bread into the oil and brings up very tiny shreds of hard-boiled egg or tomato: he forces himself to repeat the gesture as often as possible, afraid that the sheikh, noticing his flagging energy, would automatically allocate him a second portion, as hearty as the first, which he would have little hope of getting through.

But at a sign from the sheikh, the steward replaces the cover on the plate, which disappears. Lassalle uses the opportunity to stretch out his legs and to lean his back more comfortably against the cushions.

The first of the three windows, to the right, looks out on the casbah entrance, lit by the lantern: seated on a wall of dry stones, a switch in her hand, a little girl is humming a melody repeated indefinitely without the slightest variation. At her feet, squatting on the hard-packed earth strewn with blades of straw, another little girl is playing with pebbles which she tosses in the air and catches awkwardly. Her face is hidden, but the braids on her shoulders are, on the contrary, fully lit, as well as her companion's forehead and the stick swaying midway between the two heads.

— Aren't you eating? Ba Iken questions. The sheikh is not going to be happy.

Lassalle notices a second course is awaiting him, identical to the first in its basic ingredients, but this time garnished with potatoes and cauliflower.

— Yes, yes, of course! He corrects his position in a hurry and begins to pick here and there through the sauce. Ba Iken observes him with his gray-blue eyes. Alongside the sheikh he looks as "foreign" as Lassalle. It is hard not to resist the suspicion that he has expropriated his outfit.

— Ba Iken, tell me something.

— Yes, Mr. Lassalle.

— You must have heard about it yesterday, in Assameur . . . in the morning? Some people from the mountains brought someone into the infirmary, a wounded girl . . . She died soon after she arrived.

Ba Iken lowers his eyes, and seems to think for a moment.

— Yes, I remember. There was talk about it yesterday afternoon in the médina. But I was told it was a woman, not a young girl. Why? Did you see her?

— Yes, I saw her in the infirmary. The people came from the Aït Andiss. That's why . . . I thought that you knew all about it, that perhaps you knew them . . .

— They came from the Aït Andiss, you're sure?

— Yes, the attendant said so to the captain in front of me. Isn't that the tribe from Imlil, the Aït Andiss?

— The Aït Andiss is the whole tribe around the Angoun jebel; there are three offshoots: the Aït Baha to the south, the Aït Ouguenoun to the east, and the Aït Imlil to the north.

— So maybe they came from Imlil then?

— If they're people from Imlil, Mr. Lassalle, I'm immediately informed in Assameur. Everyone saw me there yesterday.

— Then they're from the other offshoots you mentioned: the Aït Ouguenoun . . . or the Aït Baha . . .

— Perhaps. But you know the attendant can be mistaken, he can be confused with another tribe . . .

Lassalle mechanically takes some more cauliflower at the exact moment when the plate is being taken away. It has been a long while since he's been hungry. But a third plate arrives almost immediately: a stew with cucumbers and onions. Luckily, large glasses of cool water are also brought.

The sheikh is first to sample the new dish, soon followed by his guests. For a few seconds all three eat in silence. Outside, the child can be distinctly heard humming, below on the terreplein: the girl is still sitting on the stone wall. Her companion has not moved either; but she has stopped juggling with the pebbles: she is leaning forward, her elbows on her knees, her head between her hands; her braids, slipping down on either side of her shoulders, are resting against her breast.

— Maybe they came through here on their way down to Assameur?

— Who's that, Mr. Lassalle?

— The people who brought in the wounded girl.

– I don't know about that . . . It's not known exactly where they come from . . .

— Maybe the sheikh is one to know . . . Don't you want to ask him? Maybe he knows all about it.

Ba Iken turns to the sheikh and speaks to him. From the first sentences the sheikh shakes his head and lets drop a monosyllable: "La!" whose meaning is immediately accessible: it is an absolute denial. The head gesture is accompanied by a clipped movement of his wrist: the index finger traces a very short half-circle, the end of the curve coinciding with the falling syllable whose function it is to emphasize. Then the conference resumes. As the choppy guttural sounds multiply—the two men are surely expressing themselves in dialect—Lassalle only catches the familiar names in passing: Assameur, Tafrent, Iknioul, Ouzli, Imlil . . . That's quite all he understands. Nevertheless, in a way, they contain the salient elements of his itinerary, uttered in fragments, at times in the order he actually accomplished each stage of the journey, sometimes in the reverse order, as if it all came down to the total or partial realization of well-established routes—Assameur-Ouzli, Imlil-Iknioul, Tisselli-Assameur—whose particular adventures it would only take a few lines to relate . . . Ba Iken comes back to him:

— I asked the sheikh: he saw nobody coming down with a wounded woman.

— And nothing was brought to his attention?

— He says no. He has heard nothing about it . . . You know, if they came from the Aït Baha or the Aït Ouguenoun, they passed through Iknioul.

— That's not possible: the forest warden saw them in Tafrent.

— In Tafrent?

— Yes, he spoke about it yesterday evening . . . I thought that they had come through here . . . Now, maybe they came through at night, no one spotted them . . . Or they forgot to tell the sheikh.

— The sheikh knows everything that happens, Mr. Lassalle, even if it's nighttime.

The sheikh sharply raps the table twice and the servants arrive to take away the stew with cucumbers. The next one is with quinces. Lassalle is not one bit hungry anymore. To do justice to the dish, he meticulously labors at detaching a quarter-slice of quince. The sheikh is not eating anymore: he raises his eyes to the ceiling; the grease is running off his right hand, drop by drop, onto the table edge.

— Did the attendant say what happened?

— What happened?

— Yes . . . why she was wounded?

— No . . . They had just arrived. She had been stabbed twice. That's all they knew.

Ba Iken takes a crust of bread and dips it into the sauce.

— You know, those sorts of incidents happen often . . . arguments. Fellows get angry over nothing at all. They're overwrought . . . It's the sun, the heat . . . That's the way it always is in the summertime. There are always incidents like that, throughout the mountains.

The stew with quince only made a brief appearance. An enameled metal basin replaces it, containing a remarkable mound of semolina, shaped in a truncated cone: the cone's summit is occupied by pieces of meat and all sorts of vegetables.

— This is couscous, Ba Iken explains, while taking some semolina in his cupped palm. Wait, I'll ask for a spoon for you. It's easier with a spoon.

A spoon is brought to Lassalle, while Ba Iken shakes his semolina rhythmically until he obtains a smooth consistent little ball that he pops with his thumb into his wide-open mouth.

— There's another pathway that goes to Tafrent, which bypasses Ouzli. You pass through the mountains. It's shorter. You arrive directly in Tafrent. The Aït Baha often pass that way.

Lassalle eats a few spoonfuls of semolina and drinks a glass of water.

The sheikh has prepared a small ball for himself: he swallows and leans back on the cushions. Then he contemplates his guest's baggage, the three bags set in a row upon the carpet near the door, and converses in hushed tones with Ba Iken.

— The sheikh says that you're going to sleep here . . . That way, you have a good rest and tomorrow the sheikh gives you two good mules to go up to Imlil.

Lassalle thanks the sheikh. His head feels heavy and his eyes are burning . . . The cushions and the mattress will do the job quite nicely . . . All he longs for is sleep; he catches himself yawning shamelessly.

Fortunately the sheikh does not seem to want to prolong the evening any further. A tray loaded with fruit is whisked in and out. The last cups of tea are drunk down rapidly. The basin circulates once again from one to the other, and the servants clear the table.

After a short while, Sheikh Agouram and Ba Iken retire and Lassalle finds himself alone in the large room. The carbide lamp, whose smell was becoming annoying, has been taken away. A tall candlestick, more simple, replaces it.

Lassalle goes over to get his sleeping bag and stretches it out on the mattress along the windowless wall, in the spot where the sheikh had just been sitting.

Fearing drafts, he shuts, in turn, each of the three windows over-looking the casbah entrance: the terreplein is now in darkness; an uneven light, coming from the porch, allows a glimpse of the post where the lantern has been hung and, below, the beginning of the drystone wall. A girl is sitting on the ledge of the wall, switch in hand. The light seems to run along the ground, magnifying the bumps of the hard-packed earth, lingering on the first blades of straw, on a small pile of pebbles, and, a little higher, on the bare feet of the child, which are now and then brushed by the tip of the switch.

The only window left open is the one which, perpendicular to the three others, looks out on the terraces.

Once the candle is extinguished, the leaves of the walnut impercep-tibly grow more precise, then the watershed on the opposite bank; higher still, the stars. But the fields, and the lower branches of the trees and the footpath running along the wadi away from the sheikh's residence are invisible. The landscape will only come alive in several hours, the hidden elements of the relief gradually emerging and coming together: the rocks in front of the casbah, the steep incline climbing the red bed peak, the thorn bushes at the outer edge of the plots, the patches of lichen on the walnut trunks, the row of poplars on the sand bank in the middle of the wadi, the shimmering water—a mule coming around the turn of the footpath, several mules walking in single file, moving across the valley floor, men en route to Ouzli and beyond the plain, pulling on the reins, clicking their tongues or kicking with their heels.

In the deserted valley all that can be heard is the trampling of hoofbeats, the clicking of stones flung from the footpath, and sometimes someone calling out, the interspaced notes of a song, a shout from the other side of the torrent.

VII

Far upstream from Tisselli, enormous walnut trees shelter the terraces on the shore of the wadi, but the mule path, pushed to the edge of the slopes, runs in broad sunlight among the tracts of rock and the clumps of dwarf palm trees.

Then the large trees are more interspaced, the fields themselves disappear and the brush descends to the immediate vicinity of the torrent. The cypresses, the junipers, the thuyas, along with the holm oak bushes and tufts of cytisus, compose a limited number of forma-tions arranged in layers—copses, curtains, clearings—that are repeated indefinitely, with slight variations due to the nature of the soil or the angle of the slope. This is a forest with man-sized dimensions, a "scrubland": whosoever ventures into it soon finds that he drops out of sight from head to toes.

The two riders, with Ba Iken in the lead, ascend the footpath in the steps of the first mule which, having set out an hour before under the leadership of one of the sheikh's servants, they still have not caught up with.

The trail line yields to the demands of the terrain, closely hugging the slightest rises and falls, plunging into the ravines which cut across at right angles, perpetually changing course, to such an extent that two men on foot walking at the same pace three-hundred meters apart would have almost no chance of ever spotting each other.

But those riding fare much better: upon reaching the midlevel of the bushes, they receive an overview if not of the full extent of the undulations, at least of the journey's immediate prospects. Since the footpath often branches off so as to better penetrate the copse, or doubles back on itself to circumvent a crevasse, they are sometimes surprised to find themselves very close by each other, but each at one pole or the other of the obstacle, watching each other move past in the opposite direction, for the space of a second, only a few steps apart—the head rises up, the shoulders and even the entire torso if the copse is not too lush—then they lose sight of each other just as suddenly.

Elsewhere, the footpath climbs on the hillside, threading between the thorny bushes: they pass by without seeing each other, on either side of an embankment or a rock, until a falling stone alerts them, or a slender vertical fault unmasks them, one overlooking the other, at two neighboring stages along the trail line, almost within arm's reach.

Then for a long while they remain unaware of their respective positions, each persuaded that the other has speeded up—or slowed down—his pace, and then here comes one of them looming up at an unexpected point, trotting forward, it seems, to meet the other. But the confusion quickly dissipates, the disruptive presence shortly veers off, doubles back or rises several meters due to a steep incline beyond reach of his pursuer.

In this miniature relief, a virtual chassé-croisé establishes itself, wherein the distance between the two moving objects seems subject to constant fluctuations. However, the actual gap hardly varies at all and the climb continues onward, on foot alongside the mules or riding at a trot for hours at a time upon the loose pebbly soil, under the sun, within a maze of bushes too entangled to allow a breath of air in, too scraggly to block the rays.

Gradually however the bushes are more sparsely strewn, the copses thin out: the footpath emerges from the forest, leaves the valley of the Issoual and begins to climb back northward, on the right bank, along a dried-up affluent.

From the outset the trail rises very quickly. After several hundred meters, ruins loom up on the left upon a projecting shelf: low crumbling walls, dismantled towers, partitions built of cob which rainwater has melted away like sugarloaves.

Ba Iken dismounts, takes a few steps forward, his nose lowered, and shows Lassalle a mosaic tile half-buried in clods of earth.

— This was the casbah of the sheikh of the Aït Issoual, before Agouram's father, he explains. A great battle took place in this valley. It lasted for three days . . . After, the casbah was burned down.

The outer walls can be located here and there along the perimeter of a vast rectangle; the fortified dwelling is now no more than a pile of rubble overrun by thistles and wild grasses.

The guide is squatting in the shade, at the other end of the casbah. Near him, the mule, relieved of its burden, grazes on singed twigs. The bags are set standing up along a wall.

Ba Iken sits beside the guide and unpacks the supplies the sheikh has provided them with: round loaves of rye, meat, olives, figs, watermelon . . . There is even a jar of honey wrapped in a fringed napkin.

Lassalle sets himself down beside Ba Iken, tastes the olives, the figs, but the morning meal at Sheikh Agouram's—rice, noodles, butter, dates, honey, coffee, cakes—was so hearty that he has not yet got back his appetite. He does proper justice only to the watermelon and to the mint tea with which it occurred to him, today, to fill his flask.

His two companions do not seem to be very hungry either . . . The watermelon is quickly gulped down; the flask is soon emptied.

The guide stretches out at the foot of the wall, his head behind his hands. The three mules, hitched side by side, scrape the ground with their shoes; their tails tirelessly chase away the flies.

As yesterday at the pass, approximately at the same time, Lassalle goes over to get his map, spreading it out across his lap and studying it at great length.

It is a section of the administrative map at 1:100 scale labeled "Assameur," for Assameur, despite its outlying location, is the only sizable agglomeration to figure on it: the others—hundreds of others— are merely isolated hamlets scattered on slopes or huddled on valley floors. Opening toward Dar el Hamra, the hub of the network of trails, Assameur is the point of departure for penetrating into the mountainous backcountry; and, in many cases, and regardless of the projected circuit, it also is often the way out.

On the map, in spite of everything, it is only one name among so many others, in capital letters of course, but not all that much larger, brushing the upper margin, whose black line monopolizes attention. And the drab, bulbous, opaque mountain with its lines of force, its folds and traps, covers the entire sheet, except for two small diametrically opposed triangles: up to the left, a few leagues of the great plain where the Issoual empties; down below to the right, a glimpse of the high southern plateaus, where settlements stretch out along intermittent streams.

Everywhere else there is the dark brown tangle of watersheds and sheer slopes. The most powerful ranges establish the general south-west-north-east orientation, but their offshoots diverge in almost every direction. The plateaus are often chaotic, their folds swept along and swelled to the breaking point. The torrents plunge through the breaches and reach parallel valleys where they resume their initial direction; most of them rather quickly join the tortuous gully leading them toward the plain; a few nevertheless remain imprisoned over long distances and owe their escape only to the conjunction of altogether exceptional tectonic phenomena: the Issoual, downstream from Tisselli, stretches out interminably westward; at the moment it is about to disappear in the left corner of the sheet, it veers abruptly and flows due north. But the other wadis surmount obstacles without any undue delays. Only a few streams are named, and these names change on several occasions, each offshoot of a tribe baptizing as they wish the irrigating stream.

Overall, the map is stingy with details. There is something rather striking at first glance: the more you drop southward, the more the reading leaves something to be desired. Along the borders of the plains, information is plentiful and precise, but down farther the notations are more widely interspaced or are quite simply absent. In the high mountains the map is practically mute; three or four ranges are mentioned, just as many passes, but with no altitude markings. As for the valleys, they are seemingly deserted, and their centers uninhabited.

Only Ouzli and Tisselli figure on the Issoual: the blue line slinks anonymously between a double sheaf of contour lines, heedless of the four or five douars along the irrigated zone. A little farther on, what's more, it disappears, absorbed by the white patch, elliptically-shaped, about fifteen kilometers long, at the center of the inner fold of the map. Just two words run across it by way of explanation: UNCHARTED ZONE; but this is not even an explanation.

On the near side of the hazy perimeter is a void: the map is as white as the sky. Before the Issoual is interrupted, a very tiny black line—a mule path—breaks away from the valley and begins to climb northeastward. It soon disappears, toppling over as well, after a few millimeters—after several hundred meters, at the approximate location of the casbah ruins.

Lassalle folds up his map and puts it away. The others are already on their feet, busy hitching the large bag to the mule's back.

It is a little after two o'clock. Ba Iken sets out first. The sheikh's servant follows him several meters behind, pulling on the bridle. Lassalle brings up the rear; from time to time he turns his head and contemplates the curve of the valley, down below, where the Issoual is concealed by two wooded slopes.

The road to travel is still long: they must climb back up the entire ravine, cross the pass, then plunge into the Imlil basin and reach Asguine, the first douar. Ba Iken is talking about a five-hour trek, with a difficult descent, and arriving after dark.

The torrent bed is completely dry. The pathway, on a narrow strip of earth, swings back and forth between the rocks and the stones. On the bottom of the wadi, arid, torturous and hemmed in, the sun beats down as it had not ever yet since Assameur, and for the first time Lassalle admits the necessity of protecting himself.

— You mustn't stay like that, Mr. Lassalle. It's very bad . . . I have an old army forage cap at my place. Tomorrow I bring it to you. It gives good protection. It's light.

Meanwhile, Lassalle only has his shirt at his disposal: he takes it off, slips it over his head and pulls down the collar as far as his eyebrows. But this is a rather mediocre makeshift: the forearms and a part of his lower back are now exposed. A towel and a sweater would do the trick more nicely. Unfortunately, the bags are no longer accessible.

The slope is steep, the pace steady. Along the sheer passages, the mule marks a pause, gathers up its strength and violently whips its back. The rider has some trouble staying in the saddle: his knees are shoved up in fits and starts as high as his chin, the rug slips backwards . . . The best solution is to pull the sandals out of the blanket folds and let them dangle along the animal's sides. In addition, if ever the creature came to lose its balance, this position would allow a quicker jump.

Ba Iken whistles, a twig between his teeth. The guide lets out inarticulate grunts. Lassalle, as the hours pass, begins to doze off: at one time he is leaning his elbows on the edge of the packsaddle, his head between his hands, at others he straightens up and strives to replenish the flow of thoughts which his listlessness imprisons within the narrow frame of minute superficial observations and ready-drawn conclusions: this evening he will be in Imlil, a day ahead of schedule, thanks to Ba Iken, thanks as well to Sheikh Agouram, and to the sergeant's minivan; this evening he will set up his tent in the vicinity of Asguine and will sleep to his heart's content; tomorrow he will begin to survey the surroundings, and it would be highly unlikely if, after eight or ten days of exploration, he has not succeeded in establishing a novel approach to the problem's solution, all the more so since he has the benefit of his predecessor's experience: Moritz and two or three others at the very beginnings of the project; what's more, even if he fails, the damage will not be irreparable: the Company will dispatch someone else next year or in two years; on the other hand, if it all goes smoothly, perhaps in a few months the work will begin downstream from Ouzli: the trail will be easy to open along the Issoual; it should leave the valley at approximately the same place as the mule path; naturally, it will rise less quickly than it does; allowances will need to be made for the numerous loops—they have already been made: the definitive trail line to the pass has long since been adopted; everywhere the ground clearings are sufficient to stamp it with a steady, moderate incline, with no need to assail the rock or pass along the cliff edge . . .

Meanwhile, the ravine has become much less sinuous; it climbs in large straight segments and emerges on a coomb at the bottom of which water is thinly trickling between slabs of schist: a green patch cuts off the footpath, a very tiny pasture where the animals' hooves sink into the moist grass.

Farther on, a barefooted boy, wearing a sort of black toga, a beret on his head, is watching over twenty or thirty goats clambering here and there over the rocky terrain, grazing on God knows what. Farther still, a man in a white turban is guiding a mule toward the Issoual; he gestures a quick greeting; on the mule's back a young woman sitting sidesaddle clings with two hands to a multicolored carpet; she is wearing a red ribbon in her hair and turns her head away as they pass.

The shadows filter into the hollow of the ravine and stretch impercepttibly toward the crests. His exhaustion has increased but is distributed throughout his body.

At the approach to the pass, a man armed with a long bludgeon is dropping down the slope with incredible agility. He passes by, his face blank, as if he had seen nothing.

At the pass itself, the sun has disappeared. The sheer ridge of the Angoun reveals itself gradually on the right, to the south, in the light of the setting sun: one-hundred meters of rock, where progress, measured meter by meter, is slow, uneven, laborious. The enormous escarpment soon appears along its whole length, with its cliffs which, red at the summit, turn pink, then gray, before plunging into a whitish mist. On the left, to the north, the Addar jebel comes into view, with its saw-toothed peaks.

Lassalle keeps a grip on the reins and jumps. His legs are so stiff that he stumbles with his first step and must catch himself by the packsaddle to keep from falling. Bridle in hand, he wobbles forward.

Ba Iken has stopped a little farther on. When Lassalle comes alongside him, he turns his head and, pointing out the pass, exclaims, as if to himself:

— That's the tizi n'Oualoun . . .

Then, indicating the void before them:

— Imlil is all the way at the bottom.

At first sight the screen of fog conceals the basin floor. But, once adjusting to it, the opacity of the white sheet gradually diminishes; its transparency grows more pronounced: green streaks trace themselves in the middle of the depression, most likely trees, or terrace fields; and closer, brown patches as well, perhaps the towers of the casbah of Asguine, the first douar, right at the foot of the pass, or grain lofts topped with branches; at several points, smoke rises in columns. But all of this remains indistinct.

Ba Iken has already begun to dash down. Before running along in his steps, Lassalle casts one last glance on the Angoun cliffs, aglow with a slender golden fringe. At this very second, the light vanishes: the only thing left is the rock, dull, dark, suddenly closer. While the mist slowly rises around the whole perimeter of the basin, the columns of smoke below strive vainly to reach the heights: they melt, one by one, into the shadows.

II

I

SITTING ON A FLAT ROCK, in the shade of a boulder, under this blinding sky and in this dry heat to which he has grown accustomed in a few days, Lassalle contemplates the Imlil basin, an enormous desert-like rocky cirque, except for the narrow gullies, far below, which are the wadi shores laid out in terraces—a painstaking, precarious and delusive task, at the mercy of summer tornados or the spring thaw.

Lassalle likes overall views: just as Moritz two years previously, he made it a point on the very first day to climb the Addar djebel, opposite the Angoun, so as to form a general idea of the problem to be solved, taking in with a single glance the full expanse of the slope upon which he was about to exercise his ingenuity by projecting a trail from the Asguine douar in the western horn of the basin as far as the future mine site, way up there, exactly in the middle of the Angoun.

Leaning forward, his elbows on his thighs, wearing the forage cap Ba Iken had brought him this morning as promised, he takes the measurements of this vast bowl, at times scrutinizing the particularities of the relief through his binoculars, at others letting his gaze sink more freely to the islets of greenery, then climb back up toward the summits. While his right hand falls and replaces the binoculars in the case, the fingers of his left hand scratch up against the growth of his unkempt grayish beard presently covering his cheeks and chin.

Two steps away, reclining on his side, a cigarette in his lips, Ba Iken studies a sheet of paper placed on the ground upon the pebbles. He raises his head:

— This drawing is very good. Was it done by a colleague, Mr. Lassalle?

— Yes, the person who came two years ago. Perhaps you saw him? . . . A tall blond man, in his thirties?

— No, not possible, Mr. Lassalle. I was still in the army, two years ago . . .

Ba Iken leans back against the boulder, lights a second cigarette, takes a puff, expels the smoke through his nose.

The sheet of paper remains spread out over the pebbles, within reach of the two men—a large sheet of blackish-brown paper with yellowed edges, crisscrossed with black, green, and blue lines . . . Moritz must have stopped almost at the same spot, almost at the top of the Addar, at three-thousand meters, one hour's walk from Asguine.

The scale is certainly too small for all the details to be figured in the drawing: many features are simplified, many surfaces leveled out; but the proportions are rigorously precise.

The Imlil basin is bordered on the south by the forceful rectilinear range of the Angoun, and on the north by two lower ranges, the Addar and the Ahori which, curving in semicircles, both link up with the Angoun: the Addar, in the west, by the tizi n'Oualoun; the Ahori, in the east, by the tizi n'Amerziaz.

Three torrents—three "assifs"—drain the basin. The first two come down passes and flow in opposite directions toward each other. Between the two, the Imlil assif—a deep sinuous gorge—surges down from the uppermost heights of the Angoun in the eastern part of the basin. The three torrents merge below the Ifechtalen douar and form, for several hundred meters, a rather beautiful valley which ultimately recedes northward between the Addar and the Ahori.

The morning light is quite satisfactory: the various sections of the basin stand out with perfect clarity to the naked eye, and with utmost precision through the binoculars: Anguine, at the foot of the n'Oualoun, with its stone casbahs and massive towers, its mellah with more modest-sized buildings; downstream, the irrigated zone, with its juxtaposed plots, its two chief séguias and their networks of streams slanting through the cornfields; farther seaward, Ifechtalen, at the confluence of the three torrents; still farther off, at the foot of the Amerziaz, Zegda, almost entirely hidden by a fold in the terrain; Asguine, Ifechtalen, Zegda, the three douars of the Aït Imlil, seem lost in the rocky landscape, overwhelmed by the gigantic Angoun range.

A barely undulating plateau rises from the floor of the basin to the foothills of the Angoun. These latter, very steep, topped with a sheer ridge of rock, lead up to a large projecting shelf. Higher still, enormous cliffs soar up, extending as far as the jagged watershed line, which at several points exceeds four-thousand meters.

The vein is located on the Angoun shelf, between the cliffs and the rocky ridge, approximately in the middle of the range, that is to say, five kilometers as the bird flies from the tizi n'Oualoun.

Over this short distance, a great array of obstacles accumulates: red-bed spurs, gullies, slabs of schist, scree . . . ; the ridge of rock obviously constitutes the most serious of all. Several solutions have been imagined to see the job through. None has managed to garner a majority of the support: any attempt to cross the ridge directly from the pass condemns one, for want of maneuvering room, to dangerously increase the slope's degree of incline; passing right below means embarking across a jumble of smaller cross-ridges devastated by erosion. Moritz has set out all these complications, with supporting calculations, and others had done so before him. He was categorical on this point: if one insisted on taking the Issoual valley, the only way to proceed, upon reaching the pass, was to descend to the outskirts of Asguine, then to cross the entire plateau diagonally and approach the rocky ridge by way of one of the faults which offsets it rather far eastward, and finally to come back, across the shelf, toward the vein. During the last days he had even begun the plans for such a road, setting markers to the foot of the pass. On the plateau, he noted afterwards, there were no surprises in store . . . All that remained was the approach and the crossing of the ridge . . . It is not a bad idea, all in all, but the total trip from pass to mine is twice as long this way. Yet it is better than giving up the Issoual route and falling back on the Iknioul's, with the interminable defile between the Addar and the Ahori, the obligatory passageways through the horns and the costly road work they entail . . . At any rate, the Imlil trench forms the eastern border, dividing the plateau into two unequal, virtually isolated sections: the upper fringe of the rock wall is clearly visible from several places along the meanders.

Lassalle lowers the binoculars and slips them into the case. Tomorrow, the first thing to do is climb directly from Asguine to the future site of the mine: the chances of success for the "Moritz plan" are perhaps greater than one might think. A detailed project established on this basis would surely be taken under consideration.

On the other hand, returning to the tizi n'Oualoun is essential, as much to make certain that the descent to Asguine is easily negotiable as to see the famous petroglyphs—one of the region's two curiosities, along with the natural bridge over the Imlil assif. It was really too late last night at journey's end to stop there.

The sheet of paper is still lying on the ground upon the pebbles. Before putting it in his briefcase, Lassalle examines it once more, absently at first, but soon with a greater attention as if something, a few moments before, had escaped him.

The map's edges are yellowed, covered with stains, fingerprints, smudges. The features, boldly delineated in the beginning, have grown faint: certain lines have faded away, in two or three places, most likely a result of handling, the shaded areas have merged. But the sky surrounding the crests has preserved all its purity, as well as the center of the basin as far as the boundaries of the three douars. The rest has become blurry. Held at arm's length, the image is reduced to a crude sketch: toward the bottom, a bright section, more and more indistinct, and at the very top, far away at present, the silhouette of the large mountain, as if looming up from behind the horizon.

Up closer, the design resumes its normal appearance, the secondary elements return to their role. Everything is correctly situated, rather schematically in places, but moderately so. Little green balls are even represented here and there in the valley: the rare trees which survive at this altitude, a few rows of poplars on the banks, a group of twenty or so sickly walnut trees on the terraces . . . Among which, the one under which Ba Iken helped to set up the tent last night, after eight o'clock, in the light of the lamp he himself had gone to fetch from his house.

It was a solitary tree, at the far end of the western horn of the basin, upon a high terrace overlooking Asguine, right above the spring supplying the douar.

Lassalle picks up his pencil, installs the leather briefcase on his lap to act as a blotter, places the sheet of paper upon it and industriously traces a small rectangle to the right of the last green ball.

Everything is in place now, except for the natural bridge, mentioned by several documents, but which the sketch seems to make no account of. A photograph shows a kind of arch spanning the banks, under which the waters of the torrent flow. An old report "specifies" that the bridge, "fragment of the plateau which remained suspended through some sort of miracle," is "halfway" between Ifechtalen and the Angoun cliffs. But everything depends on how such a "way" is calculated: as the bird flies or along the looping wadi, which is not by any means the same thing.

Ba Iken ought to be able to at least indicate its approximate location.

— Ba Iken? . . . Can you show me where the natural bridge over the Imlil assif is located?

— The natural bridge?

— Yes . . . The place where the torrent passes under the mountain . . . There must be a grotto there, a waterfall or something like that?

— Oh! Imi n'Oucchène? . . . There's a big grotto with waterfalls. It's called Imi n'Oucchène because of the jackals.

Ba Iken tosses away his cigarette, gets up and goes over to Lassalle. Squatting on his heels among the folds of his djellaba, he stretches out his arm toward the highest douar—Zegda—verifies that Lassalle has noted the location mark, then climbs slowly back to the right of the douar . . . His hand does not move:

— It's over there! But you can't see from here. It's behind that sort of white mountain above Zegda . . . If you want, I'll show you the way to get there.

But Lassalle has no intention of going there; he will have enough to do with the trail, and the place is almost at the other end of the basin, quite far beyond his field of operations.

He gets up, folds the sheet of paper in four and puts it into his briefcase with the plans, the maps, and the studies of the uncharted zone.

But the pencil is not there anymore: it was on the briefcase, beside the drawing . . . It must have fallen, rolled upon the pebbles, unless it slipped under the large stone serving as his seat.

With the tip of his shoe Lassalle tries to raise the rock, but in vain. So he sets down the briefcase, stoops, and with both hands grips the edges of the rock. He pulls, lifts, pushes: the rock tips up.

A scorpion has escaped, already scurrying through the dust toward the boulder close by. Ba Iken has come back, alerted by Lassalle's exclamation: he makes a dash, but too late: the scorpion has disappeared in a hole or a crevice in the rock wall.

— Those filthy creatures! They always run faster than you think.

Lassalle rubs his right thumb, slightly scratched.

— I ought to have been more careful. It's stupid . . . I might have got stung.

— You must always look under stones before sitting down, Mr. Lassalle.

Ba Iken shakes the dust out of his djellaba, readjusts his chèche, slips his bag—he calls it a "choukara"—over his shoulder.

— Well, anyway! You're not hurt, hambdou Allah!

He takes a few steps toward the footpath.

Lassalle picks up the pencil, which has indeed fallen under the stone, picks up his briefcase again and puts away his binoculars. Then he takes to his heels. But he stops almost immediately and goes back toward the rock.

The smooth wall sinks into the soil without the slightest seam visible at ground level. The pebbles, stirred around with his foot, do not seem to hide any hole. Nothing is moving in the vicinity of the stone, within a radius of two or three meters. But farther on, from the direction of the footpath, a column of ants is advancing toward the rock wall.

There are at least two hundred of them, black, very tiny, rushing along in several rows with feverish haste. Of course they are not advancing very quickly, but in relation to their size, their agility is more than a match for the scorpion's.

II

The Addar footpath plunges into the Asguine valley, goes around the grain loft, perched high on the left bank, then crosses the terraces downstream from the douar. But instead of continuing on to the mule path, at the very bottom on the wadi banks, it slants to the right and climbs back up the séguia over a short distance toward the mellah.

It took less than a half hour to come down. Ba Iken, who set out in advance, moved at a quick clip, but Lassalle did not have the slightest trouble catching up with him: the morning climb limbered up his legs and he feels very much at ease.

He walks with large strides along the stream, from his hand dangling the leather briefcase which beats rhythmically against his calves. Ba

Iken follows a few steps behind.

The entrance of the mellah is a mere fifty meters away: an elderly man with a white beard is sitting on the ground, his arms crossed over his chest, in front of the first house to the left of the pass; a woman emerges from behind a row of Barbary fig trees, an infant hanging on her lower back in the folds of her dress. She circles the wall and slips into the house; then a child wearing a sort of black apron appears in the doorway, carrying a glass—or a cup—tightly in his joined hands.

Lassalle keeps moving at the same steady pace: in a few minutes he will be back under the tent, will heat up some water for tea, will have lunch, will stretch out on the bed, will put away the things he left in disarray . . .

The séguia flows alongside the footpath. Thirty meters remain before reaching the first houses—about forty strides. The sun is invisible behind the layer of white clouds, but the glare precludes raising his eyes. The shade has shrunken to a thin fringe surrounding each obstacle. The light shimmers, blinding, uniform . . . His legs continue to move at the same rhythm but no longer seem to be touching the ground. They swing backward and forward in place, flailing in the void, while the footpath unfolds under his feet like a rolling sidewalk, dragging along in its course the elements comprising the immediate scenery—the water running a little more quickly in the opposite direction, the pebbles, the blades of straw to the right in the reaped field of rye—then the elements of the background set into motion in turn, slipping smoothly toward the foreground: the branch-thatched roofs, the patches of clay walls, the chinks between the cob-cubes, the grave, wrinkled, almost familiar face of the old Jew, his long pointed beard, his black cap on the crown of his head, the boy standing in front of the door, glass in hand, also motionless, observing the foreigner who is drawing near, counting his steps perhaps, or the number of times his briefcase bounces on his calves . . .

So, for the second time, the séguia cuts off the footpath: just as a short while ago, his foot lands on a wobbly slab, then upon the clods of earth at the edge of the other bank. Steps echo once again on the freshly tamped soil. The water flows on the right in the opposite direction he is walking. The house is now very close; with his hands joined around the glass, the old man takes small sips; standing in the doorway, the boy stares straight ahead, his eyes round, his hair tousled.

Lassalle stops a little farther on, stationed in the bright sunlight right in the middle of the pathway; then, since the chat is dragging on, comes back step-by-step toward the door, glancing at his watch, wiping the sweat from his brow. He was on the point of urging Ba Iken to move on. Naturally not understanding a word being exchanged, he tries to guess at the meaning of the intonations, the winks, the facial expressions. But only the old Jew could supply some clues: Ba Iken, as usual, remains impassive, his face inscrutable, expressionless, disconcerting. At the very beginning, the old man made a sharp movement with his chin in the direction of the newcomer. Shortly afterward, his nose in the air, his beard disheveled, he pointed his index finger inside his house. Ba Iken, meanwhile, uttered a few words in a neutral tone. This all goes on for a good five minutes, maybe more. Lassalle glances at his watch again . . . It is only at the second sign from the old man that Ba Iken turns toward him:

— This is Schlomo, he explains, the moqaddem of the mellah. He wants us to come in and have tea. I told him some other day, fine, but today you're tired, you don't have the time.

— Yes, you made the right decision. Thank him. Tell him we'll come another day. I'd like to rest a while . . .

Ba Iken goes back toward Schlomo to confirm his answer. Lassalle gestures in apology and gets ready to leave. But the young boy has knelt down by the elderly fellow: he takes hold of him by the shoulders and leans right up against his neck, as if he wanted to whisper in his ear, at the very moment that the old man, raising his face, concentrates all his attention on Ba Iken's sentences. So the child's first efforts to be heard have little result.

From a distance, he might have been taken for a ten- or twelve-year-old child, but his features are much more pronounced, more mature than they generally are at that age: his mouth is large and thick, his nose very broad, his forehead and the corners of his mouth are marked with wrinkles, his eyes, perpetually agawk, are affected by a slight strabismus; his ears bend down under a mane of such prolific blond curls that they conceal the black beret set upon, rather than buried in, the center of his hair, except, of course, when his head is bowed, which is presently the case.

The elderly man has already pushed him away with his arm several times, but each time the lad renews his assault, slinking beside him, tugging on his beard until his head pivots around and simultaneously showing him something with his finger: Lassalle himself, it seems, but more precisely, the object the latter is holding in his hand, and which, in his impatience, he is drumming against his knee.

Finally the old man surrenders and turns his head: this signals the start of an orgy of grimaces and mute gesticulations: the child places his beret on the ground, goes over to Lassalle, plants himself right by his side to clearly establish his identification with him, then begins walking parallel to the wall, opposite the Angoun, hunched over, his left hand held flat over his brows, his right sinking to his calves, weighed down by an excessive burden. Reaching the corner of the house, he turns around, points toward the sun at its zenith, amply mops his brow with the back of his sleeve, then comes back toward the small group, with a heavy wobbling gait, stopping twice to emphasize his exhaustion, his cheeks drawn, his tongue lolling between his lips, his empty stare focused on the distance. He passes by the door again, replaces the beret on his shock of hair, in the spot where long practice has packed it down, walks up to Lassalle, makes a low bow, grabs hold of his briefcase and, bending his knees, retraces the preceding circuit at half his height and full speed, with his nose pointed skyward, his mouth wide open, and an ecstatic smile. Returning to his point of departure, he restores the briefcase to its owner, pretends to take out a coin from his shirt pocket which he sticks in his hand, and winding up, bows, turns on his heels and stations himself in the doorway, imperturbable.

Lassalle, rather flustered at the outset, laughs heartily now. The old man smiles while shaking his head as if asking him to make allowances. Ba Iken breaks in without a moment's delay:

— He can be useful to you, you know. He can't talk, but he's sharp-witted . . . He saw you get in last night and he's been pestering his grandfather with it ever since this morning.

— If you think he can be helpful . . . At any rate, I need somebody to lend me a hand.

— Oh! He's very shrewd, Mr. Lassalle! And he knows the whole mountain. I'm sure that you are happy with him. You give him twenty or thirty reals a day and that works out just fine.

— Good. We can always give it a try. Tell him to come tomorrow morning at seven. We'll climb up the Angoun.

Ba Iken translates to Schlomo who, his head lowered, his expression serious once more, begins to drink his tea in the glass, half empty now, which the boy brought him shortly before: the glass has rather large dimensions, crudely ornamented in its upper section with garishly colored patterns: bright green lines against a background checkered blue, yellow and pink.

The woman has come out again on the door step, freed of the nursing infant whose shrill cries are resounding within the house.

All three gesture in perfect unison when the two men leave: the old man nods his head, the woman bares her teeth in a smile, the boy bows, his hands clasping his beret at belt level.

Lassalle and Ba Iken—khaki forage cap and khaki turban—go off into the distance side by side.

— So what's my helper's name?

— His name's Ichou, Mr. Lassalle.

Ichou . . . Ichou ben X . . . ben Schlomo, grandson of the moqaddem of the Asguine mellah, an offshoot of the Aït Imlil, a tribe of the Aït Andiss . . . Born on . . .

— How old is he?

— Oh! . . . Ba Iken frowns evasively . . . I think he was born the year of the famine, or the year before . . . That must make him ten or eleven years old, a little more maybe . . .

The footpath goes down through the mellah—thirty or so clay gourbis—then once again amid the terraces, meets up with the douar again at the bottom of the slope and emerges almost at once on a triangular open space out across by the mule path on the left on its way from Ifechtalen, heading rightward toward the pass. Three large buildings each take up one side of the triangle. On the one to the right, a white hand is stenciled in the center of the door, resembling in every detail the one adorning the portal of Sheikh Agouram's.

— That's my house over there! Ba Iken announces. If you have time tomorrow, you come have tea at my house.

— Yes, Ba Iken, rest assured! I hope I won't get back too late!

— I am going to show you the way . . .

The morning trip bypassed the douar: Ba Iken had picked up the

Addar footpath by going behind the grain loft, along the hillside. Nevertheless, Lassalle could find his way by himself. But Ba Iken seems to take pleasure in guiding him.

— The big casbah with its towers is the house of the sheikh of Imlil . . . He's not there just now. He is making the pilgrimage . . .

For the next two-hundred meters, the narrow street threads its way between dwellings of all heights, some extremely well maintained, others tumbledown: through the crevices between stretches of wall empty lots come into view, where dry grass covers over the scree.

Ba Iken leaves Lassalle in front of the last house—a small squat structure, standing alone on the left.

Beyond the douar, the mule path begins to tackle the pass. But to arrive back at the tent, one must veer off to the right and climb the incline rising toward the spring.

Briefcase in hand, Lassalle strides onto the narrow pebbly footpath, wiping the sweat on his forehead, lifting his eyes every ten meters or so toward the two walnut trees overlooking the terraces: the first, scrawny, in the vicinity of the spring; the second, more robust, under which he awoke this morning, at daybreak, utterly surprised to discover where he was.

III

Since the furrows have been virtually leveled out on this side of the tree, the groundsheet is only marked by minor embossments. The cot—covered with the padding, the sleeping bag and the gray woolen blanket—takes up half of the available space on the right, and the bags set standing up at the head of the bed fill a third of what remains. The corridor thus established on the left, about four-and-a-half feet long, assures a relative liberty of movement. As for the kettle, the aluminum plates, the portable stove and the carbide lamp, they have been slipped under the bed and do not get underfoot.

The tent's location has been wisely chosen: halfway between the tree trunk and the rocks overlooking the field, it remains in the shade from the rising to the setting sun.

The field, on the highest terrace upstream from the douar, dominates the entire valley floor—a vast amphitheater where the torrent slices diagonally across the uneven tiers. Since the douar and the terrace are separated by a fifty-yard difference in elevation, the campsite, without being too isolated, is nevertheless removed from the comings and goings of the inhabitants. Indeed, no sooner had they arrived than Ba Iken brought this double advantage to his attention: "The douar is right below us. Here, you have peace and quiet: there's only the spring a little farther down, the women who come to fetch water, but the footpath doesn't come up this far. If you need something, you come down and ask me at my house. It's not far . . ."

The choice, in reality, was very limited: the second walnut tree, lower down, is much too near the spring; another tree, at the same level, but on the shores of the torrent, suffers from its proximity to the mule path. And the young poplars, alongside the douar, do not give enough shade, and mosquitoes always pose a threat along the wadi; even when the bed is dry, puddles persist here and there among the pebbles.

From the tent only one building is visible: the fortified loft, two-hundred meters farther to the east, at the summit of a peak which the recently harvested grain—millet, Ba Iken claims—colors with pale green patches. To have a view of the douar, it is necessary to go as far as the wall of dry stones which props up the terrace downstream.

The screen of white clouds begins to dissipate toward the end of the afternoon, the sun to go down between the Addar and the Angoun, right above the pass.

Lassalle sits on the ground, leans his back up against the walnut trunk, lights his pipe, then opens his briefcase and empties it methodically, setting out all around him, piece by piece, maps, index cards, charts, reports, which he plans to consult in anticipation of tomorrow's survey . . . Much to his surprise, one last object tumbles out from the bottom of the briefcase: the small pocket diary bound in green leather which he must have taken out of his pocket at a given moment and slipped in here inadvertently. The most serious thing about this is that he was not in any way disturbed by this disappearance, nor did he bother in the least to put into practice the resolutions made at Assameur at the end of the week: to summarize his daily activities, to get into the habit of noting each evening the salient elements, without going into details, so as to later avoid confusion as to dates, or overlapping blocks of information, or mistakenly ascribing one day's happenings to another . . .

In fact, he has not made an entry since . . . Friday, in the bedroom on the hill at the Office, before going down to the souk: one single block is filled in, the one for Thursday, August fifth, which relates the first stage of the journey. And today is Monday, the ninth . . .

Two pages farther on, a small rectangle is consecrated to Monday, August ninth. Lassalle pulls the pencil out of its holder and notes: "Morning: climbed halfway up the Addar djebel. Overall view of the Imlil basin and the Angoun range. Returned at 1 P.M. Afternoon: rest; tidied up."

So much for today's salient points. Is there anything else? Crossing the mellah? Meeting Ichou? Why not, in that case, waking up in the tent, the complete itinerary of the hike, the unexpected discovery of the scorpion? Right from the outset, this would result in spilling over the originally established frame.

He goes back to the preceding page and enters, at bottom right: "Sunday the eighth— Left Tisselli at nine. Stopped at noon while climbing the tizi n'Oualoun. Arrived in Imlil at eight-thirty. Set up tent in the vicinity of the Asguine douar." Here, at any rate, he doesn't find anything else to specify.

Farther up: "Saturday the seventh— Left Tafrent at eight with two mules. Stopped at noon on the tizi n'Arfamane. Arrived in Tisselli at six. Night in the sheikh's casbah."

Finally, to fill in the last empty space: "Friday the sixth— Morning: Visited the Office. Assameur souk. Lunch at the forest warden's house. Left at four in the brigadier's van. Arrived in Tafrent at seven. Night at the forest warden's."

Lasalle rereads what he has just written: thirty words a day is obviously rather paltry for a schedule as busy as his own, but it corresponds perfectly with what he wanted to do. What's more, the space is strictly apportioned: the thirty words already fill up the entire block. If he had nursed more ambitious plans, he would have equipped himself with a notepad, or a large diary, if not a journal.

Nevertheless, certain gaps are shocking: no mention is made, for example, of Captain Weiss. Nor is the sergeant named, or the guard

(Piantoni? Pantaloni?), or the sheikh of Tisselli . . . But their role, on the whole, was merely episodic . . . All the same, Ba Iken seems to deserve more attention: he has been here for three days and will remain here in all likelihood for the entire length of stay in Imlil.

Lassalle picks up his pencil again and adds, under the heading "Saturday, August seventh," in a very tiny scrawl, under the "Stopped at the tizi n'Arfamane": "Met Ba Iken." Then he puts the diary in his shirt pocket, shifts position, lights his extinguished pipe, stretches himself out with satisfaction: he is all caught up, the diary is up to date. Now the crucial thing is not to forget to make an entry tomorrow evening . . . At the bottom, this pocket diary is quite adequate, all the more so because there is no middle ground between a three-line summary and a journal entry. Yet, keeping a journal is a much too absorbing enterprise: it inevitably means writing at least one copybook-sized page a day, often more than that in practice, certain events giving rise to commentaries, comparisons, interpretations . . .

He really has not found the right position: his lower back is still aching, his grazed thighs are very painful in those places where the skin rubbed most insistently against the mule's packsaddle. Lassalle sets his pipe down, leans his back more comfortably against the tree trunk, extends his legs, yawns . . . Assuming that he had decided to keep a journal and likewise neglected to do so up to this point, he would have had to fill up five large pages this afternoon, five large pages in a fine meticulous hand, which would have taken him a good two hours: the time needed to review the facts, to choose those which merit a detailed narration, to compose . . .

The last page would surely contain a description of Asguine and its immediate surroundings, seen from the tent or from the Addar, as well as an account of going down into the valley, of crossing the mellah, of the chat between Ba Iken and the old man, of Ichou's intervention, his spontaneous pantomine . . . but that already comes to more than a page, especially if the description, in a concern for exactitude, is extended to the behavioral nuances of each character . . . the elderly man's reserve, the lad's self-assurance, Ba Iken's shrewdness in such situations (to what extent did not Ba Iken himself make all the arrangements for this apparently spontaneous meeting? Perhaps he did not go so far as to plan the pantomine . . .).

In the preceding pages there would most likely figure the arrival at the tizi n'Oualon at nightfall, the "diffa" at Sheikh Agouram's, perhaps the picnic with the guide under the thurifer of the tizi n'Arfamane, the first impressions of the mountain on the Tafrent trail in the sergeant's minivan, observations on the heat, the hours of torpor in the afternoon, the exhaustion, the aridity, the vegetation, the forest, the habitat . . . a depiction of the Assameur souk, a portrait of Ba Iken, "the soldier come back to live among his tribe," the olive grove in Assameur seen from the Headquarter's hill, the traffic on the olive-grove road, the infirmary, the traffic in the souk, the hours of torpor, from ten in the morning until five in the evening, the hours when the sun is hidden behind the white clouds, the heat which pricks the skin, the dust, the exhaustion, the sleep, the motionless leaves of the olive trees, climbing again after the bridge over the wadi, the crowd gathered before the white facade of the infirmary, the mules hitched to the walls at the corner of the building, the car stopped under the olive trees, the front stairs with its three steps, the waiting room and at the far end the door opened a crack, the man in the white jacket leaning above the bed, the young girl's head lying straight upon the pillow, the neck raised slightly by the headrest, the hair, very black, parted down the middle, woven in braids falling on the shoulders . . . through the cracked open door, the delicate triangular face, extremely pale, with quivering lips, the raised eyelashes, the wide-open eyes looking toward the door, and behind, footsteps fading in the distance, the emptiness establishing itself between the men as they withdraw and the wall at the far end, the door cracked open in the threshold of the small room . . . the slanting pale-green gaze, clouded over with fever and exhaustion, emerging suddenly from unconsciousness or sleep . . . the sound of voices, footsteps in the hallway, the emptiness in the large white room, footsteps echoing and punctuating these few moments of unsatisfied, unfocused, impersonal waiting . . .

The attentive green eyes, unusually far from each other, seemed to be set at the borders of the temples, beyond the jut of the cheekbones. The forehead is broad and very prominent, while the lower face tapers to a point. The tilt of the head accentuates two concentric curves: the lines of the eyebrows and of the thin supple lips. The hair, very black, is parted in the middle and woven into braids which go around the ears and fall in front of the shoulders.

The arms, thrust backward, delineate the throat more boldly, more sharply. Behind the head, the right hand clutches the upper rim of a loop handle; the left vanishes, alongside the hips, toward the bottom of the jug or the bottom rim of another loop. The jug—a kind of amphora with a long cylindrical neck—presses its full weight against the lower back. The red-and-white striped dress is tied at the waist by a very wide strip of cloth patterned with alternating gold-and-black squares. The neck is adorned with a necklace of silver coins threaded on a silk string. Metal bracelets slip from the wrist toward the elbow, along the right forearm.

The silhouette stands out against the muted glare of the sky. The young girl stopped in the middle of a field, midway between the tree and the drystone wall. The bust is leaning forward, the head slightly turned: the gaze seems to drop diagonally toward the object it has just secretly caught sight of, a few meters away, stumbled upon by chance: the foreigner stretched out under the walnut tree, with head propped partly on the tree trunk, partly on a satchel placed vertically against the bark; one hand supports the head, the other is closed around a piece of wood—a pencil, or the stem of a pipe—touching the ground amid the blades of straw and leaves of paper.

Lassalle has just opened his eyes . . . Perhaps he had them cracked open for a few seconds, for she has fled . . . She was standing in front of him, three or four meters from the tree, right in the middle of the field, and now she is rushing away, she glides swiftly with supple footsteps along the furrow parallel to the wall. Drops of water escape from the neck of the jug, splattering hair, legs, bare feet . . . She runs to the far end of the field, jumps to the bottom of the wall and disappears.

Lassalle passes his hand across his forehead, sits down, notices the papers scattered all around him, the briefcase he knocked over while getting up, the pipe on the blades of straw . . . Then he is on his feet, walking, and—cutting across the furrows—he moves toward the wall. Reaching the end of the field, he stops at the wobbly stones and looks below him.

At first, the dim light suffusing the valley floor prevents anything at all from being clearly discerned. But very quickly the plains fall into order, brighter patches appear, contours grow precise: a first terrace, immediately at the foot of the wall, then another below, the round ball of a tree and, to the right of the tree, the site of the spring and the slanting line of the footpath.

The footpath leaves on the right, then curves halfway up the slope and runs leftward toward the douar. A girl—or a child—is dashing down. Coming around the bend, she stops a second, raises her head, then begins to run again and penetrates between two branchy bushes. She only appears again, still dashing along, at the crossroad of the mule path. A few meters more, then she comes to a halt in front of the first house, to the right of the entrance to the douar. She sets down her jug against the wall, right by the door, but at the very moment she is straightening up, someone emerges, grabs her by the arm, strikes her twice and, with a brutal shove, forces her back into the house in front of him.

The door closes again. It was a very brief scene: the two silhouettes struggled and swayed. The place was dark until then, but a light coming from inside the house brightened the threshold for as long as the door stayed open.

Lassalle remains straddling the edge of the wall for a long while still. Nothing is moving around the house anymore. Columns of smoke rise from several roofs. Lights flicker at two or three windows. Much farther off, a fire is shining at the far end of the basin, in Ifechtalen most likely —Zegda is invisible from this side of the valley.

Darkness has now fallen. The air is already cooler. How different from the plain! . . . But does not the chill air in fact seize the body upon waking, weigh down the eyelids, numb the limbs?

A dog—or a jackal—is barking all the way below, in the vicinity of the douar—a dry sharp yelping which echoes from one slope to the next, a sound which is dry, brutal, definitive, like a slamming door reverberating interminably from one end of the valley to the other.

IV

What first catches his attention, upon waking, is the loop handle of the teapot caught in a ray of light which is filtering between the two imperfectly overlapping canvas flaps. In the few seconds it takes his eyes to grow accustomed, the teapot itself appears, then its raised lid, then farther on the carpet on the ground, the box of sugar, the bag of cookies, the blackened metal beaker—closer by, the walking shoes, sandals, socks, the trousers whose legs are lying on the floor, the khaki forage cap. The wristwatch is placed, just within arm's reach, on the bag nearest the head of the bed: the hands indicate six-thirty.

It is the exact time set for wake-up—the time to pull off the blanket, to get out of the sleeping bag, to slip into his trousers, to put on his sandals, to splash some water across his face, to heat water for tea.

The last bonds of sleep untangle themselves, slip off, escape along the wooden uprights, the canvas walls, the furrows of light dusty earth. Uncontrollable images, which an instant before were still rising to the surface, dart off at full speed, vestiges of a diffuse passionate agitation, now subsiding, flattening out, with no ruts or crevices.

Lassalle pulls off the blanket, gets out of the sleeping bag, slips into his trousers, puts on his sandals, throws open a flap at the tent entrance.

The air is cool, the sun still invisible behind the peaks, the bluish sky perfectly empty.

— Well! The weather's going to be fine today!

Indeed, the weather's going to be fine today as it has been since the beginning of the year, as it will be until November: beautiful sunshine all day long, hot evenings, warm nights, the air dry, not the slightest hope of a beneficial shower, skies which are wonderfully transparent at daybreak . . . Lassalle smiles, grabs the canvas pail under the bed, gets up and goes out, his chest bare.

A young lad is sitting under the walnut tree, with his arms crossed, his head held erect and his eyes fixed in a stare. He is wearing a sort of black apron—or a black gandoura with pockets. His features seem much too mature for his age: a broad nose, a thick mouth, arched eyebrows . . . He is as curly as a lamb.

Lassalle recognizes Ichou. But he had completely forgotten him, and for a moment he remained confused, stopped still at the tent entrance, pail in hand.

Ichou jumps to his feet, comes up to him, bows, takes the pail, turns on his heels and darts off toward the wall, over which he bounds with his feet joined.

Two minutes later he reappears above the wall, dashes back toward the tree and holds out the pail full of fresh water.

Between time, Lassalle took out the utensils and lit the camp stove, all the while wondering how long the lad had been there. "Come at seven" surely does not mean all that much for someone from Imlil . . . Ichou must have arrived at the first light of dawn, unless he spent part of the night watching over the tent . . .

A half-hour later all is ready. Ichou accepted a cup of tea, but declined the cookies. Lassalle decided to give up the briefcase and to use the shoulder bag from now on. All he keeps on his person is the Swiss knife, the compass and the clinometer. Everything else can fit easily into the bag: the waterproof jacket with lining removed, the pair of binoculars, two flat barley loaves which Ba Iken gave him, three small cans of food, the flask full of tea, the sketches, the charts, the indispensable papers, not to mention the administrative map which can be of use, for example, in identifying distant peaks along the perimeter of the basin. The bag is not too heavy: Ichou signals that it is easy to carry.

Lassalle loops up the canvas flaps, checks the ties, makes certain the stakes are sturdily planted, throws a quick glance over the setup, vaguely anxious, even though Ba Iken has taken great care to put his mind at ease: "The tent's in no danger, Mr. Lassalle. I tell everybody that you're my personal friend. Nobody will come near your things." Nevertheless he has the impression of leaving his equipment exposed, the whole time he will be away, to every sort of risk: fire, bad weather, animals, looting, the temptation that a deserted "guitoune" represents when unguarded . . . Perhaps he would do better posting Ichou in front of the tent and setting off alone, with his backpack; or hiring a guard; or, for want of something better, to clearly show that "somebody's around," hanging a sign on top of the stake: "The engineer in charge of the future Angoun trail will be back at the end of the afternoon."

But Ichou has already gone ahead: he reaches the jujube hedge bounding the field on the west, spreads apart the thorny branches, and waits, with arm outstretched, for Lassalle to catch up with him.

The quickest way to get to the plateau consists in circling the valley, at the same height, then to attain, on the right bank, to a point approximately symmetrical to the fortified loft's in relation to the douar.

The slopes above the terraces are dense with clumps of thistles, esparto, broom, and dwarf palms. Traces of plowing persist here and there, every place where the people of Asguine desperately strive to make something grow—most likely barley or rye—in this stony arid terrain, but he is not so sure that they harvest much more than they sow.

Two-hundred meters from the tent, at the edge of the mule path, rises a tree whose light-colored leaves in any other location would be thought to be an apple's . . . Perhaps it is a pistachio tree: they can still supposedly be found on certain slopes. The evening before yesterday, this is where the small caravan, on the way down from the pass, veered off toward the campsite. Ba Iken must have used the "pistachio tree" as a landmark.

Ichou, still in the lead, crosses the "main road" of n'Oualoun, then the completely dry torrent bed, and approaches the other bank. His feet bound in rope sandals, he walks with a slanting, jerky gait: each stride alternately propels him to the right or to the left of the path line, as if the trajectory he favored was a series of rather short dashes breaking off at unexpected, uneven angles.

Gradually, a passage opens up through a tangle of pebbly ridges, twenty meters above the séguia—a little farther, there must be a spring, at the same level as the one on the opposite slope.

The valley narrows when it comes alongside the douar, caught between the peak formed by the loft and, on this side, a red bed knoll of which the trail is presently going around.

At this moment the sun's rays are lighting the major part of the Addar, as far as the grain loft, which takes on the appearance of a genuine fortified tower. Asguine, seen from here, appears more spread out: a range of low structures emerges from the valley hollow, right above the mellah. If it wasn't for the columns of smoke escaping from one casbah and the scattered fowl pecking in an alleyway, the overall settlement would look uninhabited . . . Tafrent, Tisselli were likewise deserted at this hour . . . People get up late, activity being reduced to a minimum in this season: the animals have been led out into the summer grazing ground—the "azibs," Ba Iken would say; it will be a month or two yet before the corn is harvested . . .

The irrigated zone widens appreciably on the other side of the knoll. Ichou, who is slightly ahead, drops out of sight behind a boulder. When he reappears, he is thirty meters away, stopped right in the middle of a field, near a person who is accosting him with a host of gestures and exclamations. Short and stocky, the man makes as if to block the way, or more precisely, leads one to believe, by his present position, that he was blocking it only a few moments before and has just stepped aside. He is barefooted and wearing a very filthy gray gandoura. His skull is completely shaven, his cheeks are covered with a triangular black beard. In his left hand he is holding a sort of pick or mallet. With his right he threatens Ichou, then grabs him by the arm and, badgering him all the while, with his tool tip shows him, first, the very place where his feet are planted, then the immediate surroundings, and finally the entire plot.

Lassalle draws near. The man shouts very loudly, Ichou looks over his shoulder and sees Lassalle coming closer, but he does not seem to get unduly excited and patiently strives to break free. The other continues, while gesticulating, to point out something insistently, one of the corners of the plot perhaps, indicated by a large heap of stones.

Ichou ends up by extricating himself and continues along as if nothing had happened. The other does not make one move to hold him back: he stays planted in his place, pick in hand, and when Lassalle arrives alongside him, the man scrutinizes his face for a fraction of a second—perhaps he thinks Lassalle is a policeman or a soldier—then turns around and slowly goes off toward the douar. It is not so much his baldness or the close-trimmed beard cleanly rimming his jaw which grabs one's attention, as his facial expression: obtuse, hostile, stubborn . . .

Lassalle quickens his pace and speedily rejoins Ichou who, by way of clearing things up, limits himself to a shrug of his shoulders. Since Lassalle insists, the lad turns his thumb toward the man who is receding behind his back, then hits his forehead with his index finger. This indeed constitutes an explanation, but one of a very general nature.

Here they are on the plateau now, veering southward, definitively leaving the Asguine valley on their left. About two kilometers separate them from the foot of the Angoun's rock ridge—two kilometers of gently rolling terrain covered with pebble beds and clumps of esparto.

The moment has come to take stock. Lassalle stops and calls Ichou, who immediately retraces his steps. Then he sits on the ground, rummages in his bag and pulls out the documents established by his predecessor: the sketch made of the Addar, already examined yesterday, a schematic map of the eastern slope of the tizi n'Oualoun, a detailed chart of the approaches to the douar and several pages of typed notes where Moritz describes his "alternative route," as he himself calls it, points out the chief obstacles and indicates the way to get around them. He did not have the time to finish his work, but his first conclusions are definite: the stretch of the pass at Asguine is easily practical and must comprise, according to his calculations, a little more than four kilometers.

The chart presents a meticulously detailed portrait of the irrigated perimeter to the west and south of the douar, the torrent, the mule path, the two séguias and the red bed knoll. The future trail, drawn in violet ink, begins on the right bank, passes above the séguia, goes around the knoll, then, beginning at the field where the little man gave Ichou such a hard time, turns directly southward. But the line hardly goes beyond the field . . . The last paragraphs of the report set out the plans for building the segment between the valley floor and the knoll. As for the map, it deals with the descent proper from the pass.

The pass, hidden by a protruding shelf, is not yet in sight, but the slopes observed through the binoculars seem to be uniformly gentle, with ample open spaces.

At any rate, up to this point, Lassalle trusts Moritz. His own work begins precisely at the place where he has just stopped.

He puts away the papers in his bag, gives the bag to Ichou, gets up and sets off again heading toward the Angoun, binoculars in hand.

Before him, the areas of shadow are receding one by one, bump by bump, and descending to the valley floor. In a few minutes the whole plateau will be bathed in bright sunlight.

Behind, the shadow-line is now moving to the foot of the grain loft, running as far as the spring above the campsite and circling the valley. The rays will soon touch the roofs of Asguine.

The man with the pick has not moved beyond the borders of his field: he has sat down on a stone marker, his back to the valley; he lowers his head and scrapes the soil with his iron tool.

At the edge of the field, his silhouette stands out against the web of terraces which bound the wadi, far below: a checkered weave of green, mauve and brown plots.

V

The foothills of the Angoun rise like a series of bastions in the form of truncated pyramids, topped by roughly semicircular byways which are in fact the extensions of the rocky ridge neighboring the tizi n'Oualoun. The bastions are linked to each other by dead-end ravines with sheer walls.

Above the ridge, the shelf climbs gently, then more and more steeply, up to the foot of the cliff whose upper edge constitutes the terminal arête of the Angoun. The vein of zinc rises to the surface approximately halfway between the ridge summit and the foot of the cliffs. The whole problem consists in gaining access to the shelf.

The plateau, as predicted, holds no surprises: the ripples are barely pronounced, the faults non-existent, the hollows strewn with broom, mastic trees, clumps of mugwort and of esparto, with so many different species of grass and thorny tufts that only a specialist could name them with any certainty.

Crossing the plateau—about an hour's journey—leaves time to examine the different possibilities for gaining access to the shelf. Since the ravines are impassable, there is no other solution but to climb the northern side of one of the pyramids, and once at the top, to look for a passageway between the rocks.

Two of these pyramids rise on the direct pathway from Asguine to the mine: they are almost joined at their bases, but their summits are at a seven-to-eight-hundred meters' distance from each other. It is probably the one on the right which would be the shortest way. Therefore good sense dictates exploring it first of all.

The far edge of the plateau, reached around nine o'clock, is attached to the Angoun by an area of scree, at an altitude of 2,700 meters. This is where the actual climb begins.

As far as the foot of the rocky ridge, two-hundred meters farther up, the northern slope of the bastion forms an approximately perfect isosceles trapezoid, with a very marked but regular incline, wide enough to allow for a looping road to be established without incident at an acceptable gradient. In principle, the rise should not exceed eight percent; wherever there is simply no other alternative, it can be as high as ten percent, but never beyond. In addition, the soil is good; the gullies are shallow, since the greater part of the runoff sweeping down from the shelf empties into the adjacent gorges. Furthermore, it is accepted that such a trail must be "opened" every spring to repair the damage caused by the storms and the thaw: filled ditches, blocked bridges, crumbling embankments, rock slides . . .

As for the fragment of the rocky ridge crowning the pyramid, it is fifty meters high. Its northern and western faces, which from a distance make it resemble an enormous molar, are impractical at first sight. On the other hand, the rock face is abundantly creviced, and offset in a jumble of blocks: a gulch opens between two tall walls and leads, after a right-angle bend, to the shelf level, from which it is separated only by a huge zone of rocks.

For two good hours Lassalle climbs, descends, climbs back, compass in hand, surveying the gulch, examining its every cranny, clinometer at eye-level, studying each gradient in detail, measuring heights, widths, directions, declivities, scribbling figures, making sketches, imagining a preliminary layout, exploring alternatives, constantly retracing his steps . . .

Around twelve-thirty, he climbs back to the shelf for the last time, sits on a boulder, rests a few minutes, then signals Ichou to resume their ascent toward the vein, which he would be unable to locate without looking at the maps unless he were to stumble upon it accidentally. Ichou surely knows the exact location, that is, the spot where the first excavations were carried out and the head of a gallery opened in the rock—a crew worked at it several years ago: thirty men from the Aït Imlil, under the supervision of a certain Moret (or Morel) who has long since left the Company . . .

Ichou sets off again, thumbs slipped under the straps of the bag, nose in the air, his blond curls swaying from right to left to the irregular rhythm of his gait.

At first, the shelf climbs gently. The cliffs appear quite near, the crests perfectly accessible. But the more the slope rises, the more progress becomes slow and difficult, the more the cliffs recede into the distance: soon they are out of reach. As for the crests, it is best not to glance up toward them: the very sight of these jagged tapering silhouettes, a thousand meters higher, discourages any thought of scaling them.

The goal at hand is fortunately more modest. A little before two o'clock, after a few hesitations and about-turns, Ichou triumphantly shows a narrow excavation concealed by a mass of debris. The "experimental gallery" penetrates only forty meters into the mountain. A few traces persist, in the surroundings, of the other year's labor: the vestiges of a retaining wall, a platform upon which they had at one time planned to erect a shed (but what would be left of it today?), a mound of rubble in front of the very mouth of the gallery, ditches here and there, half-filled in.

Lassalle advances a few steps into the tunnel which a collapsing wall blocks off ten meters from the entry. He reemerges, his back curved, explores the immediate area, gathers rock fragments, stumbles over some old rusty cans, even comes across a pick with a rotted handle and is surprised that no one had made off with it, since the time . . .

But he is not here to busy himself with the mine. His own problems are quite absorbing enough: the morning treks have exhausted him, and he is dying of thirst.

No matter how far he casts his gaze it does not meet with the slightest nook or cranny of shade. Ichou, questioned, advises against hunting for anything of the sort. So the only thing to do is to station themselves at the gallery entrance.

Lunch is a hasty affair: his appetite is disproportionate to his real hunger, which proves to be quickly satisfied. What remains is his thirst, afterwards as beforehand: the flask filled with lukewarm tea is three-quarters empty, and yet—is it out of discretion or abstemiousness?—Ichou has hardly drunk from it at all.

The siesta promises to be very uncomfortable in this black hole, but it is still better than being exposed to the sunlight. While Ichou, stretched on his back, his head propped on a stone, seems rather determined to take his nap, Lassalle props his back up against a wall, as near the light as possible, looks for his pipe but then changes his mind—he would parch his throat for the rest of the day—and, finally, for the second time, takes out of the bag the papers he slipped in there this morning.

The map of the vein holds only a moderate interest for him: the technicians affirm that it is a magnificent vein of zinc, mixed with lead, as in most cases, extending along a length of a hundred meters and a height of twenty through the entire Angoun massif: they supposedly discovered its trace somewhere on the southern slope, approximately at the same altitude—3,200 meters—but a coincidence cannot be ruled out. Even with this hypothesis, the largeness of the vein already documented would justify the exploitation. But there are numerous examples of such peremptory affirmations being gradually refuted by the facts.

The first map, on a 1:100 scale, matches the information of the ordinance survey map. The second is an enlargement of the first on a 1:20 scale. It is clear, precise work; the altitude markings situate the tizi n'Oualoun at 2,730 meters, Asguine at 2,420, Ifechtalen at 2,210 . . . The "alternative" route should descend to 2,005, which makes a seven-hundred meter shift in elevation from the outskirts of the douar to the mine.

However, the results of the study carried out this morning are hardly encouraging: if the second sector (northern side of the pyramid) and the fourth (the shelf) do not present any great problem, it is not at all the case with the third (crossing the rocky ridge).

Of course, the first order of business consists in blowing up the boulders where the shelf begins, but this is not complicated. More troublesome is the fact that the slope, all along the gulch, appreciably surpasses the ten-percent limit, going as high as fourteen for the last incline. Important roadwork would be needed to widen the passage, dropping the gradient to the permissible ten percent. Would this work prove to be more or less considerable than that projected (then rejected) in the plans for a direct route from the pass to the mine? That is the crucial question . . . Moritz was surely far too optimistic: when all is said and done, here exist the same obstacles as those which, two years ago, prevented the route along the immediate heights of the n'Oualoun from being adopted.

Lassalle feels vaguely disappointed . . . In a little while, on his way down, he will once again study the passage through the gulch, and tomorrow, at any rate, he will explore the northern slope of the pyramid.

Ichou has begun to snore, his mouth wide open. His beret, which he has set on the stone, protects his curly mop of hair. His "apron" is, in fact, a black gandoura, on the front of which two large pockets have been sewn.

Lassalle unfolds the survey map on his knees and superimposes over the white patch the "supplement" drawn up by the Company. The vein occupies more or less the center of the ellipse formed by the uncharted zone . . . If access were not difficult, it would have been exploited long since. But the complicated relief of the range terribly draws out distances: this Ouzli route is already very long, this Issoual valley interminable: 115 kilometers, according to the maps, from Assameur to the tizi n'Oualoun . . . However, Imlil is not so very far from Assameur, as the bird flies . . . forty kilometers at the most. It is this bend through Ouzli which makes you lose time. If it were only possible to directly link Imlil to Tafrent . . . But it would be necessary to cut through four transversal ranges, among which the Addar: four ascents, four passes, four descents, and across what slopes, over what gullied terrains . . . Didn't Ba Iken claim, the other day, Tafrent could be reached directly without passing through the Issoual valley? "There's another way to go to Tafrent, which bypasses Ouzli . . . It's shorter." Shorter as a straight line goes, there is no doubt about that, but across the mule paths, to the extent they are actually practical? . . . Four passes instead of two. Perhaps these passes are easy after all. "It's shorter, you arrive directly in Tafrent." Did Ba Iken say "shorter" or "quicker"? A route can be shorter without necessarily being quicker. "You arrive in Tafrent directly. The Aït Baha often travel that route." Indeed, the people from Imlil perhaps came down that way the other day. At any rate, the sheikh maintained that they had not passed in front of his house . . .

Ichou has just woken up: he sits up, replaces his beret on his hair and points his index finger toward his wristwatch: Lassalle notices that it is already three-thirty. He rises, folds up the maps and, leaving the boy to put everything into order, leaves the shelter and limbers up his legs over on the platform.

At this altitude the temperature is pleasant: twenty-five degrees perhaps. A cool breeze gusts intermittently. The view is far from being as imposing as Lassalle thought: he was expecting to look out over the entire mountain as far as the plain and, with a little luck, to glimpse an olive grove, a white house, a column of dust raised by a truck along a straight road . . . There is nothing like this whatsoever: behind the Addar, which he clearly dominates, a second range, far below, is steeped in a kind of pink mist which gradually merges with the sky and, in any case, hides the plain.

Behind him rise the Angoun crests. He examines them at length through his binoculars—he thinks he makes out a tree at the bottom of a fissure, but it is most likely an optical illusion. He then endeavors to scan them methodically westward: they reveal themselves to be extraordinarily tortured, chaotic (mouflons must take refuge in this rocky terrain). He abruptly stumbles upon the tizi n'Oualoun, partly hidden by a reddish spur.

Farther to the right, the Addar arête advances eastward, as far as the defile of the Imlil assif, which widens at its lowest point downstream from Ifechtalen, at the confluence of the three torrents. In Ifechtalen itself, white points are visible between the houses—people sitting in the shade—and farther to the west, climbing along the affluent on the left, the first plots of Asguine's irrigated zone, then others much vaster, and then suddenly the grain loft appears in the spyglass, curiously flattened, then the walnut tree to the left of the loft, and slightly in front of the walnut, it seems, the small white rectangle of the tent.

A man is standing in front of the tent entrance. He squats down, rises, then disappears . . . He reappears on the other side of the tent, as if he had just circled it, draws away from the tree and leaps over the small wall at the far edge of the field. Then he passes in front of the spring, dashes down the incline, reaches the mule path crossing and immediately afterwards vanishes behind the first houses of the douar.

VI

The mule path climbs between the squat cob structures spotted that very morning from the top of the knoll. It is a genuine alleyway, paved with flagstones in places, which comes out on the small triangular open space already crossed the night before on the way back from the mellah.

Three large stone casbahs each compose one side of the triangle. In the cone of shadow cast by the one rising at the other edge of the triangle, a man in a khaki turban, his back turned to the alleyway, is speaking with a young woman who, her head slightly tilted, is looking at a basket set on the ground beside her. She is barefooted. The man's djellaba partly hides the red-and-white striped dress.

Lassalle recognizes her at once: she simply appeared to be taller last night, motionless in the middle of the field, back arched under the weight of the jug.

Alerted by the sound of footsteps or the intrusion of a double black spot in the sunny canal of the alleyway, she raises her head and sees them approaching, the lad first, zigzagging, his thumbs under the shoulder belts of the bag, then the foreigner at a leaden gait, his shirt dustcovered, his forage cap askew.

As they reached the middle of the square, she picked up the basket, turned on her heels and fled toward the pathway to the pass, which begins just to the left of the house: emerging almost at once into the sunlight, she draws away with light, rapid steps, right hand supporting the handle of the basket set atop the hair, braids beating rhythmically upon the shoulders.

The man in the khaki turban has turned around: a wide smile bares his gold teeth. He lights a cigarette and approaches, his hand outstretched.

— You're coming to have tea, Mr. Lassalle?

Whatever wish he may have to change his clothes, to get back to his bed and assure himself that no one has rummaged through his belongings, Lassalle cannot decline Ba Iken's invitation, all the more so since he already accepted it last night.

Ba Iken's house has an air of affluence about it: the facade wall on the ground floor is coated with roughcast; the windows of each floor are decorated with wrought iron grills.

Ba Iken pushes against the front door—his long delicate hand lands just below the white hand stenciled in the middle of one flap—and precedes his guest into the staircase.

Lassalle sets his foot on the first step and violently bumps the beam with his forehead. Ichou, losing all self-control, bursts out laughing, his eyes closed, his mouth wide open, with an idiotic expression. Lassalle, somewhat stunned—both by the shock and by the lad's unexpected laughter—pats his forehead with his handkerchief. Meanwhile Ba Iken, coming back down a few steps, tries to comfort him as best he can.

On the second try, the three-story climb takes place without incident.

The reception room is long and narrow, but still not as long as Sheikh

Agouram's. The window is open: it looks out, through the grill, onto the square and the opening between the two other casbahs, onto the greater part of the Imlil basin, as far as the pass—the tizi n'Amerziaz—where the Ahori range meets the Angoun.

— Are you feeling better now, Mr. Lassalle?

Ba Iken holds out a mirror—a two-piece looking glass rimmed with a thin tin frame. Lassalle does not notice any scratches on his forehead— nothing but a rudimentary bump.

— Thank you, Ba Iken. It's fine, it's nothing . . . I'm an awkward fellow. I never pay attention . . .

It is not his forehead which bothers him, but his chin and cheeks: for four days running he has not looked at himself in a mirror, and now he discovers a pepper-and-salt beard, rough, uneven, in disarray, utterly at odds with his hair.

Ichou has remained below with the bag. A young boy makes his entrance into the room, carrying a kettle, then a teapot, a sugarloaf, two small cups and a large heap of mint leaves set on a tray.

— This is my son, Ba Iken declares . . . Bihi, the youngest.

Bihi bows, walks over to greet the guest and returns to his preparations, bare feet on the carpet.

Lassalle would really like to take off his shoes: he accomplished the entire descent on a run, from the rocky ridge to the torrent bed downstream from the douar, and his feet ache very much. Since Ba Iken encourages him to make himself comfortable, he unlaces his large shoes, pulls them off and deposits them rather far from him, at the carpet fringe. He feels much better at once.

Ba Iken lights a new cigarette.

— And the work, Mr. Lassalle, did it go well today?

— Yes and no . . . I climbed directly to the mine, as I had told you . . . You can go that way, naturally, but the slope is sharp up by the rocks. Major roadwork would be needed . . . I'll try tomorrow by a different route.

— And if it doesn't work?

— If it doesn't work, I'll need to look even farther, more eastward . . .

Young Bihi scalds the teapot with water, then packs the mint leaves into it.

— If it wasn't for that rocky ridge . . . You come across it everywhere after leaving the pass. . . .

Ba Iken, with eyes lowered, hands joined on his lap, slowly expels the cigarette smoke through his nose.

— And Ichou, Mr. Lassalle, are you happy with him?

— Very happy, Ba Iken. He's of great use to me . . . This morning he was there before I was even up!

Ba Iken smiles, raises his eyes and looks toward the window.

Lassalle is seated in the corner to the left of the window. Ba Iken is opposite him. Both are leaning their backs against thick cushions piled up around the perimeter of the room. The mirror has remained where Lassalle deposited it, on a low table placed in front of the window.

The wrought iron grill is very beautiful. Lassalle perceives that he would be hard pressed to refer to the ornamentations—sorts of rosaces and sideways *s*'s—in any other way than with the general term, probably inappropriate, of "arabesques." These designs are inscribed in twenty square and rectangular blocks, each framing a fragment of the countryside. Shadows already blanket the whole of the douar and a portion of the terraces downstream, except for the foliage of a walnut tree which glistens, two- or three-hundred meters away, set in a rosace whose four linear components culminate in volutes. The quadrangles of the upper rows stand out in three horizontal strips of increasing height: the first comprises the environs of Ifechtalen and of Zegda, the second the Ahori range, and the last a fringe of silver-gray sky. Two columns of smoke rise above the invisible douars, slicing through the triple metallic terracing. Closer at hand, halfway up the grill, the cigarette smoke lingers in whitish streaks which disintegrate upon contact with the iron bars and filter toward the roof.

The four lower rosaces coincide with the small open space, the facades of the two other casbahs bounding it and the last meters of the alleyway, paved with flagstones in places, emerging from the lower quarters—an extension of the mule path climbing along the wadi between the squat cob structures—and opens onto the small triangular space, or more exactly on the empty lot lying between the three stone casbahs, each of which forms a side of the triangle: the cone of shadow cast by the one rising at the opposite end of the alleyway is moving eastward, its edges parallel to the facades of the two other buildings. It has apparently grown longer since a short time ago . . . then it only reached to the middle of the open space; Ba Iken, his back turned, was chatting on his doorstep; his djellaba partly hid the red-and-white striped dress . . . Now the summit of the cone of shadow nearly reaches the entrance to the alleyway.

— That young girl who was with you . . .

Bihi draws near Ba Iken with the second cup. Ba Iken takes the cup and speaks a few words to his son in a hushed voice, accompanied by a nod toward the tray.

— That young girl you were speaking with downstairs?

Ba Iken takes a swallow.

— Ah! Yamina? . . . No, she didn't get scared. But, you know, when a stranger comes to the house, women can't stay. It's the caïda.

— Yamina?

— Yes. She's a relative, a cousin . . . Ba Iken smiles. Everybody belongs to the same family in the douar . . . That's the way it has to be.

Lassalle takes a swallow in turn: the tea was not as hot as he thought it would be. He continues drinking. When the small cup is empty, he sets it back on the table edge, then rummages through his pocket and pulls out the pipe, the tobacco pouch and the matchbox.

Bihi dashes from the other end of the room, teapot in hand. He leans over and pours the tea intently, holding the teapot a good twenty centimeters above the table. His face is flush against Ba Iken's, which is tilted in the same way with a dignified reserved air, the forehead broad, the nose straight, the complexion light, the eyes a gray-blue . . . "Everybody belongs to the same family in the douar. That's the way it has to be" . . . She's a relative, a cousin . . . face tilted as well, the forehead wide, very prominent, the cheeks hollow, the chin tapering . . . the lips twitch imperceptibly, the eyes, unusually far apart, seem to be set at the border of the temples, past the jutting cheekbones; the eyelids are closed, the lashes perfectly still; the arms dangle along the metal uprights . . .

Lassalle unties his tobacco pouch and begins to stuff his pipe.

— The incident I mentioned to you in Tisselli . . . you know, that girl I had seen in the infirmary at Assameur, who had been stabbed . . . have you heard any more information? Everyone must be in the know here, even if it happened at the other end of the tribe.

Ba Iken pushes away his cup on the table and with his finger asks permission to borrow the matchbox. He takes a third cigarette out of his pack and while drawing it close to the flame, shakes his head affirmatively.

— Of course, everyone is in the know, Mr. Lassalle. They told me all about it, yesterday . . . It was in Ifechtalen that it happened: an argument . . . Her husband was the one who stabbed her: she left the house, you see; he wanted to bring her back by force; she didn't want to; then he beat her and after he stabbed her with the knife.

— Her husband? But they would have given him twelve, thirteen years!

— It's not like back home here: girls are often married at eight, or nine . . .

Bihi, who had become invisible, returns with two plates full of cookies, marzipan, honey-cakes, sugar-coated fruit jellies, and tiny almond-paste crescents, commonly called "gazelle horns." He sets the plate on the table and invites Lassalle to help himself.

Lassalle selects a honey-cake, which he holds in his hand.

— Ifechtalen is part of Imlil, right?

— Yes, Mr. Lassalle, it's in the Aït Imlil . . . Why are you asking that?

— Because the other day you told me, at the sheikh's house, that the incident had most certainly not taken place in Imlil . . . that it must have happened in another offshoot of the tribe, otherwise you would have immediately learned of it in Assameur.

Ba Iken finishes his second cup of tea and digs into the cookie plate.

— Oh, you know, when I say Imlil, what I did mean is Asguine . . . First of all, Asguine is where I live, and also, Asguine is the biggest douar, far bigger than the two others . . . Besides, everybody says Imlil, in place of Asguine . . . That's the way it is throughout the whole tribe. When you don't want to talk about Asguine, then you say Zegda, or Ifechtalen . . . Elsewise, if you only say Imlil, everybody thinks what you mean is Asguine.

Lassalle eats his cake, then lights his pipe. The tobacco crackles and twists upon contact with the flame . . . Naturally, this type of confused terminology is rather frequent. Since the greater portion of the Aït Imlil live in Asguine, it is to be expected that the two names be popularly used each in place of the other and wind up by merging together. Yet, in

Tisselli, it did seem that Ba Iken, by excluding Imlil, intended likewise to exclude the entire offshoot of the tribe, and not simply the most populated douar.

— So then, they did come through the Issoual valley?

— Oh—Oh! (Ba Iken simultaneously raises his head, slightly askant, and his right hand, with his index finger sticking up. The second exclamation is somewhat sharper than the first, and their sequence appears as the exact aural equivalent of the parallel movement of his head and hand. Lassalle had already remarked the expressive gesture on several occasions; now he understands what the signs mean: contradiction, or more precisely, the "inscription of falsehood." At any rate, this is indeed the first time that Ba Iken has answered this way, point-blank, in his own language. . . .) No, they came by the footpath, that I told you in Tisselli. It's shorter, but you need to have good animals . . . First you climb the Addar, on the trail we took yesterday, and after you drop directly toward Tafrent by way of the mountain.

— But there must be several passes?

— Yes, but the valleys are not as deep as the Issoual's.

— But if it's shorter, why don't people always go that way?

— It's shorter for the people of Ifechtalen and Zegda, who normally go by way of Iknioul. But for those from Asguine, it's better to go by way of the Issoual. And then, that way, you cross the douars on the banks of the wadi as far as Ouzil . . . Taking the other way, you never leave the mountains . . .

Lassalle drinks his second cup. Bihi draws near at once and pours another cupful of steaming liquid.

Lassalle leans his back against the wall, elbow on the cushions, pipe in hand. He takes a "gazelle horn" from the plate and begins to nibble at it mechanically.

— And then, if you're lucky, you can find a car in Ouzil, at the end of the trail . . . That way, you get to Assameur in no time.

Ba Iken takes a few swallows of tea, bites into a cookie, lights another cigarette.

Night is falling. The greater part of the room is now in darkness. In the corner to the right of the window the brighter djellaba cloth stands out, and a little higher the red dot of the cigarette—at the other end of the room the young man's white turban and a golden reflection on the tray. All that the daylight now illuminates is the window rim, the wood shutters, the whitewashed ledge where the shadow of the grill is outlined very palely, the table with the cups, plates and mirror—the looking glass split in two widthwise, the unevenly dented white iron edging.

The image reflected in the mirror is at first glance incomprehensible: lines crisscrossing in utter disarray, at irregular intervals overstrewn with fibery sheaves, and knots, and dots . . . Considered as a whole, it recalls a spray of thorns, then a weave of barbed wire, dense, homogenous, composing in a fashion a definitive primary image, which is coherent, autonomous . . . But soon the illusion dissipates, and the reflection of the grill, most likely a bit warped by the ridges and bulges on the glass surface, gradually recomposes itself: dots, knots, interlacing loops, relate back to the spirals, winding cables and volutes of the "arabesques." Upon closer inspection, the mirror unambiguously restores every curve, every pattern of the wrought iron.

Outside, there is still some light, but all the sun brightens is the crest-fringe of the desert-like Ahori range, whose rocks take on a pale pink tint. Zegda is located at the foot of the Ahori, on the very floor of the valleys, and farther below, Ifechtalen.

Lassalle takes a honey-cake and savors it in small bites.

— Ba Iken, what happens in these sorts of incidents? Is the Kaid the one who makes an investigation?

— It all depends, Mr. Lassalle. When it's a very important matter, the Kaid comes himself, or else his Khalifa . . . Otherwise, the sheikh's the one who makes the investigation.

— And for this incident . . . in Ifechtalen?

— I don't know . . . The Kaid's gone on vacation. Maybe it's his Khalifa who's going to come.

— But the . . . husband, was he arrested?

— No, Mr. Lassalle. People say he ran away . . . And as for catching him, well, that's not so easy. They go off across the plain, they take the bus and they disappear in the big cities. There's no way of finding them.

— But maybe he's hiding out in the mountains?

— Very far away, maybe, but not here . . . People know everything in the mountains . . . People know at once where he is.

Bihi brings a carbide lamp which he hangs from a hook in the center of the room. Lassalle looks at his watch.

— I must be getting back, Ba Iken. It's already six-thirty.

— Stay a little longer, Mr. Lassalle. It's not late, and the work is done!

— I thank you, Ba Iken, but I need to go rest up. The day turned out to be very tiring, and I must be off again very early tomorrow morning.

Lassalle gets up. Ba Iken imitates him, heads toward the door and precedes his guest into the stairway, lamp in hand.

— Watch out for the steps this time!

Lassalle, his legs stiff from the siesta, proceeds down cautiously.

— You must come again tomorrow, if you're back early.

Ichou is calmly waiting, sitting on the ground in front of the door, with the bag between his legs.

Outside, it is still light enough to get one's bearings without any difficulty. Children are playing in the open square. Farther on, in the alleyway, women pass by, bare feet on the pebbles, backs bent under the weight of their jugs. A small donkey escapes from the casbah and flees on the pathway to the pass.

On the left, leaving the douar, rises the isolated house before which the young girl stopped last night. The door is closed. No light comes from within.

Scaling the incline is particularly difficult. Ichou, tireless, ascends on a run.

The canvas flaps, at the tent entrance, are intact. Nothing has been taken from within, or even moved out of place.

Lassalle, exhausted, stretches out on the cot. He would really like to cancel "dinner" and go to sleep right away: Ba Iken's sweets have killed his appetite.

VII

The footpath emerges from a tangle of short gravelly furrows, parallel to the séguia, on the right slope of the valley.

The sun's rays have already reached the foot of the grain loft and, farther to the left, the walnut's dark foliage. In a few moments they will drop as far down as the spring and shortly afterwards to the towers of Asguine's tallest casbahs: the sheikh's, in the center of the douar, between the alleyway and the torrent, two others, almost as majestic, between the alley and the loft peak, the last three discrete, not soaring as high, grouped on the small square where the mellah lane and the mule path cross.

But this bank remains in the shade within the recesses of the valley upstream from the douar, sheltered by the red bed knoll.

Ichou, who has moved slightly ahead, arrives at the end of a straight line and disappears behind a stretch of rock. In the place where he just was a moment before, a bluish smoke rises above a roof, and immediately upon entering the zone of sunlight, is drawn thin and almost instantly withers away.

When Ichou reappears, he is proceeding across the rectangular plot, teeming with pebbles and sandstone outcroppings, which is already in the broad sunlight and where each tuft of couch grass casts a cone of gray shade, stretched flat and broken up by the stones and clumps of earth.

The man with the mallet is there, just as yesterday morning, but instead of advancing to the middle of the field, and gesticulating and hollering while hopping around the lad, grabbing him by his collar and shoulders, shaking him and berating him, he remains motionless, seated at the border of the lot upon the "stone marker" to which he had withdrawn yesterday after the outburst, turning his back to the valley, his left hand flat upon his knee, his right closed around the mallet handle (or the scraper's) planted directly in front of him—like a model in rags (the gandoura, seen against the sunlight, seems to be completely tattered) or a scarecrow for sparrows.

Ichou proceeds along without even turning his head. Lassalle leaves the trail to the left—which goes down to the séguia—enters into the field and casts a glance, as he passes, upon the squat swarthy man, set a few steps away on his heap of stones, impassive, his head turned toward the Angoun along the approximate axis of the route leading to the mine, as if he were making it a point to rivet his gaze for as long as possible in this single direction.

Lassalle crosses the parcel of land slantwise—he realizes that he forgot to fill in Ba Iken on what happened—catches up with Ichou and signals him to head for the second pyramid, which is in a markedly more eastward direction than the first.

The bases of the two pyramids almost meet, but their summits are seven- to eight-hundred meters apart. The scree zone is located at the edge of the plateau—it must extend as far as the Imlil assif—formed with enormous blocks of stone scattered along the entire lower surface of the glacis.

As far as the foot of the rocky ridge, the pyramid presents the same characteristics as the one explored the day before: a sharp regular incline, solid ground, shallow gullies.

The fragment of the rocky ridge, which is also fifty meters high, resembles a gigantic dungeon topped with a sort of chaotic covered walkway. Its eastern and western faces are impractical. Only the northern face seems sufficiently offset to eventually yield a passage to the mine. But there is no need for a lengthy study today in order to bow to the facts: from one end to the other of the gulch, which could be established by blowing up a few large obstructions, the slope's percentage of incline would be far too high: fourteen or fifteen on the average, twenty along the last gradients; and this time there will be no way to widen the gap, regardless of cost, unless of course all the adjoining rock walls were also destroyed: one might just as well envisage blowing up the entire rocky ridge . . .

The chances for success of the "Moritz solution" thus remain linked, temporarily, to those related to the difficult, costly task of establishing the passage sighted the day before on the other pyramid. Yet, at first approach, even this view does not seem to present a conclusive advantage over the initial plans for a direct route. Were such an advantage to exist, it would be canceled out for the most part by the need to lengthen the road . . .

Nothing here that amounts to very much . . . Seated at the summit of the ridge, in the shade of a huge red boulder, Lassalle, flask in hand, passes in review the slim results of the first two days' exploration. Naturally, he is going to continue to search farther eastward, but he has no illusions: he will soon be stopped by the trench of the Imlil assif. If he finds nothing between here and there, he will have no choice but to climb back up the first pyramid to do a detailed study of the only practical passage, and this will be the only contribution in his name.

Two steps away from him, Ichou, still full of energy, is scraping the bottom of the pâté can with his penknife: first he digs into the center with broad strokes, then pecks around the oval perimeter with the point, while the screaking can rotates about the motionless blade. Once the possibilities for using the knife have been exhausted, he cleans the sides of the container with a piece of bread. When he is convinced that the can is completely empty, he flings it with all the strength in his wrist: leaning forward at his chest, he watches the metallic carcass drop, bounce on the pebbles, and eventually disappear behind a fold of the terrain.

Lassalle drinks the last drops of tea, sets the flask back down and, propping his back up against the boulder, arms crossed over his chest, contemplates the gray and brown uniformity of his new visual universe. The light, vertical at this time of the day, pounds down upon the mountain. It is no longer the oblique morning brightness which fashions the correct contours of forms, rendering an exact measure of the space between and surrendering it again in the evening before darkness settles in. The sun at zenith has dispersed the shadows: the light is inert, even, wherein the divided brightness recomposes itself between 10:00 A.M. and 3:00 P.M., eliminating the morning's landmarks, blurring reliefs, suggesting new relationships between distances—not insofar as the plains draw closer together and coincide midway from the horizon, but rather that the very organization of the landscape is now deprived of its most rigid bond: distances are obliterated, contours dissolve, black-and-white precision gives way to a shimmering transparence, and a layered effect to juxtaposition. Surfaces station themselves in flat range of the eyes in an unreal haze.

As far as the view reaches along the northern slope of the Angoun, it does not come upon the slightest bush (but the southern slope must be even more arid). There is no longer any trace of forest at this elevation—merely a few shreds of thorny growth. It is the last stage of a degeneration recorded day-by-day from the outset of the trip—beginning at the palm groves of Dar el Hamra, the enormous olive groves of the plain and the citrus fruit plantations wrenched from the fissured soil, and extending to the olive grove in Assameur and its old contorted trees; to the orchards at low altitudes, deep in the valleys; to the scrubby forests of green oak and junipers, cypresses and thuyas, and their "undergrowth" of laburnum and holly; to the thurifers, even higher, scattered few and far between in the rocky terrain; to the prickly blackthorns, the jennets, the mastic trees, the laburnums, the rare walnut on the terraced lots, and on the plateau below, the mugwort and Esparto grass. And now on this projecting shelf hemmed in between the cliffs and the rocky ridge, what is able to survive, buried under the snowfall, and to come to life again in the spring: a few clumps of thistle, a few small cushions of thorny plants, tufts of astragalus scattered upon the stony ground—the residue of the sandstone platform which a superficial decomposition has brought to various stages of pulverization: gutted rocks, blocks of stone balanced midslope, tiny pieces of debris spread in conical sheets, pebbles with crumbly edges, a gray-and-red dust upon the furrowed ground.

Ichou, who has put the things away in the bag, asks permission to take a short walk among the rocks. He leaves on a run, bounding from one leg to the other.

Lassalle rises, takes a few steps in the sunlight and comes back to sit in the shade. He unfolds the survey map and enjoys himself by using his pencil to fill in with broad strokes the lower flap of the sheet. But soon he breaks off: what he is doing here will not be of much use. At the very most he notes that the vein of zinc comes to the surface approximately in the center of the uncharted zone. This latter stretches from the bend in the Issoual wadi—where the n'Oualoun footpath starts up—to the ill-defined region of the upper plateaus, beyond the tizi n'Amerziaz, to the east of the Angoun. The northernmost point of the white patch seems to be the place where the Imlil assif leaves the long defile which it crosses between the Addar and the Ahori, the southernmost the drainage basin of the Issoual, on the southern slope of the Angoun . . . The blue line-trace of the Issoual, upstream from Tisselli, comes to an abrupt stop: the wadi is supposed to penetrate inside the ellipse, and since it reemerges nowhere, also has its source there. The same problem arises along the whole perimeter of the white patch—a perimeter which is virtual, indeterminate, the fruit of a series of uncertainties and indecisions, the geometric locus of the absorption points of multiple straight, curved, and broken lines which drop out of sight. The eyes move from puzzle to puzzle, questioning as they pass the origins of ultimate end point of a crest whose delineations venture a few millimeters beyond the neuter surface, or the course of a torrent springing out of nothing, or the fate of a gently undulating plateau, whose contour lines—as if it were emptied of its substance—tilt inexorably into the contiguous blur.

The pencil point slips out of control across the map . . . Lassalle raises his head.

The rocky ridge where he is located is at about three-thousand meters, at the same altitude as the Addar, and the horizon is as obstructed as it was yesterday.

The sheet of fog begins four or five kilometers from the observation post, concealing the greater part of the theoretically visible landscape. All that emerges are the Imlil basin, the Addar, the Ahori—including the two passes at each drop-off of the Angoun, constituting in a fashion the foci of the ellipse—and, beyond, a peripheral ring of unvarying width. The perimeter of this marginal ring roughly coincides with the circumference of the white zone, whose northern tip is visible, whereas the rest of the mountain, through a perfect reversal of the cartographical anomaly, disappears within a pinkish mist which is seamless, opaque, slightly fleecy.

Lassalle folds up the map. Putting away the pencil, his hand touches the pocket diary. He realizes that once again he omitted, yesterday evening, to enter an account of the day. He picks up the pencil again and writes:

"Tuesday, August tenth.—Climbed directly from Asguine to the vein. Discovered a practical passage (after major roadwork). Returned at five. Tea at Ba Iken's."

And on the next page:

"Wednesday, August eleventh.—Studied an alternative to the preceding route. Failure. Returned to Asguine around four."

Then he puts the small tablet back into his pocket and, while waiting for Ichou to come back, scans the crests of the Angoun through his binoculars, in hopes of discovering a mouflon perched at four-thousand kilometers on the point of a boulder.

But the crests of the Angoun, as far eastward as they rise, are completely deserted. Soon the drop-off of the tizi n'Amerziaz will begin . . . Suddenly his field of vision is blocked by an immense blurry gray patch, glittering with rainbow reflections: in the time it takes to focus the lens, Lassalle recognizes Ichou at the end of the spyglass: the lad is coming forward dancing on one foot; his black apron is beating against his calves; his curly locks, quivering in rhythm, resemble an oversized or loosely fastened wig.

Two minutes later, Ichou hitches the bag on his shoulders, slips his thumbs under the straps and charges downward at top speed.

Lassalle, although better equipped, with his thick shoes for running over gravel, vainly labors to catch up with him. Recognizing the pointlessness of his struggle, he slows down, stops, lights his pipe, then sets off again at a tranquil pace, contemplating the casbahs of Asguine, at the bottom of the valley, planted in the earth like the pieces of a construction set.

VIII

— I know you already came back: I saw Ichou downstairs.

All that is visible at the tent entrance are the djellaba folds, the engraved dagger sheath, the leather choukara and the left hand lifting the canvas flap. His voice seems less to project itself within the tent than to hover above it.

— Come in, Ba Iken! You've come at the right time: the tea's ready.

The khaki turban, then the close-trimmed blond beard cleanly rimming his jaw, inscribe themselves in turn within the triangle to the right of the stake. Ba Iken, doubled over, enters the tent and sits at the foot of the cot.

— It's black tea. I don't know if you like it.

— I do, Mr. Lassalle. Black tea's very good. It's as good as ours.

Lassalle holds out a tumbler full of scalding liquid and with his finger indicates the tin can set on the bed:

— If you want to try some cookies . . . They don't match yours, unfortunately, but they're all I have.

— No really, Mr. Lassalle, it's just fine like this . . . It reminds me of the army. Ba Iken takes a cookie, a few swallows of tea . . . Are you happy with your work today?

— No, not at all. The place is very bad. There's no way to pass through it . . . Tomorrow I'll look farther off. But I'm afraid I'll be reduced to the first road trace . . . to the one I spotted yesterday . . . It doesn't amount to much.

Lassalle refills Ba Iken's beaker, while his guest nibbles his cookie, leaning forward, for fear of knocking askew his turban whose points, as soon as he stands, crush up against the canvas.

— You got back early . . .

— Yes, I had finished up there at two. And we came back directly, without passing through the douar.

Ba Iken drinks his second cup in one gulp.

— And that bump on your forehead, Mr. Lassalle?

— Oh, it's nothing. It's still noticeable, but it's not serious.

— I'm very embarrassed, you see: you come to my home and you trip on the steps . . .

— But it's my fault, Ba Iken! It'll teach me to watch where I step.

Lassalle pours a third cupful for Ba Iken, who takes another cookie.

— I've come to see you because I must go up to the grain loft. So, if you want to come, maybe it is interesting for you.

— Yes, of course, Ba Iken. It's a good idea. I'll join you.

No sooner are the last drops of tea drunk down, Ba Iken rises and leaves, followed by Lassalle, who simply lets the canvas flaps fall back, deeming it pointless, for such a brief absence, to knot the laces.

The grain loft is a little higher than the campsite, but rather than pass through the rocks, it is best to drop to the terraces below, proceed along the séguia, then climb back to the peak summit.

The two men make their way along the hillside, leaping over the small walls and the jujube bushes, walking along the séguia, cutting through the fields where the pale-green stalks of millet are coming up.

On the valley side, the peak plunges fifty meters to the first houses of the douar. The slope line drops directly from the terreplein, at the summit of the peak, as far as the encircling wall of the large casbahs located north of the alleyway. A quadrangular tower, twelve meters tall, rises on the terreplein, in the shape of a truncated pyramid, with reinforced ledges, an exposed branch-thatched roof, and clay walls slit with loopholes, "like a lighthouse on the cliff overlooking the port": Lassalle has just allowed himself to be caught by this mediocre comparison and despite all his efforts does not manage to rid himself of it: the lighthouse, the cliff, the port silhouette themselves in space according to the classic layout of an old postcard; even more: the torrent, below, suggests the shore . . .

But they reach the foot of the loft. Blocks of clay, on the bottom floor, are coated with a layer of white roughcast and pierced with miniature square openings.

Ba Iken circles the edifice—the door opens on the valley—and from his choukara takes out a key as long as his forearm: the stem is a good centimeter in diameter and the ring is so large that the thought flashes through Lassalle's mind that it is some sort of a joke. But no: the lock is also enormous.

Ba Iken turns toward Lassalle and, scratching the point of his beard with the ring:

— I always have the key, he utters with a smile. I am the loft watchman.

He leans toward the door. As he is inserting the key in the lock, a bare-headed fellow springs up from behind a boulder and in a few strides scales the last meters separating him from the terreplein. He stops, short of breath, and without even glancing at Lassalle:

— Ba Iken! Ba Iken! he bellows in the latter's back.

Ba Iken turns around, his face twisted in a scowl, his arm folded across his chest, barred diagonally by the immense key.

The newcomer pours out his words in a swift, antagonistic surge: he shouts, stammers, splutters . . . The hard consonants of the dialect explode with all the more power since they seem held back for an instant behind the gums, giving the tongue time enough to collect its strength. He brandishes a hoe in his right hand and strikes the ground with it at the end of each sentence—or what functions as a sentence in such a chaotically spouted invective.

Lassalle recognizes him right away: pug nose, low forehead, long triangular sideburns connected to his mustache, a narrow chin whose hair has been reduced to a sparsely scattered fringe, the straight lines of his eyebrows perpetually furrowed over his tiny piercing gray eyes, the man has exactly the same obstinate, fierce, obtuse expression as yesterday morning in the fallow field, on the other side of the valley.

Ba Iken, postponing the opening of the door, strives to calm down the troublemaker. At first, he can only get in a word or two edgewise, those rare moments when the other is catching his breath; then he attempts to intercede at greater length. The enormous key accompanies all his gestures, passing from one hand to the other, smoothing the folds of his djellaba, beating time, rapping the recalcitrant man's shoulder who, whenever this happens, closes his eyes, pouts and hunches his sideburns down inside his lacy shirt collar, as if to let it be understood that he is not above being persuaded—or that he is already familiar with the argument. Now and then Ba Iken, worn out by his opponent's renewed onslaught, heaves a long sigh, raises his eyes skyward, clenches his teeth, then patiently resumes his demonstration.

Lassalle has taken a seat on the low wall which fortifies the loft's foundations and lighted his pipe. He follows the controversy with interest.

— Hey, Ba Iken, he looks like he has a grudge against you!

— Oh, it's nothing, Mr. Lassalle . . . a little "chikaya" of no importance.

Ba Iken makes an effort to smile, but he is visibly worried, all the more so since nothing seems to be getting settled. The small man stands up to him, screams in rage, stabs the cutting edge of his scraper into a clod of earth which flies into pieces. And now he is beginning to motion toward Lassalle with his chin, above Ba Iken's shoulder, then with his finger, his arm outstretched. Ba Iken hops to the left and to the right to hide the offensive gestures, but is not very successful. After a few minutes of this little scene, Lassalle gets up:

— But it looks like he's attacking me now?

Before Ba Iken can intervene, the other grabs Lassalle by his shirt sleeve, spins him around and insistently shows him an indeterminate point on the other side of the valley. But Ba Iken quickly forces him to loosen his hold.

— I didn't want to trouble you with this, Mr. Lassalle . . . I tried to calm him down, but he doesn't want to listen. He says you ought to know. He doesn't want to leave before you do.

— Fine, then, what does he want from me?

— He says that yesterday and today you crossed over his field, up there, on the other side of Asguine.

— Yes, I saw him, of course. He even tried to pick a fight with Ichou.

— Fine. He said you had your "boundary marking" in your hand.

— My boundary marking?

— Yes, your map, your chart . . . And your colleague, two years ago, also came to his field, and he took measurements with a chain. So he thinks you're going to make the road pass through his land and he's furious, he doesn't want to hear anything about it . . .

While Ba Iken is explaining, the man continues to brandish his index finger toward the plot of land, over there, on the right bank, above the séguia, behind the red bed knoll; then he passes his left hand, several times, over his throat—sign language whose interpretation is instantaneous: "Cut off my head if you want, but I will not budge."

— Don't worry about it, Ba Iken concludes. He usually shouts like that. He's well-known in Imlil: he pesters everybody. You just need to talk things over with him for a little while . . . Afterwards, he calms down.

— But it's a misunderstanding, Ba Iken! First of all, nothing has been decided. And also, the road can just as well avoid his field . . . go around it after coming off the knoll and pass a little above it. Tell him he has nothing to fear. And also, if even a few meters of his land were whittled off, he would be compensated . . . But we can surely do it some other way. Put his mind at rest!

— Listen, Idder, Ba Iken mistakenly begins, and then corrects himself and continues in dialect.

Idder . . . this small stubborn stocky fellow who had grabbed hold of Ichou the day before and shook him like a wisp of straw . . . Ichou, also, must know him well . . . He took great care not to be curt with him.

Idder is displaying new signs of impatience. He is pretending to scribble with a pencil in the hollow of his palm—an allusion to the "boundary markings" most likely—then once more the simulated beheading, followed by furious jabs of his scraper. However Ba Iken exhibits great talent as an arbitrator: he slips his arm around the plaintiff's neck and gently pats his shoulder, while, guided by the other arm, with the key tip draws the boundary of the lot in the dirt, then traces the eventual road. From time to time Ba Iken raises his eyes to Lassalle, to make him understand that everything is going to be settled, at least temporarily. Lassalle, on his side, does not remain inactive: he tries hard to help Ba Iken and to testify, with small hand signs, casual shoulder shrugs and pacifying smiles, how pointless the feud is.

Finally, Idder, his eyes lowered, seems to be swayed, if not entirely convinced. He nods his head, hits the ground again on principle, starts up a vehement sentence but falls silent, his eyebrows furrowed, his gaze darker than ever. Ba Iken chooses this moment to take his hand and to shake it vigorously. Idder mutters a few words, stops short, then turns on his heels, dashes downward, and soon disappears behind the rock.

— Thanks for settling matters, Ba Iken. I would never have understood a thing about it.

— Oh, it's nothing, Mr. Lassalle; but he's an impossible fellow. That's the way he always is. If he bothers you again, come find me . . .

Once again, Ba Iken leans upon the door. He thrusts the key into the lock. The door creaks as it opens.

A stone staircase leads to the first two upper floors, a wooden ladder to the third.

— You see, all these cubicles, these are for storing each family's reserves. Now there's no use for them. It was for when there was "siba" . . . But maybe "siba" comes again, one day . . .

Ba Iken rummages through his choukara and flourishes three large bunches of keys:

— I have all the keys, for all the people of Asguine.

Through a double rib-shaped window, on the uppermost floor, the douar appears, all the way below, in the broad sunlight.

— Come on, Ba Iken continues, we'll go up on the roof. You'll have an even better view from up there.

Ba Iken moves up a very narrow ladder, ending in a trap door. He opens the door with some difficulty, flapping it over on the outside.

— You can come up, the roof is solid!

Indeed, the roof is solid, but so flexible that it sways under his feet. The shafts of wood are covered with gravel and hard-packed earth.

— It needs to be repaired often, this roof. Especially when it rains. And in winter, you have to come up and remove the snow . . .

It is difficult to imagine Imlil covered with snow: its scorched, cracked slopes, its parched wadi, this dust, the bushes of dried-up thorns . . .

Asguine stretches out at the foot of the grain loft: on the right, the double row of gourbis from which the trail to the pass breaks away; in the center, a cluster of twenty or so houses, including the three large four-towered casbahs; on the left, the small triangular open space with

Ba Iken's house, then the lower quarter crossed by the stone-paved alley which, a little farther on, becomes the Ifechtalen road; even farther to the left, and higher, the mellah, at a visible remove from the agglomeration.

Lassalle does not dare venture too close to the edge, since the branches extend a half-meter beyond the wall rim. Once again he is sorry he forgot his camera: from the top of this perch ("the lighthouse on the cliff"), he has a magnificent overview of terraces and inner courtyards—assembled in a maze of intercommunicating surfaces which are juxtaposed like the steps of a large staircase.

And the lighting is ideal: the sun, on the verge of disappearing behind the pass, is grazing the roofs and facades, splendidly shaping the slightest contour, the slightest overhang . . . The most inexperienced amateur could snap a good shot.

IX

The report is straightforward: no land expropriation is foreseen in the Imlil basin. The trail goes down from the pass, crosses over the wadi, passes above the séguia and joins the plateau without traversing a single cultivated field. Idder's hostility is based on a simple apprehension: they surveyed his land, map in hand, noted a few landmarks . . . For all intents and purposes, his intervention will not have any repercussions. Anyway, the road trace Moritz settled on stops just beyond the red bed knoll . . .

The map of Asguine's outskirts, spread out on the cot, represents with the utmost precision the boundaries of the farmed surfaces to the west and south of the douar—hatched with green lines when they are irrigatible, and with yellow otherwise. The large violet stroke of the future trail approaches the knoll, circles it, and immediately breaks off. Of course, it cuts along a stretch of a few millimeters through the yellow hatching located farther eastward but it seems that is merely a projection: Moritz himself had hardly settled on the subsequent direction of the road. Whatever the case may be, avoiding the lot will not entail any complications. If only the plaintiff does not require anything else to satisfy him . . . While waiting, it is better not to show Idder the map: he would be tempted to see it—supposing that he were to understand something—as a confirmation of his fears.

The sheet of paper, carefully refolded, takes its place again in the briefcase, and the briefcase at the top of the bag, at the head of the bed.

It is a little later than nine o'clock. But contrary to previous nights, sleep is a long time in coming: the exhaustion is much less noticeable than yesterday and every trace of the first days' exertions has disappeared.

Lassalle pushes the mess tin, the teapot and the kettle under the bed, slips on his jacket, picks up his pipe and his flashlight, extinguishes the carbide lamp and leaves the tent.

Outside the air is warm, the night black. A few stars shine through the leaves of the walnut tree.

The furrows, even though perpendicular to the direction he is moving, are barely pronounced. The clumps of earth fritter upon contact with his large shoes, which pulverize them or send them tumbling in the hollows.

Soon the thornbush interposes itself, at the far western edge of the field. Beyond, the foot stumbles on tufts of grass and sprays of thistle, slips upon pebbles and slates of schist, in the hillside, slips along the entire valley rim to where he meets the mule path. But the tree—the would-be pistachio—is not there: the juncture point is most likely located at a level lower than the campsite's.

Farther upstream, the mule path runs parallel to the torrent, over-looking it for about a meter, but the bed of white and gray stones can barely be made out from the banks. In darkness such as this, bright patches appear only at the edge of the field of vision; dark patches stand out only against the sky: here is the pistachio, betrayed by its upper branches, since the trunk, close at hand, remains invisible.

Footpath and torrent merge, one-hundred meters higher, at the entrance to a limestone outcropping which the wadi cuts with a narrow tortuous trench—a miniature version of a defile where the sound of hooves, the evening they arrived, echoed endlessly from one cliff face to the other, as if the animals had been trampling in place, or turning in circles; but this was due to weariness: the crossing had probably lasted only a few minutes, the last minutes of uncertain expectation before the vista upon Asguine.

The torrent bed is completely dry, the gorge entrance obstructed by huge, round boulders with flattened, easily accessible summits—a convenient point for sitting down and smoking a pipe.

In Asguine, only two windows are aglimmer: one of the faint glows, wavering, goes out almost at once. Much farther on, a light is shining, at the other end of the basin, most likely in Ifechtalen—Zegda is too boxed in for its firelights to be visible. Nothing else emerges from the dark chasm along whose ledge shepherds keep watch, camped in the pastures, the animals huddled in the caves—nothing else but a column of smoke, ghostly and twisted, which the wandering gaze manages to discern toward the crests.

The sky is extraordinarily clear. At times, from among this profusion of stars, one point detaches itself and "shoots," with a white streak which trails behind, scattering downward in a shower. A dog barks in the distance, repeatedly, then falls silent. Closer by, in the douar itself, a man calls out two syllables into the night. Even closer, a pebble slips, hurtles down the slope, comes to a rest. The man cries out once again. Someone answers him—a series of interjections, the last of which, taken up by the repercussion, echoes a long while afterward, as if the very instant it had been uttered was itself being indefinitely divided . . . Then everything grows calm. The silence reestablishes itself once again, deeper than before, until a second pebble slips down along the rock face.

The last shooting star, leaving from the zenith, swooped right down upon the Amerziaz, then disappeared, in its wake pulling along a dust of shimmering particles. A glow dots the crests of the Addar—a twig fire, perhaps, which a shepherd has just lit. A door opens below: a reddish brightness spills out on the ground in front of the house. But the door closes again before whoever it is ventured outside.

A cool draft edges along, reaching the boulder, caressing hair, and neck, and jacket cloth, from the shoulders down to the base of the spine . . . It is nearly ten o'clock. It is best to begin walking again: now is no time to catch cold.

The rounded stone blocks strew the torrent bed, hemmed in by vertical walls that are not very high, but smooth, with no crevices. The footpath can be guessed at from one boulder to the next, wheeling around the oleander, inscribing its own twists and turns within those, much vaster, which have been sinuously carved by the wadi in the tabular platform. Certainly the overall layout of the gorge, considered in the abstract, must prove to be perfectly clear, logical, intelligible, but on pebble level the path traveled remains fragmented, incoherent, without any immediate rationale. And the darkness is such that at certain points there is need to resort to a flashlight.

Shouts—monosyllables, exclamations—most likely bellowed by the people of the douar, still reach this far at irregular intervals.

With the very first few meters, the valley has disappeared behind the rocks, and the two walls seem to be joined at the gorge entrance. Sometimes fifteen meters apart, they most often advance so close to each other that the sky, so high above, is reduced to a furrow of brightness, shimmering, tremulous, distant . . .

Progress at the bottom of the ravine is slow and difficult. A new gulch opens on the right: judging by its rectilinear edges, it must not measure more than twenty meters . . . But sleep is starting to make itself felt, and weariness to stiffen the muscles: the moment has come to turn back, now, at this very spot . . . or a little farther on, at the next bend . . .

A little farther on, the torrent bed emerges into open space. The footpath hugs the wall in places, but the overhanging rocks make walking very dangerous and necessitate going back to the middle of the wadi, at the risk of stumbling upon the rocks.

A voice bursts out once again, distinct and deadened at the same time, as if something of its original clarity persisted after running an uncertain course. The douar is not so very far away, after all: the echo must rebound from one rock wall to the other until it reaches upstream of the defile.

After thirty steps, the gulch suddenly veers leftward. Instantly the voices become closer. A clear hammering is intermingled with them, a sound of pebbles knocked loose under animals' hooves or men's sandals coming down the slope, latecomers hastening through the night . . . There are surely several of them, unless the single rider has stepped to the ground and is running ahead of his mount . . . Perhaps they are still very far away from here, at the entrance, out there, at the opposite end of the gorge. But how can an exact notion of distances be acquired?

The length of this new segment is difficult to estimate. All the same the average height of the rock walls can provide information as to the proximity of an exit.

The lamp beams, cast on the left wall, cause a dull gray rock, striped with greenish grooves, to loom up from the shadows ... A stone slipped, very nearby, just as the lamp was lit. The luminous circle moves slightly to the right, inspects the rock face: a hand appears, plastered against the rock, then an arm, a red-and-white striped cloth, finally the whole body pressed against the wall, the other arm protecting the dazed face.

A braid falls over the left shoulder; its tip drops to meet the necklace of silver coins. Metal bracelets slip, one by one, from the wrist toward the bend of the elbow ... "Jamila ... She's a cousin, a relative ..." The girl does not make the slightest move to flee. "Everybody belongs to the same family in the douar ..." The arm comes down slowly, baring the forehead, eyebrows, the blinking eyelids ...

The light drops along the dress, along the legs, as far as the knees, as far as the ankles, the crumpled toes of the bare feet upon the stones.

Then the girl bounds forward, arms outstretched. The fingers clutch the metal cylinder. The lamp goes out.

Fifty meters away, at the opposite end of the gulch where a new bend begins, a glow dances upon the wall, fanning out in a semicircle, sweeping the rock face from ground level to the upper edge. The light source is drawing near, the illumined surface gradually stationing itself along the lower third of the wall. Meanwhile, a second glow takes shape, covering the entire wall as did the first when it loomed up; a gigantic shadow sets to trembling, magnifying from a distance the bumps and jolts of a jerking trot.

Very close by, the girl, who has kept a hand on the lamp, holds out the other toward the douar, as if to urge turning back, making an about-turn, but a part of the gesture is lost in the darkness. She takes a step backward, comes forward, grabs the jacket sleeve, yanks the cloth, loses patience.

Out there upon the curved wall, the shadow, as it grows precise, assumes more modest dimensions. A first silhouette soon appears at the bend in the ravine: the man, torch in hand, is jogging forward. Behind him a mule is trotting, ridden by a figure in a white djellaba, with hood pulled down over the forehead. And already the second torch-bearer enters the scene . . .

The girl, forgoing the effort at persuasion, dashes off, alone, and immediately disappears at the turn of the footpath, which runs to the right flush against the rock face . . . But she has not gone very far: she follows the footpath, a few meters away, sweeping a hand along the surface of the rock, then stops, backtracks. Behind, the torchglows are momentarily hidden, but the shouts of the guides exhorting their animals and the racket of the pebbles sent flying by the hooves fill the whole ravine.

The girl halts before a crevice in the wall, whose mouth she cautiously explores, the arms reaching forward. Behind, the outsized reflection begins to whirl on the patches of rocks overhanging the bend in the gorge from which it has just emerged. The man in the lead approaches the turn: his shadow dwindles and takes shape, despite the wobbling. In a few seconds he will come out at the foot of the wall.

The girl again grabs hold of the jacket, pulls on the sleeve, indicates the cave interior. Hunched forward, head drawn down between the shoulders, she is first to cross the threshold; she huddles in a recess, just to the right of the entry: the vault, very low at this point, forces one to squat or otherwise risk bumping a forehead. The back leans against the rock, which scrapes the jacket cloth, from the collar down to the belt. On the ground, a thin layer of sand conceals the gravel. The lamp is set directly on the sand, between the toes of the bare feet and the large dust-covered shoes.

Outside, the brightness sharpens. A white patch wavers on the threshold—the hammering steps grow more insistent—and in a single burst the torchlight invades the cave, illuminating the vault and the smooth, uniform side walls.

The man has already gone past, and the animal following him: a misshapen shadow danced on the wall, a fleeting image of the rider.

The darkness returns, but not for long: the second torch illumines, just as briefly, the cave interior, and the second mule trots past, then a third, on the heels of the preceding one . . . But the last animal must have stopped immediately afterward, for the third torchbearer, looming up at once behind the recalcitrant mule, comes to a stop exactly in front of the cave entrance. For a second or two, the torchlight casts the man's profile upon the wall, in bold relief, sharp and precise, from the curve of the bare skull to the protruding ridge of the brows, the very short squashed nose, the chin drawn down into the shirt collar. The shadow of a bludgeon—or of a club—rises above the head and comes crashing down. The animal, struck violently on the rump, starts up at once. The light, swirling, darts off.

The girl had been sitting, face hidden in hands. Slowly the head rises, then—the sound of the footsteps fading in the distance—she gets up, approaches the entry, leans back against the rock. She peers outside, signals not to come out yet, is poised expectantly a few moments, at last makes up her mind, crosses the cave threshold, and with measured steps advances along the footpath.

Ten meters farther on, at the last bend, the gorge exit appears, very close by, with the vertical edges of its two walls almost meeting and rounded stone blocks strewing the torrent bed. The line is empty: the escort has already crossed the last gully.

The girl hastens along. Her gait becomes more assured, swift and supple, difficult to follow over this tortuous terrain, encumbered with obstacles.

Soon the walls spread apart, the stars multiply, the crests outline themselves in the distance; on each side of the basin, the footpath plunges into the dark chasm of the valley.

All the way at the bottom, the three blazing torchlights frame the white patches of the riders trotting away into the distance and shortly afterward slip between the first houses of the douar. The fiery glows loom up again, once or twice, lighting the casbah walls, then they all go out.

The girl takes a few steps beyond the rocks, stops, turns around and remains motionless for a moment, mute and rigid, eyes fixed upon the entry to the gorge. Then she dashes downward and sinks out of sight into the darkness.

Under the bare feet the pebbles slip and plummet down the slope. A dog barks, far away, then falls silent. Closer by, in the douar itself, a man calls out two syllables, then cries out once again, and someone answers him from the other side of the valley—exclamations, monosyllables, the last of which, taken up by the repercussion, echoes indefinitely . . . Then everything grows calm. The silence establishes itself, new, deep, until the moment other pebbles come slipping to the bottom of the slope.

In Asguine, a single window is lit. Much farther on, at the opposite end of the basin, a light shines, most likely in Ifechtalen. A shooting star detaches itself and dives upon the crests of the Ahori, pulling along in its wake a dust of shimmering particles which rains downward. A glow—a twig fire—dots the Amerziaz. A door opens below; a yellowish brightness spills out onto the ground in front of the house. Then the door closes again without anyone having appeared.

A cool draft edges along, reaching the rocks, caressing hair, and neck, and jacket cloth, from the shoulders down to the base of the spine . . . Ten-thirty. It is time to go back.

The footpath emerges from the torrent bed and runs along the left bank, overhanging for a good meter the gray and white stones which can barely be made out from the shores. Bright patches appear only at the edge of the field of vision; dark patches stand out only against the sky, such as the pistachio tree, a hundred meters below, betrayed by its upper branches, whereas the trunk, very close at hand, remains invisible.

Along the whole rim of the valley, on the hillside, the foot stumbles on tufts of dwarf palm and sprays of esparto grass, slips on stones and slabs of schist, as far as the thornbushes marking the western extremity of the field.

The furrows, although perpendicular to the direction he is walking, are barely pronounced. The large shoes pulverize the clods of earth or send them tumbling in the hollows.

Arriving in front of the tent entrance, Lassalle unknots the laces of the canvas flap, takes off his jacket, lights his flashlight, sets it vertically on the ground carpet, undresses and lies down on the cot.

Sleep, at present, cannot help but come quickly.

X

As on every morning between daybreak and the sun's appearance above the Amerziaz, the rays sweep the northern face of the Angoun on a slant, striking the peaks from before six o'clock, then the cliffs, dropping at a slower pace upon the projecting shelf, and toward seven o'clock finally attaining the arête of the rocky ridge. The shadow-line wheels around this immense sundial, ebbing gradually toward the rocks, then toward the plateau which it travels across unhurriedly, one ridge after the other, passing into the valley, then behind the poplars and casbahs, and later still into the last recesses on the torrent shores, finally behind the low walls, stones and thornbushes. The relief, so sharp up to that moment, then begins to blur, and the sky to fill with whitish streaks which dissipate only in the early evening.

For the moment, the shadow-line still only reaches the edge of the plateau: it is around seven-thirty and Lassalle does not need to consult his watch to understand that he is waking up one hour late. He rubs his eyes, standing in front of the tent, then spies Ichou who, on all fours under the walnut, is observing the comings and goings of ants scurrying between clods of earth.

When they set out on their way, a half-hour later, the sun is already shining along the entire height of the grain loft, as far as the terreplein and the first fields of millet.

Ichou leaves first, bag over his back, leaps over the two walls of dry stones, circles around the second walnut and dashes up the steep incline. Halfway up, he passes alongside two old women who are climbing at a deliberate pace toward the spring, their backs bent.

Lassalle circles around the second walnut, breaks into a run to catch up with Ichou and in turn passes alongside the two women, actually younger than he thought, their faces wrinkled of course, but painted with khol and henna. One of them is wearing a clover-shaped tattoo right in the middle of her forehead.

All the way at the bottom, the incline meets the footpath to the pass, ten meters in front of the douar entrance. As Ichou is moving past the first house on the right, the door opens and the girl steps onto the threshold, at the very spot where she had stopped at nightfall in a sudden flood of light, and had lingered a few seconds, wary and hesitant, before being forced back inside the house.

She comes out now, bends down, picks up a jug set against the cob wall, hitches it up on her back and pushes the door shut with her foot. But the door resists and does not close completely.

In a few steps the girl reaches the fork where Lassalle arrives running at full tilt. She moves aside, standing along the edge of the footpath, with chest turned away and head tilted to the side, an arm hiding her face.

In the time it takes to pull himself up, Lassalle finds himself alongside the house: through the door left open a crack, Idder emerges, decked out in his eternal filthy gandoura, perhaps pale blue in the beginning, but now absolutely colorless, or rather gray in front, scattered with brownish spots and purplish glints.

Lassalle moves past as fast as possible and nods his head toward Idder, but the latter remains impassive: his tiny sparkling eyes only graze the other's glance, as if they saw nothing which was worth the trouble to stare at, and they already dart off, trained more to the left toward the spring. Then the door creaks and slams and a sound of footsteps is heard, a sound of gravel crunching under sandal soles.

The small square is still not in sight: hardly two-hundred meters separate it from the first houses, but the curve traced by the alleyway spaces out the perspectives so that they can be perceived only layer by layer.

This is the hour of the day when the douar begins to come to life. Three women emerge from the casbah porch, jugs propped on their lower backs, and turn into the passage. Two men, squatting at the foot of a wall, drink tea from flowered glasses. A donkey hitched in an empty lot begins to bray and kick while turning in circles around his stake. A chicken dashes along in a flurry of wing beats, panics, and crosses the alleyway in one feeble hop.

Ahead, Ichou continues along with his jerking step. Behind, the footsteps have died off: did Idder come to a stop? Did he turn around? But the donkey's braying keeps one from lending an attentive ear.

To the left, through a large breach in a wall crumbling in ruins, the grain loft appears, at the very top of the peak now half-bathed in sunlight. To the right, views of the adjacent back streets look out upon the cornfields bordering the wadi.

Upon reaching the sheikh's casbah, to the right, the alleyway continues along a straight line as far as the crossroads. Ichou is already stepping into the square: he turns his head toward the mellah, marks a pause, then starts up again.

The little square is still in the shade. The two casbahs in view do not give any sign of activity: their windows are closed, their long trapezoidal facades are dark and silent. The place would be perfectly deserted if it wasn't for Ba Iken who is peacefully smoking on his doorstep, nose in the air, arms crossed over an impeccable djellaba.

— Hello, Mr. Lassalle. How are you this morning?

— Fine, Ba Iken, and you?

— Just fine, thanks, Mr. Lassalle.

— It feels cooler today, wouldn't you say?

— Oh, that doesn't mean a thing: the air is hot. It is going to be as hot as yesterday.

Through the opening of the footpath climbing toward the Addar, the flat buildings of the mellah can be seen, already in the broad sunlight, and the terraces below, upon which the horizontal rays cast immense spindly shadows.

— Did you come through the douar this morning?

— Yes. I expect to go much farther eastward. There's no point in climbing right at the start.

Idder in turn emerges into the square, a sickle in his hand, nodding toward Ba Iken as he continues on his way, without stopping, heading for the valley. At the other end of the square, he passes ahead of Ichou who has huddled against the wall and is whistling, his legs crossed, his hands under the packstraps.

— Did he come bother you again this morning?

— Whom do you mean?

— Idder.

— No, no, not at all: he came out of a house, at the entrance to the douar, just as I was passing in front of it . . . the house where that girl lives, who was there with you the day before yesterday . . . you know . . . Jamila?

— Jamila? Ba Iken tosses his cigarette on the ground and crushes it with the tip of his shoe.

— Yes . . . you told me that she was one of your cousins . . . someone in your family.

— Yamina, Mr. Lassalle, not Jamila!

— Oh, that's right . . . Yamina . . . Lassalle passes his hand over his forehead. Ba Iken rummages through his choukara and takes out a pack of cigarettes.

The sun had just gained the last terrace below the mellah and, simultaneously, the thatched branches overhanging the casbah's facade wall.

— It surprised me to see her there. I didn't know he lived with her . . .

— Yes . . . he lives there. Ba Iken strikes a match and brings the flame toward the end of his cigarette . . . He lives with her . . . He's her brother.

— Her brother? Idder?

— Yes, he's her brother.

Idder disappeared at the first bend in the alleyway. Presently he must be walking between the two rows of squat houses, in the stone-paved alley which soon becomes the pathway to Ifechtalen, and passing alongside the cornfields bordering the wadi.

Ichou, still leaning against the wall, is contorting his face: his eyes lost in an unfocused stare, he stretches open his mouth with his fingers, then sucks in his cheeks while crossing his eyes . . .

— That mustn't be too pleasant for her, considering his personality . . .

The sunlight now drops to the first third of the facade wall. Behind, it grazes the roofs of the lower quarters.

— I glimpsed him yesterday evening . . . I had gone for a walk on the pass road . . .

— Who? Idder?

— Yes. He was coming down from the pass, with a torch in his hand. He was escorting three riders, three . . . dignitaries on muleback. They must have fallen behind . . .

— Yes, I know . . . Idder went to wait for them at the tizi n'Oualoun. It was the sheikh from Tisselli who arrived.

— Sheikh Agouram?

— Yes. Sheikh Agouram often comes to Imlil. He stays a few days, each time . . .

The sun bursts above the gourbis of the "lower quarter." Instantly the whole facade wall lights up as well as a triangle of packed earth on the square in front of the casbah.

Two shadows now loom up upon the facade: Lassalle's, on the wall to the left of the door, and Ba Iken's, on the door itself, at the same level as the stenciled white hand in the exact center of the flap.

— What is that hand, Ba Iken?

— That's Fatima's hand, Mr. Lassalle. That's to bring luck to the house.

Upon closer inspection, it does not seem that the hand was stencil-painted, but rather sketched, schematically, with a few awkward brush strokes: five straight lines, of equal length and thickness, arranged in a shapeless patch representing the palm. Consequently, the fingers appear abnormally bony (especially the thumb) and the palm abnormally swollen, as if bloated with a soft, sickly substance. As for the monstrous wrist joint, it brings to mind a bulging rib of cloth stuffed with bran and crudely stitched up.

Lassalle looks at his watch:

— I have to be going, Ba Iken. I'm already behind schedule . . .

— Fine. Well, until this evening perhaps! Have a good day's work, Mr. Lassalle.

— Thanks. So long, Ba Iken!

Lassalle shakes Ba Iken's hand, turns on his heels and sets off for the "lower quarters."

Ichou has already begun walking again. He turns into the alley and emerges into the broad sunlight.

XI

Ichou, true to form, races through the "lower quarter," zigzagging from one gourbi to another along the whole breadth of the alley, moves along the cornfields for a stretch of several hundred meters downstream of the douar, then turns around, signals that the time has come to climb up to the plateau and without waiting for a sign of assent, heads for the torrent bed which he spans jauntily, springing from one rock to the next with great dexterity.

Lassalle follows in his steps over the pebbles and catches up with Ichou on his way up the right bank.

After leaving the small square they have not met—nor passed by, nor caught a glimpse of—a living soul. Idder has either gone into one of these houses bordering the alley or else he has hidden (but, good God, to what end?) behind a wall, a poplar or one of those jujube enclosures which after a fashion protects the plots of land, or else he has continued straight ahead without stopping until reaching a given point in the valley, some other piece of ground belonging to him, or else only as far as the confluence of the Imlil assif, in Ifechtalen, at the home of some "relative" to seal a bargain, or recount his quarrel with the new engineer who also has it in mind, like his predecessor, to make that trail pass smack through his land, as if there wasn't all the room in the world for passing alongside, across the whole stretch of the plateau—explaining his troubles, working himself up, seeking to stir up sympathy, his forehead taut, his lips antagonistic, his heel stomping furiously, his speech hurried, his tiny gray eyes, huddled at the root of his nose, slivers of rage and indignation . . . Unless he is recounting something else entirely, unless he is not talking about any engineer, or trail, or land to defend . . . Or on the other hand, he may be talking only about the engineer somehow, separate from the trail, of the mine, of the future trucks which will or will not be driving through these two or three hectares which cannot even be irrigated . . .

Idder, Yamina's brother? He looks so little like her . . . Ba Iken had not made the slightest allusion, yesterday evening, to this family tie, neither during nor after the run-in at the foot of the grain loft. He might have specified, after the fact, that Idder was the girl's brother, because he had also spoken about her the day before . . . What's more, he wasn't the one who had first spoken of her; just as he was not the one either who, just now, first mentioned the house. He simply confirmed the fact: "Yes. He lives with her." And he added, insofar as this confirmation quite naturally called for a clarification, or a hint of clarification: "He lives with her. He's her brother." To be honest, the circumstances today lent themselves better than those yesterday to this declaration. But hadn't Ba Iken established the family ties the other day, once and for all? "Everybody belongs to the same family in the douar . . ." Idder, Yamina's brother, is also Ba Iken's cousin.

He lives with her, in the last house, standing alone on the left on the way out of the douar, in this small squat house made of cob from which she came out this morning to go up to the spring . . . She opens the door and steps into the threshold, the place where she stopped the first evening in the douar at nightfall in a sudden flood of light, and lingered a few seconds, wary and hesitant, before being dragged back inside the house . . . The scene did not last very long: the two silhouettes struggling and wavering. A light from within lit the doorstep for as long as the door remained open. Not one gesture was lost to sight: the girl sets her jug against the wall, very close to the door, and just at the moment she was getting up, someone looms up, seizes her by the arm, strikes her twice and, pushing her roughly ahead of him, forces her back into the house. The door creaks and slams . . .

A dog—or a jackal—is barking all the way below in the vicinity of the douar—a sharp clipped yapping which echoes from one slope to the other, like a slamming door which would reverberate interminably through the valley.

Ba Iken was right: the weather is as oppressive as on previous days. The heat becomes bearable only above three-thousand meters. Here, this is still the bottom of the basin, airless, with no shade, or hope of coolness promised at the outskirts of the douar by the walnut foliage, and at the terraces, by the poplars and ashes on the torrent shores.

While crossing the entire plateau, Ichou has again gotten a good hundred meters ahead. Reaching the foot of the pyramidal bastion explored yesterday, he slants eastward and continues on along the edge of the Angoun, in the middle of the scree zone.

Farther to the east, a deep indentation comes up against a dead-end wall attached to the rocky spur overhanging the next pyramid. It is a cause for alarm that the ridge may reform itself at this point and continue along without a fissure, as sheerly as at the approaches to the pass, as far as the Imlil gorges.

Ichou, in any case, is quickening his pace, as if to discourage any search for a pass in this sector. As it happens, once the new bastion is behind them, the wall spreads out in a regular frieze and the spurs of the Angoun resume their original appearance: a heap of scree, strewn along two-hundred meters of uneven ground, surmounted by a steep rocky ridge. If this is the way to Imlil, the last part of the survey will merely be for form's sake. In less than an hour, at maximum, the last hopes will have been dashed. All that will remain to do in the five days ahead is to stake out a suitable road line from Asguine to the vein, through the passage discovered Tuesday on the first pyramid, beginning tomorrow morning at the exact point where Moritz had stopped, namely, at the end of the red bed knoll, south of the douar.

Beginning the road at this outermost point means finding oneself right from the outset on Idder's land—not on the land, but right in front of it— and thus, also a means for establishing a detour around it as one's first order of business. But there mustn't be great freedom for maneuvering: in practice, the stakes will be planted flush against the boundary of the plot . . . Idder is quite capable of seeing this slight detour as a mere momentary concession—eminently hypocritical—to his demands: once the day comes to break ground on the project, no one will have any qualms about crossing his field every which way, henceforth heedless of his grievances.

Certainly his suspicion has a partial explanation: numerous residents must have been bought out, within the tribe, especially along the border of the plain, whenever trails were introduced along the valley floors. But he surely ought to realize that this case is different: that it is the extreme paucity of usable surfaces which, most of the time, inevitably forces expropriations among the irrigated zones. Here, the problem is not set out in the same terms . . . Nevertheless it is better to begin work at a good distance from his field, halfway from the Angoun, for instance. It is still the best way to prevent a new scandal, since efforts at persuasion have not had any results, since the official assurances that Ba Iken had taken on himself to communicate to him do not seem to have caused him to relent.

His hostility remains what it was on the first day: willful, veiled, indirect, as if aimed more often than not slantwise at the destined target. What is the point of taking it out on Ichou, Yamina, or even Ba Iken? Naturally, the latter is the indispensable intermediary. But why treat the unfortunate man as if he was directly to blame? . . . Ba Iken himself claims, it is true, that Idder is up to his usual tricks, that he wrangles with everyone, on any pretext. "He's well known in Imlil. He usually shouts like that, he pesters everybody." Didn't he attack the girl, the first evening, the day before the "engineer" walked over his land, well before, consequently, any squabble about the trail? What had he to reproach her with? Coming home too late? He had clearly seen, however, that the meeting was perfectly fortuitous . . . He must have been lying in wait for her that evening, eyes peeled for her departure; he must have brooded over the length of her absence, up there, on the terraces above the spring, lying in wait for her return . . . He burst through the door which suddenly flew open. He rushed upon her like a madman, seized her, beat her, forced her back into the house . . .

The outskirts of the douar are plunged in shadows, but gradually the plains fall into order, brighter patches appear, contours grow precise. A glow from within lights the scene: the arm rises and strikes, then the light swirls, darts off, the door creaks, shuts again with a sharp bang. The light grows still: the man's profile is cast upon the wall, in bold relief, sharp and precise, from the curve of his bare skull to the protruding ridge of his brows, his very short squashed nose, his chin drawn down into his shirt collar. The girl has hidden her face in her hands. The man takes a few steps forward in the room. She lifts her head and looks at him. He takes another step. Then she bows her head, moves backward to the wall and remains leaning against the packed earth, her eyes staring, her hands folded together over her braids. The shadow of a bludgeon—or a knife—rises upon the wall, above the smooth curve of the skull, sweeps downward, rises again, sweeps down a second time . . . Nothing moves around the house anymore. Columns of smoke climb from several terraces. Lights blink at two or three dormer windows. Much later, a fire shines at the opposite end of the basin . . .

Later, toward eleven o'clock, Ichou, who has not stopped walking faster and faster, finally comes to a halt, turns around, stretches out his arm toward the mountain, then, making it swing from right to left, traces in front of him, at ground level, a line break still invisible to the observer who, slightly below, has striven in vain, for two good kilometers, to catch up with him.

Five minutes later, the edge of the plateau is reached. A mule path runs along the gorge borders. Ichou, his back turned, contemplates the precipice.

The Imlil assif hollows out a trench whose depth—fifty meters upon leaving the mountain—seems to decrease as it moves downstream, parallel to the even inclination of the plateau. Upstream, a fold of the terrain conceals the twists and turns of the defile.

On this bank, the Angoun's outposts culminate in a cone-shaped redoubt whose access is forbidden by its rocky ridge. On the opposite bank, talus slopes drop to where they overhang the gorges: their angle of incline varies, though is gradual on the whole. As for the rocky ridge, it has disappeared: a few chunks of rock here and there testify to its recent disintegration.

Ichou, in the lead, begins walking again. He climbs the footpath with a swift deliberate step, as if he himself had established the day's agenda at the outset. The configuration of the left bank, however, leaves little hope remaining. But Ichou does not allow any time for reflection: he turns around every fifty meters, his finger indicating with admirable obstinacy an ill-defined point directly in front of him . . . In less than a quarter of an hour, he arrives at the entry to the defile and vanishes at once behind the fold in the terrain. The gorge, at this spot, traces a meander and its two banks are not any more than thirty meters apart.

Once the hillock is scaled, Ichou appears once again, but in a quite surprising position, gesticulating and leaping at the summit of an immense rock vault which joins the two banks of the precipice, then running from one edge to the other and stopping to scrutinize the gorge bottom, his hand held horizontally above his brows.

The natural bridge is at the same elevation as the plateau: its clearing is very ample; it is accessible on the same level without the least difficulty. On the other bank, just below the axis of the bridge, an old thurifer rises—dark shriveled leaves upon a tattered trunk.

Ichou, beaming, waits beside the bag. Lassalle proceeds as far as the summit of the vault:

— Imi n'Oucchène?

The lad bows his head, then, positioning himself in the direction of their walk, mimics working a lever, a pedal and something at chest level which is perhaps a steering wheel, suggesting at the same time, with a circular movement of his hand, a simple, practical, and perfectly unexpected itinerary: leaving Asguine, the trail climbs straight to Imi n'Oucchène, spans the torrent across the natural bridge, scales the Angoun foothills by way of the right bank of the Imlil, heads westward and rises on a gentle incline right up to the vein.

Ichou, very proud, goes through his demonstration three times.

XII

Since the natural bridge spans the Imlil at the end of the meander, the gorge bottom is visible upstream only along a hundred-meter stretch.

A stream edges in between the pebbles of the torrent bed itself, while patches of green reemerge here and there upon the shores: bushes of willow and agnus cactus, tufts of oleander huddling at the foot of huge round boulders behind which puddles persist at times, surrounded by beaches of cracked clay.

Upon the sheer walls, the rare patches of shade are cast by the over-hanging stratum. Between two vertical walls a steeply inclined glacis wedges itself in where the scree seems on the point of sliding down again and tipping over into the void. Elsewhere the rock walls are articulated in enormous steps interrupted every so often in the distance by an impassable lane. Leaning forward a little, red stalactites come into view, hanging from the vault and, down below, the shadow-line marking the entrance of the underground gully. Coming out of the gorge, it is clearly deeper as if, equivalent to the distance the mountain falls toward the plain, there corresponded a similar difference in levels under the vault. A glance upstream is accompanied by a slight feeling of dizziness, which a reminder of the present position, balanced above the void, hardly helps to dissipate.

Even though Ichou's pantomime is clear, Lassalle, at the time, does not grasp its implications. One thing prevents him from training his full attention upon it: the surprise which swept over him upon discovering a natural bridge far more imposing than he imagined. Among all the photographs in his possession, one alone shows Imi n'Ouchène, and framed in such a way that it is impossible to judge either the depth of the precipice or the dimensions of the arch "straddling" it. In reality, it is an enormous mass of rock which, right at the bend in the gorge, withstood collapse: its width at the center exceeds twenty meters; it is linked to the banks along such very wide bases and the bedrock foundations of the vault are so extensive, that the torrent, seen from the plateau, seems to surge up from an immense tunnel; the entrance to the gully upstream remains hidden. The picture would have more likely brought to mind an ordinary walkway ten meters above the pebbles. But this is not the only element of surprise: after the directions provided by Ba Iken the first day halfway up the Addar—directions which he has thus interpreted rather badly—Lassalle situated the natural bridge in the immediate vicinity of Zegda. Yet Zegda is located far lower on the other bank. The Company's map, which omits indicating the bridge's location, on the other hand mentions the elevations of the douar and the foot of the Angoun: Imi n'Oucchène would be at 2,700 meters, that is, 250 meters above Zegda.

Thus absorbed in his analysis, somewhat unawares, Lassalle presides over an impromptu inauguration: Ichou, stationed at the controls of the first vehicle taking the trail, is laying out the broad outlines of the itinerary for the visitors. He aims his pantomime to be convincing, his enthusiasm contagious. He plays this out three times, then stands there, with arms akimbo and a questioning look.

Lassalle smiles, scratches his beard upward against the growth, then breaks into a laugh and heartily slaps the lad's shoulder:

— And the torrent? The torrent . . . up there?

Facing the Angoun, with his finger he extends as far as the crests the gaping trench which, before as well as behind them, excluding the observation post where they are perched, irremediably isolates the two sectors of the mountain.

Now it is Ichou's turn not to understand at the outset . . . Lassalle becomes more explicit: his left hand rises on the new bank, reaches the shelf, tilts westward and comes up against his right arm stretched along the general axis of the gorge.

— The torrent, up there, is there a way to cross over it?

Ichou was expecting this objection. He assures him that the torrent does not pose an obstacle; the gorge is not very long; it begins only at the rocky ridge; above, you come across only shallow ravines. The image is simple: his elbow represents the bridge, his forearm the gorge upstream of the bridge, his wrist the entrance to the gorge, his fingers the ravines of the drainage basin. The upper passage would be located on the shelf, at the gorge entrance.

Evidently, Ichou is very familiar with the locale, but isn't he proceeding a bit too quickly by asserting that a trail can be laid down through there? His ideas on the question must be rather perfunctory . . . Yet he seems self-assured. At any rate, since the possibility of using the left bank has been eliminated, surveying the right bank is imperative. It would have become imperative, on principle, even if Ichou had kept his plan to himself, even if he had not nurtured a plan.

The lad, triumphant, once more hitches the bag on his back, sets off again and in a few strides reaches the right bank, where the pathway forks to each side of an old skeletal tree; the segment on the left stretches off along the edge of the plateau—it would lead to Zegda or to the tizi n'Amerziaz, according to Ichou; the one on the right rises southward in the mountains. Ichou goes to the right: all that need be done now is to climb "directly," so he motions: the pathway, up there, emerges right at the gorge entrance.

The mule path ascends through the rocky terrain along rectilinear gradients strewn with enormous quadrangular blocks whose shadows have been retrenched to a paltry fringe. Veering away from the gorges at the outset, the footpath cuts across a very sheer spur, probably to rejoin the Imlil upstream from the meander. But already the Imlil is no longer visible from the spur's summit: beyond the immediate twists and turns, it traces a large loop westward.

The climb lasts two good hours, during which the gorges appear only once, narrow, contorted, much shallower. Above, shelf level, the torrent is reduced to a gravel bed twelve meters long, fed—during the rainy season—by a network of ravines connected to the last slopes of the Angoun.

Arriving first at the predetermined spot, Ichou struts about, proud of himself, waving his arms in both directions to clearly show that there are no more obstacles.

After a quick meal, the inspection of the torrent shores proceeds along the whole length of the shelf, as far as the foot of the cliffs. This takes a good deal of time, not to mention the attempt to explore the entrance of the gorges, out of pure curiosity, an attempt quickly ended as soon as the going gets rough, but which sets them back a good hour.

Beginning downward, around five o'clock, Lassalle suddenly experiences a great weariness: the climb in the broad sunlight has really taken its toll; lunch, although meager, has stayed on his stomach; he feels the first stabs of his migraine. The road to Asguine is still very long and the flask is empty.

In order to bear his pain patiently, he concentrates on studying the problem methodically, from every angle. But the various features of the problem come to the fore on their own, chaotically, for his inspection. No sooner does the idea of having found a practical access route set him at ease (although he must still wait until tomorrow to have his mind absolutely clear, since meeting an obstacle on the shelf cannot be ruled out), than the new itinerary strikes him as being far too extravagant to be really viable (is it not the result of a series of fortuitous discoveries: a very large bridge on the Imlil assif, an accessible right bank, an easy passage toward the shelf at the gorge entrance?). But upon reflection, nothing along this route is unfeasible. Sending trucks over Imi n'Oucchène? Why not? The bridge is large enough, and none more solid could be built. Constructing a revetment upstream of the gorges? That is a simple matter. Naturally, this revetment will be swept away every year—or several times a year—but that is the common fate of every makeshift revetment established on the slopes; every spring, those points which gave way during the onslaught of the spring floods are patched up; it takes two or three weeks work and a few rows of gabions. Obviously, the entire trip, from the pass to the mine, would become decidedly longer, but the opening of the trail would not pose any insurmountable questions. Among the three possibilities compiled this very day, the last one could well prove to be the most economical . . .

Despite everything, this solution seems at the same time to be too simple and too unconventional. Perhaps there is the added reproach of not having thought of it before: it would have been necessary to obtain more thorough information on the position of the Imi n'Oucchène, to go out on a survey mission on Monday, to have the idea of using it . . . But Ichou was the one who had the idea.

Now Ichou is going down the last gradient on a run and continues on to the bridge in the same rush. Lassalle has only reached the spur summit, from which he once again has a view on the Imlil, its mouth where it comes out of the mountain, its short underground gully and the deep trench it hollows out across the plateau.

It is nearly six o'clock. The sun is still shining above the n'Oualoun, but the heights of the left bank intercept the rays. The entire gorge bottom is in semidarkness. The shadow-line runs horizontally across the rock walls of the right bank, then slants toward the redrock foundations of the bridge, and cuts the roadway along three-quarters of its length.

Lassalle in turn breaks into a run. Nevertheless, when he reaches the fork at the thurifer, Ichou, on the other bank, has already disappeared behind a fold in the terrain which, this morning, in the opposite direction, concealed the bend in the gorge.

Lassalle steps onto the bridge, crosses the shadow-line. He feels the chill fall at once upon his sweating forehead and over his shoulders where his damp shirt is sticking to his skin. As he reaches the middle of the bridge, he spies Ichou who is coming back waving his arms; he races down the hillock, trips on a stone, and falls full-length upon the gravel.

Lassalle rushes forward, but the lad, already on his feet, seizes him by his sleeve and drags him forcibly off the footpath.

Standing behind a rock, fifteen meters from the bridge, Lassalle tries in vain to get an explanation: Ichou, whose watchful eyes remain fixed toward the talus, signals him to crouch down.

Idder, walking briskly, comes into sight at the summit of the hump, enters into the zone of shadow, descends and soon appears at the entrance to the bridge. In his right hand he is holding a short-handled tool—perhaps the pick he has a habit of carrying with him. He crosses the bridge at the same brisk step. Here he is once again in the sunlight: he stops, wipes off his forehead with the back of his hand, leans over the chasm, upstream, and looks into the bottom of the torrent.

It is not a pick he is holding in his hand, but a sort of bludgeon. Lassalle, who has straightened up a bit, seeks to identify the object, but unsuccessfully. Then he crouches down, rummages through his bag— Ichou is squatting right beside him—opens the leather case, and aims the binoculars toward the bridge.

Idder, motionless, is still looking at the bottom of the torrent. The object is made of reddish terra-cotta, but it is apparently not a bludgeon: the globe, disproportionate with the handle, is pierced with myriad tiny round holes; it sways at the end of the handle. The swaying grows more pronounced: the object leaves the field of vision.

Idder has begun walking again. He arrives in front of the thurifer and veers off along the footpath on the left. Twenty meters farther on, he disappears at the first turn.

Lassalle gets up, puts away his binoculars in his bag, then holds Ichou back by his sleeve and inquires about the meaning of this ploy. Ichou, evoking Idder, brings his right index finger to his forehead, exactly as he did Tuesday morning, after the first altercation. But this time, he embroiders his answer with an allusion to Idder's torrent of abuse, with another to his belligerence, finally with a third—which Lassalle, at the time, finds grossly exaggerated—to the "danger" being run. Exaggerated or not, the allusion is clear: Ichou brandishes a fictitious club above his head and lets it drop full force on his companion's skull.

Lassalle shrugs his shoulders, turns on his heels and, heading out in the lead, strides up the hillock. Reaching the summit, he turns around and contemplates one last time the entrance to the defile: the shadowline on the bridge has joined the one which, upon the gorge walls, was slowly climbing between the rocks. The plateau, on the other side of the chasm, is deserted.

Ichou retakes the lead. They are in the sunlight again, but not for long.

Lassalle somewhat resents the boy for engaging in that ridiculous evasion. Obviously Ichou believed he was acting correctly by avoiding, on his own, another confrontation with that troublemaker. But the meeting would not have inevitably degenerated into an argument. They would have crossed paths without saying a word, that's all . . .

Ichou has just passed by the place where he had turned into the torrent at morning's end. Nevertheless he continues along the footpath. Lassalle lets him do so for a short while, then grows anxious: hasn't the time come to veer off westward through the rocky terrain? But no: Ichou is not mistaken: the footpath leads directly to Asguine; most likely he'll come into the irrigated zone at some point downstream of the douar.

Five-hundred meters farther on, indeed, the mule path, veering away from the gorge, bears westward. The sun has disappeared behind the pass.

Six-thirty . . . Lassalle calculates that they will not be back before nightfall. His migraine, at the moment, is solidly entrenched. And in addition, as a result of that stupid misadventure, he has the feeling he has caught a chill.

XIII

The instant before, everything was dark—not black: dark. Contours stood out poorly in the gloom. But now it is bright. The gaze scrutinizes space—the portion of space still available—and sees a stone to the right, very close to the head: a gray stone with rounded edges, and smooth facets striped with green streaks; it seems no bigger than the head, but maybe it is an extension of the large boulder, a little farther along to the right? What way is there to know? At the very top a furrow of bright whiteness is shining, hemmed in between two dark walls. A silhouette leans above the void at the edge of the white strip. On the left (when the eye reaches the left, at the end of its journey) a second stone rises, bigger than the first, more prominent, probably isolated from any immediate background. And that's all . . . What remains escapes from view. But maybe this is all there is to see . . . It is not important. What needs to be done is remove the stone: the neck is resting against a cutting edge . . . All that would be needed is to slightly shift the stone, or to turn it over, to expose another face. Only a minor displacement is required for the position to become bearable: if the head could move a little, attempt on its own to push the stone away, with repeated nudges, until the pain abates . . . But the head cannot move. The right arm, folded over the chest, cannot move either: only the thumb and two index knuckles are visible. The left arm has most likely slipped down along the body, at a much lower point; the nails must be grazing the sand, the fingers playing with the pebbles. As for the legs, they are out of reach. But only the head hurts. Perhaps by extending his body full-length, and turning over on the chest, and bringing the cheek against the stone . . . But no: the previous attempts produced no results. The stone—the cutting thing emerging from the stone—continues to press its weight, to dig a hollow at the edge of the head. There is nothing to be done. The eyes alone are mobile: opening, shifting about, closing, opening: on the left the large stone, standing alone; on the right the small gray stone, divided, fragmented, which itself is perhaps only a part of the large boulder over there, in the background. And at the very top a furrow of shimmering brightness, the two walls of shadow pressing in around it and the silhouette leaning above the void . . . Then everything becomes dark again—not black: dark. The stones are still there, surely, but their contours have melted into the gloom . . .

Outside a light breeze slinks along the canvas walls and flutters the flaps, whose laces have come unknotted. Now and then, a flap folds back inside the tent and the moonlight plunges on the stake, the ground carpet and the foot of the bed.

Lassalle has just opened his eyes: he is almost entirely outside of the sleeping bag. The pillow has fallen on the ground: his head sits directly upon the transversal metal beam of the frame.

He gathers up the pillow, puts the bag in order, and stretches out on his right side: very close, the watch hands indicate three-thirty.

As in previous moments of wakefulness, the scratching in his throat is an unpleasant surprise. The pills swallowed yesterday, as soon as he got back, did not have the radical effect he counted on . . . He will have to take some others at breakfast. Or else boil some water immediately and prepare a grog? But getting up, lighting the lamp, running to the spring, lighting the camp stove, looking for the bottle of rum in the bag, it all figures to be such a terrible bother in the middle of the night. It is just as well to bide his time until daybreak.

It was that unplanned pause that is at the origin of his illness. Already, while crossing the bridge, the chill had swept down in one blow upon his forehead, and shoulders, along his whole sweat-soaked body. He would have needed to go back into the sunlight without delay . . . Lying in wait for several minutes, in ambush behind the boulder, proved to be fatal. Ichou thought he was acting correctly, obviously. There is no reason to resent him. But why had he become such a willing accomplice of the "sideshow" which the boy decided upon and immediately put into practice? Surprise played the most important role: Ichou, visibly unsettled, seemed to flee an imminent catastrophe. But later, once Idder emerged at the summit of the hump and the supposed danger was revealed, nothing kept them from coming out of their hiding place and peacefully resuming the Asguine trail—or from pretending to study the topography of the sites: what could be more natural than meticulously exploring the approaches to the bridge? On the other hand, remaining hidden behind the scree implicitly recognized, insofar as he participated in the ploy, how well-founded the lad's precautions were. In addition, using the binoculars to more conveniently observe Idder on the sly shamelessly flaunted a curiosity which the lad was perhaps far from suspecting until then—a curiosity pushed to the point of spying upon the least gesture, the least facial expression, as if the little man had been on the verge of giving himself over to some flamboyant exhibition: dancing on tiptoe at the edge of the chasm, juggling with his club, plunging headfirst into the void . . .

Such a mania, too, this never leaving the house without carrying a pick, a hoe, a mallet, or some other tool of the sort . . . and for no other apparent purpose than the sheer pleasure of holding it in his hand, at arm's length . . . Anyway, that was not a club yesterday, but rather a terra-cotta utensil, an example of which was prominently displayed on the mantelpiece, in the captain's office, between the jug and the candle holders: a very short handle with stippled ribbing, a spherical mass, probably hollow, pierced with myriad tiny round holes. Ba Iken could certainly say what the object is used for . . . At any rate, Idder must have a knife on him—not a display dagger such as the village dignitaries wear, but a solid highland knife carried deep within his greasy choukara . . .

He was surely coming from Asguine, yesterday evening, for if he had continued on in the morning to Ifechtalen, he would have immediately found himself on the right bank of the Imlil and would not have need to take the bridge. On the other hand, considering the late hour, he could have reached Zegda—Imi n'Oucchène is most likely the shortest route from Asguine to Zegda . . . Unless, of course, he had really gone up there to find them and do them a bad turn: he had been following their comings and goings since morning, knew that they would go down through the Imi n'Oucchène at the end of the afternoon and had resolved to wait for them there . . . But no: in that case, he would have been the one to hide . . . So he passed through without any bad intentions whatsoever and meeting him was a result of pure coincidence, which proves at the very least that Ichou is in a perpetual state of alert and truly seems to fear the worst . . .

All the same, doesn't this ascribe to Idder rather shady intentions, quite out of proportion to what is substantially at stake? What is more banal, in these regions, than a quarrel over a piece of land? Sometimes the quarrel turns vicious, that's understood; yet the point of contention must be clearly defined, or the bad faith of one of the litigants involved absolutely self-evident; the antagonist is wrongfully working the plot, chases off the owner, prevents the latter from reaping . . . In the present instance, there is nothing of the sort; nothing irreparable has been carried out. On the contrary: every desired assurance has been given, everything has been done to ward off suspicion . . .

The wind is still blowing steadily, swelling the sides of the tent inward, now and then lifting the right flap, which bares a triangle of parched earth, bathed in a milky light, over which walnut leaves and blades of straw scurry with a sound of rustling paper. Lassalle turns over on his left side. He must have forgotten to tie the laces last night, otherwise the canvas would not be shifting around like that. But it is not worth the trouble to fasten them anymore: the sun will rise soon.

The only clear point, last night, was Ichou's allusion to the "danger," exorcised by the measures he took: the lad brandished a bludgeon—or something analogous—above his head and let it drop full force. He is dramatizing, certainly, all the more so since he knows whom he is dealing with. When in doubt, he cannot be blamed for being over-cautious. Anyway, during the five days left, the rules of conduct are simple: avoid meetings, to the greatest possible extent, and in the event of an argument pretend to give in, acquiesce and move along your way . . . When all is said, perhaps Idder quite simply went to station himself on his field, this morning upon leaving the douar, if for no other reason than to declare his presence, as he did yesterday morning. For he did not budge from his spot yesterday morning, he did not intervene in the slightest, whereas the "detriment" done him was exactly the same as the day before. But he let Ichou pass without saying a word, without raising a finger, and when the "engineer" trod across the ground, just as the day before, along its entire length, he did not move a muscle either. The day before, he had squarely blocked Ichou's path, then had stepped aside, gripped the lad by his arm and had shaken him, berated him, at times showing the very ground where he was stamping his feet, at times the whole plot . . . But he was turning his back; Ichou as well. It was possible to have misunderstood the meaning of these gestures apparently stripped of all artifice. Perhaps he was speaking to Ichou about something else entirely, perhaps he was speaking to him about the other scene, the day before, when he was unable to stop himself, yet another time, from shouting, stamping his feet, assaulting, beating . . .

Lassalle shifts position yet once more. The white light is still filtering through the canvas slits. Everything is calm outside: the wind has dropped off. Yet the right flap folds back, but inwardly: the triangle of packed earth appears, then a cord sandal and a patch of black cloth, finally, flush against the stake, Ichou's lower profile and his round eye.

Lassalle looks at his watch: a quarter-to-seven. He leaps to his feet.

The schedule (for this Friday) was established like so: climb to the mine by the direct road (Tuesday's); arrive at the mine toward ten o'clock; survey, from ten to one in the afternoon, the still unknown sector, between the mine and the entrance to the Imlil gorges; descend, as the day before, along the right bank of the Imlil and the Imi n'Oucchène.

But the result of waking up late, a heavier heat than usual and the shortness of breath due to the first effects of the flu, is that, right from the outset, the timetable is not respected: the rocky ridge is reached only at ten o'clock, the "gallery" at eleven.

Afterward, fortunately, the exploration of the shelf—three good hours, as foreseen—proves to be free of surprise: the soil is good; the shift in levels (two-hundred meters over three kilometers) very moderate; the ravines, numerous but shallow, are easy to span.

Lunch and the siesta occur at the same place as yesterday, in the shade of the huge boulders where the Imlil, dry at present, begins to hollow out its gorges. A hundred meters away runs the mule path, after looping steeply up the left bank, and continues to climb eastward . . . or southward. Its destination remains a mystery: does it also rejoin the tizi n'Amerziaz, or does it span the crests of the Angoun instead? Ichou, consulted, seems to want to give validity to the second hypothesis, but his arms sweeping above the terminal arête are accompanied by a rather discouraging pout . . . Ba Iken will surely be more explicit.

At four o'clock on the dot, Lassalle gives the signal to leave. Two hands in his pockets, his forage cap askew, he goes down on a run, almost as quickly as Ichou, lively, light-footed, his extinguished pipe in his mouth, careful to slow down only at the twists and turns of the footpath, all the while ruminating upon two or three satisfying subjects which put him into a rather cheerful mood: first, the state of his health, which has improved—his throat problems have disappeared, thanks to the pills, of course, but also to the bottle of rum he slipped into his bag at the last moment; next, the relief of not having met Idder on the way out of Asguine (as an extra precaution, he had preferred to scale the red bed knoll, so as to pass a good distance from the field, but, as he was able to ascertain afterward, Idder was not at the rendezvous); and last, the certainty of measuring up to the task of submitting to the Company a proposal for a coherent roadway, a bit bizarre naturally at first glance, but easy to carry out and very worthwhile in the end.

The first stretch (Asguine–Imi n'Oucchène) and the last (entrance of the gorges–vein) offers no category of difficulty. The second—the one he is presently tracing for the third time—will perhaps be a more delicate matter to perfect, even though the clearings are quite adequate at all points.

The boy's idea was a good one . . . more precisely, his intuition, if not his calm, simple conviction, from his first working hour, that their investigations would lead there sooner or later, by force of circumstances— by force of the very configuration of the landscape to be explored.

In any case this is what allows him to organize tomorrow, with a perfectly clear conscience, a "day of relaxation" at the tizi n'Oualoun which he had been planning since the day after he arrived.

As the day before—but one hour earlier—Lassalle looks out upon the Imi n'Oucchène from the top of the last gradient, and a few instants later, leaning back against the trunk of an old juniper, once again he contemplates the loop of the Imlil emerging from the mountain, the bridge directly in front of him, and to the right the sheer trench dropping across the plateau.

Ichou goes as far as the other bank, then comes back, and designating in succession the sun, still high over the tizi n'Oualoun, the bottom of the gorge downstream, the underground gully, the bottom of the gorge upstream, he launches into a long demonstration in pantomime which can be translated in the following way: "Since we have some time to spare today, we would be able—if it interests you and you're not too tired—to go down to the gorge bottom along the steep incline you see over there two-hundred meters lower down and which I'm familiar with, then pass under the bridge along the torrent bed, which is feasible in summer, since it is almost completely dry, then go up over there along another incline, a little higher . . . You'll see, it's worth the trouble and it'll take us just under a half-hour, no more."

Lassalle hesitates a moment, consults his watch, then seduced despite everything by the lad's proposition, accepts, lights his pipe and rises.

In order to move more freely, Ichou slips out of the bag which he hangs from a tree. Then he proceeds along the edge of the precipice, downstream of the bridge, as far as the place where the incline heads upward.

Lassalle is suddenly gripped by anxiety: is he really going to venture out on this crumbly granular red bed wall with no other support than these few tufts of esparto grass and dwarf palm? The shift in levels is a good fifty meters . . . Seen from here, Imi n'Oucchène resembles a gigantic scaffolding scantily camouflaged for an inauguration: a triple white, pink and gray strip-edging that surrounds the tunnel entrance, garlands of red stalactites, multicolored blocks of stone heaped from top to bottom of each pillar . . . Curiosity carries him along.

In any case, Ichou did not wait for the outcome of this discussion: he set off down the incline, sometimes backwards, facing the wall, sometimes squatting, slipping along on his sandals. Lassalle soon sees himself forced to imitate him and to sit back on his heels on several occasions to maintain his balance. Midway down the slope, fortunately, a rock outcropping provides a more solid ground for their maneuvers. But the red bed soon resurfaces and not far from their goal he loses his footing, slips and goes down the last meters on his back. While falling, his pipe and cap went rolling off into the gravel: Ichou retrieves them, with a joyful expression.

In the approximate axis of the gorge, a thread of water trickles peacefully from one plane to the other, plunging into the puddles that persist in the shade between the huge boulders. Crescent-shaped sand banks bound the stone alignments. At the edge of the theoretical bed, the splotched branches of the agnus cactus and oleander bushes give evidence of the sweeping force of the last flood. The arch of the natural bridge, one-hundred meters upstream, seems to block the way. Yet, upon drawing closer, the other opening can be made out through the zone of darkness, at the end of the curving corridor, but much higher on the right—like the oblique section of an offset prism.

Lassalle shakes the dust from his trousers; he washes his hands, throws some water over his face, his eyes, his cheeks where the hair growing every which way creates the caricature of a rather ridiculous beard. When he goes through the motions of drinking from the hollow of his hand, Ichou intervenes and strongly advises against doing so.

Beginning at the entrance to the underground gully, the gorge grows constricted, flattening out in stages as it rises. The torrent bed itself is impassable: the breaks between levels attain several meters. They must circle around every "waterfall."

Drops fall from the summit of the vault, making some surfaces very slippery. But on the whole they have a sure foothold, and the climb is easy. The light coming from downstream signals the obstacles rather distinctly, thus anticipating any surprises. Soon its task is taken in hand, beyond the highest level plane, by the opposite light coming from upstream. The corridor then slants westward and the gorge gradually regains its normal width.

Lassalle hurries his step. He is in a sweat and he fully realizes that a relapse, after yesterday's warning, will prove critical. He emerges into the broad sunlight, walks a few meters along the stream, dips his handkerchief in the water and once again refreshes his face. The daylight dazes him. Spotting a flat rock, not far from the stream, he settles himself down, out of breath, rather light-headed, his legs wobbly, facing this underground passage which he has just crossed through, when all is said, much more easily than he thought.

Ichou scurries back and forth, enjoying himself by turning around the rocks and the copses of greenery, or else charging from one bank to the other, with elbows tucked in, and a loud clattering of pebbles.

Lifting his eyes, Lassalle perceives on the right the dark green leaves of the thurifer extending just barely beyond the edge of the plateau, exactly within the angle formed by the upper arête of the trench and the wall-juncture arch which, seen from here, more closely resembles an arc of a globe balanced on the gorge than a genuine bridge. In any case, the bridge platform is concealed by the side wall of the vault—a slant-wise slice through several layers, the last of which, a reddish purple, is drawn out, due to seepage, in festoons of swollen stalactites. The sun is still shining on two-thirds of the bridge surface. More to the left, in the shade now, the vault bedrock is fused to the gorge wall, itself extended, in the background, by the rock face of the last foothills of the Angoun and its rocky ridge, rising fully against the sunlight. Seeking to climb back along the left bank would be vain, even though the gorge is half as deep as it is downstream of the bridge.

All the way below, the gray rocks come into view, the gravel bed, then the sun, the thread of water upon the smooth stone, the rocks again, flanked, on this side, with oleander bushes: the dust has drained their pale green leaves of color; between the stems whitened by the over-flowing surges, there are accumulations of twigs, clods of earth, tufts of esparto, tiny slivers of glass or metal which glint intermittently.

The silence is broken, now and then, only by the clear tumbling click of the stones, farther upstream, where the tireless lad is carrying out his operations.

Once again a spark jumps from the oleander bushes, drawing his attention beyond the fringes of his gaze. The breeze is nonexistent, but the most infinitesimal shift of a stem or leaf can be enough to bare a reflecting surface and expose it to the sun's rays.

Lassalle rubs his eyes, yawns, stretches out, pulls himself to his feet and approaches the bush. He spreads apart the branches. Straight-away, his hand touches a leather thong clinging to a small branch. At the end of the thong comes a case, also in leather, lodged between two stems at the foot of the bush.

He stoops and pulls the object free: the lid, furnished with two snap fasteners, is open, the case empty. The strap supports are made of chrome-plated metal, as well as the two rings used to adjust the length of the straps and the oval trim reinforcing the lid's jutting rim. The whole, lightly dustcovered, is in good condition: the leather bears a few super-ficial scratches but does not seem to have suffered from the dampness. The shape of the box suggests a piece of photographic equipment.

The bush is located at the base of the arch edge, a few meters from the right bank. The object could not have been carried there by the waters: the leather is intact (in any case it hasn't rained since April). Either it was forgotten (or lost) at the bottom of the gorge, or it fell from the top of the bridge.

Depositing the case on the gravel, Lassalle methodically inspects the bush, which stretches for a few meters along the rock. First he explores the foliage, then stoops and rummages with his foot among the dead branches, the melding leaves, the dried grass. His prospecting is effort-less: oleanders are not very lush. In his wish to be thorough, he probes the very rock crevices, but finds nothing more. When he reaches the last tufts, he gives a start backward; his movement is instinctive, disorganized: a serpent huddled under the leaves unfurls itself and slithers off, slinking slowly between the stones.

Perhaps it was only a common snake (very long, slender, its skin speckled with black and green diamonds), but it leaves a very troubling impression.

Lassalle wipes his forehead and makes an about-turn: Ichou is there, standing still, his arms hanging flat against his body, lost in contemplation before the case and the leather thong . . .

Ichou has no precise ideas on the origin of the object: Ba Iken will be able to say who came to Imlil in the recent past (Ba Iken, as usual, is an arm wave toward Asguine, followed by a swift allusion—more and more swift—to the close-trimmed blond beard cleanly rimming his jaw, and sometimes with another, to the cigarette).

Lassalle meticulously covers the zone bounded by the stream and the right wall of the gorge, along a twelve-meter radius around the bush. Returning to his point of departure, he again inspects the branches, but in vain. Finally, he gives up.

Ichou has slung the straps around the side of his shoulder and is striding toward the incline that climbs along the right bank, one-hundred meters upstream of the bridge.

The slope is as sharp as on the way down, the soil as slippery, but the change in levels is half as slight. As they are scaling, which they do most often on all fours, Ichou constantly fiddles with the case, opening it, closing it, turning it in every direction.

Lassalle arrives on the plateau out of breath. The climb, short but rugged, has all at once revived his appetite. The scratching in his throat has started up again . . . As soon as he is back under the juniper, he opens his bag, grabs hold of the bottle and takes a huge swallow of rum, just in case, to check the flu's progress.

The watch shows six-thirty—the time when, yesterday, they were passing exactly the same spot, just before Ichou made an about-turn . . . Lassalle drinks one last swig of rum, replaces the bottle in the bag and beckons Ichou to return his find.

Ichou frees himself from the straps, but instead of handing over the case, presses the snap fasteners, opens the lid wide and extends it toward him upside down, slightly slantwise, in such a way that the inside catches the full sunlight.

Lassalle looks at the boy without understanding. Ichou brings the lid closer and shows the inner edge with his finger, above the leather tongue supporting the snap fasteners.

On this edge, which is a little more than a centimeter high, a small white paper rectangle is displayed, held in place by two elastic bands. Two lines have been typewritten onto the paper, first a proper name in capital letters:

DR. H. LESSING

then, immediately underneath, in small letters:

B.i.a.g. Rotheim.

The paper is a Bristol board, analogous to the type used for calling cards: the length is the same, the height a third of what's customary. Nothing is written on the back. Placed this way within the lid, the paper usually escapes notice.

Lessing . . . Doctor Lessing ? . . . "Mr. Lessing?" The name does not seem to stir any echo: Ichou, imperturbable, is still holding the case with both hands. With a vacant gaze, and his lower lip protruding, he shrugs his shoulders with an evasive air . . . But perhaps the stranger did not stay in Imlil; perhaps he merely passed through . . . He may not even have necessarily gone by way of Asguine . . .

Lassalle turns around the narrow strip of white card-paper in his fingers, then replaces it under the bands, shuts the lid and puts the case away in the bag.

Ichou unhooks the bag, slings it over his back and sets off in the lead.

Reaching the entrance to the bridge, along the last meters in the sunlight, Lassalle draws near the brink, leans over and sees down below, right under him, the oleander bush, now in the shade. Then he comes back to the middle of the bridge, proceeds along the left bank and catches up with Ichou.

He feels fairly dizzy: perhaps he overdid it with the rum today. Yet the crucial point is to firmly check the flu's progress.

Walking at a fast clip, he will be back in Asguine at seven-thirty, just before dark.

Ba Iken will certainly be at home at that hour.

XIV

They did not get back until eight, in reality. Ba Iken was not at home: a tall fellow of the same age and stature—his brother perhaps—came down to chat with the visitors and launched into abundant, voluble explanations, which were unfortunately incomprehensible. Ichou, more sparing, simply showed with his finger, in passing, the lighted windows of the sheikh's casbah, specifying that Ba Iken was in the middle of dinner, up there, on the second floor.

The walk having sobered him up, Lassalle now felt only a tenacious muscle ache. Immediately upon getting back to the tent, he went to bed without consuming anything more than a little cold tea.

As on the previous night, his throat problems disturb his sleep: kept awake by a pain which is benign, but precise and irritating, he twists and turns on the cot, clearing his throat, swallowing his saliva apprehensively, knotting and unknotting around his neck the gray woolen scarf he found at the bottom of the bag and which threatens at times to choke him, and at others sets off such a flood of sweat that its very presence becomes intolerable.

Along toward morning, his sneezes multiply, his left nostril begins to run. Certain, nevertheless, that he does not have a fever, Lassalle gets up when Ichou arrives, goes himself to get water at the spring—in order to "react"—prepares a copious breakfast and sets off for the tizi n'Oualoun, as planned, without experiencing anything other than a vague pain stretching from his shoulders to the base of his spine, and sometimes a shiver, starting in his lower belly, and which briefly runs over his chest and neck before lodging itself between his eyebrows, right at the base of his nose.

His itinerary is extremely simple: all he has to do is follow the mule path, from the pistachio to the pass, first of all by taking the torrent bed across the limestone outcropping which obstructs the valley for three- or four-hundred meters. How constricted it seems, this defile—which can be climbed in under a half-hour—with its short vertical walls, compared to the Imlil gorges, or any other ravine frequently referred to as "gorge," or even compared to the memory which the first two nocturnal forays left behind—the first along an unknown road, at the end of a wearing stage of the journey, the second during a night which was darker still, in a total gloom where perception of distances, of contours and shapes does not originate in sight but in a confused intuition of what is all around present.

At any rate, the trail will not pass that way: it will go down from the pass along the left bank of the valley, circle around the obstacle and span the torrent at the end of the defile.

The footpath, oblivious of curve radii and degrees of inclination, mounts along the steeper right bank, emerges upon a broad col expanding outward and linking the Addar to the Angoun, and then arrives directly at the pass.

With slow, regular steps, they reach the pass toward ten o'clock without being too winded. Ichou heads at once for the petroglyphs—the goal of the hike—which are located twelve minutes north of the pass on the first crests of the Addar.

These famous drawings which Moritz spoke about (and of which he had taken several rather blurry photos, even though he had diligently chalk-coated the ridges carved into the stone), these drawings, deemed to be "prehistoric" by some—but others are more circumspect, and there are those who even believe there are signs of a forgery—are engraved in no apparent order upon the surface of schist slabs strewn along a twenty-meter stretch.

Numerous slabs are bare, the majority are rather poorly illustrated, but one of them gathers together a complete collection of all the design figures inventoried in the vicinity: double circles with a serrated or stippled halo evoking a sun, a wheel, a gear part; straight lines slicing through triangles or circumferences and creating clubs, or lances or arrows; schematic outlines of human bodies; animal silhouettes much closer, in their expressive stylization, to bears and giraffes than to horses and mules.

Elsewhere, in a very balanced composition, a warrior crouched on the hump of an enormous animal (a camel?) is holding out a sort of javelin at arm's length (crouched this way, he seems to be hiding behind the creature's neck).

But on a rib-shaped stone half hidden by a tuft of mugwort, a more complex compositional design captures one's attention. A person straddling a moderately-sized quadruped (a small donkey?) brandishes a mallet with which he threatens a child prostrated with joined hands beside him, to the right. On the opposite side, a body is reclining behind the animal, arms flung wide. In the absence of perspective, the body is shown standing up, but at a lower level than those of the other characters, as if the animal, upon passing, had plowed him straight under the earth: the man has just been struck and lies there, dead or fatally wounded. Still farther to the left, at normal level, a second animal is receding with a raised hoof.

While Ichou pushes away the twigs of mugwort with his foot, Lassalle, one knee on the ground, tries to retrace as faithfully as possible, on the last sheets of his pocket diary, the five figures he has under his eyes and which he cannot help considering, every now and again, as a single tableau. But obviously nothing proves that such an intention inspired the engraver: many relationships are a result of simple juxtaposition, with no logical constraint necessarily governing the enterprise (or at the very most, a certain material constraint: want of space).

Between the three figures on the right—the child, the rider and the donkey—the connection is probable, if not manifest. Between the two others (and between the two groups thus constituted), it is much more debatable. Nevertheless there is a great temptation to link the two figures on the left to the first group and to thus infer a unity of action capable of lending the scene a novel dramatic interest. This means postulating a double murder and already ascribing all sorts of motives to it: hate, ritual, treason, vengeance . . . The man has just been struck, his mount has abandoned him. The rider then turns toward the child, who is going to undergo the same fate . . . The chief argument supporting this thesis resides in the position of the "victim" with regard to the "path" followed by the rider. But it is far from irrefutable, and nothing more solid exists to prop up the demonstration. On the other hand, the spectacle of disarray so complacently strewn on the other slabs revives a scepticism which, beyond interpretations, daydreams, and premonitions, invariably conducts one back to the point of departure: a flat, roughly rib-shaped stone, about a meter high, buried under the leaves and pebbles, as enigmatic when all is said and done (or as obvious) as it was at first sight.

With all the precision required by the scant amount of room at his disposal, Lassalle draws men and animals side-by-side such as they are assembled on the stone, scrupulously respecting the directions they are facing and the spaces between. Later he will reproduce them, in their actual size, gauging his proportions by the child's height, that is, nine or ten centimeters—a charcoal reproduction, for example, on a beautiful sheet of white paper.

The stone disappears once again under the tuft of mugwort. Lassalle comes back toward the large slabs of schist and rapidly sketches, on the neighboring pages, the most characteristic figures.

At the very moment he is closing his diary, he remembers not having made an entry for the past two days due to getting back late. Therefore, he notes, after the other summaries:

"Thursday.—Survey of the Angoun foothills as far as the natural bridge of Imi n'Oucchène. Discovery of a second negotiable passage across the Imlil assif, upstream of the gorges. Returned after dark."

"Friday.—Direct climb to the mine. Survey of the mine—gorge entrance sector. Possibility of having the trail pass across the natural bridge, then along the right bank of the Imlil. Went down to Imi n'Oucchène at the bottom of the gorge. Returned after dark."

Then he closes the diary, blows his nose, sits down on a slab and remains fixed a long while in his contemplation of the landscape. It is the first time, when all is said, since Sunday, that he has come back to the edge of the Imlil basin.

The schist outcropping dominates the pass for fifty meters. On the other slope, but markedly higher, starts the rocky ridge which runs almost without interruption to the Imlil assif. It obviously seems very difficult, leaving from the pass, to climb directly to the shelf, unless enormous rock walls are blasted away, and even more . . . That is precisely the constraint which obliged the Company to renounce its plans for a direct route. And yet, from here, the vein is no longer very far off . . . A direct road would have measured six to seven kilometers . . . One from Imi n'Oucchène would come to fifteen, sixteen, seventeen at the most, but the construction would not entail any difficulties.

To the right of the pass, a long valley gradually slopes westward: the other day it took the whole afternoon to go up it in a sleepy listless state. In the evening, the shadows had seeped into the hollow of the ravine. At the pass itself, the sun had disappeared. The sheer arête of the Angoun had come into view, gradually, on the right, in the sunset, and soon the enormous escarpment had appeared along its whole length, with its cliffs red at the peak, then pink, gray, plunging into a whitish mist. Green streaks traced themselves in the center of the depression—the twenty-some walnut trees of Asguine, the lines of poplars and ash on the shores of the wadi, the cornfields downstream of the douar—brown patches as well—the casbahs, the grain loft . . . Columns of smoke were climbing above the roofs.

Then the golden fringe which was shining over the Angoun had dissipated. Ba Iken had started downward on a run.

Upon setting out, it was still light and the tiny bright specks which had sprung into sight all the way below gave an idea of the distance still left to travel. Then darkness had fallen, the footpath had merged with the torrent bed, the lights had gone out and the sound of hooves slipping on the stones echoed between a double rock wall for a length of time which, magnified by weariness, had seemed interminable. But it had probably taken only a few minutes to cross through, the last minutes of uncertain expectation before the vista upon Asguine.

Suddenly the lights had reappeared, very nearby. Ba Iken, leaving the footpath, had veered leftward and stopped under a tree, a little farther on . . .

This happened six days ago.

It would have been useless, that evening, to climb to the slabs, upon arriving at the pass. Night was falling quickly . . . It would have pointlessly drawn out his journey: those strokes a few millimeters thick carved into the dull brown stone would have gone unnoticed.

Today, the circumstances are no longer the same. It is in broad daylight, soon after having lunch and a nap, that he will proceed down to Asguine . . . but on foot, and with the first serious signs of the flu.

Lassalle gets up and motions to Ichou to come down to the pass, where a single boulder, very close to the footpath, simultaneously provides abundant shade and a convenient landmark.

This is probably where Idder, the other evening, waited for Sheikh Agouram.

XV

Lassalle folds the mattress, carries it outside the tent and sets it up at the foot of the tree between two large roots in such a way that the opposite edges, bent upward, serve as armrests.

— This way, we'll be more comfortable . . . He invites Ba Iken to have a seat. This walnut is not all that tall, but its shade is quite pleasant . . . For that matter, it doesn't have many nuts, or so it seems.

Ba Iken sits on the mattress.

— Oh, as far as the nuts go, Mr. Lassalle, we won't have any this year yet.

Lassalle smiles, leaves for the tent, penetrates inside and comes out again shortly afterward, carrying the camp stove, the kettle and the teapot.

— I've just gotten back . . . I went up to the pass this morning: I wanted to see the engravings . . .

He sits down on the mattress and lights the stove.

— I would have come by your place, in any case . . . I was sorry that I didn't find you at home yesterday.

— Yes, it's dumb . . . I was at the sheikh's. My brother did tell you, but you didn't understand . . . It's idiotic: he ought to have brought you over to the sheikh's.

— Is he still here, Sheikh Agouram?

— Yes. He's living in the sheikh of Imlil's house, every time he comes . . . He leaves tomorrow morning. By the way, he asks you if you want to come have lunch tomorrow. He would be delighted to see you again.

— I would like to, Ba Iken, but I was planning on being gone the whole day . . .

— Listen, Mr. Lassalle, you are not going to leave for the whole day tomorrow. You are tired, you have walked all week long in the sun, from morning to night. You're going to get very sick, what with this flu . . . So then, tomorrow, you get up late, you come have lunch at the sheikh's and after that, you rest up all afternoon long. That way, on Monday, you feel better.

— Yes, you're probably right. I'll see how I am tomorrow . . .

Lassalle sneezes, blows his nose . . . Despite the heat, he has kept his jacket on: sitting at the edge of the mattress, he keeps an eye on the water which is beginning to boil.

Leaning his back against the tree at the other end of the mattress, Ba Iken slowly lifts his head: before him, beyond the circle of shade cast by the walnut, he sees the parallel, but not straight, furrows running to the far edge of the field, then the first gravelly slopes and, much farther off, the bright green patches on the hillock around the grain loft. But his gaze soon wanders back and settles, inside the circle, upon the pale earth scattered with twigs.

— Did you find a way for the trail?

— Yes, I think so . . . Lassalle takes the kettle off the flames, turns off the stove and pours the water in the teapot . . . I think the trail can be made to pass over the natural bridge and then be established along the right bank of the Imlil and from that point proceed right up to the mine. I surveyed the entire route. It's easy: there is no rocky ridge on the right bank.

— But what you're talking about there is very long. It's twice as long than from here straight up to the mine.

— Oh no, not twice . . . Twelve kilometers maybe, instead of seven or eight. But, you see, when there are no rocks that need to be blasted away, it goes much faster and costs far less. A few extra kilometers don't matter much.

Lassalle gets up, enters the tent and comes back with the can of tea, the cookies, and the metal tumblers. He empties the teapot, throws in several pinches of tea and again fills it with boiling water.

— I think it might work. I had never thought of it before . . . I pictured the bridge as being much lower and much smaller.

— But I told you the other day: if you want to see Imi n'Oucchène, we go tomorrow, I show you the way . . .

— Well, yes, I should have accepted . . . Mind you, at any rate, I had to begin by surveying the direct route. No time was lost.

Lassalle sneezes again, blows his nose and clears his throat.

— It was on Thursday that I caught cold, when coming down from up there. Believe it or not, we met Idder. He was on his way up. He was just arriving on the bridge the same time we were.

— Did he bother you?

— No, no! Lassalle breaks into a laugh. Ichou had seen him coming:

he made me hide. You see, I couldn't figure out what he was after, Ichou, so I followed him . . . Idder passed very close by, but he didn't see us . . . What a farce!

— Ichou acted rightly, you know. It's better than getting into an argument . . . You never know where arguments lead . . .

Lassalle raises the teapot lid, pours a little steaming liquid into his beaker, then lowers the lid.

— He stopped a few moments on the bridge, then he left . . . He didn't climb the Angoun: he went off to the left on the pathway which rejoins the Amerziaz.

— He certainly wasn't going to the pass at that time of day. He must have been going to Zegda . . . Zegda's a little lower: you're there in twenty minutes . . .

Ba Iken bites into a cookie, while Lassalle sets to pouring the tea into the tumblers.

— By the way, before I forget, can you tell me where that pathway goes, the one which keeps climbing, all the way up, after the gorge entrance?

— The one that climbs along the right bank after the bridge?

— Yes.

— It passes along the southern slope of the Angoun. But it's very hard. The pass is very high in the rocks. You have to walk on foot and pull the mule along. You can't continue on the mule.

— But where does it go?

— It goes into the southern tribes, along Ksar el Jdid. But it's very far. It takes two days to go to Ksar el Jdid . . .

Lassalle filled the two tumblers. He offers one to Ba Iken, who begins sipping it.

— Yesterday we went up to the mine. We followed the entire slope as far as the gorge entrance . . . We came back, like the day before, by way of Imi n'Oucchène. It wasn't late . . . We went down to the bottom of the torrent. It's not very convenient for going down to the bottom of the gorge, but passing under the bridge is a rather easy matter . . .

Lassalle breaks off, takes a pill from a tube, swallows it and drinks a little tea to help it down. Ba Iken takes a second cookie.

— Coming out of the other side, I was a bit winded. I sat down on a boulder . . . I saw something shining in the leaves. I went over for a look and I found . . . Wait, I'm going to show you . . .

Lassalle gets up, disappears into the tent and soon reappears, case in hand.

Ba Iken sets the tumbler on the ground, takes the object and inspects it from every angle: he examines the straps, the joints, the chrome-plated edge of the lid, springs open the snap fasteners, opens the case wide and begins to scrutinize the interior—first the inside of the box, then the lid; turning the box upside down next, he studies the bottom of the lid and runs his finger along the bottom of the projecting edge.

— What's there written on the paper?

Ba Iken shows with his finger the white rectangle held in place by the two elastic bands.

— It's the name of the owner, apparently: "Lessing" . . . "Doctor Lessing" . . .

— That's all?

— No. There are also four letters . . . probably the initials of a company, and then "Rotheim," the name of a city . . .

— Lessing, you say?

— Yes. Maybe you have an idea who that is? Not all that many people must have come through Imlil since spring . . . Maybe you met him ? . . . The case was lost very recently . . . You see, it's in good condition, nothing's damaged . . .

Ba Iken turns the case around, sets it on the mattress and closes the lid. He picks up his tumbler of tea again.

— I think it's the foreigner who had set up camp in Zegda . . . I saw him once on my way to Zegda. We chatted a little, but I didn't understand too well. He had a horrible accent . . . I think that his name was something like that . . . Ressing, or Messing . . . He told me, but I don't remember exactly.

Ba Iken drinks what's left of his tea and turns the tumbler around in his hands.

— But it's been at least three months since he came . . . It was, let's see . . . it was in May . . .

Lassalle pours a second serving of tea. Ba Iken looks for his pack of cigarettes in his choukara.

— You found it in the oleanders, by the bridge?

— Yes, there's a big oleander bush, right at the base of the bridge, right-bank side.

Ba Iken lights a cigarette.

— And you found nothing else?

— No, nothing. I looked all around, but I didn't find anything.

— He must have dropped the case from the top of the bridge.

— Maybe . . . Or else he came down to the gorge bottom and misplaced it . . . He must have reported that he lost something?

— Maybe he said so to the people in Zegda.

— At any rate, if he lost the case, it doesn't seem that he lost the camera. That's the essential point.

— Yes, that's what's most important.

Ba Iken takes a few quick swallows of tea, drags on his cigarette, expels the smoke through his nose.

— The best thing is to hand it to the Office, when you come back to Assameur . . .

When Ba Iken has finished drinking, Lassalle fills his cup again. The cigarette smoke climbs between the walnut branches. Gradually the shade spreads over the field in the direction of the grain loft. The silence is broken only by the strident braying of a jackass, the clucking of a hen or a shout, sometimes followed by an answer, long afterward, much farther off . . .

Leaning his back against the trunk, Ba Iken casts his gaze over the rocks which the field comes up against upstream, the peak of the loft, then the plots of corn downstream of the douar, finally along the right bank, as far as the red bed knoll in the full sunshine.

Lassalle drinks his tea methodically, head bowed, looking drowsy.

Between the two men lies the closed case in the middle of the mattress, its unfolded straps touching the ground.

— When do you want to come back to Assameur, Mr. Lassalle?

— On Friday.

— Friday evening or Friday noon?

— Friday noon, preferably.

— Then you must leave Wednesday morning.

— Exactly, that's what I was planning on doing. It's a little less long by way of Iknioul, I think?

— Yes, a little less long. And you can find a truck in Iknioul: Thursday is souk-day.

Then Ba Iken lifts his gandoura sleeve and glances at his watch:

— Excuse me, Mr. Lassalle. It's five o'clock already. I have to get back home . . . He gets up . . . So can I tell the sheikh that you come tomorrow at noon?

— Listen . . . If I'm going to work, I'll stop by your place on my way. Otherwise, I'll go to the sheikh's at noon. All right?

— Fine. Agreed. But you need to rest, Mr. Lassalle, it's more sensible!

Ba Iken shakes Lassalle's hand, walks out of the shade, crosses the field and jumps to the bottom of the dry stone wall.

Remaining alone, Lassalle deposits the case on the ground beside the teapot and stretches out full length on the mattress.

The engineer's schedule, the itinerary he followed during the day, the minor incidents, the unexpected meetings—it is quite certain that Ba Iken has Ichou inform him of all these matters every day, if only as a distraction. The lad manages to explain everything he wants; through a series of apposite questions, the salient features must be quickly passed in review.

Ba Iken had obviously been filled in on the discovery of Imi n'Oucchène, on his flu, on the new road line imagined for the trail (did he inspire Ichou's gestures when tracing the journey by way of the bridge?). He also knew about meeting Idder, the day before yesterday at the end of the afternoon . . . On the other hand, Ichou surely could not hold himself back from talking about the find. He was even able to specify to Ba Iken who the case's owner was, since he had heard the name. The list of people passing through Imlil must not be all that long: five or six names at the most since the beginning of the year. Ba Iken must not have had much trouble listing them. Perhaps he even realized at once who the person was.

Things are quickly learned of in the tribe. No sooner does a foreigner arrive than everyone gets wind of it. And Ba Iken is in a position to enter into relations with him . . . He must have made a trip to Zegda on purpose to see the man whose name he is now mangling: "Ressing . . . Messing . . ."

The captain had mangled the name also: "A certain Hessing, or Gessing, or something close to that . . ." Lessing . . . "Like you, he was heading toward the Angoun, to Imlil, or perhaps farther on the southern slope. A geographer, or a geologist . . . That was two weeks ago."

Just now, Ba Iken mangled the name in a similar way.

But "two weeks," at the latest that would be July twentieth . . .

XVI

The servant deposits his slippers in front of the door and proceeds ahead of him barefooted on the carpet, holding a basin full of hot water with both hands.

Ba Iken dips the napkin in the water, folds it in four and moves it toward Lassalle's left leg. Lassalle rolls up his trouser cuff.

— Leave it be, Ba Iken, I'm going to hold it.

He himself places the compress over the wound, where the grazed flesh has taken on a reddish discoloration; then he stretches his leg out on a cushion and gives the signal to relax: Ba Iken, Sheikh Agouram, and the master of the house, very formal up to this point, brighten up and break into broad smiles.

— Such bad luck you have! First it's your forehead, then your leg . . .

— Yes, you see, I haven't got used to your stairs. This time I was very careful of the beams but I forgot to look at the steps.

Sheikh Agouram sits to Lassalle's left, Ba Iken directly opposite the latter. As for the master of the house—the brother of the sheikh of Imlil, or so it seems—he has slipped off.

— Does it feel better now, Mr. Lassalle?

— Yes, thank you, Ba Iken. It'll go away. It hurts right now, but it's only superficial.

The servant returns and sets down a copper tray filled with kebabs on the low table. An old man concealed by an enormous teapot gets up, crosses the room and holds out a plate with small brimming cups.

— You did right not going to work today! It's more sensible!

— Yes, I followed your advice . . . And then I had a bad night. I had a slight fever yesterday evening . . . But I had a good rest all morning long. Now, I feel fine. I think the flu has passed.

Sheikh Agouram offers Lassalle a kebab, then says something to Ba Iken with a laugh, who translates at once:

— The sheikh says that with your beard like that you look like somebody from the tribe. You are exactly like us!

Lassalle rather believes that Ba Iken is the one who looks like a "Christian." As for being related to Sheikh Agouram, with his swarthy, almost purple skin, his plump cheeks, his large white eyes . . .

— Marhababik! The sheikh, completely overjoyed, stretches his two arms toward Lassalle in a great burst of hospitality. Ba Iken explains:

— The sheikh wishes you welcome. He is very happy to see you. This place is like his own home. He comes to Imlil often . . . He takes care of the tribe's business when the sheikh is not here.

— And the sheikh of Imlil has been absent for a long while?

— Yes. Two months already. He left on . . . how do you say it ? . . . el Haj ? . . . for Mecca?

— For Mecca? Oh, the pilgrimage!

— Yes, that's right, the pilgrimage! Sheikh Agouram has also been on the pilgrimage. Three times.

— And he's the one who takes care of the Aït Imlil when their sheikh isn't there?

— Yes, you see, this week he stayed for three days. In a little while he's going to go down to Assameur to see the Khalifa of the Kaid . . . He goes by way of Iknioul. He is in Iknioul tomorrow and in Assameur Tuesday . . . If you want to give him a letter he can post it for you.

— No, no, really, I thank you, but there's no need. I must telephone from Assameur on Friday. That's the way it was arranged with the Company.

Ba Iken offers Lassalle a second kebab.

— Thank you, Ba Iken. These kebabs are very good.

— It's sheep liver. It's very good with tea.

Lassalle dips his compress into the hot water and presses it against his shin. Then he picks up the kebab and chews at it hungrily, deciding to do justice to a meal which is such a pleasant change from what he is used to.

The sheikh's residence, in the center of Asguine, is a large casbah which rises several floors, hemmed in between four massive towers. The stone walls, reinforced with wooden beams, are slit with loopholes and pierced, somewhat chaotically, with miniature windows. On the southern facade, on the last floor, the outer wall is replaced by a long wrought-iron grill. This place, transformed into a solarium, is where the men come to warm themselves in the winter, swaddled in their black burnooses, facing the snow-covered Angoun . . .

Today, the adjoining reception room is more appropriate. It leads to the solarium through a twin door. At the opposite end, a narrow door opens onto the vestibule and the stairway. The master of the house, standing in front of this door, gives instructions with signs and monosyllables.

His kebab finished, Lassalle shifts his injured leg a little and half reclines upon the cushions.

Along the entire perimeter of the room, a vermiculated frieze displays its bright greens and garish reds. Between this frieze and the edge of the ceiling, Arabic texts have been painted in black letters— probably phrases from the Koran—and, above the doorways, some quite unconventional representational compositions figuring flowers, trees, birds, and even, in profile, a long sky-blue automobile, perched high on its uneven wheels.

The sunlight penetrates the room through the twin doors. Stretched out this way upon the cushions, Lassalle has a view on the right half of the balcony, on the terrace roofs through the grill patterns, the corn-fields on the other bank of the valley, below the séguia, and finally, much higher, the red bed knoll and the footpath circling around it.

His hosts are involved in an animated discussion. Amid this concert of abrupt syllables, strewn with aspirates and sibilant shushing, now and then he locates a place name—Asguine, Zegda, Imi n'Oucchène— or even a proper name . . . They are surely speaking about him at this moment, but with what name are they referring to him? There is a rather rich choice: the Engineer, the Christian, the Foreigner, the New-comer . . .

The kebabs have disappeared. A young lad brings over some round barley loaves and three glasses filled with water.

Ba Iken leans forward:

— The sheikh asks if you are satisfied with your work. So I told him about what you are doing . . . You understand that this trail interests him a great deal: if it comes past his place, he buys a car!

— Listen, I'm not too sure about when the work will begin. Next year maybe . . . In any case, to get as far as Tisselli won't take long. It'll be three weeks', a month's work.

Ba Iken smiles.

— He finds it amusing, having the trail pass over Imi n'Oucchène. But he says that it's dangerous. If he goes there later, he gets out of his car and crosses on foot.

But the entire trip will be dangerous . . . All these mountain trails are dangerous: the pathways are narrow, the ground slippery, the bends hidden; and there are neither warning signs nor parapets nor, more often than not, any room to make a U-turn or even to pass by another traveler. The Imi n'Oucchène passage is no more dangerous than any other . . . But it is quite obvious that a plunge from the top of the bridge, with or without a car, would prove fatal.

— Did you speak to the sheikh about what I found the day before yesterday in Imi n'Oucchène ? . . . Maybe it's possible he also met this stranger?

Ba Iken shakes his head.

— No, he was not able to see him. The other man came through Iknioul and afterward continued southward. He did not come back down to Assameur.

— What was he doing exactly?

— I'm not quite sure. I think he was looking for rocks, pebbles . . .

— Did he stay in Imlil long?

— Oh . . . Five or six days maybe. You know, he was in Zegda . . . I saw him only once.

Ba Iken breaks the round loaves and distributes the pieces. The sheikh silently watches him do this.

— It was in the month of May he came, you told me?

Ba Iken raises his head, makes like he is counting.

— Wait . . . Three months ago, at least . . . Yes, that's correct, in the month of May. That's just what I told you.

Ba Iken is categorical. The captain was also: "This was two weeks ago"—that is, now, a little over three weeks . . . .

A commotion arises in the vestibule, dominated by the piercing voice of the master of the house. A servant enters, bearing a heavily laden tray at arm's length.

Lassalle takes off his compress, lowers his trouser leg and signals the lad that he can take the basin away.

— It's going to be better now.

— Fortunately you came today, Mr. Lassalle. Otherwise . . . you are among the tribe two weeks and you don't eat any méchoui!

A whole sheep, roasted on a stake, takes up the entire tray. The grilled skin is peeling off, slightly scorched in places, exposing pink flesh under a thin layer of fat. Three saucers containing salt, pepper and cumin are arranged around the tray at the edge of the table.

— Bismillah! Sheikh Agouram, with two deft fingers, detaches a chunk of scalding meat.

The méchoui is succulent. Lassalle compliments the sheikh: rarely has he tasted such good meat. But the experience of his first diffa (without a méchoui) inspires him to temper his enthusiasm. So he sets himself to dividing up his hunger into myriad tiny morsels, each of which is acquired by means of several accompanying gestures. Most of these gestures are useless, but their repetition gives the impression that he is steadily satisfying a vigorous appetite. Frequent recourse to the barley loaf—crust or soft innards, for dipping—contributes to perfect the illusion, as well as his downing numerous swallows of water, but this latter is not as cool as might have been expected.

Ba Iken and Sheikh Agouram have resumed their conference. Just as before, only certain syllables capture his attention: those which evoke familiar places or people. Once again the double consonants and the "sh" recur so often—Ichou, Icchène, Ouddame, Oucchène, Idder— that, while listening, he loses his way. In addition, it cannot be ruled out that the supposedly recognized fragments are themselves part of more complex wholes; there also exist variations of accent which are difficult to grasp, determining a vast quantity of secondary or derivative meanings; not to mention homonyms. Furthermore, at least one proper name has been the object of periphrasis.

Only intermittent whispering reaches them from the vestibule. There is absolute silence on the lower floors. The casbah seems deserted. All of Asguine seems deserted. Not one sound rises in the hot dry air of this early afternoon. Yet the room looks out over half of the douar and the doors are wide open. Is it due to the hour, to the layout of the premises, or the direction they are facing? Not one shout is heard, not a cry, not even a bark, all those signs which, up there, under the walnut, constantly recall the proximity of the invisible douar. Here, in the heart of Asguine, the sounds appear to be floating, or deadened, as if smothered as soon as they arise, or ill-designed to echo beyond a certain neutral zone.

The right hand moves to-and-fro, from the round loaf to the roasted animal carcass, from the small pile of meat gathered at the table edge to the spice saucers, the glass of water, the lips.

The muted guttural dialogue drags on at length. Each man speaks in turn less frequently, the silent pauses grow longer, as if henceforth the interlocutors, their subject exhausted, made due with restating, after widely spaced intervals and at a slower and slower pace, their unchanging conclusions.

The sheikh is the first to break off: he wipes his fingers on a crust of bread and leans back. Ba Iken, still bent forward, hand in the air, lifts his eyes and, smiling toward Lassalle opposite him:

— It's too bad . . . the sheikh doesn't understand what you are saying, and you don't understand the dialect.

— But I do understand: you were just talking about Idder!

Ba Iken, amused, translates for the sheikh, who bursts out in a loud guffaw which is utterly unexpected and out of proportion to the "surprise" provoked by this revelation.

— That's true, we spoke about Idder . . . The sheikh knows him well. He says Idder's a "chitan."

— A "chitan"?

— A "chitan" is a person who always causes trouble.

The sheikh, firmly nestled in his cushions, is still laughing, his chest shaken by slight tremors which he has no power to repress.

— By the way, Ba Iken . . . I wanted to ask you this yesterday, and then I forgot. The other evening, when he passed by us, at Imi n'Oucchène, he was holding a sort of terra-cotta tool in his hand . . . I don't know what it can be used for . . . The handle is not very long, but the ball is rather large and riddled with tiny holes . . . From a distance it looks like a club. Do you know what I'm talking about?

— It's made of red clay?

— Yes.

— Oh, I see . . . It's for bees. His brother, in Zegda, has . . . how do you say it? Small huts for bees?

— Hives . . .

— Yes, that's right, hives. The instrument is for making smoke in the hives . . . Hives in our country are baskets placed on flat stones . . .

Upon an unspoken invitation from the sheikh, who has finally regained his composure, Lassalle digs into the plate one last time, out of politeness, then signals with his hand that he has finished . . . He chews silently . . . A smoker, that sort of terra-cotta club . . . Idder really had it in his head to wield it like a weapon.

— I haven't seen him since . . . It's true I got back late Friday, and yesterday I went up to the pass.

— He went to his brother's. He goes there, now and then, over to Zegda . . . His sister is the one who told me.

— Jamila?

— Not Jamila, Mr. Lassalle, Yamina!

The two names are so close, so easy to confuse one with the other. It is probably not the first time such a mistake has been committed—a confusion of names, of faces, of a gaze . . . Yamina hasn't shown herself since . . . since Thursday morning, when leaving, at the bottom of the slope. Jamila appeared only once, at the infirmary, in the small white room all the way at the end of the corridor . . .

— Yamina, not Jamila.

Had Ba Iken already pointed out the error the other morning?

— Yes, indeed, I'm confusing them . . . Jamila's the girl who is . . . who was stabbed . . .

The sheikh quickly raps the table three times: the master of the house, with his back leaning against the door, raises his head and makes a sign toward the vestibule.

— This girl who was stabbed, in Assameur . . . You know, we spoke about it at your house the other day. There was supposed to be an investigation . . . You told me that someone would be coming to make an investigation . . .

Ba Iken nodded slightly to the right:

— Sheikh Agouram's the one making the investigation.

Lassalle looks at the sheikh, who has struck a formal posture now, eyes lowered, right hand resting in his lap, fingers spread wide and dripping with grease.

— He came to take care of matters in Imlil. So the Khalifa of the Kaid asked him to make the investigation.

It was the simplest solution, obviously . . .

— But you had told me that the . . . matter had taken place in Ifechtalen, and not in Asguine?

— Yes, that's right, in Ifechtalen . . . Ba Iken sits a little farther back and leans against the wall. The sheikh went to Ifechtalen Thursday morning. He saw the house. He interrogated the witnesses . . .

Thursday . . . that was the day they went down to Asguine, at the start, the day they met Idder, along the alley between the casbahs, the second meeting—just barely avoided—at sunset, on the way out of the gorges, after the discovery of the Imi n'Oucchène . . .

— And . . . did he learn something new?

— Oh no . . . What I told you the other day is all there is: the argument . . . she wanted to leave, he stabbed her with the knife . . . Everyone knows all about it . . .

— And the . . . husband?

— I told you: he ran off right afterwards. He left for another tribe . . . Maybe he'll be back in a few months. Then he settles with the family about paying the "dia."

— The "dia"?

— Yes, the price for the dead woman . . . That's settled between families. When the dia is paid, it's over. Everything's set right.

The méchoui carcass is carried off. The table remains empty an instant, then the first "stew" makes its appearance.

— He left for another tribe, probably in the plains . . . For instance, he works in a garage, in the city, to get some money. When he has the money, he comes back to Imlil and pays the dia to the parents. And it's all over . . .

The servant removes the lid: the first tajine is made with tomatoes. The sheikh, stirred by a reflection, sits up and reaches a hand toward the stew. Ba Iken draws closer as well.

Lassalle dips a crust of bread in the oil . . . Nothing can be more logical, when all is said, than to have entrusted the investigation to Sheikh Agouram, in his capacity as regular substitute for the chief of the tribal group. That is not what surprises him, but rather that someone came to make the investigation, and in any circumstances did so and is now on the point of leaving to report to his superiors—and all this happened without his getting wind of it in any way whatsoever (Ba Iken might have thought to mention it; but Ba Iken only speaks to specific questions) or even suspected for one single second . . . But, to tell the truth, he was no longer thinking about this investigation: his treks, his immediate worries made him lose sight of it. And now that it is on his mind again, for the first time in several days, here he finds the investigation is over. "Everything's set right at present." The murderer has run off, but he'll be back in Imlil, one day, to pay the blood money and take his place once more among his people.

— The dia is the price for buying the pardon . . . For women it's half of what it costs for a man . . .

Ba Iken chews with gusto. Lassalle imitates him, but with restraint, and a good thing too, for six other stews are paraded out—one with cauliflowers, another with cucumbers, then potatoes, turnips, fried eggs, and quinces—followed by two couscous—one salty, the other sweet—honey cakes, dates and enormous slices of watermelon.

When everything is finished, when the watermelon slices have been consumed and the cups of cinnamon coffee drunk down, then after that, yet once again, cups of mint tea, Lassalle rises, thanks the sheikh and the master of the house, takes leave of his hosts, proceeds cautiously down the three floors and finds himself in the alley, quite happy to be exercising the leg which has fallen asleep.

Inside the douar, as always at this hour, the men are invisible. Only the women stick their noses outside, old women for the most part, with furrowed faces, bent down under the weight of jugs and bundles of wood —a few children as well, draped in old sacks, barefooted, mud-encrusted, playing in the dust with something or other.

XVII

— A foreigner . . . a certain Hessing, or Gessing, or something close to that. Like you he was heading toward the Angoun, to Imlil, or much farther along the southern slope . . . He came by way of Iknioul . . . Maybe he's here on the same business as yourself?

— Certainly not. I've never heard him mentioned.

— He came here the other day—it's the room which makes me think of it—this was two weeks ago.

Two weeks ago ... that is, at the outermost, July twentieth, the twenty-second to be exact. He must have left the next morning, reached Iknioul that very evening, and two days later arrived in Imlil, where he would have stayed, according to Ba Iken, five to six days, from (the evening of) the twenty-fifth to the thirtieth or the thirty-first.

Captain Weiss was positive, in his lack of precision (but he had no reason to be precise, and he would certainly have been able to find the exact date, if he had been asked, so sure was he of his facts: "It was two weeks ago: I was out on an inspection tour, my assistant was the one who spoke with him"). Ba Iken, for his part, is equally categorical: his second answer at the sheikh's, even clearer and more elaborate than the first, eliminates the hypothesis of a stray error, a lapse of memory or a simple oversight: "It was three months ago at least ... Yes, that's correct: in the month of May."

If there had been mention of "a month or two" in the captain's words, or even "a few weeks," the two versions would not be irreconcilable. But "three months" and "two weeks" are mutually exclusive. Yet the allusion to Lessing, in the office at Assameur, was a mere parenthesis, opened by a play of associations: spontaneous, touching upon a subject unknown to the interlocutor, it is placed right from the start above all suspicion. Ba Iken's situation is different: it was the result of an unexpected discovery, and in response to precise questions, that he was led to speak of events that he would have had as much reason as the captain to bring up himself, if not more (the frequency of conversations, his presence at the sites of the action), but which, in any circumstances, he did not mention. And even if both theses would be equally suspect, the inspection of the found object would plead indisputably in favor of the first ...

The pipe smoke slowly climbs through the hot dry air, lingers around the lower branches, then trails off in the walnut leaves. The taste of tobacco is particularly pleasant after such a copious meal, after countless cups of tea and cinnamon coffee.

On his aching leg, a large black-and-blue patch marks the place where the bone was scraped in the poorly lit staircase by the sharp edge of one of the high uneven eroded stones. But walking brought him some definite relief: the shooting pains are less pronounced than a while ago when leaving the sheikh's casbah.

The shade of the walnut begins to stretch toward the dry stone wall consolidating the field in the east. The customary sounds—an iron pot falling, a mule braying, the piercing shout: "Oh Moha!" let out each time in one single burst, the first syllable heavily stressed, the second glided over as the breath wanes—now and then remind him of the proximity of Asguine, from which Sheikh Agouram is now withdrawing, all matters set aright, every arbitration settled, the investigation concluded (the dossier is complete, the testimonies are in agreement: a misunderstanding, a falling out, an argument, a stabbing, flight, the murderer's exile to a faraway tribe) . . .

Ba Iken is surely accompanying the sheikh as far as Ifechtalen, perhaps a little farther upstream, up to the tribal boundary: their animals trot in single file on the slopes, side by side on the wadi floors . . . Ba Iken turns to the sheikh and speaks to him in a hushed voice, but the only elements which stand out in the course of their speech are already familiar place names: Assameur, Iknioul, Imlil, Angoun . . . The rest escapes . . . Yet, in a way, that is precisely where the salient elements of the itinerary are contained, uttered in fragments, at times arranged in the actual stages of the journey, at others in the reverse order, as if it was all reduced to the total or partial realization of well-established routes: Assameur–Iknioul, Imlil–Tisselli, Ouzli–Assameur . . . "I asked the sheikh: he didn't see anyone coming down with a wounded woman . . . He didn't hear about it." Ba Iken started to eat again, then the sheikh rapped the table twice quickly. Was he an accomplice to this subterfuge? But perhaps the question had not been put to him . . . Two days later, the circumstances surrounding the meeting with Ichou had proved able to keep the suspicions alive (but shouldn't Ba Iken rather be reproached with a penchant for embroidering, for an oblique presentation of people and incidents?), all the more so, the day after this meeting, due to the precariousness of the "details" furnished on the girl's murder. But the physical weariness, the unaccustomed constraint of the heat and the necessarily unfaithful transposition of the tortuous course of the dialect, adorn facts and gestures with a fringe of inconsistency behind which they retreat, resistant to any interpretation, inaccessible, insignificant . . .

The new element, today, is the recently acquired certainty that on one specific point (the date Lessing passed through Imlil) Ba Iken deliberately sought to misrepresent the truth. His previous omissions are revealed in a clearer light . . . Nevertheless, even at that time, the hypothesis of a mule path allowing the trail to cut through the mountain, from Imlil to Tafrent, was difficult to maintain upon examination: during his only trip through the charted zone, it would have been necessary to cross over four passes. In such a relief, a straight line has no meaning, especially for such a delicate expedition: the distance can be shorter, but not necessarily the length of time to make the trip . . .

The reality, in all likelihood, was simpler: going down to Assameur by way of Tafrent, the small escort had followed the usual Issoual route, passing through Tisselli and Ouzli, and if Ba Iken had been led to imagine the "shortcut" it was surely because he could not do otherwise, having affirmed beforehand that no one had passed through Tisselli (a rather imprudent affirmation; it might have occurred to him that in Tafrent, if not in Assameur, the news had been commented on in the newcomer's presence) . . . He had started out by claiming that the infirmary aide had been mistaken, had become confused with another tribe, then that the wounded girl, a native of the Aït Andiss, had come from a tribal offshoot other than the Aït Imlil, from one of those offshoots facing Iknioul. Finally he had imagined the "shortcut" at a high elevation, "often followed" by the Aït Baha. Three days later, after having "informed himself," he had confirmed this itinerary (with no more mention of the Aït Baha for that matter, who, leaving south of the Angoun, should not even pass through Iknioul, much farther eastward) and recognized that the incident has taken place in Ifechtalen, slipping free of the last contradiction ("If they had come from Iknioul, I would have been told in Assameur") by means of a terminological pirouette.

When all is said, Ba Iken had successively "located" the incident, from one stage to the next, along a cautious line of retreat: somewhere in the jurisdiction of the Kaid of Assameur (in the case of error or confusion on the part of the infirmary aide), then in the tribe of the Aït Andiss, then in the Aït Imlil, finally in Ifechtalen. One last stage, which he did not reach, was Asguine, either because the murder did not take place in Asguine or because he had wanted to "distance" it from his douar.

However, as Ba Iken himself had admitted: "The people of

Ifechtalen and of Zegda usually pass through Iknioul; for the people of Asguine, it's better to pass along the Issoual." On the other hand, it was in Asguine, evidently, that Sheikh Agouram made the investigation; otherwise, coming from Tisselli and leaving through Iknioul, he would have set matters right in Asguine first, then in Ifechtalen, on the Iknioul road. Did Ba Iken want to "shift" the murder site by a few kilometers, as he just "shifted" by a good two months the foreigner's stay in Imlil? Perhaps he also "distanced" the foreigner from Asguine? Perhaps Lessing had set up his camp in the vicinity of Asguine, not Zegda?

There also, twice over, Ba Iken showed himself to be very definite. To come back to this point would most likely draw an identical response . . .

A shout rises from the douar after a long silence—Oh Moha!— identical to the others, as if the man, after having dozed off, had just woken up and was resuming his litany . . .

Ba Iken would unfailingly provide the same answer . . . The only way of knowing would be to question Ichou. Ichou could surely answer, if he wanted to. But would he want to? And how to make himself clearly understood? It would be running the risk, in addition, that Ichou would report to Ba Iken at once and that the latter would take offense, and justifiably so, at such a flagrant sign of distrust. But how to put his mind at ease without questioning the lad? Without questioning him tomorrow, or the day after tomorrow, one of the two days remaining— tomorrow morning, for instance, as they begin staking out the plateau? . . .

The extinguished pipe soon rejoins, on the ground, the matchbox, the tobacco pouch and the small leather-bound pocket diary, opened to today's date.

Yesterday's block is unsullied, as expected, but how great is his surprise to ascertain that the two preceding blocks are empty as well. Hadn't they been filled in the day before yesterday at the tizi n'Oualoun?

A quick glance at the previous pages shows that the summaries for Tuesday the twelfth and Friday the thirteenth had been mistakenly entered in the space for Thursday the twenty-ninth and Friday the thirtieth of last month.

Fortunately, the mistake is not a serious one. The undesired notations are voided with two broad diagonal strokes across the whole length of the page, then recopied word for word in the correct place, and immediately followed with a brief synopsis of yesterday's and today's schedule:

"Saturday, August fourteenth—Morning: Climbed to the tizi n'Oualoun. Petroglyphs. Afternoon: flu; rest."

"Sunday, August fifteenth—Morning: rest. Diffa at Sheikh Agouram's. Afternoon: rest."

Thursday, July twenty-ninth . . . Friday the thirtieth. Lessing was still in Imlil at that moment, at the end of his stay . . . Unless he stayed longer than Ba Iken says . . . unless he really set up camp in Zegda and can still be found there . . . But this is hardly plausible: he would have surely come, once during the week, to tour the area around Asguine, if only to try to recover his case. He would have spotted the tent under the walnut . . . Nevertheless, if Ichou confirmed that the foreigner was really in Zegda, it would be interesting to push on that far, tomorrow or the day after, on the off chance, provided that there was still a little free time left. The detour would not be all that long: Ba Iken talks about a twenty-minute trip from Imi n'Oucchène . . .

Now the walnut shade is stretching midway between the tent and the dry stone wall marking the far end of the field. It must be four o'clock, four-thirty. Last Sunday, at the same time, the mules were getting winded while climbing the tizi n'Oualoun, in the oppressive heat. And the whole week was spent scaling the foothills of the Angoun, planning out a trail line among the arid, rocky, scree-strewn slopes, climbing, dropping down, retracing steps, forehead dripping with sweat, ankles bruised by the unevenness of the ground . . .

The week might have flowed along at a completely different pace: waking up late, strolling around the outskirts of the douar, leisurely lunches in the walnut shade, long siestas lasting until sunset . . .

Last Sunday, the animals were creeping up the road to the pass one step at a time, numbed by heat and exhaustion . . . The Sunday before, Lessing had already set off . . . unless he stayed longer than Ba Iken says . . .

Meanwhile, there was Dar el Hamra on the fourth, Assameur the fifth, and on the morning of the sixth, the souk, the infirmary . . . Meanwhile, there was Jamila's murder, the fourth or the fifth, in

Asguine in all likelihood . . . the fourth or the fifth . . . probably the fourth: the trip down lasted a full two days.

XVIII

The swaying grew more pronounced: the object left the field.

Idder then set off again: arriving in front of the thurifer, he took the leftward footpath and went off to the edge of the plateau. Twenty meters farther on, at the first turn, he disappeared.

He certainly wasn't going up to the tizi n'Amerziaz at that hour. He was going to Zegda, to his brother's—Zegda, that's twenty minutes from Imi n'Oucchène, 220 meters farther down along the right bank. He goes to his brother's, just like that, now and then . . . He stays there five or six days, a week or two . . .

A few hundred meters farther on, leaving the trail to the pass on the right, he turns leftward at the second fork and begins to go down toward Zegda.

His brother set up hives on the slopes upstream from the douar. They are simple wicker baskets, propped on flat stones. To harvest the honey, the bees must be smoked so that they will be powerless to sting. The smoker is a sort of hollow terra-cotta globe, riddled with myriad tiny round holes, and probably with a much wider opening where the combustible material is inserted. As for the handle, it is very short and striped with parallel ribbing. An identical utensil was located in the captain's office, between the jug and the candlestick holders. Several others were for sale in the souk at the potter's stall.

Idder, facing upstream, was watching something on the torrent bottom, just at the foot of the vault. He was holding the tool in his right hand: the ball was swaying slowly along the folds of his gandoura. Then the swaying grew more pronounced and the object left the field.

A little farther on, Idder turned to the left and receded in the direction of Zegda. He disappeared at the first turn.

He still has not reappeared.

But perhaps he has come back by this time . . .

In any case, he was absent the three days following the sheikh's arrival. Thursday, he left his place early in the morning, proceeded along the alley to the small square which he crossed without a word, and then set out on the Ifechtalen road. He lingered on the way, perhaps paying a call on relatives or friends. He only reached Imi n'Oucchène toward six in the evening, stopping a brief moment on the bridge, then he resumed his trek to Zegda, where he must have arrived around six-thirty.

He left for his brother's. His sister is the one who said so, his sister Yamina, who has not reappeared either, since Thursday morning. Perhaps she left to join him? (Why didn't she leave with him?)

His "sister" Yamina: there is no more excuse for the confusion at present. Ba Iken clarified things yesterday at the sheikh's, as he had already done Thursday morning, on his doorstep. But the confusion dates from the day when he pronounced the name for the first time: "Yamina? She's a relative, a cousin . . ."—that day (Tuesday) when the three syllables echoed, somewhat belatedly, the three twin consonants heard for the first time at the infirmary, in the small room at the end of the white corridor. Her name is Jamila . . . The aide had leaned over the bed, had tied a strip of cloth around her waist. The girl's neck was slightly raised by the headrest. The forehead was broad, prominent, the lower face tapering; the cheeks were hollow, the lips twitching imperceptibly . . .

His "sister" Jamila: her eyes, unusually far apart, seemed to be set at the borders of the temples, past the jutting cheekbones. Wide open, they were looking in the direction of the door, effortlessly, without the sudden light appearing to bother them, each at the far edge of the face, one alert, near, insistent, the other faraway, calm, impersonal . . .

There is no more excuse for the confusion at present—confusion of names, of faces, of a gaze: the ambiguity arose the first evening, under the tree, at nightfall . . . It was rekindled two days later, at the same time Sheikh Agouram was coming down from the pass, was approaching Asguine in the torch light, guided by the small squat black man, the "brother" of the two girls.

The Khalifa of the Kaid commissioned Sheikh Agouram to make the investigation, in his capacity as regular substitute for the chief of the tribal offshoot . . . The news of the murder reaches the Khalifa's ears on Friday. He has the first information gathered, interrogates the people in the escort . . . Sunday, he composes a letter addressed to Sheikh Agouram and dispatches it by messenger the following morning. The messenger leaves on muleback, arrives in Tafrent that very evening, the following evening in Tisselli, and Sheikh Agouram sets out on Thursday morning, the letter in his pocket, followed by one of his servants and his scribe, who has had barely enough time to slip his pencase in his choukara, as well as the bottle of ink and his notebook with exercise-lined pages. The sheikh rereads the letter two or three times during the interminable climb of the ravine: ". . . make the investigation. The incident happened in Asguine. An argument . . . Her husband's the one who stabbed her: she had left the house. He had wanted to bring her back by force. She resisted. Then he beat her and, after, he stabbed her with the knife. People say he ran off . . ."

He fled to the mountains. He was absent during the sheikh's investigation. The sheikh noted his absence. He mentioned it on the papers . . .

The murderer fled. In a few months, or a few years, he will come back to the tribe with the price of the dia. He will pay the blood money. The family will pardon him and all will be set right once more. He will come back as soon as he has the money . . .

Perhaps he has come back by this time.

He has not yet reappeared, in any case, on this Monday morning.

Idder is not here: Ichou, planted in the middle of the field (the nono irrigated field, situated well above the séguia—for that matter, the highest of all the fields apparently cultivated on this slope), waves his arms in every direction to show that the way is clear.

The sun is already shining upon the major portion of the Addar on the left, as far as the roof of the loft, but the tent and the walnut are still in the shadows.

The red bed knoll advances alongside the douar perpendicularly to the valley, shrinking even further the irrigated zone, virtually nonexistent in this spot on the right bank of the torrent. Asguine, silent at this hour of the morning, seems deserted. A column of dust rises above the sheikh's casbah, fifty meters farther down. Exactly opposite, along the same axis, the loft takes on the appearance of a genuine fortified tower.

The footpath which has gradually emerged, beginning at the torrent, from a tangle of gravelly furrows, curves to the left along the border of the field and drops toward the séguia.

Ichou waves his arms and runs every which way along the plot of land sown with stones and tufts of dwarf pine—this doom with thin, stiff, small leaves, colored a dull grayish-blue like blades of tarnished metal.

Idder is not here, there is no two ways about it, but that is still no reason to abandon all precautions. To avoid any new quarrels, the stake-laying must begin at a good distance from the disputed ground. The road line emerging on the rock face, the one studied by Moritz, comes from the knoll, so it is of little importance that the trail is not marked out along a straight line extending three- or four-hundred meters. There will always be time to settle the matter later, either by circumventing the obstacle or by seeking a friendly settlement (a plot of land two-hundred meters by one-hundred should not cost very much in non-irrigated territory) or purely and simply through expropriation: this will be the only expropriation along the whole stretch of the journey from Tisselli.

Ichou has set off again. He goes forward with an uneven step, his black gandoura beating against his calves, his feet bound in rope sandals. His progress seems to follow a broken line made up of short dashes, as if each stride threatened to carry him off the straight path. He veers southward, definitively leaving the Asguine valley on his left.

The stones are scarcely more numerous on the plateau than on Idder's land. Three-hundred paces from the border of the field lead to a hillock from which the jagged outline of the right bank of the Imlil can be made out in the distance—or more precisely the patch of shade cast by the heights of the other bank, for the sun has just appeared above the Amerziaz . . .

According to the Company's map, the distance from Asguine to Imi n'Ouchène does not exceed five kilometers. No sizable ravine cuts through the plateau—only a few furrows easy to assimilate—the two days ahead ought to be sufficient in theory to carry out the staking as far as the natural bridge. Afterward, if the project, as probable, is adopted, not more than four or five days will be needed to finish up the last few kilometers: one half for scaling the foothills of the Angoun on the right bank, the other for climbing along the shelf up to the vein . . .

Another fifty paces and Idder's field disappears behind the fold in the terrain: the moment has come to drive in the first stake.

Ichou, on a signal, stops, deposits the bag on the ground, opens it and takes out the pair of binoculars, the leather briefcase and the chain measure. The bag contains, in addition, thirty stakes which he had gone to whittle from young poplar branches the night before on the wadi shores.

He sticks the first stake in the ground, goes to gather some big rocks round about him and, as if he was long used to this work, quickly constructs a roughly cone-shaped marker around the stake.

XIX

The footpath runs along the cornfields on the left bank of the torrent, penetrates the douar between two rows of squat cob structures and emerges in the small triangular open space which the shade cast by Ba Iken's house already covers in its entirety.

Pulled along by an old man at the end of a long rope, a camel trudges up toward the mellah, bobbing its large flat head sideways.

Farther on, the alley slips between the stone walls, passes before the sheikh's house, then before the empty lot beyond which rises, radiant, the grain loft in the sunlight.

After the last houses, the way to the pass continues along a hundred-meter stretch before climbing toward the pistachio tree. The incline to the spring begins to ascend as soon as it leaves the douar.

Ichou, hardly affected by the day's efforts, sets out at a brisk pace for the bottom of the slope and slips out of sight at the bend of the footpath, only to reappear at a higher level, standing in front of the hollowed-out tree trunk from which a thin trickle of water runs between the stone slabs, before rejoining the head of the séguia.

In order to drink, it is necessary to bend down very far or, better still, kneel on the rocks, even if it means dirtying one's trousers.

The cold water, gulped down too quickly, causes an icy shiver to shoot up to the head, numbing the brain and provoking a brief but brutal dizzy spell.

Ichou has left again, passing under the small walnut which shades the spring, scaling the first low wall, then the second.

While crossing the field, all that can be seen are the upper branches of the large walnut sheltering the camp: the sun's rays strike them slantwise before dropping to touch the ground, much farther to the right, and landing upon the pieces of millet which ring the grain loft.

The second wall, lower than the first, is easily spanned in a single stride. Ichou has deposited the bag in front of the tent and labors at untying the laces. When the two flaps are open, he picks up the bag again, sets it as usual on the cot and disappears, clearing the entrance.

Since the night before, the empty case has remained wrapped in the jacket lining, at the bottom of the clothing bag, flush against the head of the bed.

Ichou considers the object without surprise, as if he had expected it to be displayed. But is he going to understand the question from the start? The question, to be effective, should make do with associating three words: "Lessing" (show the case so that the only thing which stands out in his mind is the owner's name, traced inside the lid on the small rectangular card); "guitoune" (show the tent so that only the idea of it is retained); "location" or "campsite" (which constitutes the interrogation proper, more difficult to formulate than the first two terms; there is no other way but to illustrate it empirically by designating in turn, as examples, certain privileged points upon the entire basin, such as Zegda, Ifechtalen, the outskirts of the loft, the spring, the pass . . .).

For a good minute Ichou remains impassive, his head tilted sideways, with a vacant gaze and a simpering smile, giving the impression he has seen and heard nothing, or simply did not understand. Then he slowly moves his hands from the back to the front of his hair, smoothing down his curls over his eyebrows, making him look horribly overwrought, dumbfounded, inaccessible . . .

He was most likely collecting his thoughts, for he abruptly rises, grabs the case, places it on the bed beside the bag, closes the tent and, with a complicitous gesture, sets out across the field, along the rocks, away from the douar.

After having crossed over the jujube hedge, he proceeds along the hillside, with a lithe, steady step in marked contrast to his usual gait, and swiftly reaches the pistachio.

He marks a pause, facing the valley, observing the comings and goings of two young girls filling jugs at the spring and getting ready to go back down toward the first houses of the douar. Then, turning around, with his finger he points toward the pale, cracked, slightly sloping ground under the tree.

The place is out in the open, the branches sufficiently high. Ichou circles around it, designating with the tip of his foot, here and there, narrow, precise, evenly excavated holes, then, a little off to the side, a block of darkened earth.

The location is certainly usable, but too near the footpath and perhaps not as well protected as the field, over there, at the same height, above the spring.

"Lessing?" . . . Ichou bows his forehead several times, once again showing the traces left by the tent stakes on the ground cleared of large stones. But the same name, the other day, immediately after the discovery, had found no echo, as if it evoked nothing in particular or had never been heard before. Since then, there was the sheikh's investigation, his departure, Idder's prolonged absence . . . Ba Iken was nevertheless categorical on two occasions: "He had set up his tent near Zegda. I saw him only once on my way to Zegda . . ."

"And Zegda?" . . . Zegda, over there toward the east at the other end of the basin? . . . Ichou shakes his head with determination and juts his index finger, for the third time, toward the rectangle of brown leveled earth under the pistachio. Then he casts a quick glance toward Asguine, bows low, wheels around and dashes downward.

The two young girls have arrived at the bottom of the slope. They are walking slowly, with bended knees, each right hand gripping a handle above the shoulder, the other hand supporting the jug against the lower back. They reach the crossroads—Ichou passes ahead of them on a run—move along the facade wall of the first house standing alone at the douar entrance, and recede into the alleyway.

A husky-voiced dog barks.

Columns of smoke come out of the terrace roofs, rise a hundred meters, then spread out in a bluish sheet which gradually covers the whole breadth of the valley.

The sunlight has withdrawn from the slopes. In the north, a rocky fringe shines on the crests of the Addar. To the south, the cliffs of the Angoun begin to take on the reddish hue that they will keep until darkness falls.

The light-colored foliage of the pistachio stands out against the sky. The campsite is exactly symmetrical in relation to the tree trunk and to the mule path running along the torrent. The Asguine assif is dry and will remain so until the next rains, until the next storm. Storms are frequent in September, they say, rarer in August . . . The place was not well chosen at all . . .

So this is where the foreigner set up camp upon arriving in Imlil at the end of last month—only for a few days, five or six days . . . But perhaps he was still there at the beginning of August, perhaps he had stayed in Imlil for the very first days of August, a few days before the arrival . . .

A few days before going back to Imlil—normally three days—he arrives in Assameur, coming in all likelihood from Dar el Hamra. He pays a visit to the captain, is received, in the latter's absence, by his assistant and spends the night in the guest room at the Office, between the four blank, impeccably whitewashed walls, in a steady temperature of 30 or 33 degrees centigrade, the window closed for fear of mosquitoes and noises rising from the olive grove. The next day, he sets out for Iknioul, which he reaches that very evening, unless he lingers in Assameur to stroll around the souk (since in theory he finds himself there on a Friday) or to visit the médina and take some photographs, certain despite everything about arriving that evening in Iknioul, having located a vehicle making the journey that afternoon. The twenty-fourth, he begins to climb the course of the Imlil assif, pitching his tent that evening in the vicinity of the douar (the survey map mentions a whole series of small black blocks along the wadi), or sleeping more comfortably at some dignitary's home if he had the good fortune to make the acquaintance of someone in the tribe. The twenty-fifth, he spans the defile between the Addar and the Ahori, emerges in the middle of the afternoon into the Imlil basin, and travels until evening across the four or five kilometers separating Ifechtalen from Asguine. At twilight, he sets up camp under the pistachio. Ba Iken arrives with his lamp and offers his good services . . .

Only the Angoun cliffs remain shining for a few moments longer. The golden fringe has disappeared from the crests of the Addar. Above Asguine, the columns of smoke struggle vainly to reach the heights: the bluish sheet stretches eastward along the whole length of the basin, merging with the smoke from Ifechtalen, then that of Zegda.

Below, in the douar itself, a dog barks.

The light-colored leaves of the pistachio stand out against the uniform grayness of the slope. The tent is set up under the tree, facing the valley. It is open. A camp stove, a teapot, a kettle, a few more objects, are deposited on the ground near the tent stake nearest the trunk.

The foreigner is reclining under the pistachio, head partly propped on the tree trunk, partly on a sort of satchel set up vertically along the bark. One hand supports the neck; the other, flush against the earth, is closed around a long piece of wood—a switch, a pencil, a very slender pipe stem. Sheets of paper are strewn on the ground within hand's reach.

The footpath, which has emerged into the open from the torrent bed, passes under the branches on the other side of the trunk and, a few meters farther on, forks toward the first houses of the douar.

Light, serious, attentive, Jamila has stopped at the side of the footpath, a few meters from the tree. The girl's arms, thrust backward, delineate the throat more boldly, more sharply. The right hand clutches, behind the neck, the upper edge of a handle; the left hand disappears, at hip level, toward the bottom of the jug or the downward curve of the other handle. The jug—a "goulla," a kind of amphora with a long cylindrical neck—presses its full weight on the lower back. The bust is leaning forward, the head turned away, as if the gazing eyes had just seized upon their object by chance, secretly. The green eyes, oval-shaped, motionless, seem to be set at the far edge of the face, at the border of the temples. The forehead, very broad, is slightly bowed. A part line divides the hair which, woven in braids, curves around the ears and falls upon the shoulders. The feet are bare and she is wearing a multicolored, flower-print dress, pulled around the waist by a white-and-black checkered belt. The sleeves are rolled back to the elbows. The collar, closed, is decorated with a necklace made of old silver coins strung along a silk thread. Metal bracelets slip from the wrist to the elbow along the right forearm.

The girl's silhouette stands out against the lingering brightness of the sky, a few meters from the tree, at the point where the footpath heads downward.

The foreigner has just opened his eyes. Perhaps he had them cracked open for a few seconds already, for the girl has fled. Did she suddenly notice that he was watching her? Did she take fright? She was in front of him, three or four meters from the tree, and now she is rushing off, swiftly dashing along the footpath, with small lithe steps. Drops of water escape from the jug, splattering hair, dress, legs, bare feet . . .

The foreigner passes his hand across his forehead, sits up and sees the sheets of paper in disarray all around him, the briefcase he knocked over when getting up, the pipe on the blades of straw . . . Then he rises to his feet, takes a few steps, approaches the edge of the footpath.

The darkness commanding the valley floor at first prevents him from discerning anything whatsoever. But soon the plains fall into order, brighter patches appear in the immediate surroundings.

The footpath proceeds in a straight line to the bottom of the slope, where the running girl arrives. Farther on, contours become indistinct and along the last level segment of the footpath shapes are engulfed by the semidarkness. The bright patch of the dress reappears at times, then vanishes from view. Yet a reddish glow is cast on the ground, coming from one of the first houses.

A door has opened. A silhouette rears up in the threshold, gesticulates, swirls around . . . The light darts off.

The sound of the slamming door has arrived very attenuated, but clear and precise, and its repercussions seem to last a long time afterward, as if all the doors in the village were slamming one after the other, closer and closer, all the way down into the lower quarter.

Columns of smoke climb above several terrace roofs. Lights blink at two or three dormer windows. Much farther away, a fire shines at the other end of the basin, most probably in Ifechtalen—Zegda is invisible from this side of the valley.

A dog—or a jackal—is barking in the vicinity of the douar, down below.

The dark foliage of the pistachio stands out against the lingering brightness of the sky. For about a meter the mule path overhangs the gray-and-white gravel bed which can barely be discerned from the banks.

Along the whole rim of the valley, on the hillside, feet stumble over tufts of esparto grass and doom palms, slip on the stones and blocks of schist, as far as the thorn hedge marking the western border of the field. The furrows, though perpendicular to the direction traveled, are scarcely noticeable. Clods of earth crumble upon contact with the large shoes, which pulverize them or send them rolling off into the hollows.

A few stars shine through the walnut leaves.

The tent is closed up.

On the cot, to the right, the bag is still in the same place, and the case, empty, beside him.

XX

At present, sleep cannot be long in coming.

The wind makes the sides of the tent swell inward. A slight draft edges in, as far as the bed, caressing hair, neck, the shirt cloth along the spine.

The blades of straw skip over the furrows, blow flat against the clods of earth, come up against the canvas. This noise is unbearable . . .

The door should be closed, the window—one should rise, the lamp should be extinguished, the door closed . . . Close the windows because of the mosquitoes. In Assameur, the mosquitoes slip through the trellis mesh and hover around the bed. But once the window is shut, they can no longer get out; as for the others, those which have remained outside, they cling to the mosquito netting, clumped in groups of ten, twenty, a hundred . . . There are thousands of them scratching up against the metal wire. The heat is much heavier in Assameur: not a breath of air penetrates within the room.

The wind glides along the canvas walls . . . which swell inward like sails . . . as if the tent were beginning to glide gently along to the end of the field . . . It is going to come to a stop in the thorn hedge.

To close the door . . . The spring is thirty or forty meters away, the mosquitoes cannot fly this far. Perhaps there are no mosquitoes around this spring. The temperature at night is too low for them to survive: they are all dead; they die at once.

All the same the door should be closed, the lamp extinguished: such brightness would end up attracting them.

Sleep, which has been such a long time in coming, begins to arrive.

To close the door—to lean an elbow on the pillow for balance, heave himself up and simultaneously turn over, stand up, stiffen the legs, advance, go as far as the door . . .

Outside the air is warm, the night black.

The tent light causes to loom up along the ground enormous clumps of earth whose fanning shadows run to the far edge of the field, cutting across the furrows which are inevitably not straight. It depends on the small donkey (on the mule, the camel . . . not the horse, horses are reserved for the warriors, for distinguished warriors) which has pulled the plow (the hoe, the piece of wood . . . a steel plowshare would wedge between the stones instead of gliding around them).

The jujube bush is brightly lit. But farther on, the foot stumbles up against tufts of doom, upon thistles, and slabs of schist. In order to make one's way correctly along the hillside without sliding down the slope, the wisest thing is to keep an eye on the tent, broadly illuminated over there under the walnut, walking backwards, if possible, along the intermittent clearings.

The mule path, for instance, is in a clearing.

The pistachio, on the other hand, is very poorly lit: the trunk, though very near, remains invisible.

Lessing slips on his jacket, extinguishes the lamp and leaves the tent. Outside, the air is warm, the night black.

Under the walnut, the light is extinguished. But a glow flickered nearby the spring—someone is going up to fetch water (at this hour?)—other flame glows flicker from the first houses of the douar, ten, twenty, a hundred; hundreds of glows flare up one after the other, closer and closer, all the way down into the lower quarter—and after waiting a few moments, a spray of merging sparks above Ifechtalen, and shortly afterward still others above Zegda. The entire Imlil basin becomes lit up . . .

The footpath to the pass runs along the torrent. The gray-and-white gravel bed can be barely discerned from the banks. A hundred meters higher, footpath and torrent merge. The bed, now dry, is half-obstructed by huge, round blocks of stone.

A dog barks in the vicinity of the douar, another answers it. At once dozens of dogs—or jackals—bark around the douars, others answer them in the mountain; the noise becomes progressively louder: an extraordinary din rules the entire Imlil basin.

Suddenly, barking, yapping, yelping, come to an abrupt halt as if by magic. Silence settles in once again, deeper than before.

Behind, the lights have gone out. Nothing more rises up from the chasm.

The rounded blocks strew the gorge bottom. The footpath swings around the oleander bushes. On each side, very low, but smooth, regular, seamless, the vertical walls press against the corridor passage, at times so close together that the sky is reduced to a furrow of stars.

Progress at the bottom of the ravine is slow and difficult. Sleep is becoming more and more urgent. The trail reappears in places, flush against the wall, threatened by the overhanging boulder. About twenty more steps and the corridor veers leftward, forcing one's way back to the middle of the torrent. But soon the left wall interposes itself, curving in the opposite direction.

The passage looks very narrow, with the possibility that the walls join together, or the defile heads into a waterfall or leads to a dead end. Yet, a little later, the situation remains unchanged: one rock face leads to the other, more and more quickly, but does not impede the movement forward. At each new encounter the hands verify the reverse curvature of the rocks, but do not yet succeed in touching them at the same time.

The darkness has deepened: up above, not one star shines anymore, not the slightest recess of the sky appears. For that matter, there is no longer anything to be seen all around, not even in the torrent bed itself. The stones have disappeared. Sandals land upon a soft, light, very smooth soil.

The moment has arrived to resort to the electric lamp—to take it out of the jacket pocket, to push the button.

An enormous glow blazes up, bluish, even, ubiquitous, lighting every feature of a circular cavern with smooth walls and a perfectly spherical vault. In the center of the cave stands Jamila, slender, svelte, motionless, arms raised, hands joined behind the neck, head thrown backwards. She is wearing a very short, multicolored dress, pulled tightly around the waist by a silver coin belt. The bracelets fall one by one along the forearm. The toes of the bare feet play with the sand . . . Then she takes a few steps, dances, spins around, gradually moving away from the center of the cave, tracing a spiral which soon brings her flush against the wall: as she passes, she seizes hold of the lamp, leading the intruder after her.

The light swirls and darts off.

The course is halting, indistinct, uneven. The hands often brush up against the rock; patches of wall loom up in a flash of light and sway.

Suddenly, nothing is moving anymore. The two arms are leaning against the wall, which the forehead fitfully bumps. A clear hammering can be heard, a sound of stones escaping under animals' hooves and echoing between the walls.

The daylight returns in all its sparkling radiance. At the other end of the corridor, Idder is proceeding along on his mule, torch in hand: he approaches the girl, seizes her by the waist and installs her on the saddle behind him. The mule makes an about-turn and speeds off, disappearing at the bend in the ravine.

Once again there is darkness. The footpath reappears in places, flush against the wall. The end of the gorge is very nearby: the walls spread apart, the stars multiply, the outlines of the crests in the distance come into view. The way is open. The path plunges into the gloomy chasm of the valley.

A hundred meters farther down, the upper branches of the pistachio stand out against the shimmering brightness of the sky.

A hundred meters farther down, in the small house standing alone to the right of the douar entrance, the man's profile is cast on the wall. The shadow of a knife rears up above his head. The girl, on her knees, has hidden her face in her hands. Her braids drop to her breast.

The man unhooks the lamp, takes a few steps forward and appears in close-up, his tiny gray eyes swell to an exorbitant size and soon cover all the available space . . .

Outside the air is warm, the night black.

Sleep is long in coming—if it has come for a few instants, it has already dissipated. The head has slipped down into the alley-like aisle between the bed and the bags. The eye contemplates the carbide lamp, hooked to the ceiling and still burning despite the late hour. The shirt, unbuttoned, is turned down upon the trousers. As for the pajamas, not even unfolded, they are still lying on the clothing bag.

The tent must be closed up—one must lean one's elbow on the pillow for balance, heave oneself up and simultaneously turn over, stand up, stiffen one's legs, move forward, go as far as the tent entrance, untie the laces fastening the flaps, come back to the head of the bed, get undressed, unhook the lamp, extinguish it, get into bed . . .

Very close by, the hands of the wristwatch indicate eleven-thirty. There are still eight hours left before Ichou comes to press his nose up against the tent entrance . . .

The wind makes the canvas walls swell inward. A slight draft edges in, despite everything, as far as the bed, caressing hair, neck, the arms resting on the blanket.

Later, the moonlight has succeeded in filtering in through the crevices of the flaps. A narrow white beam of brightness falls on the foot of the bed, then on the center stake, on the ground carpet, on the right wall of the tent, and disappears.

The air is cool in the early morning. Dawn has just broken. Streaks of mist slowly climb along the eastern sector of the basin, toward the Imlil gorges.

When Ichou arrives—late for the first time—the shadow-line on the northern face of the Angoun touches the foot of the rocky ridge and begins to drop toward the plateau.

Showing Asguine, then evoking Ba Iken with the two familiar whirling arms, Ichou announces that the latter is waiting for them below, in the douar itself—or that he would like to see them before they go, that he has something to tell them, now, at once.

Things are almost ready—compass and clinometer are in his short pocket; papers, binoculars, and measuring chain in the bag, with the rest of the stakes (yesterday twenty were enough for the two-and-a-half kilometers marked out).

Ichou then hitches the bag over his back and immediately sets out toward the spring.

Ba Iken is not waiting for them in his house, but at the entrance to the douar, standing, cigarette in his lips, wrapped in conversation with Idder in front of the latter's house. The two men raise their heads at the exact moment when Ichou, passing in front of the spring, darts downward as fast as his legs can carry him.

Idder is leaning back against the door, opened a crack, whose flap he is rocking forward and backward, mechanically, as if he was hesitant to shut it. All the other dwellings are quiet and closed up.

Ichou reaches the bottom of the slope and continues headlong as far as the second house, sitting down at the foot of the wall to catch his breath.

Ba Iken holds out his hand. Idder does likewise, without all the while relinquishing his fierce, stubborn expression. Drops of blood have oozed from his cracked lower lip, coagulating on his chin hairs. A scar line slants across his right eyebrow.

Ba Iken smiles:

— He had an argument with Ichou, the day before yesterday, on his way back. They fought . . . But, you see, Ichou knows how to defend himself!

Idder, his forehead lowered, continues to sway back and forth at a steady rhythm, his back pressed against the door. A little farther on, in front of the other house, Ichou is whistling a tune and pulling on his fingers, playfully.

Right behind Idder's house, long fields of corn stretch to the wadi. Farther on, the torrent draws very near to the douar and the irrigated plots reappear on this bank, only much lower downstream.

The door squeaks with each swing. Not one sound reaches them from inside the house.

Ba Iken lights a second cigarette and begins, self-consciously:

— Idder came looking for me yesterday . . . He wants me to speak to you about it now, since it's the last day . . . He told me about the land, up yonder . . . Ba Iken gestures vaguely in the direction of the knoll . . . Well, it's just that he thought about it, since the other day: he agrees to the trail . . . You understand, he has other plots of land in the valley. That one has no water . . . So he is willing to give up a part of it . . . if the price is right, of course. But it's not expensive, when there's no water . . .

A sliding sound is heard on the other side of the door. The flap draws backward and Yamina appears in the gap: arms raised, jug against the lower back, she slips along the wall, with face turned away, and rapidly recedes toward the pathway to the spring.

Idder, who had come forward a step, returns to his original spot. Ba Iken stirs the dust with the tip of his shoe:

— It's not very expensive . . . Without water, you understand . . . Here, in the mountains, a hectare costs fifty-thousand reals, more or less . . . If the Company agrees . . . You see, he has made up his mind, the trail can pass through. In any case, it's much simpler?

Ichou has gone back to the middle of the pathway, as if he understood that the essential points have been made and that soon he was going to have to leave. Ba Iken, more relaxed now, looks for a cigarette in his choukara.

— It's much simpler in any case? That way the Company can decide more easily . . .

Ichou, without waiting any longer, sets off again. Ba Iken holds out his hand:

— Tomorrow morning, at eight o'clock! You can count on me: I'm going to take care of the mules.

Idder holds out his hand as well.

In the alleyway, Ichou is already fifty meters ahead.

XXI

The trail crosses the entire plateau diagonally, climbing slowly and steadily along a two-hundred meter shift in elevation which separates Imi n'Oucchène from the immediate surroundings of Asguine.

Two-thirds of the way along, it rejoins the footpath which, leaving the wadi downstream of the douar, follows in its manner a shorter mule path governed by the laws of an age-old logic. From that point the two routes—the modern single-lane route and the tribal route with its myriad variations—proceed along in concert, parallel along the level segments and markedly divergent as soon as a hollow or a hump arrives to break the monotony of the relief, the footpath heading directly across the obstacle which the single lane approaches slantwise. Together they arrive at the edge of the gorges, along which they run on the left bank up to the summit of the hillock giving access to the bridge.

That is the place where Ichou, overjoyed, plants the last stake marker.

The total length of the trip—four-and-a-half kilometers—proves to be slightly shorter than anticipated. Thirty-five stakes have been stuck into the ground, thirty-five signposts at the salient segments of the road line, signaled by large cone-shaped markers which could well have been overzealously covered in whitewash. But it would have been a waste of effort: between now and next year most of them will have disappeared, flattened by bad weather or kicked down by shepherds.

At least the chore is accomplished now, without having called upon any resources other than perseverance, since no complications arose. It was sufficient to survey and to verify now and then the direction they were facing. Strictly speaking, this road line could well have been roughly improvised with the naked eye by training one's sights on the downslope of the Angoun on the left bank of the Imlil.

It is only four-thirty, but the advance on their schedule came at a great price: lunch, of necessity in the broad sunlight, had to be shortened, and the siesta eliminated.

Ichou climbs over his last piece of work, turns toward Asguine and, measuring in a glance the full extent of his accomplishments, rubs his hands together vigorously, delighted, it seems, to have done with it so early. Then he jumps upon the pebbles and comes to sit on the other side of the mound, which is sheltered by the heights of the left bank. On the bridge itself, the shadow-line has already advanced three or four meters toward the old tree half-dashed by lightning, which seems by its presence alone to determine the fork.

The chore is now accomplished, precisely nine hours after having left the douar (an hour to get back to the place where the work was broken off yesterday, a half-hour for a snack, seven-and-a-half hours spent measuring, drawing, calculating, sighting, choosing, noting . . .), nine hours after the conclusion of this brief interview at the bottom of the mountainside, this brief discussion with Idder—with his mouthpiece more precisely, who finds himself, by force of circumstances, to be the mouthpiece of everyone in Imlil.

Idder was swaying against the door, his eyebrow ridge disfigured, his lower lip split, his chin spotted with blood—the unexpected result of a scuffle with the lad. "He had an argument with Ichou the day before yesterday on the way back" . . . The day before yesterday, that means Sunday . . . Sunday afternoon or Sunday evening, because he had not yet reappeared by the time of the diffa at the sheikh's. Sunday . . . It was the next day that Ichou revealed the foreigner's real campsite . . .

Idder, back since Sunday, therefore stayed away from Asguine for three days—a little more than three days, during which Sheikh Agouram saw his investigation through . . . And the morning of the last day, Idder makes it known that he has reflected on the matter, that he agrees, all things considered, to give up the strip of ground necessary for the trail passage to this friendly fellow in return for a "reasonable" compensation, naturally (fifty-thousand reals a hectare is obviously far too expensive for a plot of land without water rights, but the surface to be acquired is so reduced . . .).

Idder was swaying back and forth, his back leaning against the door flap whose to-and-fro movement he himself regulated, his eyes lowered of course, his brows furrowed, with that unchanging, gruff, surly look, but infinitely calmer, more discreet, as if he had made up his mind, after taking a gallant last stand for honor's sake, that the time had been sounded for a serious talk.

Last week, a similar shift in attitude would have seemed incomprehensible. But wasn't it last week's perspective which was false? The recent events—Lessing's traces discovered, Ba Iken's dissimulations confirmed, Ichou's revelations—have cast Idder's behavior in a new light, both rawer and more direct. His "evolution" appears much less surprising from the moment that the hostile gestures of those first days can be ascribed to the strict demands of the "farce" to be played out concerning the land. The mistake most likely consisted in viewing as a mere pretext—a parallel quarrel whose ultimate goal was to mask some secret subject of discord—what ought to have been understood literally. Indeed, any oblique interpretation of Idder's conduct was probably superfluous: Idder was "chikaying" for the land, and for nothing else, and if jealousy, anger, and hatred had inspired him, it was not during those few days when he stationed himself as a sentinel over his field or when he sprang up at the grain loft to remind them of his rights and his determination to defend them, but rather at the end of the last month, shortly after the foreigner set up camp one evening in the vicinity of Asguine, on the footpath to the pass, under that tree from where he dominated the entire valley, from where he could keep an eye on the comings and goings of the girl climbing twice a day to the spring and at times venturing as far as the tree, as far as the gorge entrance, in the dry torrent bed, her bare feet running upon the stones. Most likely at that moment he lost all good sense, all his composure. And if, shortly afterward, the second foreigner's arrival had been of a nature to irritate him, his hostility was rather quickly brought back into direct line with its object: the opportunity for blackmail centering on the land changing hands. Being obliged to absent himself during the investigation, he had come back as soon as the "danger" was eliminated and had proposed a friendly—and advantageous—settlement to the newcomer with regard to the only point of contention which might have kept them apart. His feigned aggressiveness had become tempered to the exact extent that the dispute was heading toward a resolution.

It was a few days previously that he had lost all good sense, all his composure, that he had let anger bring him to unequivocal words, to extreme gestures . . . An argument . . . A quarrel . . . Everyone in Imlil is aware of what's going on . . . Ichou is surely aware of everything that happened. He answered with no difficulty yesterday evening, but this time he will probably not answer . . .

Ichou got up, packed the things away in the bag—the measuring chain, the binoculars, the sheets of paper covered with notes and numbers. Then he went off to sit in the sun on a heap of stones. He is contemplating the landscape—that is, the pebbles, boulders, sheer walls of the gorge and the parched earth spread out all around him as far as the eye can see.

The question does not seem to surprise him. He does nothing, in any case, to pretend as if he hasn't understood. He clearly heard the two names, following the arm dropping in imitation of the gesture . . . He keeps his gaze fixed on the falling hand for a moment, perhaps waiting for it to describe a new trajectory, then lowers his head and remains motionless, his extended legs joined at the heels, his arms akimbo, his fingernails grazing the uneven surface of the large stones which he gathered from all around and piled up over the stake.

A second attempt proves to be as fruitless: the two names are sounded once more—Idder, Jamila—and his arm simulates delivering a blow twice over. But the syllables die out without any repercussions, as if they had been cast far beyond the target to be reached, and the mere isolated gesture is susceptible of any number of interpretations (driving a stake into the ground, for example).

At the very most, the lad shrugs his shoulders with an imperceptible twitch, which can signify: "I don't know" or "It's none of my business," as well as "There's nothing to be done" or "That's all over now, it's not important anymore."

Then he gets up, picks up the bag, hitches it over his back and inquires as to which direction to take.

This is a good opportunity (as well as the last) to go on a surveying expedition as far as Zegda. Zegda is just under a half-hour away from Imi n'Oucchène, according to Ba Iken. The time they gained setting the stakes allows them ample time to make the round-trip journey before sunset.

The shadow-line now extends one-third of the way along the bridge. At the bottom of the gorge, it just reaches the middle of the ravine. Opposite, on an exact line extending from the bridge, the twisted skeletal branches of the old thurifer stretch out on each side of the trunk like a rudimentary road sign—on the right: the gorge entry, the Angoun crests, southern tribes; on the left: Zegda, tizi n'Amerziaz.

A fifteen-minute walk at a fast clip through a scree zone leads to the second fork: whereas the Amerziaz path proceeds straight ahead until it meets the Ahori, to the left an even narrower footpath, whose traces are barely visible through the rocky terrain, veers northward and gently slopes along the border of the valley.

The torrent, down below, is dry. In order to reach it, the footpath describes a series of very short loops. But there is no need to go down: Zegda appears at first glance, flush against the right slope of the valley, in the broad sunlight, as if sculpted in the rock wall: only the small rectangles of the doors and the far ends of the branches jutting beyond the terrace roofs allow the structures of the neighboring slopes to be discerned, interspersed with tatters of thornbushes.

The valley is very arid: there is not a single tree—or vestige of a tree—not one walnut in the vicinity of the douar, not one poplar along the torrent. A green patch, far downstream, announces, perhaps, an irrigated zone.

Zegda seems uninhabited. Not one column of smoke climbs above the roofs. No one is standing on his threshold or sleeping between two cob walls.

But this customary listlessness is suspect. The people of the douar have probably spotted the two silhouettes looming up above, for a few minutes now, at the edge of the plateau. They are observing them through the crevices between the cubes of packed earth. If the strangers decided to draw near, they would continue to observe them, remaining invisible—to keep an eye on their progress along the loops of the foot-path, from the top to the bottom of the slope, as far as the boulders in the middle of the wadi, then once again on the foot trail, now climbing toward the first houses of the douar, straddling the jujube bushes whose layout has been disturbed by gusts of wind ever since the harvest. At that moment, they would send out a boy to scout—one of those children whose belly and buttocks are hidden by an old torn grain sack and whose single braid drops from the top of his skull, decorated with two melded nickel coins or a row of multicolored balls held together by a knucklebone.

But going down would be too long, painstaking, pointless. Curiosity is satisfied. Zegda surely has nothing else to reveal.

All that remains is to make an about-turn, to go back to the Amerziaz fork, then to the Angoun's, where the half-scorched, dislocated juniper tree offers some mediocre yet satisfying shade: Ichou stretches out on his stomach, head between his hands, nose in the dust.

It is nearly six o'clock. Just time enough to smoke a pipe, and then they will need to set off again on the Asguine trail, so as to be back before dark and to have Ba Iken confirm that everything has been seen to for his departure.

The tobacco pouch is almost empty: just one pipe bowl left, and it will be finished.

The wind is imperceptible. The smoke trails off peacefully through the stationary air.

The pocket diary opens, as usual, upon the middle pages where the summary of the daily activities now fills a dozen blocks, from Friday the fifth to Sunday the fifteenth inclusive. Yesterday's agenda can be summed up, as follows:

"Monday, August sixteenth—Extended Moritz's road line in the direction of Imi n'Oucchène. Stakes set on the plateau along two-and-one-half kilometers of the new road line."

And today's:

"Tuesday, August seventeenth—Finished setting the stakes on the Asguine-Imi n'Oucchène stretch. Total length: four-and-one-half kilometers. Hiked as far as Zegda."

Farther back, on the last pages of the tablet, figure the pencil drawings, awkward but precise, taken from the slabs of the tizi n'Oualoun—club, spear, serrated wheel, sun—and on the next page, the complete reproduction of the engravings on the rib-shaped stone: the man astraddle and brandishing the mallet, the child bowed before him, and on the other side the flattened body with outflung arms, lying on the ground or buried feet first in the dirt, finally the second animal, with raised hoof, which is turning away or receding . . . The man has just been struck, his mount abandons him; the rider turns at present toward the child and makes ready to have it undergo the same fate . . . But this entails postulating a double murder and already ascribing all sorts of motives to it: ritual, vengeance, treason, jealousy . . . Obviously nothing prevents one from considering the five figures as forming a single tableau: a good many relationships arise from simple juxtaposition, even where no global conception governed the enterprise . . .

The relation between the child, rider, and donkey is immediate. Between these two figures, and the remaining two, it is more debatable, more ambiguous. Nevertheless there is a great temptation to link the first group with the three figures on the left and to thus infer a unity of action capable of lending the scene a novel dramatic interest. But that entails postulating a double murder . . .

It is nearly six o'clock . . . The shadow-line on the bridge is drawing closer to the right bank of the Imlil. Two or three meters more and it will meet the other line, the one which on the gorge wall slowly climbs between the rocks. The foreigner gets up and, leaving his belongings under the tree, proceeds to the middle of the bridge, camera in hand. At once he feels the coldness fall upon his sweating forehead and over his shoulders where his damp shirt is sticking to his skin. This is the perfect moment: the slanting light wonderfully shapes the slightest folds of the relief. In the torrent bed itself, a stream is edging between the stones, while green patches come back to life here and there on the shores: willow bushes and agnus cactus huddle at the foot of huge, round boulders behind which puddles persist at times, surrounded by a beach of cracked clay.

Lessing comes back toward the tree and enters the sunlight. He draws close to the edge, leans over and sees far below, in the shade, an oleander bush, right under him.

Idder, walking at a fast pace, appears at the summit of the rise, on the other bank. He penetrates the zone of shade, descends and soon appears at the bridge entrance. In his right hand he is clutching a short-handled tool—a pick, a mallet, a bludgeon, a club . . . He crosses the bridge with the same swift, nervous steps. He draws toward the right bank. Here he is once again in the sunlight. The weapon sways back and forth at the end of his outstretched arm; the swaying grows more pronounced, his arm rears above his head . . .

Idder leans above the chasm and looks at the bottom of the ravine. He sees the dark masses of the boulders on the shores of the torrent and, right below him, flush against one of the two rocks, the oleander bush.

The contours are poorly delineated in the gloom. Gazing eyes scrutinize space—the portion of space still available—and see a stone to the left, very close to the head: a gray stone with rounded edges and smooth facets striped with green streaks. It seems no bigger than the head, but perhaps it is an extension of the large boulder, a little farther along on the left? What way is there to know? To the right a second stone rises, larger than the first, better circumscribed, probably isolated from any immediate background . . . The neck rests on a rock. The head does not move . . . The right arm, folded across the chest, does not move either. The left arm has slipped along the body, much farther down; the nails must be grazing the sand, the fingers playing with the pebbles. As for the legs, they are invisible . . . The stone continues to press down, to dig into the edge of the head. Only the eyes are able to move: opening, shifting about, closing, opening: to the right the large isolated stone, to the left the small gray one, split apart, fragmented, which is perhaps simply part of the large boulder located in the background . . . Then everything goes dark—not black: dark. The rocks are still there, certainly, but their contours have melted into the gloom . . .

Idder has set off again. Reaching the thurifer, he follows the footpath on the right which rises along the mountainside, passes in the vicinity of the gorge entrance, spans, much higher up, the cliffs of the Angoun and penetrates, beyond the crests, into the southern tribes . . .

The shadow-line on the bridge meets the one which, on the gorge wall, was slowly climbing between the rocks. On the right bank, a single line now draws near the two footpaths and the old tree which marks the site of the forking.

The wind is imperceptible. The smoke trails off peacefully through the stationary air.

III

I

THERE ARE AT LEAST two hundred of them, black, very tiny, scurrying about at a furious pace without marking the slightest pause, harnessed to an exceptional task worthy of mobilizing all their energies.

They have already devoured well over half of the creature, beginning at the stinger and the curling extremity of the appendix. They are now attacking the last segments of the abdomen, the pincers, the head, the claws still unfolded in a walking position.

The scorpion's carcass seems enormous. The very tiny black dots slip along the rugged shell, as if they could not reach the end of it, and yet they chip away at it, split it open, infiltrate it, empty it of its contents, suck it dry, digest it and bustle about the debris which imperceptibly dwindles, fritters away, vanishes into thin air.

It was probably a black scorpion, of moderate size, a member of the most widespread species in the region, small and very poisonous. But at present it is gray, the color of dirty sand, virtually colorless . . . Deprived of its curved weapon, each and every part amputated, reduced to a few linear elements of tough matter, to a few transparent surface planes, it suggests an old, forsaken celluloid toy.

The dismemberment is carried out with meticulous detail. The hard, withered substance disintegrates crumb by crumb, immediately swallowed up. The ants are too numerous: several at once scramble over the legs, jostle each other, climb on top of each other, tumble on their backs, turn themselves over and dart off to the attack. Some, incapable of reaching the spoils and carving out their share, resign themselves, gather off to the side and helplessly witness the banquet's progress.

The eight unfolded legs are in walking position, ready to set out on their way, as if the catastrophe had surprised them in midstride, and the entire creature, still clinging to the boulder by the abdomen and the tips of its legs, seemed to have passed without transition from lively animation to annihilation.

The boulder is in the shade. The whole field is in the shade, the whole valley floor: the sun has not yet reached the grain loft. Opposite, the shadow-line is dropping slowly upon the plateau: in a few moments, it will touch the pinnacle of the red bed knoll.

Standing in front of the boulder, Lassalle watches these operations unfold. It was while pulling up the stakes, a while ago, on this side of the field, that the commotion alerted him. But before coming back, he folded the canvas, put away the tent equipment in the first bag, the cot, the mattress, the blanket and the utensils in the second, the clothes in the third, along with the leather briefcase, the backpack, the camera case, the measuring chain and a few cans of food necessary for the rest of the trip. He shared the surplus provisions between Ichou and Ba Iken. The lad was especially delighted by the sugar, apart from the money which was owed him in any case for his eight days of active collaboration.

Ba Iken procured three mules, two as agreed upon and the third for his personal use, for he decided to go down to Iknioul "for the Thursday souk." He arrived at the set time, followed by an old man with a bare head, shaved skull, and black pointed beard: the owner of the animals. Both worked to secure the baggage upon the sturdiest beast. The bags are a little less heavy than on the way here and the task is accomplished without incident. Ba Iken begins to knot the ropes around the baskets.

A few steps away, dozens of small black ants are scurrying back and forth upon the scorpion's transparent carcass, sure of gnawing away at their prey until the last bite. The labor has been going on for several hours, and it is far from approaching an end. He must come to terms with the situation—witnessing the finale of the scene would seriously compromise their timetable for this stage of the journey—and make the decision to take to his heels.

But his curiosity comes to the fore again and the irresistible temptation arises to double back, with the feeling that the action is going to lunge abruptly forward or that an event of capital importance is in progress. But everything that happens is merely very normal and exasperatingly slow.

— Did you finish setting the kerkours yesterday?

— The "kerkours"?

— That's what the markers are called, the piles of rocks . . .

Lassalle gathers up his jacket and military cap which he had left at the foot of the tree, puts the cap on his head, runs his hand irritably over the horrible beard which is itching him more than usual, then throws the jacket over his shoulders and goes up to Ba Iken.

— Yes, it went well. We staked as far as Imi n'Oucchène . . . It was a quick job, but the route was easy.

— Then the trail is really going to come through there, Mr. Lassalle?

— Well, I still can't tell you for sure, but chances are . . . I hope I haven't done all this work for nothing.

After a few protests for form's sake, the old man tacitly recognizes that the load is not excessive. He assures himself of the stability of the arrangement one last time and checks the straps. Ba Iken sets him at ease and arranges the blankets on the packsaddle of the other mules.

— There! Now we can leave, Mr. Lassalle!

— Perfect, Ba Iken. Let's go!

— Bismillah!

Lassalle casts a last glance under the walnut, where everything is now in order: the place has become once again what it was the evening he arrived, with its leveled furrows strewn with blades of straw—except for the holes left by the stakes and a narrow circle, not far from the tree trunk, where the ground has somewhat darkened.

The three mules, guided by Ichou, Ba Iken and the old man, pass over the small, dry stone wall, cross the field just below and disappear, beyond the second embankment, behind the small tree to the left of the spring.

That is the point where Lassalle meets up with them. Ba Iken helps him into his saddle, then leaps in turn onto his mount, while the old man proceeds along ahead, tugging on the bridal of the third animal which reluctantly starts on the path downward.

Kneeling on the slabs, bust motionless, Yamina maintains the neck of her jug under the gush of water flowing from the hollowed-out tree trunk. She lowers her head, her braids fall on each side of her throat. Her necklace of small coins slips along the brown skin of her neck.

Farther down, her ankles extend beyond the folds of her dress and the toes of her bare feet are bathed by the cold water.

But the mule teeters forward. When Lassalle catches his balance, he has already traveled several meters and the spring is lost to view: all he makes out, behind him, are the leaves of the walnut tree, and much farther up, long grayish streaks on the rocky crests of the Addar. Immediately afterward, the incline veers to the left and heads in a straight line to meet the footpath to the pass.

Idder, his arms crossed over his foul gandoura, is leaning back against the cob wall of the first house at the entrance to the douar.

Ichou reaches the fork on a run and continues on without slowing down, without even raising his nose. The old man passes by at a trot, pulling up his djellaba folds with his left hand. Ba Iken stops in front of Idder and exchanges a few words with him. Lassalle also stops and holds out his hand: Idder shakes it, scrutinizes him a brief instant, then turns away and goes back inside his house.

Ba Iken sets off again, and the three mules file along the alley between the three casbahs in the center. Through the breach in the crumbled wall, the loft appears on the left, just as the sunlight strikes the roof branches.

Ichou has stopped in the small square, in front of Ba Iken's house, and lets it be understood that he is not going any farther, that he no longer has anything to say in the matters at hand, that he is going back up to the mellah right away. He takes off his beret sunk down in his disheveled shock of hair, goes up to Lassalle and kisses his fingers. Lassalle, surprised, pulls back his hand sharply, then smiles and gestures in farewell to the lad who, serious and ceremonious, remains bowed, his black beret clutched against his chest with both hands, until the last mule has disappeared at the other end of the square, at the entrance to the lower quarter.

Beyond the last buildings, the small caravan moves past the stunted poplars growing on the shores and sandbanks amidst the stones; five-hundred meters lower down, it leaves the mule path on the right which, after having spanned the wadi, crosses the entire plateau as far as Imi n'Oucchène, scales the cliffs of the Angoun and descends into the southern tribes.

It is eight-thirty. The sunlight, which touched the valley floor upstream of Asguine, rapidly sweeps eastward. The heat is already very heavy. The sky, as every morning, is laden with whitish clouds, but for the first time large clouds ring the crests.

— There is going to be a storm today . . . Where there are clouds like that in the morning, that means there's going to be a storm. We must hurry and pass through before the rain.

— To pass through the gorges after Ifechtalen?

— Oh, the gorges are easy! . . . It's passing through the wadi, after that, in the Aït Mezdou.

Ba Iken shouts something to the old man who, without balking for a single instant, breaks into a jogtrot. His slender, muscular legs rhythmically slacken and spring back with an astonishing litheness. Lassalle, whose mule has begun to trot, begins to seek out a more comfortable position, but the blanket is too short: his knees, instead of hugging his mount, flap about in the air, which ruins his balance. In desperation, he frees his feet from the blanket and lets his legs dangle along the animal's sides.

— I had a little time left over yesterday at the end of the afternoon. I used the opportunity to go as far as Zegda.

— You were in Zegda?

— Yes. I wanted to see Zegda . . . There was a little free time left . . . It's even drier than in Asguine. I didn't spot one single tree! I really wonder where Lessing could have set up his campsite.

Ba Iken props himself on the animal's rump with one hand and turns his chest more directly:

— A little lower down . . . There are some walnuts, lower down, with the fields below the séguia . . . They aren't as big as Asguine's, but they still give a little shade . . .

Then he resumes his original position. The old man has gotten a few meters ahead.

Now the fields have disappeared. The valley has shrunk: almost the whole plain surface between the two slopes is taken up by the stones.

Lassalle turns around to contemplate Asguine one last time. But the course of the torrent has curved northward: Asguine has disappeared. The last rises of the Addar seem to have merged with the plateau, filling in the valley, leveling the casbahs, obliterating the few hectares of greenery under the rocky terrain. It is as if the valley continued to rise, grim and deserted, up to the last slopes of the n'Oualoun, whose regular parabola stands out against the white sky.

It is this fictitious line—the threshold of the basin—which the footpath crossed at the end of a wearing stage of the journey, ten days earlier, the evening he arrived.

II

The whole morning long the clouds bank up. The long gray streaks which, since daybreak, have been clinging to the crests, imperceptibly drop altitude and merge on the n'Oualoun and the Amerziaz: the two passes disappear, then the shelf of the Angoun and its rocky ridge; tattered ribbons of mist slink along the border of the plateau, slipping into the ravines, venturing as far as the valleys.

Toward ten o'clock, coming from the west, another system bursts onto the scene, superimposing itself on the first one and within a few minutes invading the entire basin. The heat becomes stifling. Abrupt gusts drive up whirlwinds of red dust which fly above the footpath and drop back after a short distance, interpenetrating clothing, infiltrating eyes, throat, nostrils.

At the outskirts of Ifechtalen, as the incline of the slope sharpens, lightning bolts proliferate from one end to the other of the leaden sheet now covering the whole sky. Ifechtalen gradually appears on the right bank of the Imlil, at the confluence of the three wadis, in staggered rows on a hill, barely more extensive than Zegda, but surrounded with walnuts and cornfields and dominated by a large casbah from the top of which a man, his elbows leaning on the solarium balustrade, greets Ba Iken from the distance and shouts something while showing the clouds.

The footpath veers leftward and follows the Imlil assif along this brief stretch of its run where, having emerged into the open from the plateau hemming it in from Imi n'Oucchène, it spreads out, broad and peaceful, for several hundred meters downstream of Ifechtalen before heading for the mountain once again. Then it crosses the torrent. The water is clear, shallow: the animals' hooves striking the stones splash up shimmering sprays.

At the entrance to the defile between the Addar and the Ahori, the old man stops to rest the mules. Ba Iken does not view this halt too kindly ("If the storm breaks immediately, we won't be able to cross the wadi to the Aït Mezdou"), but the old man insists and winds up by having his way. The three men take advantage of the opportunity to have a bite to eat.

At present the thunder rolls without breaking off, the sound repercussing from one rock wall to the other along the whole rim of the basin and farther off along the invisible slopes, along the whole stretch of the immense range hidden all day long—for several days perhaps—under a thick layer of restless, opaque clouds.

The pause does not last longer than a half-hour. Shortly after noon, Ba Iken gives the signal to be off, jumps on his mount and opens the way, preceding Lassalle and the old man who, despite the difficulties of the terrain, the heaviness of the atmosphere and the threatening tornado, is softly humming between his teeth.

For two hours the path draws out along the cliff edge, climbing and falling, circling around the large rock overhang where palm rats scurry about, their bushy tails bounding up and disappearing in a hole, while underneath, now close by, now hidden in the hollow of a meander, the torrent slips between the two mountains, edging its way through the talus slope at the foot of which are scattered bare, polished tree trunks, lodged there since the last thaw.

A little after two hours, the storm bursts and the rain sweeps down, heavy and warm, upon the parched earth which months of dryness have transformed into a light, resonant crust: the first drops raise up small flakes of red dust.

— If we reach bottom in a half-hour, we can pass across, Ba Iken shouts over his shoulder, but we must hurry . . .

Drops as large as coins dash against his nape and penetrate the canvas of the gandoura. All the while trotting along, Ba Iken leans backward, shifts his saddle rug and exposes a large piece of blue cloth set on top of the packsaddle. He tosses the burnoose over his shoulders and pulls the hood down over his turban.

All Lassalle has at his disposal is his jacket, folded on his lap. He slips into the sleeves and raises the collar. But the protection quickly proves to be illusory: the water runs directly from the rim of his cap over his shirt.

Behind, the old man shelters himself, in desperation, under his djellaba hood. He stops from time to time to rearrange one of the bags—theoretically waterproof—which was knocked off balance upon hitting a rock.

The water streams along, more and more plentiful, dragging along everything in its path: pebbles, large stones, roots, tufts of thistle, chunks of rock and blocks of earth already worn away by erosion. The debris tumbles down the slope and solidifies in the mud, filling in the footpath which becomes unrecognizable, furrowed by the horizontal segments of countless ravines and, as soon as it begins to descend, converted into a yellowish rivulet where the mules' hooves flounder and stumble.

The poor visibility deprives the traveled route of any coherent overall perspectives. The clouds pass very low. The eyes see no farther than a few hundred meters. The slope of the Addar, on the other side of the gorges, has totally disappeared. The torrent itself is hidden behind a sheet of mist.

On several occasions, they must wait for the old man who is having a difficult time of it, even help him along a tricky passage, then slow their pace to allow him to follow them.

The half-hour Ba Iken announced has nearly slipped away. The footpath now goes steadily downward. The valley of the Aït Mezdou is most likely not very far off: in clear weather, the douars ought to be visible down below, the walnuts, the irrigated fields . . .

Strange shapes have been filing past for a while now at some distance from the footpath: holm oaks with twisted branches and roots cleaving to the rocky terrain; but there are not very many of them: the majority, nestled at the foot of boulders, are half reclining on the slope.

Also in the rear, new shapes loom up: men bowed forward, bludgeon in hand, heads sinking into canvas sacks. Trailing one behind the other, they arrive at a jogtrot, pass by the old man, draw closer. There are seven of them, who wave as they proceed past, lifting their eyes without lifting their heads, then exchange a few words with Ba Iken, without stopping.

The footpath no longer curves. It goes down, in a straight line, between two rows of holm oaks. The thunder has moved off into the distance; it can be heard rolling more to the east—or more to the south, since the ramified echoes create false leads. At present the rain falls in a fine shower, cold and nourishing. The clouds have regained altitude. The trees part, revealing the wadi, twenty meters farther down, which is flowing very rapidly between two muddy banks. Then another rumbling arises, clearer and closer: the sound of thousands of stones rolling along the torrent bed.

Ba Iken succeeded in persuading the seven men to help him. "We must cross at once, Mr. Lassalle! Maybe in five minutes, it's too late!"

Two men draw near on the right: the first grabs hold of the bridle and pulls; the second clutches the packsaddle and pushes. The mule enters the turbid water, shallow on this side. Lassalle frees his feet from the blanket just in case and leans on the edge of the packsaddle.

"Don't look at the water, Mr. Lassalle! If you look at the water, you get dizzy and you fall!" The swelling wadi spreads out fifty meters, the deepest place located in the neighborhood of the left bank, more precipitous than this one. The two men make slow progress, jumping from one foot to the other to avoid the stones which clash together in a deafening roar.

Lassalle makes an effort to observe Ba Iken's recommendations, but soon he can no longer help himself, the temptation is too great: he raises his eyes and sees the water flowing before him from left to right. Instantly he feels himself slipping leftward, as if he was moving headlong up the wadi. Out there, opposite, the other shore also seems to be shooting upstream, while circles form on the gray still water, turning slowly, then faster and faster, proliferating, swirling. "If you look at the water, you get dizzy and you fall!" Lassalle shuts his eyes, clutches the mane . . . Then once more he sees the head of the mule which wants to turn away but is dragged along by the bridle and a hand pressed against its neck. The two men bellow hoarse cries intended to cover over the noise of the pebbles and reassure the animal—perhaps also to reassure the rider. Lassalle notices that they are now walking on the gravel: they have reached a strip of sand, two-thirds of the way across. Ba Iken follows behind a few meters; two men support his mount. He himself has turned his head in the direction of the third mule, guided by the old man and held onto by three strapping fellows who seem to be having no end of trouble, despite their vociferations, to stay on course.

Fifteen meters remain to be spanned, quite likely the most dangerous:

over there, small waves attack the shore, from which chunks of earth detach themselves, fall in the water and are swallowed up at once. Once again Lassalle closes his eyes. The guides' shouts become even more violent. The mule seems to stop, sets out again, advances a meter or two, stops again, refuses to go on, sets out again in spite of itself, then buckles, slips down, almost to its knees. The wadi is much more deep on this side, the current much more swift. Lassalle feels the flood rising to his knees and even passing over his hands. Someone grabs him by the arm. He opens his eyes again: the shore is one meter from him. The man explains that it is too high for the mule to gain access to it, that he is going to go a little farther down, but that he, the rider, must make ready to leap off at once. Lassalle crouches on the animal's back and, without having the time to steady his balance, springs forward.

He has touched the bank and holds himself there, braced upon his forearms. But his legs plunge into the water without coming across anything to lean upon. He tries to free his right leg: at the very instant his foot is set on the shore, the earth collapses and his foot falls back into the water. The soil is also threatening to give way under his elbows. After several attempts, his leg finally catches hold. He heaves himself up on the bank and for a long while remains stretched out, exhausted, his head buried in his arms.

The mules were able to approach the shore twenty meters downstream. Having caught his breath, Lassalle gets up and draws near, floundering in the mud. Ba Iken and the old man are busy setting a bag up straight. Already the improvised guides are off on their way, hopping in single file along an indistinct footpath.

— Fortunately we met them!

Ba Iken passes the rope over the baskets.

— The mule laid down in the water. The top bag went away . . . We really had trouble catching it. It got a bit torn on a boulder, but I think it's nothing serious . . .

— We'll see about that in a while, Ba Iken. We passed across, that's the main thing . . . Is the first douar far off?

— It's very close, now, Mr. Lassalle. Barely ten minutes . . . I know someone. We're going to go to his house. We can't stay like this . . .

They get back in their saddles in their drenched clothes.

The rain has stopped, but clouds still blanket the sky. Superimposing itself over the clear rolling of the stones, a more muffled rumbling can be heard from time to time, coming from the south or the east. The storm is receding, but the waters are continuing to rise. They will surely continue to rise through a part of the night. Fording the wadi again would already no longer be possible.

Soon the douar comes into sight, built against the left slope of the valley. Large streams run down from the terrace roofs along the stone walls. The water flows in torrents in the alleys between the houses.

Ba Iken stops in front of a casbah to the right of the foot trail, on the way out of the douar, and knocks at a door signaled by a large white hand stencil-painted high on the flap.

The door opens a crack, then swings wide.

The master of the house, named Si Abdesselam, arrives shortly afterward and has the three men come up to the reception room, on the third floor, where a wood fire is crackling in a narrow fireplace in the corner.

A few instants later, kneeling on the carpet, Lassalle sets about drying his clothes—those he had on his back and the others in the immersed bag.

The bag is marked, near the bottom, by a twenty-centimeter long rip. All the clothes are there, which had been piled at the top of the bag, but most of the cans of food have disappeared, as well as the measuring chain. Lassalle did not find the camera case either. He rummaged through the other bags to be thorough, but in vain: it was in the damaged bag that he had put the case this morning.

The papers in the leather briefcase have seriously suffered from the immersion. All the same, the notes and calculations are still legible: they must be recopied as soon as possible. The Company's map is washed out, but the survey map proved very resistant.

Lassalle sorts the papers very cautiously, spreading them out one by one in front of the fire. When he has finished, he unfolds the survey map on the carpet.

In the center of the lower fold of the sheet, a few millimeters from the uncharted zone (just to the left of the blue line which seems to spring up out of it as if by magic), three small black square blocks are lined up along the edge of the wadi: these are the douars of the Aït Mezdou. Taking the scale into account, the boundary of the white zone ought to be located approximately at the place reached on the cliff trail of the Ahori at the moment the storm broke.

The contour lines have reappeared, as well as the brown hatching highlighting the crests, the blue lines the waterways, the green patches the forests . . .

The torrent has changed names for that matter. It is not the Imlil assif anymore: it is now called the Mezdou assif.

Outside, the rain has begun to fall again.

III

Si Abdesselam grabs the clay pot and lavishes a long stream of melted butter over the vermicelli. Soon the whole dish is awash in the golden liquid which infiltrates every last recess.

Lassalle helplessly witnesses this procedure and sets his spoon down after a few mouthfuls of a preparation which is much too difficult to digest at such an early hour of the morning.

Shortly afterward, in any case, the servant takes the vermicelli away and comes back with two plates, one filled with honey, the other with a very white butter. Then he replenishes the barley loaves and presents each guest with a large glass of cinnamon coffee.

The honey is exquisite, very limpid and aromatic. The flies, heavy, awkward, in far greater numbers than in Imlil, stick to the plates, the greasy table, on the fingers, the nose. One of them is in the midst of drowning in the coffee; Ba Iken catches it between thumb and forefinger and deposits it on the table: the legs shake themselves off, twitch about madly, skid across the wet wood; then the fly darts off and begins to circle around.

The master of the house leans toward Ba Iken and speaks to him in a hushed voice. Ba Iken leans, in turn, toward Lassalle:

— Si Abdesselam asks you if you slept well.

— Yes, very well, Ba Iken. Thank him. I had a very good night . . . I had a good rest.

It is best not to mention the fleas: the fleas and the shadows of the flames dancing on the walls troubled his sleep all night long. At least the clothes and baggage have dried properly.

— Thank him also for having had the bag resewn . . .

Si Abdesselam listens attentively to the thanks which Ba Iken communicates to him, then bows toward Lassalle with a slight smile.

Ba Iken takes a piece of bread and dips it into the honey.

— You haven't found the case, Mr. Lassalle?

— No. I looked everywhere . . . But I'm sure about putting it in that bag. It was all the way at the bottom, under the clothes . . .

— It's dumb . . . Yet we ran after it at once. It's hard, you know, with all those stones . . . It must have got torn the first thing after falling in the water . . .

Ba Iken brings his hand to his mouth and chews slowly for a few moments.

— Listen . . . I'm going to speak about it to Si Abdesselam . . . The people of the douar can find it in the wadi between the stones. It's possible . . . You never know . . . If they find it, they turn it in to the Office in Assameur.

Ba Iken fills in Si Abdesselam about the matter. The verb "to see," "to look for," or "to find" is accompanied by the customary pantomime gestures: the index finger pulls down the skin under the eye, baring the lower half of the eyeball, as if to solicit the interlocutor's utmost attention, as much to the words being uttered as to the object itself whose search they are requesting. Si Abdesselam lowers his head gravely on several occasions—the last time with his eyes fixed upon Lassalle so as to assure Lassalle that he can count on him.

The servant pours a second serving of cinnamon coffee, then brings over some little cups which he fills with mint tea.

Lassalle spreads out the survey map upon the cushions. The paper is completely dry at present, but crinkled. The white patch, fifteen centimeters long, occupies the center of the lower fold of the sheet. Only two words run across it by way of explanation: "Uncharted zone." This is obviously not an explanation, but it is the only notation figuring in the entire white area, the water having washed away the few pencil strokes traced out the other day with the intention of filling in the gaps. It was at the very beginning of his stay in Imlil . . . The project had been confined to extending the Issoual, to drawing the arête of the Angoun, to marking the location of the passes, to sketching out the courses of the three torrents . . . The water erased everything: the Issoual disappears once more at the boundary of the void, a few centimeters after the miniscule footpath of the n'Oualoun detaches itself from the valley floor. Farther northward, small black square blocks are stationed as sentinels along a blue line springing up from nothingness: the Aït Mezdou. An elevation marking, at the bottom of the valley, indicates 1,800 meters . . . Ifechtalen was at 2,200, Asguine at 2,400 . . .

— This is Timirit here, the first douar of the Aït Mezdou, Ba Iken explains, also leaning over the map. In a little while we are going in the Aït Mellal. Iknioul is in the Aït Mellal . . . You follow the wadi nearly the whole time as far as Iknioul . . .

The rain stopped in the early morning. The sky is clear, empty of clouds. The wadi, whose rumbling could be heard through a part of the night, is already moving along at its normal speed: it flows tranquilly at the foot of the casbah, a little murkier than usual, but barely more swollen than the day before in Ifechtalen, before the storm broke.

The wadi flows tranquilly at the foot of the douar, and farther down along the footpath where the mud will surely take several days to dry: the mules' hooves become encrusted and flounder in the puddles. A few large walnuts shade the terraces. A dozen or so men labor to dislodge the branch-thatchings swept by the floodwaters into the torrent bed. The valley is rather broad, but not as broad as the Issoual's upstream of Tisselli. The footpath goes down through holm oak, cypress and juniper; it even crosses a stand of cork oak one kilometer downstream of Timirit.

Farther on, landslides have hurled down huge masses of red bed to the bottom of the ravines: uprooted trees lean over the edge of the excavated terrain; others have tumbled to the bottom of the slope; still others have stopped midway down and are strewn in every direction across the scree.

Behind, the end of the defile is in sight, five-hundred meters upstream of the douar—a narrow fault between the Addar and the Ahori, whose northern slopes, moderately wooded, do not recall in any respect the grim desert-like ranges which seal the Imlil basin. The Angoun is invisible; perhaps it will not appear again before Iknioul—perhaps not before the plain . . .

The mule path crosses the five douars of the Aït Mezdou one after the other, then proceeds along the wadi, at times running on the shores, at others twenty or so meters above the irrigated fields. It proceeds along the wadi nearly the whole time as far as Iknioul, except when, rising up the left bank, it cuts across a rocky escarpment which the valley, slanting off at a right angle, seems to want to circle around to the east.

The footpath climbs above the forest. The old man is walking in the lead, taciturn, contenting himself with delivering a blow of his bludgeon periodically against his mule's rump. The animal in any case is following on its own all the detours and zigzags of a trail with which it surely has been familiar for a long while. Even without anyone behind it, it would most likely reach Iknioul this evening as planned.

Ba Iken brings up the rear, his still damp burnoose folded up on the edge of the packsaddle. His gandoura and shoes have suffered somewhat, but his khaki sheche is intact. Now and then Ba Iken whips his mount's neck with a sharp, brisk flick of his wrist. He whistles a tune, a straw blade between his teeth . . . This evening he will be in Iknioul and tomorrow he will take the same route again in the opposite direction. He will most likely spend the night once more in Timirit at Si Abdesselam's. Friday he will go back up toward Imlil, just as he went up to Imlil two weeks before, from Assameur to Tafrent, from Tafrent to the tizi n'Arfamane where he met up with the engineer, then, along with him, from Ouzli to Tisselli at Sheikh Agouram's, and the next day from Tisselli to Asguine, the whole day long in the forest and across rocky terrain, under the relentless sun, up to the tizi n'Oualoun where they arrived at nightfall . . .

Upon reaching the pass, the footpath widens: actually it merges with a pebbly glacis spreading from one slope to the other along the whole stretch of the passage. Ba Iken quickens his pace, moves up alongside Lassalle, pulls his animal next to his. He smiles: "Is everything all right, Mr. Lassalle?"

Lassalle glimpsed, upon the quickly turned away face, only the blue eyes and two gold, strictly symmetrical teeth. Ba Iken has already passed ahead. He is chatting with the old man and now appears in profile: the nose, very straight, rather short, the forehead high; the blond beard with glints of red nearly covers his whole cheek and the rim of his chin. He is humming, a straw blade between the lips . . . Tomorrow he will set out again for Imlil, will go back up the course of the torrent as far as the gorges between the Addar and the Ahori, as he went back up it perhaps one month before, escorting the foreigner from Iknioul to Timirit, and the next day from Timirit to Asguine, and still farther upstream of Asguine, on the footpath to the pass, up to the tree to the right of the trail, under which he helped set up the tent after dark . . .

Several days later, all that remained was the trace of the stakes on the cracked ground, a small square block of darkened earth, and the leather case buried in the oleander bush . . .

At present, the case has disappeared. All that remains are the holes in the ground under the pistachio, similar to the other holes in the ground, a little farther on under the walnut, on the side of the spring . . .

— How are things, Mr. Lassalle? It's not as hard today!

Ba Iken stopped at the border of the first trees.

— If you want, we are going to have lunch and rest here. Iknioul is not very far . . . We get in around five o'clock: you set up your tent and I go to see if I can find a car. Today's the souk; tomorrow, maybe there's a truck going back to Assameur.

Ba Iken helps Lassalle get off the mule. The old man begins to untie the bags.

All the way below, downstream of the meander, the wadi flows between two rows of cornfields. Farther on, beyond the gray-green smoothly rolling wooded crests, a blue and pink sheet stretches to the outer edges of a whitish zone—the plain, where at times a point shimmers, darts a flame and goes out: a puddle of water, the windshield of a truck, a steel blade . . .

IV

Soon it will be an hour since everything has been ready: the nine or ten passengers squeezed onto the bench seats, their baggage—suitcases, sacks of grain, bird hampers, straw baskets of pottery—piled up very high on the roof and held in place by a thick rope, the vehicle—people call it the "taxi"—already pointing, at the far end of the souk, toward the trail that emerges in the north between two brushwood hedges.

But the driver—in a red shirt, black seroual, a green wool-knit bonnet

—has disappeared once again inside the Moorish café. Everyone is patiently waiting for him to come back out.

The brown parched earth—the storm passed farther to the south yesterday—is strewn with sheaves of straw, wooden planks, perforated baskets, crushed olives and rotted vegetables. A few small donkeys are still hitched in a small enclosure. Dogs come and go in the slaughter-yard, their tongues lolling, their eyes half-closed. A horse led by a young boy proceeds along the séguia up to a cement slab serving as a trough.

The "taxi" is a small fifteen-seat bus. Its dark blue paint, filthy and peeling, bares large patches of rust. The carriage leans sharply left-ward; seen in profile, it dips markedly toward the hood which, as an extra precaution, is fixed in place by two long patchwork straps. A double door located in the rear of the vehicle opens onto the wooden bench seats. Four words are painted in black, above the windows, on a lateral yellow strip: "Assameur—El Arba—Iknioul," followed (or rather preceded) with the original Arabic characters.

— El Arba is another souk in the plain. The taxi goes to the Arba on Wednesdays and up to Iknioul on Thursdays. It returns to Assameur the same evening, or else it leaves only the next morning . . . You were lucky it stayed.

Ba Iken has arranged everything with the driver. The old man has already set off on the Iknioul road with his two mules.

Lassalle once again thanks Ba Iken, then uncovers his head and holds out the forage cap:

— I was going to forget to give you back your property! . . .

Ba Iken smiles and puts the cap away in his choukara.

— For the next trip I'll think to buy a hat!

The driver comes out of the Moorish café, cigarette in lips, and suddenly in a hurry, heads with swift steps for the taxi. One last time Lassalle shakes Ba Iken's hand and goes to sit down on the back bench while the driver turns the crank, succeeds in starting up the motor after several fruitless attempts, then comes to station himself behind the steering wheel.

A large jolt rocks the metallic carcass. The taxi starts moving and immediately draws onto the roadway. Already the dust is spraying up from under the wheels.

In front of the Moorish café, at the boundary of the souk, directly in the road axis, a small group watches the vehicle recede into the distance. Standing in the shade, leaning back against the facade wall, a little off to the side, nearly at the corner of the building, Ba Iken gestures in farewell. He is looking straight ahead, toward the car, toward the men who are leaving, or more simply toward the dusty foliage of the fig trees bordering the road. His right arm is waving: the left, armed with a switch, is mechanically whipping the folds of his gandoura.

Then it all disappears at the first bend: the Moorish café, the douar itself, except for the casbah on the hill overlooking the souk, not far from the terrace where the tent had been set up that night in the shade of the carob trees.

The roadway follows the valley for a dozen kilometers. The taxi progresses along, bumping over the ruts, beeping at the slightest obstacle, even though the din of its loosely fastened metal sheets gives warning far in advance of its arrival. Behind, a thick streak of dust throws up a screen between the valley and the backcountry.

At the end of a half-hour, the taxi slows down and stops at a cross-roads. A wooden post indicates, on the right panel: "El Arba, Ten Kilometers," and on the left, "Assameur, Twenty Kilometers." Two men get on, sit in the back seat, and Lassalle huddles against the window.

The taxi sets out again, turns left and, leaving the valley, begins to climb through the forest along a narrow road where it seems impractical to pass by other travelers. The ground is very uneven: the surface is broken by limestone layers which the runoff has stripped and isolated with a complex network of rivulets. The motor wheezes along in second gear, then in first, and the vehicle crawls upward, tossing from one pothole to another. The curves are so short that the driver must often maneuver in reverse one or two times to get around them.

The odors go right to one's head and make it spin: odors of cumin, mint, rancid olive oil, sweat and grime, drowned by those even more sickening smells of gasoline fumes and sheets of overheated metal which stream in nauseating whiffs from the back of the vehicle. The heat is stifling; one single window out of six is lowered; the others are wedged in their frames, their handles twisted or broken. An elbow does not even have room enough to lean on the window ledge. Inevitably the eyes close, the head rolls forward and the forehead bumps the rattling window with every large jolt. From time to time, at imprecise intervals, the valley appears down below, between two holm oak bushes, then the eyes close once again.

At a given moment, the taxi, rolling up upon the right embankment, slowly moves past a car which has parked between two boulders to facilitate the vehicle's passing: the driver in a khaki gandoura, standing in the middle of the roadway, gives advice on how to maneuver, supervised by the passenger, seated in the rear of the car, face pressed against the window.

Then the taxi regains speed and the purring of the motor, the reverberations, and the merciless glare of the sky work swiftly to stir up the nausea again.

A little later, the vehicle is motionless, its wheels firmly sunk in the ruts. The road is flat. The strident racket of the crickets drowns out the noise of the idling motor. Three or four travelers have stepped off. Leaning over the hood, the driver pours the contents of a large can into the radiator. The people go back to their places on the bench seats. The forehead begins to bump the window, the elbow to slip off each time it tries to hold itself on the window ledge, the odor of gasoline to supplant in waves those of the spices interpenetrating the clothing.

It is as if the old bus had been creeping along for hours through the scrub, along this roadway which could have been that of the first stage, two weeks earlier, if the sergeant's minivan (or any other available vehicle) had had business that day in Iknioul, instead of in Tafrent.

The valley—but perhaps this is not the same valley anymore—spreads out far below: a dry wadi bed separates two vast strips of bluish foliage. The road descends gently along the mountainside, then the angle of inclination becomes more pronounced, the holm oak bushes are substituted by rows of Barbary fig trees. A house looms up, and soon after about a dozen others: the taxi crosses a cob-built douar, then fallow fields and a second, larger douar, on the way out of which olive trees file past on the roadside.

A few hundred meters farther on, Lassalle recognizes the forking of the roadways, then the ramparts with the storks' nests perched on the merlons of the crenels.

The taxi proceeds along the tufts of castor oil plants at the foot of the ramparts, then, honking long and hard, edges its way through a solid crowd of men in turbans, of women in vivid dresses, and of children balanced on bicycles without brakes. The jackasses placidly draw off along the verges, but the mules circle around themselves, panicked by the clanking metal, or buck out of control, casting their riders to the ground. As for the rare camels, they remain unrattled, stationed directly in the middle of the path, or break into a pointless gallop.

The taxi penetrates the Assameur souk and stops in the main thoroughfare behind a large empty bus.

Climbing a ladder, the driver unties the rope binding the baggage to the roof, and one by one holds out the straw baskets, hampers, and suitcases to their owners, then takes down Lassalle's bags and deposits them between the bus seats. After which he locks the doors.

— I'm going up to the Office in an hour. If you want to eat, you have the time to go to the canteen.

The driver gestures vaguely with his arm toward the médina and recedes into the crowd.

It is eleven-thirty . . . The heat, odors, noise, and absence of ventilation within the vehicle ended up by triggering a heavy, devious migraine. To go to the canteen means traveling a good kilometer on foot, entering the médina, sitting down in front of a plate of tough lamb and shriveled fried potatoes . . . To wait here means lingering in the souk in the dust and the crush of people . . . Lassalle looks for a third prospect, but does not find it. So he sets about searching for a patch of shade in the souk.

A few meters from the main thoroughfare, puddles of blood and scraps of meat soil the terreplein of the slaughterhouse where a dog lies, flattened on its side across the drain furrow. Another dog ventures on the cement slab, its fur sticky, its tongue lolling. But the man who slaughters the dogs is no longer in the area.

Opposite is the string of crates serving as butcher stalls. Very close to the souk entrance, on the mountainside, the circular lane begins which leads, between two rows of oil and spice merchants, to the small white structure where the sergeant had done the honors and shown him around. Neither the sergeant nor the captain is there. Perhaps they have already left . . . But the crowd is such that you can barely recognize anyone until coming up nose to nose with him.

The other branch of the circular lane is reserved for the craftsmen, whose works are exposed flush against the ground in compartments blocked off by low walls of packed dirt: shoemakers, slipper makers, weavers, coppersmiths, tanners, blacksmiths, and finally potters, whose glaze, this week, has come out of the ovens with a dark green hue, grained with black and white dots.

Lassalle draws near and examines the oil lamps, the perfume burners, the ink pots, the candlestick holders which the potter presents to him. On the point of deciding on a perfume burner, in the left-hand corner of the compartment he spies, buried amid the unglazed utensils, a smoker which in every way resembles the one Idder held at arm's length one evening while crossing the Imi n'Oucchène.

The potter, at first crestfallen, follows with his eyes the finger designating the object in the heap of minor products, bends down and, elated, hands over the instrument to Lassalle who puts it under his arm and holds out a bill in payment. The potter, in high spirits, gives back a few coins while nodding, then, taking his colleagues as witnesses to the transaction, breaks into a playful, voluble commentary which his customer, dumbfounded, cuts short with a knowing smile and a swift gesture of farewell.

Lassalle then attempts to directly return to his departure point across the block of stalls of the fruit and vegetable merchants. There he gets lost, circles around the grain merchants' area, makes an about-turn, retraces his steps back toward the fruit and vegetables, while passing through buys a measure of olives, toasted almonds and a slice of watermelon covered with flies, finally glimpses the line of buses, ten meters from him, dashes forward and finds himself back on the main thoroughfare.

Seated on a stone wall in the shade of the taxi, he nibbles a few olives, then devours the slice of watermelon.

The driver returns only a half-hour later. While he is starting up the motor, Lassalle wraps the smoker in his jacket, puts it away in his clothing bag and sits on the first bench.

When a half-dozen travelers have taken their seats, the taxi sets off, once again edging its way through the mob, crosses the souk portal and emerges a little farther on the asphalt-paved road coming from the médina.

The pace accelerates at once and the vehicle begins to zigzag in the olive grove around the plots of land and stands of trees. Coming off a curve, the facade wall of the infirmary, blindingly white, suddenly appears to the left of the road, then the front steps near which the patients wait in single file, finally the olive tree under which the captain had stopped his car, fifteen days before, upon spotting the gathering—the olive tree from which the car set off again, a few minutes later to drive to the souk, starting up, climbing up the roadway, moving past the wall before which only a group of three men remained, surrounding the old man: two of them had their backs turned to the road; the third, cigarette in lips, was leaning against a mule.

Already the road is turning—the building wheels away into the distance and slips behind a curtain of trees—dropping toward the wadi, which it crosses on the single-lane bridge. At the bottom of the dry torrent, tufts of oleander bristle between the boulders.

The taxi ascends the right bank with difficulty, reenters the olive grove and moves toward the hill upon which the Office rises, the red barracks of the men-at-arms and the modest residences in the shade of the eucalyptus.

V

The migraine is there, yet once again, a morning migraine, which persisted through sleep, sharpened by a three-hour ride in the wheezing bus, under the light refracted by the white sky, surrounded by intermingling odors—those familiar smells of cloth and baskets, and the other one, forgotten for two weeks, filtering from the front of the vehicle, cradled by the listless vibrations of the air above the hood.

The migraine was already there, this morning, upon waking up. The night, which was too short, too restless, did not repair the wear and tear of the journey. Quite the opposite, the gust of scorching air which greeted him upon entering the lowlands, once the protective screen of the high summits was crossed, plunged the organism into a state of complete prostration. It was not a good idea to leave on an empty stomach: a light meal could have allayed the rising pain, whereas at present this cramp in midforehead, this weight swinging from one temple to the other at the border of the eye sockets leaves little cause for hope.

The small door at the back of the courtyard opens on the captain's office. But the office is deserted. The orderly explains that the captain is not there anymore: he went away on leave last week. His assistant is replacing him. The lieutenant is going to be back at any time now. The best thing is to wait for him in his office.

The shutters, drawn over the whole breadth of the bay window, plunge the room into a welcoming coolness and semidarkness. Halfway up the door-flaps, jalousie blinds allow a view, in parallel horizontal strips, of the entire range of foliage set in staggered rows upon the northern slope of the hill: through the lower slits, the fly-covered rosemary bushes; above, bordering the terreplein, the tapering stems and long leaves, partly fence-enclosed, of the poinsettias; farther off on the slopes, the glazed balls of the carob trees, the almond trees, the light green of the Aleppo pines; finally through the upper slits, the muddy specks of the eucalyptus on each side of the road climbing the hillside from the olive grove on the plain, down below, up to the small square where the administrative buildings are grouped.

The three chairs with adjustable backs are lined up side by side in front of the bay window, facing the fireplace from which the pottery has disappeared; the mantelshelf is covered with ledgers, forms, and technical reviews. The substitution was probably carried out only after the captain left: the assistant lost no time in upsetting his commander's arrangements, even those purely decorative in nature. The deep-pile wool carpet has given way to a woven mat of red circles and diamonds. The two global views of Assameur have disappeared. All that remains, beside the large survey ordinance map pinned behind the desk, is the portrait of the general, in three-quarters profile, right hand raised horizontally to the cap visor.

The door opens without any sound in the courtyard having warned that someone was approaching. A man enters, tall and skinny, the sleeves of his khaki shirt rolled up to the elbows, with eyes protected by black glasses. He closes the door and comes forward, helped along by a steel-tipped cane.

— Lieutenant Waton!

He raises his hand to his cap, then holds it out to Lassalle, sets his cane and cap on the mantel, goes around the desk and sits on the swivel chair.

— I believe we've already met.

— You must be mistaken, Lieutenant. I saw Captain Weiss when I arrived.

The officer takes off his glasses, sets them on the blotter, stares at his visitor for a moment, then takes out a handkerchief from one of his trouser pockets and begins to slowly clean the dusty lenses.

— Yes, indeed. That's correct . . . The captain himself drew my attention to your passing through. I got mixed up, at the time . . .

He removes the worst of the dust, then breathes on the inner face of the glasses and meticulously wipes off the fog with a corner of his handkerchief, controlling at every second the smooth operation of the task, his extended arm slanting toward the window, his glasses level with his forehead.

— Yet I should not have . . .

He rubs the glasses a moment longer, then sets them back on the blotter.

— It was a geologist whom I met with . . . A geologist who had come through shortly before you did. A foreigner, whose name was . . .

— Lessing.

— That's it, Lessing. Do you know him?

— No, not at all, but Captain Weiss had spoken to me about him, in this very spot, with regard to my itinerary in the mountains.

— He got killed on his way down the southern slope. An accident . . . The news was relayed to me only within the last few days . . .

Lassalle, uneasy facing the fireplace, moves his chair forward a few centimeters and shifts it more to the left toward the desk.

The lieutenant passes in review the pile of dossiers rising beside the lamp, chooses one among them, opens it and begins to consult it.

— Lessing . . . He had come through twelve days before you . . . I must have noted the exact date somewhere.

He rapidly runs through the first items of the dossier, then takes a key ring from his pocket, opens one of the right-hand drawers, takes out a large strap-bound file which he sets in front of him, undoes the strap and after shuffling around a little, exhibits a leaf of blue paper covered with handwritten signs.

— Here we are . . . I had noted it all down . . . He had arrived exactly on July twenty-third . . . Left the next day toward Iknioul . . . Wanted to study the Imlil basin and the northern face of the Angoun, then go down to Assameur by way of Ouzli or else, if he had any time left, pass along the southern slope and then reach the Ksar el Jdid post.

Lieutenant Waton closes the file, puts it back in the drawer, then picks up the dossier, which he examines again for a few moments before pulling out a yellow folder containing two letters, the first with an official letterhead, typewritten across the entire width of the page, the second handwritten, arranged in two columns: on the left the original Arabic, on the right the translation. He joins the blue sheet to the two previous items and rereads the text of the bilingual letter.

Lassalle gets up, once more adjusts the direction his seat is facing and sits back down, now opposite the desk.

— He stayed in Imlil five or six days, according to what I was told up there.

— That's right. I had the Khalifa of the Kaid asked for details, as soon as I had word from Ksar el Jdid . . . He stayed in Imlil five days, from which he left on the thirty-first with, as guide, a certain Moha ou Baha, from the Zegda douar. They crossed over the Angoun directly by way of the tizi n'Taazit and camped on the southern slope, a little above the valley of the Aït Tiziatine. August third, the guide came back down to Aguerd, the first douar of the Aït Tiziatine, to ask for help, his boss not having returned the day before from a hike on the Amsoud djebel . . . They found the body on the afternoon of the fifth and brought it back on the sixth to Aguerd, where the authorities of Ksar el Jid came to get him.

— But the . . . Were they able to . . . establish how things had happened?

— Things?

— The accident? Were they able to find out exactly what took place? How he had been able . . .

— Oh, it's a quite simple matter. The unfortunate fellow was unlucky . . . Surely, he did something foolish. That mountain is very dangerous: the rock is rotted, unstable . . . All there is are loose stones, walls crumbling to pieces . . . A firm foothold is impossible. The schist . . . Every year there are accidents of this type . . . And what's more, setting out alone, that way, all day long . . . It's really not very sensible . . .

Lassalle moves up to the very edge of the chair, leans forward, elbows on knees, and hands joined.

— The people of Asguine spoke to me about an . . . "engineer" who had gone through there shortly before . . . most likely the one the captain had referred to . . . At any rate, one day I found, quite by accident, an object which belonged to him, a camera case . . . He had lost it, or dropped it . . .

— And you have it here?

— Unfortunately no. I lost it when crossing the wadi at the Aït Mezdou, the day before yesterday. A big storm broke and we had no end of trouble passing across . . . One of my bags got ripped after falling in the water: some of my things were swept away, including the case . . . There was a name on a card inside the lid . . . I wanted to hand it over to you, naturally . . . Now, I believe it is lost for good . . .

— And where had you found it?

— At Imi n'Oucchène, Lieutenant.

— Imi n'Oucchène?

— It's a sort of natural bridge across the Imlil assif.

— Ah yes, I see . . . It has been mentioned to me, but I haven't had the time yet to get out there.

— He must have forgotten it there, or dropped it . . .

The lieutenant rips off a page from his notepad and scribbles a few words.

— Nevertheless it's curious that you stumbled upon it . . .

— Yes, it was really by chance . . . I don't have it anymore, unfortunately . . . I found it at the end of last week.

— In any case, the unfortunate fellow was already dead by that time . . .

The officer writes another line or two, then files the sheet in the yellow folder, after the three previous pages.

— It was a mishap, of course. Carelessness as well . . . To set out like that, all alone . . . A mountain that is still not known very well, difficult . . . The sun, storms, . . . An extreme foolhardiness . . .

— What campsite in Imlil did they indicate to you?

The lieutenant picks up the bilingual letter.

— The Zegda douar.

— Yes, that's what I was told. In the Zegda douar . . . On the other side of the Imlil assif, on the right bank, a little farther down than Imi n'Oucchène . . .

Lassalle settles more comfortably into the chair, shoulders leaning on the leather back, hands set flat upon the armrests.

Behind the desk, along the whole breadth of the panel, stretches the large ordinance survey map encompassing the mountainous massif in its entirety, a triangular portion of the plain in the northwest and in the southeast the onset of the high desert plateaus. The Assameur region is hidden by the lieutenant's left shoulder, but farther to the east the whole itinerary of the return trip is visible, from Iknioul to the Aït Mezdou, and farther down the eastern half of the white zone, which ought to represent the Angoun, the Addar, the Ahori, the Imlil cirque and its three torrents . . . More southward the three lines reappear, the hatchings and the contour lines. A thin blue stroke descends from the mountains toward the oases: the valley of the Aït Tiziatine, most likely.

— Does the mountain you were speaking about just now figure on the map, Lieutenant?

— The Asmoud djebel? I don't think so . . .

Lieutenant Waton swivels his seat around, turns toward the wall map and, without getting up, follows with his finger the blue stroke to the south of the white patch.

— Here are the Aït Tiziatine . . . No, you see: the map stops a little before Aguerd. The Asmoud is southeast of the Angoun. It can't be seen on the map.

He turns back around, swivels his seat, puts the yellow folder back into the dossier, replaces the dossier on the pile near the lamp and begins to wipe his glasses again, but the outer faces of the lenses this time, upon which he huffs quickly and repeatedly, his mouth pouting.

— And with regard to your work, did you end up with something interesting?

— Yes, I think so. I laid the groundwork for a relatively simple project, which ought not to entail any enormous difficulties to carry out . . . It will certainly raise fewer objections than the preceding ones.

— We are taking a great interest in this new trail, as you can well imagine. Everyone will benefit. And ever since the matter was first raised . . .

— The road I traced crosses the entire plateau from Asguine to Imi n'Oucchène before going up to the vein. It passes over the natural bridge . . .

— Do you want to have trucks drive across it?

— Why yes, there's no reason why not, it's quite wide enough!

— Oh yes, undoubtedly . . . In any case, the essential thing for us is that the trail reach Imlil . . . Listen . . . Could you send me a brief word on this subject? It would be very useful to me . . . Something clear and succinct . . . Won't you? You would be doing me a great favor . . .

The corner of the handkerchief passes and repasses over the smoky glass which his right hand brandishes now and then toward the window to verify that the smudges and fingerprints have been completely wiped away.

— Do you plan on leaving today?

— No, Lieutenant. I must telephone Dar el Hamra for a vehicle to be sent for me tomorrow morning. As a matter of fact, I wanted to ask you if you would find it possible . . .

— For tonight? Yes, of course. The room is free. I'll give orders for it to be prepared.

The officer rings for the orderly, who appears at once in the door frame and stands stiffly at attention. After a quick exchange in Arabic, the lieutenant turns toward Lassalle:

— It's settled. He's going to put the room in order. The best thing is for him to go with you now. He'll carry your baggage.

Lassalle thanks the lieutenant and rises. The lieutenant rises as well, slips on his glasses, comes around the desk and, passing in front of the mantel, picks up his cap and steel-tipped cane.

The door opens again on the courtyard, oppressed by the heat and light. Drawing level with the porch, Lieutenant Waton takes leave of Lassalle and goes off to the left along a lane lined with flamboyants.

Lassalle finds himself in the rectangular yard around which the administrative buildings are grouped: barracks on the left—a long wall coated with red roughcast, bracketed by towers on each end, with an entrance in the center where a sentinel in a khaki djellaba keeps watch; a cube-shaped edifice with a covered courtyard under which white figures are dozing; a villa with a green tile roof, an acacia bush, a tamarind tree and a clump of aloe. The leaves are covered with a film of red dust. All the walls are of the same purplish red, crumbling, filthy, with long black streaks under the waterspouts.

A hundred meters away the small pavilion rises, opposite the mountain, on the southern slope of the hill.

The orderly pushes open the wooden gate and heads for the door. Not a single blade of grass is growing from the hard cracked soil.

It is one-thirty.

Outside, the temperature is at least 45 degrees centigrade.

VI

The telephone office, grafted onto the left wing of the Office building, is a miniature recess one meter by two: the roughcast is warped, the cement strewn with greasy papers; the only piece of furniture is a garden chair which the worker yields willingly to the user for the entire length of wait, more bearable in spite of everything within these windowless premises than outside in the broad sunlight. The operator remains standing the whole while, leaning back against the index board, fez askew, humming a kind of twangy recitative, with lips open a crack and eyes half-closed.

The call is put through to Dar el Hamra within forty minutes—a particularly brief delay, to judge by the employee's triumphant expression. Everything is settled quickly with the Company: a car will leave tomorrow morning at daybreak to arrive in Assameur around seven-thirty.

The afternoon is drawing to a close: it is six o'clock; the shadows lengthen upon the gray dust. Under the building with the arcade, the white figures have gotten up and are waiting in single file.

The wooden fence has remained open; the sun still lights the greater part of the hard, cracked dirt courtyard.

The entrance door opens directly onto the bathroom, where a few hours earlier the orderly deposited the bags, swept the floor tiles and verified that the shower worked smoothly—and immediately after he left, a siesta imposed itself as an absolute necessity: begun in a long, half-conscious state of suffocation, punctuated with heart palpitations and sudden waves of sweat, it issued upon an imperceptible, uncertain awakening, subsiding and rising up again to the point of exasperation. The migraine did not dissipate for all of that: henceforth it rules a nauseating dizziness, wherein the wear and tear of the journey merge with the disorders following upon the change in the climate.

In the bathroom, the bags have been laid side by side along the closet, the two towels, still damp from the shower, spread out to dry on the edge of the bathtub. Above the sink, the slightly warped mirror reflects a more drawn face, a complexion barely colored by the mountain sun, hair which is too long, a wild grayish beard, stiffly bristling and destined this very evening for the razor. The window is closed; the shutters are drawn, but the brightness filtering between the cracks is sufficient to light up the room.

In the bedroom, everything is closed up as well: the small window looking out on the garden and the shutter flaps which were repaired, or changed, since the other day. In the upper half of each panel, a section carved out in the shape of a five-point star allows a beam of light to penetrate.

The bed, pulled for the siesta to the middle of the room, has resumed its original position in the corner between the window and the vestibule door. The painted night table still occupies the same place against the head of the bed. The piece of candle stuck into the Roman lamp has only two or three centimeters left: large beads have flowed onto the mauve glaze. Between the window and the fireplace, the cane chair has been replaced by a wicker armchair with leather-covered armrests and a swivel back. On the mantelpiece are the same ocher glazed candle holders arranged symmetrically at each end of the shelf.

Through the windowpane, the mosquito mesh, and the openwork stars of the shutter, a corner of the garden appears—the palm tree on its clump hemmed around with tufts of holly, then a fragment of the outer wall topped with the green balustrade—and, much farther away, all the way at the bottom, the first rows of the olive trees. The view does not extend to Assameur: it stops midway from the olive grove.

The sun is still high over the plain: the sun rays touch the yellow block tiles of the plinth between the closet and bathroom doors. Higher up, a map is pinned to the wall—a map of the mountain, furrowed with crosshatchings and dark patches—right in the middle of the panel, in the spot where had been hanging the other week that gray image, that blurry engraving representing a shore in the foreground, an inlet, waves breaking on the reefs and farther away, on the open sea, a long rolling line of foam, like a subsiding tumult or the harbinger of a tempest. But the contours were faded, and the memory is as imprecise as the image was itself the evening he arrived, when, in the half-light, it was reduced to a sheaf of curved lines suggesting in turn a large insect, a sheer rocky landscape, or a creeper with branching offshoots. . . .

The engraving has been removed; its hazy aesthetic character did not really blend with the pavilion's sober geometry. A map of the mountain has been substituted in its place, a rectangular sheet extracted from the survey ordinance map, entitled "Assameur," in every point similar to the one still to be found in the bag, after having withstood its immersion in the swollen torrent. All the same, the imprint is more recent: the features are better delineated, the blue of the streams more marked, the green of the forests more vivid. The paper is not wrinkled and bears no trace of creasing; at the very most, the sheet was rolled up before being affixed to the wall. But it is indeed the same map, with the same gaps and the same imprecisions.

The black lines of the trails zigzag, south of Assameur, through an apparently depopulated mountain. A blue line—which is already no longer the Imlil assif—climbs the valley of the Aït Mezdou up to the point where it should slip between the Addar and the Ahori, but it drops out of sight into the uncharted zone, even whiter and emptier than on the old crumpled map, a result most likely of the clearer and more careful reproduction of the present edition. And farther down, to the south, on the other side of the white patch, along the exact theoretical extension of the preceding line, another torrent springs up, draining the southern slope of the Angoun, soon irrigating the Aït Tiziatine. A few douars are mentioned along the valley, but the first one, the one Lieutenant Waton spoke about, is not figured on it: Aguerd is probably nothing more than a miniscule hamlet stuck in a hillside—four or five gourbis concealed by tufts of jujube.

Aguerd is the highest douar of the Aït Tiziatine. That is the place where the authorities of Ksar el Jdid came to pick up Lessing's body.

Lessing did something foolish: he had a fall . . . He had a shaky hold; his foot slipped, a chunk of rock broke away, the body began to fall along the rock face. He was found at the bottom of a ravine, on the eastern face of the Asmoud djebel, his neck broken by a large rock. When the people of the douar arrived, jackals were sniffing the cadaver, jackdaws and vultures were hovering over the spot.

Aguerd does not figure on the map, but can be located more than a kilometer from the preceding douar, that is just at the border of the white zone, some five kilometers from the crests of the Angoun. The sole passage on the Angoun is found above the Imlil gorges: Ba Iken spoke about it as of a risky journey, fraught with peril . . .

The mule path going up from Imi n'Oucchène passes very close by the entrance to the gorges, slants southeastward and ascends onto the shelf. "It passes along the southern slope. But it's very hard. The pass is very high in the rocks. You must dismount; you can't continue along on muleback . . ." The climb from Imi n'Oucchène to the pass should require at least four hours, the climb down upon the Aït Tiziatine five or six, that is a maximum of ten hours for the total trip (eleven, actually, if you leave from Zegda, and twelve if you leave from Asguine). But the southern slope is perhaps easier . . . "It goes into the southern tribes, upon Ksar el Jdid. It's very far: it takes two days from Imlil." Ba Iken surely reckoned on it taking two days to go as far as Ksar el Jdid. Otherwise, ten or twelve hours ought to be sufficient to reach Aguerd, by day as well as by night—there was moonlight that week, very early in the evening . . .

"They directly crossed the Angoun by way of the tizi n'Taazit". . . Setting out from Imlil on July thirty-first, they must have passed the watershed at the end of the afternoon and camped that very evening above Aguerd. So they had been there for two days and three nights when the guide came down to seek help, on August third—and Lessing would have had a fall the day before (the second), or the day before that (the day after arriving), unless it happened the very day of the journey, or just before leaving . . .

Whatever the case may be, the body was found on the fifth and brought back to Aguerd on the sixth, "where the authorities came to pick it up." But when? The seventh? The eighth? And what were they able to do, other than to certify that the death had occurred several days before—at least five days, but possibly six or seven—and make note of the statements of the people of Aguerd, specifying that they had discovered the body in such and such a ravine, that the tent had been set up in such and such a place, in the vicinity of such and such a footpath? As for everything else, they were reduced to recording the guide's naked assertions, the sole companion and sole witness of the last days of the hike.

By way of compensation, numerous witnesses were assembled on the foreigner's campsite in Imlil. The information communicated by the Kaid is unambiguous: Lessing had stationed himself in the Zegda douar. But the Kaid himself did not go to Zegda; what's more, he was absent from the tribe. His Khalifa did not put himself out either: he commissioned the chief of the tribal group with the task of the investigation, namely (the nominal sheikh having gone off to make a pilgrimage) Sheikh Agouram. And everyone testified that Lessing camped in Zegda.

Not in Zegda proper: a little downstream of Zegda. "There are some walnut trees, farther down, in the irrigated zone. They aren't like Asguine's, but they still cast a little shade"... Ichou had marked a pause, then designated with his finger, under the tree, the traces left by the stakes in the cracked ground. Would he renew his gesture before the people of the tribe? Would he confirm the revelations provoked perhaps, that previous evening, by the resentment resulting from a very recent quarrel? It is highly unlikely. And would he do so if it meant that his testimony would stand alone?

Besides, the case disappeared, swept away by the torrent's waters. Of course, neither Ichou nor Ba Iken would deny having seen the object, but Ba Iken was not present at the time of discovery, and Ichou could also pretend that he no longer remembers the exact spot where it had been found. Furthermore, since neither one nor the other knows how to read, one person alone could confirm having deciphered the owner's name.

As for the precise dates of Lessing's stay in Imlil, Ba Iken, upon being questioned again, would have an easy time proving evasive and even casting doubt upon the answers he had provided the day of the diffa at the sheikh's.

In any case, the Kaid's investigation clearly indicates that Lessing arrived in Imlil in the last week of July. Sheikh Agouram most surely took great pains to secure every guarantee relevant to his work. His report coincides exactly with the witnesses' statements: Lessing arrived in Imlil on the twenty-sixth, stationed himself in Zegda, set off the thirty-first toward the south, got killed on August second on the eastern slope of the Asmoud, on another tribe's territory, under the jurisdiction of another Kaid . . . The third or the fourth, a certain "Jamila bent X" . . . was the victim, in Ifechtalen, of conflicting passions: stabbed twice with a dagger by her husband, she expired on the sixth in the infirmary at Assameur. As for the murderer, he fled: he left the tribe; God knows where he is hiding . . . But that belongs to another investigation, for which Sheikh Agouram also had to take every precaution. And no one in "high places" drew a connection between the two incidents.

No one could have done so for that matter, unless it was by sheer chance, the official reports having taken care to localize the events in such a manner that the bonds that could unite them were stretched to the breaking point. As a result of having its spatial elements exploded, the problem became insoluble, the very urgency of the problem unapparent. And, when all is said and done, among all the characters mixed up in the action, two alone are found officially mentioned: the two victims.

From this perspective, the Kaid's version is perfect. Since it also benefits from general approval, it is positioned at the outset—in the absence of proof to the contrary—safe from any attack.

Lieutenant Waton replaced the Kaid's report inside the yellow folder and put it back into the dossier. Brought to his attention once more, he would pick up the bilingual correspondence again, reread the conclusions of the investigation, make inquiries concerning any allegedly discordant data. But what concrete facts to oppose it with? The gesture of a mute child? A lost object, found, then lost again? Two dates conforming with each other? The identity of two pairs of gazing eyes? The memory of awkward lies?

Perhaps at this very moment Ba Iken, come down to Assameur by some way or other—he would have had the time since this morning, even on muleback—is keeping watch over the small pavilion, or the Office entry, a hundred meters away? Perhaps he sent someone to do the watching in his place? . . . But no, Ba Iken had no doubts about the outcome of the debate, even less so since he supposedly is unaware of Ichou's admissions . . . As soon as the bus disappeared at the first bend, he set back along on the Imlil path, switch in hand, cigarette in lips . . . The "Lessing dossier" will remain pending until the captain gets back, who will then rapidly familiarize himself with it, then routinely file it in the office a hundred steps from the pavilion, on the other side of the hill, on the side looking out on the plain . . . Lessing fell from the top of a cliff, on the eastern slope of the Asmoud djebel (the tribe of the Aït . . . the Ksar el Jdid Office), during the course of an especially ill-advised, solitary survey mission . . .

The Asmoud djebel does not figure on the map either. It is located to the southeast of the Angoun, below and to the right of the white patch. A little farther down the mountain reappears, the high desert plateaus, the valleys where the populace stretches out along the intermittent waterways . . . The paper is smooth, spotless, and bears no crease marks. At the very most it was rolled up before being pinned to the bedroom wall, in the middle of the panel, between the closet and the bathroom doors.

The sun beams now strike the wall, at a point equidistant from the plinth and the lower edge of the map. They penetrate the room horizontally by way of the star-shaped openwork of the shutters.

The sun is on the point of disappearing behind the row of hills separating the plain from the olive grove. At the other end of the basin, bluish streaks spiral upward above the terrace roofs of Assameur.

Leaning to the left upon the whitewashed window ledge, the three superimposed crest lines can be distinguished, and in the background, dominating them all, standing out clearly against the white sky, a gigantic sheer-sided bastion: the Angoun, with its grayish slopes, glistening in places, deeply incised by gullies.

At the foot of the terminal arête Imlil lies hidden—a large mountainous cirque, with narrow valleys, high casbahs slit with loopholes, and rare trees here and there, vestiges of forests, landmarks in the rocky terrain.

VII

Each page of the pocket diary sums up in a few lines four days of activities, each block retracing a fragment of the journey, a stage in the progress of the work, an investigation, a failure, a success.

An account of the last four:

"Wednesday the eighteenth.—Left Asguine at eight o'clock. Stopped downstream of Ifechtalen, at the entry to the defile. Storm. Forded the Imlil assif at the Aït Mezdou. Night in the Timirit douar."

"Thursday the nineteenth.—Left Timirit at nine o'clock. Arrived in Iknioul at five o'clock. Night under tent in the vicinity of the douar."

"Friday the twentieth.—Left Iknioul by bus. Arrived at eleven-thirty at the Assameur souk, at one at the Office. Interview with the captain's assistant. Night in the Headquarters' guest room."

"Saturday the twenty-first.—Left at seven-thirty for Dar el Hamra."

. . . seventeen blocks henceforth bear witness to the complete circuit, in the form of succinct notes which, upon reading, will later allow the facts to be reconstituted in their day-to-day detail: arriving in Assameur, the first contact with the mountain, setting up camp in Asguine, the fruitless attempts to reach the goal directly, the discovery of the natural bridge, the study which traced a trail across it, the trials and errors, the doubts, the ultimate success, going back down to Iknioul, returning to Assameur.

These short sentences will help memory, if the case arises, to weave a tighter web of the various episodes. The essential thing is to avoid mixing up dates, recording information in overlapping blocks, mistakenly ascribing one day's happenings to another, or facing the abrupt void of memory.

Still figuring on the last pages of the tablet are the pencil drawings, awkward but precise, taken from the slabs of the tizi n'Oualoun: clubs, lances, cog wheels, gear parts, suns, as well as the complete reproduction of the engravings on the rib-shaped stone: the man straddling his mount, brandishing the mallet; the child bowed before him, on the right, its hands thrust forward; on the other side, the large reclining body flattened with arms flung wide or buried standing up in the ground; finally the second animal, with raised hoof, which is turning away or receding—five figures engraved upon the stone, one beside the other . . .

The slab was utterly constricted, the available space particularly constrained. The relationship is perhaps due merely to the simple want of space . . .

Once the miniature pencil is slipped into its holder, the leather-bound tablet rejoins, on the night table, the wallet, pipe, tobacco pouch, near the smoker and the Roman lamp whose flame wavers as the hand passes by.

The bed is once again pulled to the center of the room, a good distance from the walls. The window is open, the shutters pushed back and out. Only the mosquito netting interposes itself between the room and the garden, where the temperature has noticeably dropped since nightfall. Brief flows of air filter in between the mesh links and come to caress the forehead, eyes, and freshly shaven cheeks, delivered from their itching discomfort.

The stars, in great numbers at the zenith, are more widely spaced in the west, where the outline of the hills bordering the plain still stands out clearly against the brighter sky.

On the left, in the corner of the garden, the eucalyptus branches are hardly discernible against the background of the high ranges lost in the gloom. Closer by, the palm tree signals its presence only by the intermittent swaying of its lower leaves.

A car passes along the roadway a hundred meters from the small pavilion, but almost at once the streak of the headlights dips down at the point where the road descends. The sound diminishes and holds steady, more softly along the entire loop which the road traces on this slope of the hillside, up to the last bend before the olive grove. Then a double beam of white light shines on the first stands of trees, and shortly afterward arises the rumble of the swiftly accelerating motor. The car speeds headlong between the clumps of olive trees. As the humming recedes and dies, the white patch reappears here and there, at times propelled toward the right, at others toward the left, on one occasion straight forward, probably after the bridge over the wadi, in its climb up toward the infirmary; finally it comes back, the whole range of its beam aslant, along the right line preceding the ramparts, and is extinguished at the entry to the médina. Perhaps it is going to come out again in two or three minutes on the other side of the city, along one of the mountain trails.

In Assameur itself, twenty or so lights twinkle along the walls of the high casbahs. But not one fire is blazing in the south or in the west on the basin rim.

A dog is barking insistently in the distance, as if it were seeking an answer. Since not one creature echoes it, the dog ends up by falling silent. Nearer, at the foot of the hill, the toads are croaking ceaselessly, but their concert, even and monotonous, appears less aggressive than on the first day.

A burning itch at the wrist suddenly recalls the necessity of protecting himself against mosquitoes, the necessity to cover up, to cut himself off from the only source of coolness, to condemn himself to sleep in the damp, stifling, stationary air, impossible to renew. The mosquito netting is still as defective—a badly fitted frame, irregular mesh links—the protection it offers just as paltry.

With the window closed, the croaking of the toads, although deadened, seems to have intensified in its insistence and unflagging tenacity. Outside, an immense glow looms up in the heart of the olive grove; the reflected image of the flame which, agitated by the intake of air, continues to waver weakly on the glazed lamp. But when the forehead draws up against the windowpane, the lights of Assameur spring up again, somewhat distorted by the imperfections of the glass, which make them merge into each other and then unfold over the whole city sky.

The mountain outskirts are still as dark. Not the slightest fire betrays the location of the douars or the trail lines. The car did not come out again from the other side of the ramparts, south of the médina.

Inside the room, objects and furniture parsimoniously distribute the shadows along the walls coated with a dull, grainy, very clean white-wash: the shadow of the armchair, partly on the upright of the fireplace; those of the two candlestick holders in the corner of the wall above the mantelshelf; the shadow of the bed on the black-and-white block tiles, then on the lower third of the panel between the fireplace and the closet; the shadow of the night table on the tiles; and finally, on the wall behind the table, that terra-cotta utensil's shadow, defying the laws of symmetry, with its short sideways handle and its disproportionately swollen spherical mass—the shadow of this smoker spotted for the first time the day after arriving in the captain's office, seen again that very day in the souk from the top of the mahakma's terrace roof, and much later still in Imi n'Oucchène, one evening at sunset, brandished at arm's length like a weapon.

The object is there now, within hand's reach, rediscovered by chance in the souk thanks to the elbow-to-elbow jostling under the relentless sun, extracted for a modest price to the potter's astonishment, shortly after when the captain's assistant had made it disappear from the office mantel in order to substitute a new decorative arrangement: stacks of technical reviews, ledgers and paper forms.

Its color is not actually red, but pink ocher, and when all is said, drab, dull, dark—except for infinitesimal glistening patches—as if the pink (or the red) had been applied on a gray background. The clay is coarse, bumpy, covered with blisters and very tiny bits of gravel.

The tool is essentially composed of a hollow receptacle to which three pieces are added on: a flat bottom providing the instrument with a sturdy base, a kind of neck around the main orifice, and a solid, vaguely cylindrical handle, stuck in sideways at midpoint on the ball, in a position halfway between the perpendicular and the tangential. This ball is spherical only at first estimate: molded on a wheel, with a diameter in the neighborhood of ten centimeters, its form rather recalls that of certain huts or shacks in the bush, slightly cone-shaped and ridged in the middle section. An oval, thumb-sized orifice punctures the globe at a point equidistant from the base and where the handle is attached, a little to the right of the latter. The lip of the neck, analogous to a jug's, is whittled away along its entire rim by a slight chipping. The globe itself, in its upper half, is pierced with several dozen small round holes, on the face of it rather evenly distributed. But their distribution, upon closer inspection, seems regulated by nothing more than two semicircular alignments of two holes each, cutting across each other at right angles at the summit of the sphere. All the other holes have been pierced haphazardly within the confines of the four equal sectors previously established. But since the total number of holes is approximately the same everywhere, the impression of order persists, whereas in reality, outside of the two aforementioned axes, the widespread scattering is a matter of pure anarchy.

A similar absence of method—one even less disguised—presides over the ornamentation of the handle. The basic decorative feature is a chevron composed of two straight dotted lines cutting each other most often at acute angles, but also at right angles and on one occasion on an obtuse angle. A dozen of these chevrons stripe the back of the handle, pointing toward the sphere; but three isolated dotted lines interpolate themselves in the series. Furthermore, several aberrant dotted lines score the left side of the handle, two of which form a cross and two others a square. To the right figure five regular chevrons linked in a garland.

The material itself is molded very roughly and the handle ends in a sort of upturned beak at the prow.

Whether it is considered head-on (the handle sticking out in front), in profile, or even from above (such as it is seen by the user approaching the hive), the most striking feature of the instrument is its complete and permanent asymmetry, principally due, it seems, to the contiguous relationship of the handle and orifice neck, and this independent of the fact that neither of the two elements is perpendicular to the sphere. Indeed, the handle, inclined at a thirty-degree angle, touches the globe at a point slightly higher than the upper edge of the orifice, whereas the distended lip of the neck, a little farther to the right, extends slantwise under the black hole which resembles an empty eye.

The shadow of the sphere traces on the bedroom wall, on the other side of the bed, a large circle truncated at the base, grafted on the left with an atrophied, unexpected protuberance, which at first sight is inexplicable. At first suspended horizontally a short distance from the flame, the smoker produces an immense image stretched flat along the whole length of the panel, then, brandished above the head, a large dark patch which, elongated by the images of the hand and forearm, covers nearly the entire ceiling surface.

The arm drops; the object comes back down to table-level and takes its place again behind the lamp whose flame is tapering down to its last sputter.

In the time it takes to run into the bathroom, rummage blindly through the bag, grab the electric flashlight, wheel around and to close the door again, the candle has gone out, brought to an end by the draft.

Standing vertically on the table, the flashlight casts a clear, precise disc of light on the ceiling, in contrast with the previous glow which was wavering, uncertain. But the dash to-and-fro and the last few gestures have brought on a sweat. The heat is so heavy that the slightest movement sets off an immediate flow, out of proportion with the energy expended.

The bed is pulled an equal distance from the walls, head toward the window. The night table is moved forward to within arm's reach, in such a way that the two most necessary objects fall directly under the hand: the electric flashlight, shut off at present, set flat upon the wood; the wristwatch, whose phosphorescent dial face stands out clearly in the semidarkness.

It is midnight. In a few hours, it will be necessary to get up, have a quick wash, and put the bags in order. The car is supposed to arrive around seven o'clock, seven-thirty; it will leave at once and be back in Dar el Hamra at the end of the morning. So there are a little over six hours remaining, provided that sleep arrives quickly. But sleep could not possibly be far off at present: it was not the afternoon siesta which drained it away. Added to the wear and tear of the work, to the muscle stiffness caused by the ride on muleback, to the nausea in the bus, this return to the intense heat of the plain upsets accustomed ways and, before imposing new ones in their stead, leaves the body panting, short of breath, with wobbly legs and a heavy head . . . Two days hence perhaps a balance will be reestablished, the listlessness vanquished.

The head rests upright upon the pillow, one meter from the window. The outstretched body thus coincides with the central axis of the room, traversed by the sun's rays in midday filtering through the shutters' stars.

Above the head, only the barest hint of a glow is outlined, perhaps lighting the windowsill, but it does not even reach as far as the bolster. Between eye and object darkness interposes itself; planes merge together, perspectives cancel each other out. Attention gradually slackens, space decomposes and fades away: the fireplace, night table, and beyond, the bare white walls, so close a short while ago, have disappeared, flooded in such a dense gloom that the hands themselves, closed on the folded edge of the sheet, have become invisible.

Sudden starts momentarily reestablish the precise perception of uniformity, but these reactions are short-lived, numbness again sets about its task, gradually invading the limbs, paralyzing the joints, neutralizing the reflexes, giving over the inert body to the exploration of zones of shadow, which are more and more distant, more and more opaque, until, at a much later point, a grayish halo breaks into view along the rim of the circle and slowly infiltrates the sphere.

The eye already probes space, the portion of space once more available. But contours stand out poorly in the semidarkness . . . There are stones on the right, near the head, small gray stones striped with green streaks, with smooth facets, and rounded edges, and farther off, boulders in the background. Above, there is a corridor of white light, bordered with a double-margin of shadow. On the left, other boulders rise, other stones, other pebbles, on the left, on the right, as far as the eye can see . . . The head rests, motionless, upon a large flat stone. The right arm, folded upon the chest, also remains motionless. The left arm has dropped along the body. The legs are out of reach . . . The eyes alone are mobile: opening, stirring, moving from left to right, returning, closing. And everything goes dark, black. Things are there, within hand's reach, but their contours have melted into the gloom. The hands themselves are invisible, clenched on the folded edge of the sheet. The whole body is streaming; sweat is flowing along the forehead and neck; the hair is sticking to the pillow. . . . A faint glow traces itself in the margin of the window.

The hand falls directly onto the electric flashlight case, set flat on the night table. The finger pushes the switch: the cone of light casts on the ceiling a clear and precise circle of light which, dropping along the wall, passes over the map from which only the brown patches emerge, furrowed with curving lines—from a short distance it might be taken for a large insect or a creeper with branching offshoots.

On the floor, the black-and-white block tiles alternate in a checkerboard pattern. Most are broken. The plinth—small yellow tiles with chamfered edges—runs along the foot of the wall all around the room. A certain number of tiles remain hidden behind the armchair and the night table. But there is no cause for alarm: the bed has been pulled far enough away from the walls and insects cannot climb on the metal uprights.

The lamp resumes its place on the table beside the wristwatch, whose hands mark a quarter to one . . . A little over five hours are left. Sleep will not be long in coming. The dogs fall silent; the noise of the toads no longer arrives except very deadened, and no trace of light is to be feared before dawn during this moonless night.

Behind the closed eyelids, the image of the square checks persists, cast on a rectangular screen which edges from top to bottom in small even lurches. As soon as the rectangle has disappeared below, another springs up on top, exactly identical, as if there were two diametrically opposed screens, drawn downward by a vertical disc triggered by a switch. Each time that the eyes close, the same mechanism is activated. After a while, minute modifications intervene from one image to the next, either in the number of squares, or their shape, their size or their distribution.

A little later, the rate of rotation unchanging, the original frame has become enlarged to the point of filling all of space. Henceforth everything is reduced to a single rectangle, within which the variations are effectuated: shifting lines, translating surfaces, the appearance of new ensembles which, no sooner constructed, disintegrate with an implacable slowness.

The checkerboard has been offset; the black squares have grouped themselves in parallel strips which trace an unbroken interlinking design against the white background of the screen: first of all, meanders, then diamonds, chevrons, intertwining lines, immediately super-imposed in a single shifting sinusoid from left to right, creeping from one edge to the other, writhing faster and faster to the point of bursting into myriad, short, unequal fragments—a chaotic vermiculation melting into the grayness.

And once again calm is restored: the surface is now disturbed only by imperceptible wrinkles; ripples arise, propagating along the whole breadth of the screen, small waves curled by the wind, water flowing from left to right, gray water upon which circles form, turning slowly, multiplying, swirling, while the reclining body glides against the current, motionless, with legs stiff, arms clasping the chest, neck straight, and eyes wide open.

Afterword

The Mise-en-Scène, awarded the first Prix Médecis in 1958, arrives in English thirty years after its initial publication during the heyday of the New Novel movement in France. The authors comprising this loose group have long since entered the postmodernist canon, even in Anglophone circles: Samuel Beckett, Marguerite Duras, Alain Robbe-Grillet, Michel Butor, Claude Simon, Robert Pinget, and Nathalie Sarraute, among others. *The Mise-en-Scène* initiates Claude Ollier's series of eight novels, structured in a parallel sequence of four narratives, entitled *Le Jeu d'enfant* (Child's Play) that constitutes one of the hallmarks of the postmodernist literary enterprise. Nevertheless, Ollier's novel remains at once one of the most accessible examples of the "school" as well as one of the most subtly provocative in the challenge it poses to the conventions of realist fiction.

For it is apparent that the diverse technical innovations and procedures of the New Novel were essentially determined by the aesthetic constraints of the nineteenth-century, post-Flaubertian novel. Consequently, the presuppositions of this aesthetic—an author invisible like God in his creation, a transparent language providing a window on a purportedly unmediated reality, a text that suppresses its awareness of itself as an organized verbal patterning—formed the prime targets of their assault. This subversion of realist technique also entailed a rejection of the thematic preoccupations of serious realist fiction: the depiction of everyday life or of a society or of a social group in its sweeping complexities. The majority of New Novels, at least of this first period stretching from the midfifties to early sixties, are nothing less than experimental hothouses in which the transplanted fragments of popular fiction and the steamy stuff of melodrama thrive unchecked and assume fantastic dimensions. The remote and often explicitly exotic locales and sexual obsession of Marguerite Duras's seaside Sturm und Drang, of Robbe-Grillet's *The Voyeur* and *Jealousy;* the gruesome death rattle and inheritance squabble haunting

Claude Simon's *The Grass,* or the generalized murder and mayhem of *The Flanders' Road;* the stranger in a strange land stumbling upon a triple murder—mythic, remote and recent past—of Michel Butor's *Passing Time* (Ollier's original title for *The Mise-en-Scène,* which presents an uncanny parallel rendering of a similar theme); finally, being itself at the brink of decomposition in Beckett's *Molloy, Malone Dies, The Unnameable* trilogy—we are quite far from the detailed evocation of a shared social world populated by representative characters. Likewise, *The Mise-en-Scène* is set in a remote, un- specified land, most likely a French colony in North Africa; a murdered girl opens the protagonist's journey and another death closes it, each mysterious in its circumstances, and perhaps interrelated. Looming over these actual deaths are the petroglyphs, perhaps prehistoric, depicting an ambiguous double murder.

According to Webster's, the word *mise-en-scène* has been part of the English language for over 150 years. It can refer to the physical setting of an action as well as to the arrangement of actors and scenery, whether in the space of a stage, or a slab of rock, or before a camera. Indeed, the cinematic connotations may be most present to an American reader. For a roughly ten-year period beginning in 1958, the same year as the novel's publication, Ollier wrote passionately and articulately about films (his articles have recently appeared in French in *Souvenirs Ecran,* 1981). But his rapport with film narrative cannot be described in terms of the *ciné-roman,* a term indissolubly linked with the work of Robbe-Grillet. A brief comparison with *Jealousy,* pub- lished the year before *The Mise-en-Scène,* will do much to illuminate Ollier's particular concerns.

Robbe-Grillet sets the elements of his narrative in an unspecified tropic land, ever since infamous for a certain meticulously and repeatedly described banana plantation. Robbe-Grillet's mise-en- scène is a stationary, static, sealed world: the husband, wife and lover are isolated in a villa, along with a few native servants drifting about silently. The interplay of light and shadow is rendered in terms of what Ollier will call a "sober geometry." The rapid textual movement is not a motion within the frame, so to speak, but a movement between frames, abrupt juxtapositions corresponding to this "contrée sans crépuscule," this region without twilight. Movement within a scene, when it does occur, is infinitesimal: fingers running through a barely undulating shock of hair, a centipede craning its head. Indeed, it is indicative of the novel's aesthetic character that the central action of *Jealousy* concerns a very particular destructive gesture: the crushing into immobility of the centipede, a death which haunts the novel in the form of a stain on the wall. Furthermore, Robbe-Grillet structures his drama around a simple pun: jealousy referring both to the emotion and the blinds through which the husband peers, imprisoned by his obsession. The horizontal slats inevitably recall the horizontal bands of white and dark across the page: we too are prisoners of the static, self-enclosed labyrinth from which there is no exit. Robbe-Grillet elegantly explores the possibilities of a novel, implicitly rejecting the popular commonplaces of the conventional colonial narrative within the novel which the two lovers are reading and commenting on naively "as if the events had really happened." Yet even these various plot lines and characters of traditional fiction are subjected to Robbe-Grillet's procedures: the narrator climactically juxtaposes all the possible story paths in the last pages and thus renders them mutually self-canceling.

There was an inevitable confluence of Robbe-Grillet's concept of the "eternally present" quality of the cinematic image—even flashbacks happen before our eyes—the primacy he ascribed to visual description, and abrupt "cinematic" transitions, with the film work of that other "New" French movement of the late '50s, the New Wave in cinema. Robbe-Grillet collaborated with Alain Resnais, whose Rive Gauche group not surprisingly created its innovative effects primarily through an unconventional use of montage, of the juxtaposition of various shots.

But cinema is also, quite simply, moving pictures, and Ollier's world is one of ceaseless movement. Shadow-lines wheel around the landscape; light bursts in darkness, plunges, swirls, darts off. The language of the novel is rife with what linguists refer to as "shifters," those parts of speech whose meaning changes according to context, "now," "here," "there," "beyond"—and more particularly—"upstream" and "downstream." More often than not, movement loops back and forth, is jerky, slanting. Even Ichou, the protagonist's mute helper, suffers from a strabismus (i.e., one eyeball is slightly askew). "A straight line has no meaning in such a relief." Ollier ramifies Robbe-Grillet's linguistic procedure with his proliferation of volative words, those which jump along the horizontal axis of contiguity from noun to verb to adverb. Some of these specific shifts are lost when moving from French to English ("une plaque," "se plaquer"; "une échappée," "s'échapper"; "les contours," "contourner"—but things have contours, and in English, maps have contour lines); but others make the transition ("une trace," "tracer"; "une figure," "figurer"). Yet since this is indeed the nature of language itself, other correspondences assert themselves ("edge," "to edge—in/through"; "trail," "to trail—off/after"; a "drawing," "to draw—out/through/up," etc.). We also speak of a "beam" of wood, or of light, of a happy person beaming; a gorge has an "entry," a house and a city, as well as a diary. In both languages a mountain "rises," or a column of smoke, or a person after sleep, movements related more by analogy than by identity. Even the simple word *girl* is subject to a shifting denotation. Lassalle sees a dying "girl" at the beginning of his journey, but Ba Iken, his native guide, informs him that he had heard it was a "woman." Indeed, "things are not like back home here," and "girls" are married off at eight or nine.

Ollier's procedure constantly reminds us of Nietzsche's insight that language is full of coins that have lost their exchange value and are treated as mere metal, that language is built up of primary metaphors whose original impact is obscured. Even the simplest, most innocent expressions take on new meaning: "What *way* is there to know?" In this perspective the foreign vocabulary—*wadi, douar, djebel,* etc.—is a point of stillness, or perhaps an opening into the void of the unsaid and the unsayable, those crevices between languages, those uncharted zones. For the English reader this list is multiplied by a much smaller array of French words which are an accepted part of the geologic lexicon: *defile, arête, cirque,* etc. Not to mention the very title of the novel itself, or the refractions in French of Arabic place and proper names—Ichou, Ou.chène—the "ch" representing an "sh" sound. Or the metric measurements.

Might we not see all proper names as convenient sheaves of perceptions, thoughts, and actions? Lassalle—whom Ollier refers to as an "itinerant perceiving center"—may be said to be "Lassalling." Perhaps he is "Moritzing"? But Moritz, a miner from the Company who preceded Lassalle by two years, was not the first. Ollier pushes to the limit an "impersonal style" in the description of body parts—

characters in several critical passages are not so much described as inventoried—to further blur the boundaries between fixed identities (a particular usage of the article which English, infrequently, cannot always accommodate [e.g., "She hid *the* face in *the* hands"]).

Ollier's genre displacement suggests a kinship with the other branch of the New Wave, that group formed by André Bazin's concept of mise-en-scène, or movement within the frame—as opposed to the imposed movement of montage—and whose initial work consisted in the displacement of American B-movie genres—Godard's *Breathless* and *Band of Outsiders;* Truffaut's *Shoot the Piano Player* and *Farenheit 451.* His world of "moving edges" is diametrically opposed to Robbe-Grillet's fixed borders. Indeed, the blurry picture which Lassalle first spots in his bedroom in the first chapter of the novel has been removed at the end: "Its hazy aesthetic design did not blend with the sober geometry of the pavilion." Ollier's insect, a scorpion, is swift, illusive, no sooner spotted than disappearing into an imperceptible crevice. And even the body of the scorpion in the final pages that has passed "without transition from lively animation to annihilation" (and the circumstances of whose death remain a mystery as do those surrounding the deaths of the two human victims) is the site of a feverish, voracious activity. Ants, dark as printed words, are tearing it to pieces. Finally, even jalousie blinds make an appearance; but in Ollier's work they do not represent a fixed perspective but immediately schematize the other linguistic axis, the vertical axis of substitution: ". . . jalousie blinds allow a view, in parallel horizontal strips, of the entire range of foliage set in staggered rows upon the northern slope of the hill." The enumeration of vegetation which follows is one among many games of substitution and exhaustivity that parody the realist novelist's mania to name and describe, to inventory, to tell all and not to repeat oneself, a mania paralleling Idder's, the troublemaker, who always goes out wandering with a different utensil in hand—pick, hoe, mallet, bee smoker. The text itself, as the nouns accrue, gradually refuses to choose among the possibilities: "In his right hand [Idder] is clutching a short-handled tool—a pick, a mallet, a bludgeon, a club. . . ."

There is a rare wit and light humor to *The Mise-en-Scène* which distinguishes it from most of the other New Novels. Lassalle himself finds Ichou's antics funny—the lad's pantomimes, his weird, celebratory scampering. However, we smile at Lassalle's expense as we witness the protagonist's gaffes—he daintily dips his fingers in the water bowl which the natives plunge their hands into, soaping up to their forearms; he bumps his forehead, his shin, much to his host's bemused embarrassment. But we also, in turn, can laugh at the consequences of this "fringe of instability" surrounding objects in Ba Iken's deadpan explanation of place-naming customs which is a version of Abbott and Costello's "who's on first" routine: "Besides, everybody says Imlil, in place of Asguine . . . That's the way it is throughout the whole tribe. When you don't want to talk about Asguine, then you say Zegda, or Ifechtalen . . . Elsewise, if you only say Imlil, everybody thinks what you mean is Asguine."

Also rare among the New Novels is a narrative which makes no mention of other written narratives. There is virtually no writing in *The Mise-en-Scène* other than the protagonist's pocket diary, which is in many ways the very antithesis of the novel we are reading, "relating in a few lines" not so much the particular adventures of the trip as the schematic outline of a voyage which might generate any number of stories—Lessing's, the geologist, among others. With the exception of the fragment of what is supposed to be the Koran decorating a casbah wall, there are no books or references to books. There are simply documents, official files, papers, and maps in various stages of completion.

Ollier's is an oral universe. The natives are mostly illiterate. The "fringe of instability" surrounding language is imparted by the floating quality of speech itself: shifts in dialect, Ba Iken's use of the informal "you" in the original and his irregular grammar. Spoken words can be forgotten, denied, misquoted, and the official investigations simply draw the boundaries of sense as best they can with these "moving edges." Language itself is a map, with uncharted zones, a mere map in an empire of signs, with paragraphs that trail off. Non-verbal communication proliferates: there is the recurrent white hand, the mute Ichou's pantomime, and the petroglyphs, "deemed to be prehistoric by some—but others are more circumspect, and there are those who even believe there are signs of a forgery," and whose main panel evokes an ambiguous double murder. But perhaps this is merely a result of juxtaposition in space: "A good many relationships result from simple juxtaposition, even where no global conception governed the enterprise." Or, perhaps, the mere lack of spatial juxtaposition means that a story will not be woven: the deaths occurring within the space of the text will not be related, at least officially, because "the spatial elements . . . have been exploded, and the problem became insoluble." The written text participates in this shifting, this movement, situating itself along the dissolving boundaries where Lassalle is Lessing, and so many others, where Jamila is Yamina, and so many others.

But the story has already unfolded. This oral universe is one in which something has already happened, always, where multiple trails follow an "age-old logic," where knowledge is passed on in stories told and retold, the one, for example, concerning spiders in the first chapter: "Things like that always happen in the mountains." Indeed, this something-which-already-happened is perhaps a shorthand definition of what genre is. But could one not also describe *The Mise-en-Scène* as recounting the story of a mine surveyor in a foreign land and everything that *does not* happen to him? Lassalle moves through the narrative landscape, an itinerant "uncharted zone" that is traversed by the traces of his exploration, which "do not survive immersion" in the final section's flash flood sweeping the wadi, the usually dry streamed that furnishes the immobile traces of past movement.

With its widely disseminated foreign vocabulary, alien landscape, and two maps, *The Mise-en-Scène* resembles not so much those tales of action and adventure set in foreign climes (Kipling's, for example, or Hemingway's) as it does the fantastic fictional worlds of Tolkien's *Lord of the Rings* or Frank Herbert's *Dune,* to cite two of the most popularly known examples. Ollier himself notes the presence in Jacques Rivette's film *Paris Belongs to Us* of "the apparent fixed spatial ordering which reinforces, in our view, instead of weakening, the story's echoes of the fantastic." Indeed, these other-worldly elements find their fulfillment in the fifth novel of the series, *La Vie sur Epsilon,* the novel which begins the second sequence, thus paralleling *The Mise-en-Scène* and, as Ollier states, placing the textual "system into orbit." Not only is genre once again displaced, explored, burst open, but language touches its outermost limits. Simple, minimal nouns— "sand," "snow"—become ways of speaking, refer to a something which is "sand" and "snow" only by analogy; and the fifth planet in the system is itself finally revealed to be only a planet—by analogy.

In the end, *The Mise-en-Scène,* similar to many New Novels, circles back on itself, but the symmetrically structured text (three sections divided into multiples of 7, 7 x 3, 7) is perpetually shifting. The symmetry of the spider's web has given way to the weird asymmetry of the smoker's shadow. The boundaries of Lassalle—both as person and as place, for, in French, his name means "the room"—are dissolved. We must resist the temptation to normalize the narrative, or as French critics have now taken to saying, "recuperate" the elements of the story, by explaining away, for example, Lessing's recurring presence as Lassalle's hallucination or imagining. The text itself is exploring its possibilities and we ourselves, verbal map in hand, are tracing its activity. The image of water is flowing from left to right, fraught with whirlpools, moving in the direction of words across a page, words of a Western language, and we are as motionless as the consciousness present at the end, with body as motionless and eyes as wide open . . . as a reader's.

—Dominic Di Bernardi